Our Wasted Vows

Riley Andrews

Disclaimer:
This is a work of fiction. All characters, locations, and businesses are purely products of the author's imagination and are entirely fictitious. Any resemblance to actual people, living or dead, or to businesses, places, or events is completely coincidental.

ISBN 978-8-9932369-0-2 (paperback)
Cover design by David Gardias
Edited by Hannah Lynn & Sapphic Library Editorial
Interior art by Mariia Ovsianikova

To my husband, who believed in me before I ever believed in myself.

Author's Note

This book contains fictional depictions of violence, murder, crime, domestic violence (depicted on-page once, then mentioned after), PTSD and anxiety disorder, character death, explicit sexual acts, manipulation, and cheating (not between the main couple). Please be advised that the following content may not be suitable for all audiences.

Chapter One

Adeline

Two days ago

Shattered glass littered the kitchen floor.

What had once been an apology from an argument long forgotten now sprawled before me in a heap of wilting limoniums and tattered roses. Careful not to slice my already aching knees, I lowered myself to the wood floor and started the strenuous process of cleaning up yet another one of Noah's messes. It seemed like lately, I was constantly picking up the pieces between us. Grappling at the tiny shards of glass all while frantically trying to mend them back together, salvaging what little I could. It didn't take long after moving in six months ago to learn that burden was mine, and mine alone.

What Noah and I had was something akin to a dying flame —persistent in nature if given the right conditions, but wholly capable of being extinguished if all went well. Recently, I felt like an outsider, watching the flames dance with glee, close enough to burn me. I would wait and watch, a prayer on my lips as it dwindled in size. I couldn't find it in me to feed the flames of his own ambitions. But Noah didn't need me to stroke those flames to keep them burning.

Always taking something in return—the more I fed, the less I learned.

I swept up the last of the vase and walked to the trash can.

Having lived in the chaos for so long, I should have been accustomed to the piercing silence that always followed one of our arguments. A strange sense of calm washed in after a storm, swearing the worst was over. When in reality, it was the absence of chaos that forced me to dissect every troubling thought, letting them fester and grow into an unformidable beast that couldn't be tamed, forcing me to wallow in every what-if and missed opportunity. I always hated the silence that followed. While it should have been the end to my torment, it was always just the beginning—I was done with Noah, but I still had myself to answer to.

The glass hit the bottom of the trash can, slicing through perpetual silence. I kept my eyes trained down the hallway, searching through the darkness for any signs of movement. Noah was likely sulking in our room, licking his wounds after an especially bad fight, while Andy, our other roommate, was staying the night with his girlfriend as he often did.

Within the confines of our apartment, each of us had a role to play. Andy was meant to be the buffer—a blessing that was only as good as the promises he failed to keep. Most nights were all the same. Noah and I alone, without anyone to diffuse the situation from escalating any further. Tonight had hit its crescendo, and I prayed he would leave it at that, but as I tossed another pile of glass into the trash, the clattering wasn't enough to drown out the old wood groaning under the weight of each step.

Every muscle in my body stiffened as the footfalls grew closer. Trapped in the corner of the kitchen, there was little I could do as Noah approached me from behind, snaked his arms around my middle, and gently burrowed his face in my neck.

"It's time to come to bed, love," he whispered, dragging his chapped lips along my skin. "Please, Adeline."

My fingers dug into the hard plastic of the dustpan, making the beds of my nails ache as his hands left my hips and explored with the familiarity of a lover. It was an invitation to forget, a promise to put aside our differences and pretend as we had so many times before. It meant stroking the flames of desire in lieu of repairing what couldn't be fixed. Despite being in my life for such a short amount of time, I'd become accustomed to the highs and lows that careened our relationship. If I gave in, it meant for a little while longer, I could have him like this—I could have the Noah I fell for back.

From the way his fingertips skimmed the waistband of my shorts to his breath hot against my skin, it was all an attempt at an apology that would never leave his lips. Forcing us back down a vicious cycle doomed to repeat over and over until I would surely go mad. Noah knew how to distract me. He knew how to blind me with pleasure and make me forget all that had come before and was promised tomorrow.

A wave of nausea slammed into me with the force of a crushing wave as Noah's hand slipped beneath my shirt. His hand inched upward like the sweetest call of temptation.

Was this all I was good for? Destined to stroke the flames.

I wasn't sure I could do this anymore.

His fingertips strummed over my ribs.

I was so tired of playing his games.

Before I could talk myself out of it, I jerked out of his hold.

I was quick. But Noah was quicker.

He had me by the wrist, pulling me back into submission. In that split second, our eyes met like two storming colliding as one. By the time I lowered my gaze, it was too late.

"Really?" Noah snapped, startling me. "Are you seriously crying again?"

"I'm fine," I said weakly, wiping away the hot, angry tears rolling down my cheeks. One quickly replaced the other.

Noah plucked his reading glasses off and ran the heels of his palms over his eyes.

"This is so goddamn exhausting, Adeline," he groaned, visibly shaking. "We can't even have a simple conversation without you bursting into tears."

"I already told you, I'm fine."

The tremors were always the first sign—a silent promise that nothing good was to come.

Noah shook his head and huffed out a strained laugh. "I don't know what the hell to do with you."

I didn't dare dignify that with an answer.

"Huh?" he snapped, flexing his fingers. "If only you weren't so sensitive, we could have an actual conversation without you using your emotions to get what you want every time. It might have worked in past relationships, but I'm not going to coddle you like a child because you can't handle your own emotions. You need to act like a *fucking* adult and—"

"I—" The word spilled from my lips before I could stop myself.

"You what?"

Noah towered over me, his hazy brown eyes burning through me.

"I told you not to say that anymore."

He leaned in, bringing himself dangerously close to my face.

"Well, then stop acting like a child, and I will."

Having danced this dance before, I knew once the tremors were shaking him down to the bone, there was little reasoning with him. I knew where this conversation was headed, and I didn't give him a chance to finish as I bolted for the hallway, willing my legs to move faster. The sound of footfalls chased after me. My heart thrashed within my chest as I turned the corner, not sure if the mere seconds separating us were enough. By the grace of God, I managed to lock the bathroom right as his fist collided with the wood. I was spared from the verbal onslaught, but that didn't stop Noah from pounding his fist so vigorously against the wood that I feared it might splinter.

"Open. The. Door."

I sank to my knees and heaved.

"Adeline," he roared, his voice echoing through the apartment as loudly as the constant thrumming in my skull.

I snapped my eyes shut, covered my ears, and gently rocked back and forth.

"Make it stop," I mumbled to myself. "Make it stop. Make it stop."

As a creature of habit, I knew exactly what to expect from Noah. Knew the relentless shouting would subside, then eventually be replaced with his hopeless pleading when he realized raising his voice wouldn't coax me out of hiding. The calculated silence meant to guilt me into submission when he neared the last stages of his plan. Instead of crawling into bed and finishing the vicious cycle, I curled up in the bathtub and wrapped myself in a mess of towels to keep warm. The silence had returned, but I drove it away, counting the drips of water leaking from the faucet I'd asked him to fix months ago.

It wasn't until I lost count that I came to terms with the inevitable—just because something is broken, it doesn't mean it should be fixed.

And what Noah and I were had been broken from the start.

Chapter Two

Adeline

Stars may rise and fall, but only those destined for greatness will prevail.

For greatness was not given, it was earned, and despite the selfish desire or star-studded dreams that enacted greatness, it was those willing to put their body through hell in pursuit of a higher purpose who would live to see their endeavors come to fruition.

Tatiana Antonenko had fallen from her good grace. Crumbling to the ground, center stage, she clutched her ankle with unshed tears brimming in her blue eyes. The rest of the company held their breath—as they so often did when the soloist rolled her ankle—waiting to see if greatness would prevail once more.

I stood on the sidelines along with the rest of the dancers, giving enough space for the staff to check on her. The soloist clung to her dignity, desperately fighting the tears begging to be shed.

"Someone, run to the physical therapy room and find Noah," Jin, our artistic director, called out, taking a knee beside her.

"I'm okay," she weakly mumbled, more for herself than anyone else.

While all eyes were on Tatiana, her gaze was fixed on the shadows of the mezzanine. Two figures lingered in the back of the theater, their presence a not-so-subtle reminder that Margot Vishneva had retired last season and her replacement as principal had yet to be announced. It was a rare opportunity to have such an audience, which made it sting that much more when they rose to their feet and made for the exit. Only then did Tatiana allow herself to finally give in.

Halle's tutu brushed up against mine as she leaned in and whispered, "Do you think if she stays down long enough, her role will be up for grabs?"

"You might have to fight the others for it," I replied.

She playfully jabbed her elbow into my side, her golden locks glinting under the stage lights. "A small price to be one step closer to principal."

The comment earned Halle a few sideways glances from the male dancers within earshot.

There were whispers of who might replace Vishneva as principal, Tatiana being the obvious choice given her rank in the company and years of experience, but that didn't stop the rumors from spreading that a guest principal might be invited for the spring season, given how little time there was left before opening night. Having only been a part of this company since the fall season, it was fascinating to see how starved they all were for fame and glory. With two promising choices for the season, everyone watched the soloist with hungry eyes, indulging in a little wishful thinking—myself included. Each of us was a cog in the machine, but actively working to feed the flames of our own ambitions.

The life of a ballerina, especially a corps de ballet, wasn't a lavish one by any means, but climbing up the ranks did provide better financial opportunities for those willing to claw their way to the top. While passion might spark the fire, the flame provided a sense of freedom that I simply couldn't obtain on my own. A means of survival that didn't rely on the emotional whim of men.

A jaded sense of optimism, perhaps, but a chance at freedom, nonetheless.

It was several long minutes before someone could hunt down Noah from wherever he'd been hiding. Armed with a first-aid kit and a troublesome look gracing his features, he rushed in to assess her ankle and determine whether or not she'd sprained it again.

Halle didn't seem to be the only one betting on the misfortunes of others. All it took was one look around the stage to notice how the collective audience seemed to be holding their breaths, waiting for an answer they weren't sure would ever come. To everyone's disappointment, Tatiana rose once more—not without a little help from Noah. As if learning to walk for the first time, she clutched onto him for dear life, one wrong move away from a career-ending injury. Despite the more crestfallen of the ballerinas, there was a wave of applause sending her off as the duo made their way backstage, cutting a path directly toward me. The crowd parted, and my vision tunneled, eyes fixed on a man I hardly recognized anymore.

Nothing with Noah Hernandez had ever been easy—even in the beginning stages of our relationship, when things were meant to be exhilarating and new. It made moments like this, when there was no escaping him, especially difficult. There was no rest, for Noah was an all-consuming presence in both my personal and professional life.

Despite not having spoken in two days, I found myself unable to look away.

There was something about those chocolate brown eyes that used to be filled with such longing—now they were trained on Tatiana, empty as ever. I couldn't have looked away even if I tried. It was as if I were searching for any sign of who he used to be. An ounce of hope that this hell was over. Any shred of humility that could be found and a promise that when I came home tonight, I would have nothing to fear.

Even if nothing could truly be mended, that reassurance could buy me more time.

The last few days had been hell—a waking nightmare that I couldn't escape. I tried my best to hold my ground and not fall for old tricks, but where had that gotten me? Sleeping in the bathtub had taken its toll on my physical health, while living with the ramifications of that night was having a similar effect on my mental well-being. And despite the tightness in my lower back, the burning in my knee, and the cuts lining my toes, I couldn't willingly put myself in a position where I could get hurt again without knowing the worst was over.

Please look at me, goddamn it.

Fussing with the tulle of my skirt, invasive thoughts started to buzz within my head like a swarm of vexed bees, determined to drown out any sense of rational thought. Relentless in nature, the buzzing worsened with each step he took. No matter how many times I tried to break the cycle, I couldn't stop the words from looping over and over inside my head. The buzzing was going to drive me mad—

Noah walked by without a passing glance.

The buzzing stopped so suddenly that it took a moment to realize what had happened.

I sucked in a shaky breath.

All that followed was a deafening sense of silence—nearly as empty as Noah's eyes—making me regret ever cursing the buzzing in the first place. The silence chased after me for the remainder of practice, haunting my every move. Living in a frenzy of what-ifs and perpetual fear was somehow better than sitting with confirmation of what I might have known all along but refused to believe for months. That was the funny thing about the truth: once it takes hold, there's no turning back.

Chapter Three

Adeline

I peeled off my pointe shoes, cursing the damned things.

"All I'm saying is" —Halle plopped down on the ground beside me, a bag of ice wrapped around her ankle — "if Jin took a chance on any of us for once, he would see Tatiana isn't the star everyone thinks she is. She's good, don't get me wrong, but it isn't enough for the role she's been given."

"I'm not sure the artistic director has as much power as you assume he does."

"Well, he has more influence on the owner's decision than Anastasia ever has—God forbid the woman who spends the most time with the dancers has any input in the company's future. I mean, come on. I trust her decision more than anyone else's," she continued, rambling on about blatant favoritism while stripping off her shoes. "Oh, I forgot to tell you. Anastasia's friend finally got back to her with the name of that Japanese restaurant she was raving about. If you want to keep the tradition alive, we could check out Nova."

"Sorry, I can't tonight," I said, flexing my sore toes. "I have dinner plans with Noah."

Halle opened her mouth to speak, but I shushed her as a tall figure approached out of the corner of my eye. "How's your knee holding up, Hartwell?" Jin asked, nose pressed to his clipboard.

"Good," I answered quickly.

There was a dull aching that constantly rattled the very marrow of my bones, but the artistic director didn't need that. I could dance, and that was all that mattered.

"This stays between you and me, but if Tatiana isn't feeling well, I'm going to need you to step in tomorrow for her. Do you think you can manage? I know it was bothering you last week."

"That won't be a problem, Mr. Collins."

Those dark brown eyes of his found mine. "Call me Jin. Please."

"That won't be a problem, *Jin*," I corrected myself, gazing up at him.

He was ten years my senior, and his name felt odd sliding off my tongue, especially given his title within the company, but I preferred it over the familiarity of it all.

"Good. I'm counting on you," was all he said before turning on his heels. As quickly as he appeared, he was gone, venturing off toward the next group of dancers as he made his rounds backstage.

"What?" I turned to Halle.

Halle rolled her eyes. "No. I'm happy for you. I promise," she said, rolling out the word in a playful manner. "Anyway, back to what I was saying, invite Noah for all I care. Though I'll admit, the selfish part of me likes when I have you all to myself."

She shot a wink in my direction.

"We have reservations uptown," I vaguely explained, hoping she wouldn't question me further. "Next time, I promise."

Halle, much like myself, grew up out west, then moved to the city in pursuit of a promising ballet career—the young prodigy of the Benson household, looking to carve her name amongst the greats like the rest of us.

Acclimated to the fast-paced lifestyle, Halle was quick to take me under her wing and introduce me to all the Entertainment District had to offer after I stumbled into the corps de ballet, looking as lost as could be.

I wasn't aware of it until months later, but it turns out the majority of the dancers had been expecting my role to be given to a promising apprentice favored by the lot, so it came as quite a surprise when I appeared out of the blue before the fall season. While you may be able to strip the stonemason of his tools, if they have already brought hammer to stone, it's difficult to reshape their biases if they never give you a chance to do so. And then there was Halle, who had made it her personal mission to chip away at my hard exterior little by little until I broke out of my shell.

Once a week, we would sample all the district had to offer, dining at quaint little coffee shops that prided themselves on their fresh beans and decadent pastries, strange hole-in-the-wall restaurants that made me question more than the food as I followed her to odd parts of the city, to little bookshops that felt more like a labyrinth older than the city itself. We gorged ourselves on those first few weeks exploring the city—a precursor to all that would come next.

Halle started bringing me around her other friends, a charming physical therapist and his clinical buddies who welcomed me with open arms. And suddenly, a big city felt a little smaller.

I hadn't stood a chance.

With a recurring knee problem that landed me in his office almost daily, it became painfully difficult to ignore the attraction any longer. Which was odd, because if I were a betting man, I would have put my chips elsewhere. However, Noah possessed the type of allure that could have had an entire audience swooning over him had he chosen dancing over medicine; perhaps it's why I got so easily trapped in his orbit—he was an extension of Halle's promise of a fresh start.

Though promises can be hard to keep.

Sometimes I wonder what would have happened had I not accepted Noah's offer and moved in together during the beginning stages of our relationship. At the time, it didn't feel like I had much of a choice when the college students I was housed with during those first few weeks in the city had wildly different priorities in life than I did. With an ungodly sleeping schedule and friends visiting at odd hours of the day, their carefree lifestyle had started to take a serious toll on my own ambitions. Halle offered to house me, but she hardly had any room for herself, let alone me. It felt like a no-brainer when I packed up my belongings once more and thrust myself into this new chapter of my life. A choice that I didn't realize until it was too late, that I didn't have the finances to reverse once it was done. Not yet, at least.

"Next time it is." She smiled. A beat passed before she placed a tentative hand on my knee. "Are you doing all right, Addie? You seem distracted."

"Yes. Just tired," I replied, and she nodded in return.

If she sensed the lie, she didn't make it known. Instead, Halle rambled on about the various nightclubs in the Entertainment District worth sampling, some names I recognized, others I didn't. Somewhere along the third or fourth name, I'd tuned her out completely, rifling through my dance bag for my phone.

I wasn't sure what I expected when I scrolled through the unread notification, but it surely wasn't the prickle of disappointment centered deep within my chest. I guess some part of me was still clinging to the hope I might find an apology that would mean nothing to me at the end of the day, but it would be confirmation that the worst was over—that there was a reality where I could sleep in my own bed tonight without fear the tremors would return. Noah was prone to finding creative ways to buy my forgiveness, and while I wasn't in a position to accept any half-assed apology he came up with, I was so damn tired of playing games.

I wanted to pretend everything was okay, just for a little while longer.

Adeline: What time will you be home tonight, sweetheart?

Minutes dragged by without a response to show for it.

Halle, so engrossed with her one-sided conversation, didn't notice that I was starting to retreat further into myself as she attempted to narrow down her choice, which seemed to be an impossible task given all the district had to offer. She breathlessly went on, raving about the wild nightclubs, hidden dive bars, and scandalous cabarets as we made our way through the empty theater—last to leave per usual. I heard bits and pieces of the conversation, but with each step bringing us closer to the exit, her pitchy voice bled into a gentle whisper.

Stay.

It started as a low rumbling in my head but grew with each step.

Stay. Adeline.

It drew closer and closer until I couldn't ignore it any longer.

Don't leave. Stay.

It roared in my ears.

Stay! Adeline! Stay!

"... supposedly, since the fire, they remodeled, and it's better than ever—" Halle stopped short when I did, a perplexed look gracing her soft features. "What? We don't have to go there if you don't want to. I heard The Velvet Rope has good drinks too."

The voice whispered one last time like a lover's caress.

I swallowed the lump in my throat and glanced down at my phone. "Noah texted me. He's going to pick me up here so we can go straight to dinner."

"Do you want me to stay with you and wait?"

"No," I said calmly, despite my racing heartbeat. "You can go without me. I'll text you later tonight with my pick."

It didn't take much convincing to get rid of Halle. Once she disappeared through the stage door, I retreated deeper backstage, prepared to evade the custodial staff as they made their nightly rounds. It wasn't easy per se, but with a theater of this size, there were plenty of spots that were conveniently overlooked by the staff. Mr. Sinclair worked weekends and was the most careless of the bunch. With retirement on the near horizon, he gradually started neglecting his duties, hoping no one would notice after decades of unwavering loyalty—but I did.

Hiding in the props department, it would only be an hour or so until I was confident that I could leave without being caught. Like so many nights before, the theater provided me with a sense of peace so painfully absent in my life that it made my chest ache, thinking of what I'd been missing. I could have spent a lifetime carving a home for myself between these walls.

Constructed in the late 1800s, the Republic City Opera House was the pride and joy of the Entertainment District. The theater featured a neo-Renaissance design with baroque elements that were heavily inspired by the Hungarian State Opera, which was still under construction at the time of its conception. As stunning as the building itself was, it was nothing compared to the grand chandelier that made everything the light touched look like the heavenly embodiment of divine faith. Standing center stage and peering up at the sprawling fresco that blanketed the ceiling, blushing cherubs, and fluffy clouds was something akin to love at first sight.

I stopped short, catching sight of my reflection bouncing off the arched mirror propped up against the back wall. Daring to venture forward, I passed a row of shelves lined with an arsenal of prop weapons: foam axes crafted with faux battle scars, wooden daggers splattered with red paint, and rubber morning stars so intricately painted, it was hard to tell what was real and what wasn't. Each told a story of a bloodied war, a hero's mighty beginning, and a tragic ending yet to unfold, but the fabricated horrors were nothing compared to the image that stared back at me. I hardly recognized myself.

The lightest shade of pink stained my cheeks, a stark contrast to the sickly appearance of my fair skin. The pop of color highlighted the discoloration under my eyes after days of little rest, only further drowning out the normally vibrant flecks of green and gold in my hazel eyes and the ebony tone of my long hair. It made me curious if the soul could reshape itself into a physical manifestation of all that weighed heavily on one's conscience—it certainly felt that way, because I looked nearly as terrible as I felt.

Maybe if I curled up on one of the prop settees, I could get a little sleep. It wouldn't solve all my problems, but it was a start.

The sound of a distant crash shook the old bones of the theater.

I froze, my heart hammering so fiercely it shook me nearly as badly as the building did. I strained my ear, sifting through the silence, hoping I was only hearing things again.

While the crash might have startled me, it was the groan that accompanied the sound that set my nerves on edge. An image of the seventy-year-old custodian lying on the floor flashed into my mind. I didn't think twice before rushing for the exit. Those nerves electrified with each step. Fear might dictate motive, but naivete would not be my downfall. I grabbed a pair of scissors on my way out in case my ears were deceiving me. I plunged into the darkened theater, chasing after the relentless banging echoing off its acoustics, making it hard to pinpoint the source. The sound took me every which way as I chased after something I wasn't sure I could ever find, scissors poised outward in case it wasn't the old man lurking in the shadows.

"Mr. Sinclair," I called out.

Bang.

"Mr. Sinclair," I repeated, a slight tremble to each word. "Are you okay?"

The next crash sounded closer than the last—coming in short, frantic secessions. I turned the corner and came face to face with a familiar sight. The physical therapy room stared back at me, demanding something in return that I didn't quite know how to interpret.

Bang.

Bang.

Bang.

"Hello," I croaked. "Mr. Sinclair?"

What had once been a gentle caress from the ever-present voice in my head now felt like I was being shoved in the back repeatedly, pleading with me to walk despite the inability to move my legs. My every instinct screamed at me to turn away and run, but the voice was relentless.

It's okay, the voice whispered. *It's okay.*

My hand hovered over the doorknob as another groan echoed.

It's okay, Adeline. It will all be over soon.

I threw open the door.

Noah stood with his pants wrapped around his ankles, his hand fisted in a mess of dirty blond hair. I watched in horror as he bent Tatiana over a treatment table and drove into her.

Chapter Four

Adeline

Betrayal was meant to be the willful slaughter of hope—the breaker of souls and imminent damnation. No matter the degree, it always whispered a lethal promise, swearing to shatter all that had been pieced together. Betrayal was the be-all and end-all.

Yet as I stood there, frozen in the doorway, I felt nothing.

Watching someone I had once loved relentlessly thrust into another woman, I waited for the imminent slaughter. It felt as if I was kneeling before a headman's block, counting the seconds until the final blow—but the blade never hit its mark.

The corners of my lips twitched, the subtlest hint of a smile.

Noah had betrayed me, sullying our relationship and all it stood for.

And yet, all I could do was smile.

"Tatiana," he moaned, his voice echoing through my skull.

It struck me so violently that I clutched onto the doorknob to keep upright.

It was relief. Overwhelming, undeniable, soul-crushing relief that this waking nightmare was finally over, that it wasn't me pinned beneath him, hearing him croak my name. It wasn't me anymore. Financially, I didn't have enough to afford a place on my own yet, but it would give me the head start I needed to finally be free and buy me time to figure out my next step.

My smile wobbled as I shook with ease, tears spilling down my cheeks.

Noah had chosen someone else, so for once, I would choose me.

This was my chance to leave. I needed to run. I—

Something crunched under my boot as I dared a step back. Tortoiseshell frames and broken glass lay beneath my heel, along with the rest of the discharged clothes I didn't notice upon entering the physical therapy room.

By the time I lifted my gaze, Noah's blazing eyes were already fixed on me.

A shrill scream filled the room. I was vaguely aware of a strangled sob, shadows dancing about the room, and flashes of bare flesh as Tatiana scrambled to collect her belongings and shove past me. Everything in my proximity dulled in comparison to each sense connected to Noah. His gaze burned into me, leaving me utterly petrified as he stuffed himself back into his boxer briefs and closed the distance between us.

"Jesus Christ, Addie," he hissed, pulling on his T-shirt.

Move, the small voice in the back of my head wailed. *Move. Move. Move. Move.*

Anticipating me before I could even move, Noah grabbed me by the wrist. Each individual nail bit into my flesh with enough force to slice through the first layer of skin.

He slowly shook his head, jaw clenched. "What are you doing here?"

I choke out a laugh. "Seriously? You have no right to question what I'm doing."

Noah snapped his eyes shut, his chest rising and falling with each deep breath.

"You were never meant to see that," he said slowly. His grip fluctuated with each word, loosening then tightening as if he were at war with himself. By the crazed look in his eyes, I wasn't sure what side was winning. "You were never meant to see that, baby. If you'd just listen to me—"

Another deep breath in.

"Goddamn it, Adeline," he snapped, as if this were somehow my fault.

We'd spun this dance enough times to know that was exactly what he was attempting to do. Charm, intimidation, guilt trip, beg, and rage—a never-ending cycle that relied on the fact that at some point, I would roll over for him and give in. Noah was doing what he did best because he knew, as well as I did, that I always would.

Over and over again.

Noah had chosen someone else, so for once, I wanted to choose me.

I stared down at the crescent-shaped imprints lining my wrist and mumbled, "I'm done."

"Addie. Let me—"

"I'm done," I said, as a shaky laugh tore through my throat, "and there's nothing you can say to keep me from leaving you."

I tried to break free, but he wouldn't budge.

"I've wasted too much time loving someone who never deserved it," I added.

It wasn't like me to speak to Noah in that tone. He must have been just as surprised as I was, because when I tried to yank free for the second time, he let me go. I only managed to make it a few feet before Noah came to his senses and rushed to block my path with his towering frame.

"You're joking, right? You catch me with another woman, and all you have to say is, 'I'm done,'" he scoffed. "You know, it's just like you to give up when things start getting tough. Pathetic."

My molars ground together. "It doesn't matter now."

Noah took a large step forward, and I took one step back.

"It doesn't matter now?" he chided. "Well, tell me this, Adeline. Did it matter when I took you in after you had nowhere else to go and were about to be homeless? Did it matter when you came home crying after practice, too weak to even stand on your own two feet, and I was the only one who could lessen the pain? Did it matter"—he leaned in, his face mere inches from mine—"when you were stepping closer and closer to the edge, and I was the only one who cared enough to keep you from falling? You have no idea what I sacrificed for you. What bullshit I had to put up with. I gave you everything, and this is how you are going to repay me? I guess I can't say I'm surprised. It's not as if you put any effort into our relationship."

"Don't blame me for *your* mistakes," I choked out. "Trying to justify your actions with whatever bullshit excuse makes you sleep better at night doesn't take away from the fact that this relationship was over long before you ever slept with Tatiana."

"You aren't *listening*." He bared his teeth, chest heaving.

"I'm done listening to your—"

Noah grabbed either side of my head roughly, forcing me to meet his gaze.

"You need to listen, Adeline. Listen to me."

The tremors were back.

"Noah," I shuddered, eyes widening.

"Shut up. Shut up. Shut up," he exploded, splitting my eardrums.

The silence that followed was deafening, carrying on for several beats before he dropped his forehead to mine, still slick to the touch from his time with Tatiana. As I was trapped in his proximity, he spoke more gently than before, switching tactics when I didn't give in as easily as he wished I would. And while his tone might have shifted, his punishing grip didn't.

Pain erupted along the base of my skull and the underside of my jaw.

I latched onto his wrist, trying to pry him off.

"Do you have any idea how hard it is to love someone like you?" he asked, his breath hot against my skin. "To give myself over to someone who's constantly worrying about the future instead of appreciating all she has. How do you make me feel invisible in my own relationship, as if all that I'm good for is picking up the pieces every time you start to spiral?"

"Noah, it hurts," I sobbed.

He shook his head. "I didn't want to hurt you. You were pushing me away—"

"Please. Let me go."

"—with your constant worrying and panic attacks. You were always pushing me away as if I didn't matter anymore. So yes, I needed someone—someone who didn't make me feel like an afterthought in my own life. That's on *you*, Adeline. You did this to us."

"Noah."

"Don't you fucking cry. Don't act like you're the victim when you have no one else to blame but yourself for throwing away this relationship. I've put up with your bullshit longer than anyone else ever would, and this is the thanks I get. No one is going to love you as I do. You're nothing without me, Adeline. Nothing."

A constellation of blinding white lights erupted behind my eyes, shimmering with each wave of pain that throbbed from the back of my skull. I repeated Noah's name like an incantation, begging—no, pleading with him to stop, but he wasn't listening. The tremors had worsened, and I knew deep in my heart that there would be no reasoning with him.

Reason was for those willing to listen, and Noah didn't want to listen.

Refusing to complete that cycle once more, I rammed my knee upward as hard as I could, colliding with his groin. The attack was sloppy and didn't land as well as I intended, but it did give me the biggest blessing I could have asked for—a head start.

I pumped my arms harder, willing my short legs to move faster.

My name left his lips like a curse, damning me to a fate unseen.

The sound of footfalls wasn't far behind, closing in with each passing breath.

In a mere test of strength and endurance, Noah would always win. There was no outrunning when he trumped me every which way. As I barreled down the hallway, I feared the only chance I stood was finding a corner of the theater that he couldn't reach. If I could only reach the end of the hall—

Freedom was short-lived. Nowhere as fleeting compared to the splintering pain that erupted along my side as I collided with the nearest wall. The air rushed out of me in one fatal blow as Noah pinned me beneath his crushing weight. It took several gasping breaths to realize what had even happened before it all became so painfully clear.

"This isn't how we end," he grunted. "I can't lose you like this, Addie."

A deafening sob tore through me as Noah snaked his arms around my torso and lifted me off the ground before I'd been able to suck down a proper breath. I thrashed within his hold as he dragged me back toward the physical therapy room. I was weightless for a brief moment, leaving Noah's arms as we crossed the threshold. My hip bone collided with the linoleum flooring first, and with no way of slowing my momentum, the side of my head cracked against the ground next. A constellation of stars blurred my vision as bright as the night sky. I was vaguely aware of the sound of metal sliding against the floor, but it wasn't until the sudden wave of nausea subsided that I realized the pair of scissors and phone I had tucked in my waistband had skidded across the floor.

"I can't lose you, Adeline," he repeated.

Fighting a wave of dizziness, I scrambled to my hands and knees. I only managed to crawl a few feet before Noah kicked the door shut behind him and pounced.

"Help!" I shrieked as his hands wrapped around my throat. I kept trying to repeat the plea, but with each attempt, I could feel my airways slowly closing in with every gasping breath.

"Please don't leave me, Addie," he pleaded, choking down a sob.

Noah shifted forward, applying more weight onto his hold— I clawed at his hands and wrists, drawing blood, but the more I struggled, the more he squeezed. His body eclipsed the fluorescent lighting above, and despite the absence of light shifting the contours of his features into an ungodly sight, it was his eyes that were what nightmares were made of. Fueled by violent passion and animalistic delight. One look was all it took to know —Noah never intended for me to leave.

He leaned in, molding his body with mine. "Say you love me."

Noah's chapped lips grazed mine in a mockery of tenderness.

"Say it so I can stop hurting you," he breathed, voice low and commanding.

When I didn't answer, he squeezed harder. My airways thinned, and my chest heaved as the edges of my vision blurred. The scissors were right there—so close—but his crushing weight kept me from closing the gap. The world darkened with every agonizing second, and I felt myself slowly slipping away.

My fingers skimmed the cool metal.

"Please. Love me."

A pained moan left my lips, and Noah loosened his grip, expecting me to reciprocate.

"Adeline—"

Whatever he was about to say died on the tip of his tongue as I drove the shears into his side. Air rushed back into my lungs like a dam breaking under the weight of its own raging waters. I sucked down as much as I could, desperate to regain consciousness and smudge out the stars lining my vision. Bowing over, I fell into a coughing fit, too consumed by my weakened state to notice all the pressure atop of me had suddenly lifted.

"Adeline," he whimpered.

The stars subsided, and the cough subdued; only then did I notice Noah's trembling hands reaching for the pair of scissors lodged in his torso. Blood seeped between his fingers, soaking his black scrubs, making it impossible to tell how much he'd already lost. Despite the pained expression twisting his features, his eyes remained sharp and focused. It was the same look he had in any serious medical emergency.

"God," I gasped, lifting a trembling hand to my lips.

"My liver," he rasped, voice strained. "You need to call for an ambulance."

"I—I didn't mean to. It was an accident. You wouldn't—"

"Now."

Time held no meaning within the confines of this room. Every frantic breath blurred into the next, seconds slipping through my fingers faster than I could grasp them.

"Goddamn it," I swore, trying to unlock my phone. My fingertips sliced against the shattered glass. "Come on."

"Baby..."

Steady breaths turned frantic, slowing with each inhale. The sound of my name left his lips in the softest plea for forgiveness. What little fight he had left in him wavered as he started to succumb to the blood loss. Time sped back into place as I rushed to his side, narrowing and catching him before he could fall face-first into a pool of his own blood.

"It's okay. It's okay," I sobbed. "I got you."

Gone were the chocolate brown eyes I'd gazed into a thousand times, making me long for something more. Gone was the man who'd cradled me in his arms as such, whispering his hopes for tomorrow. Gone was the girl who fell for it all, too naive to see the snake hiding in the tall grass. As Noah died in my arms, I gazed into his eyes one last time and wondered what I had done.

Chapter Five

Adeline

The silence was back.

No more wheezing breaths.

No more whispers of forgiveness.

No more broken promises.

Even the sickening sound of his blood dripping in sporadic fits had stopped altogether. I wasn't sure how long I stayed cradling Noah's lifeless body in my arms, but the blood soaking my tights had run cold. I couldn't bring myself to move, besides the involuntary tremors that jolted through my limbs.

The silence had won, and there was nothing I could do but wallow in it.

It wasn't long before the whispers crept from the shadows. Starting as a singular voice that slithered its way into my subconscious, it gorged itself until it had its fill, then multiplied into disembodied voices—some I recognized, others I didn't. There was nothing I could do besides absently stare at the pair of scissors sticking out of Noah's corpse as the whispers festered upon me.

My entire body had gone numb beside the aching in my arms. It felt as if hundreds of thousands of pins and needles were being pierced through my skin over and over again before I'd become accustomed to the pain. From the top of my head to the tips of my toes, my body felt foreign, as if it wasn't truly mine—except for the crushing weight of Noah's lifeless body draped over my arms.

No matter how much my muscles ached, it was my burden to hold, and I couldn't unfurl my fingers from his cold flesh even if I tried.

"It wasn't your fault," a gentle voice whispered through the chaos. That tiny flicker of optimism—of relief—was quickly extinguished like a dying flame before I could even get a hold of it. The whispers fed upon that glimmer of hope as if a beast starved after a harsh winter, leaving only vile thoughts in its wake.

You killed him. Noah is dead because of you.

He would have apologized. He always does.

I squeezed my eyes shut, throat constricting.

Noah loved you. He wouldn't have let it go that far.

You can't undo this.

You can't undo this.

Stop.

You can't undo this.

Stop.

You can't undo this. You can't undo this. You can't—

The scissors hit the floor, and it was several heartbeats before I realized what I had done—what I couldn't undo, no matter how much I tried. It took a few more beats before I noticed that one of the voices roaring in my ears didn't reside within my head as the others did. This one was coming from behind.

"Noah," a familiar voice called out.

There was always something about her smile; the mere suggestion of it could warm an entire room and spread with the quickness of wildfire. I often looked toward her on especially hard days, hoping to feel an ounce of her happiness in any capacity. Which is why it broke my heart to see Halle in the doorway, that smile of hers slowly fading as she took in the sight before her. Frozen in place, her eyes grew wider with each drop of blood splattered across the linoleum flooring. Only when our eyes met did she become wholly aware of where she was and what had happened. All it took was two long strides before she was kneeling at my side, lifting a trembling hand to Noah's neck to check his pulse.

"No." She shuddered. "No. No. No."

Hope still glimmered in her forest green eyes, but with each passing heartbeat, I watched it slowly leach away as the initial shock wore off and reality finally set in.

"No. No. No," she repeated, falling back on her heels, a sob bubbling up her throat.

I couldn't bring myself to watch as she unraveled before me.

"Why?" she wailed, trying to scramble to her feet as if she couldn't get away fast enough. "No. Addie. No."

Supporting Noah with one arm, I brushed away a bloodied curl from his face.

"I didn't mean to," I whispered.

Shadows danced in the corner of my eye, but I paid no attention to them as Halle sprinted for the exit, a cell phone in hand. As our final moment approached and the inevitable prevailed, I took what little time the universe could spare me to drink in every inch of his face, categorizing him to memory. This wasn't how I wanted to remember him, but I couldn't recall a time when he looked so peaceful. As I dragged the pad of my thumb over his cheeks, I said my goodbyes and attempted to find it in myself to leave him, as I failed to do so many times before.

Somehow, in death, it felt harder to let go.

"They're over here," Halle's voice echoed through the hallway.

In those final moments together, I bent down and pressed a kiss upon his forehead with trembling lips. "I'm sorry, Noah."

"I wasn't sure who to call..." she continued, a shaky edge to her voice.

It would be any moment now when the silence was broken by chaos.

I waited for the inevitable shouting to pierce the air. The cool bit of metal to dig into my skin. The soul-crushing moment I would be ripped away from him with a final goodbye on my lips. I was prepared to let the chaos win, but instead of succumbing to the consequences of my mistakes, I was greeted by the soft clicking of shoes against the linoleum floor. A gentle hand tipped up my chin, forcing me to look up into a set of piercing blue eyes. Charles Blanchet, owner of the Republic City Opera House, loomed over me, meeting my gaze for a heartbeat before dropping to Noah.

"Come," he said softly.

I shook my head, pulling Noah in closer despite the way my muscles screamed in protest.

"Very well," he said under his breath before pulling up a nearby chair. "Do you care to explain what happened?" Blanchet schooled his sharp features in a way that seemed to speak to his true nature—a hint of the man who liked to be seen from the shadows of the mezzanine but rarely spoke unless he felt the need to do so. The overwhelming sense of calmness he commanded was downright intimidating. He didn't flinch at the sight of spilled blood, nor did he falter at the twisted limbs curled around me. It set my nerves on edge to be pinned beneath his gaze.

"He—Noah—"

My eyes darted to Halle, standing on the outskirts of the room.

"Start from the beginning," Blanchet prompted.

"I—I walked in on Noah having sex with Tatiana."

Something preternatural shifted in her expression. She wordlessly excused herself from the room, and the wail that echoed through the hallways fractured what remained of my broken heart.

Charles cleared his throat, drawing my attention back toward the aging owner. Time had been his closest confidante, giving him streaks of gray that peppered his black hair and skin that was weathered but still radiated some warmth. Blanchet may have been in his late fifties to early sixties, but time had only shaped him in its favor.

"Ah, a crime of passion—"

"No," I snapped, then took a deep breath. "No, this wasn't an act of jealous rage. That's not what happened, but you're staring at me as if I'm lying."

"The living can speak lies"—he gestured toward Noah—"and the dead can keep them."

"You think this is what I wanted? I didn't—he wouldn't stop. I didn't mean for this to happen. I never meant to hurt him."

Blanchet was sitting close enough that all he had to do was lean forward a little to brush a strand of hair from my neck. He made an unamused sound deep from within his throat, then said, "So pretty. They're going to eat someone like you up in prison."

I jerked back out of reach.

"He attacked me. It was self-defense—"

"And what proof do you have to support that?"

"Noah—he was choking me. I thought I was going to die."

"Simply saying it aloud doesn't make it true," he retorted. "Where's the evidence, Hartwell? What's going to stop a jury of your peers from charging you with voluntary manslaughter? Because from where I'm standing, it doesn't look pretty. If I didn't know better, I would think you walked in on your boyfriend fucking another woman, and you took matters into your own hands when he wouldn't stop. This"—he gestured to the blood—"speaks more to my claims than yours."

"No!" I snapped my eyes shut. "That isn't what happened. I was trying to leave—he wouldn't let me go. He was hurting me."

Charles sighed. "What a shame—for someone so young to lose everything because of *one* mistake. Every time you graced the stage with your presence, I could sense you were made for greatness. You were so close to being something more," he said solemnly. "I can't say this is the future I envisioned for you, and I have a feeling this isn't what you imagined either."

My body swayed. It was becoming more difficult to keep myself upright.

"No," I breathed. "I never wanted this to happen."

With one fatal decision, I had ruined two lives in the process.

Tethering myself in a mess of dreams seemed to be the only way to wade through the darkness. It was the hope that being trapped was only temporary and escape was on the near horizon, giving me the means to finally be free. It was the promise that if greatness could prevail, there would be a reality where I could find true peace.

Charles was right. Noah was gone, and he took my dreams with him.

"Which is exactly why I'm going to do what I can to help you."

"I thought—"

"Shh"—he raised his hand—"while I may not be able to make this entire mess disappear, that doesn't mean I can't flip the narrative in our favor—I have people who work for me who can defend you in court. I can make this night a distant memory overshadowed by the future you deserve, but you need to do exactly as I tell you. Can you do that for me, Hartwell? Can you play along until I can make this right?"

The alternative was a wasted life. A future written in Noah's blood that I didn't have the means to wash away. The promise of tomorrow had been ripped away.

"You've suffered enough. Let me take that burden from you," he said softly.

Blanchet extended a hand toward me.

I was so tired of pretending. I couldn't carry on like this.

Ever so gently, I lowered Noah to the ground. Accepting this path meant putting the past behind me and finally putting myself first. And although I wasn't innocent in my crimes, taking Blanchet's hand in mine promised more than Noah had ever given me.

Chapter Six

Jin

From: Careers@operabastille.com
Subject: Thank you for your interest in employment

Dear Hyun-jin Collins,

We thank you for your interest in the Artistic Director position at Opéra Bastille. After careful consideration, we regret to inform you that we have decided to move forward with another candidate—

I hit the trash icon in the top right-hand corner.

Determined not to let the sting of disappointment ruin my day entirely, I dragged myself out of bed and ventured to the gym located in my building. I started the morning as I so often did and, without fail, by the time I hopped on the treadmill and tossed my phone on the device tray, it lit up with a frenzy of notifications. The sun had barely broken the horizon, and I was suddenly being ambushed on all fronts: updates from department heads, feedback for the musical composers, scheduling issues with new dancers, and, most importantly, news of potential salary changes we'd been advocating for the company. There never seemed to be an end to the torment. Even in the dead of night, that damn screen would pull me from my dream-less sleep with yet another "emergency" that couldn't wait until tomorrow.

I increased the speed and incline, ignoring another email flashing on the screen.

Mile by mile, I pored myself into what little free time I had before I would inevitably have to go to the one place I couldn't outrun. With a mere seven weeks separating us from the opening show, it had become common practice to work outside of contract hours, and while it wasn't below me to give up my evening for the theater, I drew a hard line when it came to my mornings.

Somewhere between the third and fourth mile, the team had switched from emailing one another to the group chat, which could only mean one thing. With sweat licking down my spine and my already aching muscles screaming in protest, I hit pause on the machine and swiped through the notifications while I caught my breath.

Emmanuel: What do you think....

Anastasia: Let me guess. A big fat no?

Anastasia: I wish I could say I'm surprised, but I'm not.

Anastasia: (sent a GIF of someone diving headfirst off a cliff)

Emmanuel: Bingo! We have a winner.

The choreographer and stage manager went back and forth, voicing their grievances over the failed salary proposal. Emmanuel, taking matters into his own hands, had privately emailed Charles after the initial rejection and questioned his decision on our behalf, then proceeded to send us a screenshot of the conversation.

"Much like a diamond, talent will always thrive under pres-sure, not gratification. It's in our company's best interest to allo-cate our resources accordingly and focus on the upcoming season instead of rewarding empty promises. Make this season the best yet, then come talk to me about your salary," I read the email aloud under my breath. "Jesus Christ."

Given my years working under Blanchet, I couldn't say I was surprised. I guess you can only get so many rejections before you begin to expect them.

I shot my brother a text, needing another minute to rest.

Jin: Are you still looking for another worker on-site?

Caleb: I would rather take a hammer to the head than give you a power tool.

I snorted, and a woman on the rower gave me a sideways glance.

Jin: That's an OSHA violation if I ever heard one.

Caleb: Get fucked.

Caleb: Are you bailing on class tonight again?

Caleb: I get lonely without you (kissing emoji).

My finger hovered over the keyboard as I thought up a witty response. Before I could, my screen lit up with a picture of Anastasia sitting on my broad shoulders, a beer raised in one hand, the other threaded through my black hair for stability—a distant memory of a bar crawl from my first year with the company. Her dark brown hair was woven into a crown atop her head. If you looked close enough, you could still see a glimmer of hope in my dark brown eyes.

"Jin." Her voice cracked on the line.

Not wanting to disrupt anyone else's workout, I walked into the lobby.

"I know," I said. "I saw the messages, and I don't really want to talk about it right now." Several beats passed. "Anastasia, are you there?"

"Yeah. Yeah, I'm still here," she said softly in a thick Slavic accent. "I need you to come in early. Do you think you can be here in thirty minutes?"

"Er, is everything okay?"

"No," she responded quickly. "Just get down here quick. Now. Please."

And that's the thing about setting boundaries: you draw the line in the sand as many times as you like, but that doesn't mean anyone has to respect them. Had it been anyone else, I would have told them no, but for Anastasia, it didn't feel like I had much of a choice.

Forty-five minutes later, I was arguing with a disgruntled officer outside the theater. Even with proof of identification, he refused to let me inside. It took calling Anastasia to come rescue me for the cop to reluctantly let me through.

The place was a madhouse—first responders circled the lobby with systematic precision. There was something about the way they collectively buzzed around the theater that reminded me of hive mentality. Little worker bees, hard at work, collecting their evidence bags.

I was so mesmerized by the flashing camera lights and chaos that Anastasia had to drag me to a secluded portion of the lobby to get my full attention. Beneath the archway, the shadows started to mingle, hiding part of her soft features. A nearby sconce provided enough light to see the dullness in her gray-blue eyes and the redness surrounding them. Something unspoken passed between, and before she could explain herself, I wrapped her tightly in my arms and refused to let her go as she shook with the weight of whatever burden she was carrying. It was several long minutes before she regained composure.

"I know. I know." She took a step away, wiping her tears with the back of her hand. The laugh that came deep from within her throat was breathy and exhausted. "Some—ah—

someone called the police early this morning. They found Noah's body in the physical therapy room." Her body convulsed as a sob bubbled up her throat. "I don't know what happened, but I keep hearing the police whisper something about a pair of scissors, but...I don't know. Um. I'm just having a really hard time wrapping my head around this news."

There wasn't a tear worth shedding on Noah's behalf, but my heart ached for Anastasia and the rest of the company that would be devastated by the news.

"Blanchet is calling off rehearsals for the day, and I don't want to really be here right now. Can we please go somewhere else, Jin? Anywhere else," she mumbled against my chest.

"Yeah, of course. We can go to my apartment in the meantime," I responded, rubbing her back. "Has anyone reached out to Hartwell and checked up on her?"

If no one had, I wasn't sure I had it in me to be the one to tell her.

"Not that I know of."

"We should probably—"

"Hyun-jin Collins?" an unfamiliar voice called out.

A female officer approached, hands braced on her bulletproof vest.

"Yeah?" I answered, hesitantly.

"Officer Taylor," she introduced herself. "Do you have a moment to speak?"

I looked at Anastasia, then back at Officer Taylor. "Yeah, what can I help you with?"

Anastasia excused herself to give us some privacy. Once we were alone, Taylor started her relentless questioning. She took her time dissecting my every response, asking the most trivial of questions about Noah's employment at the company, to complex and systematic ones that further explored his character. After two and a half years of mending my dancers, there didn't seem to be an end in sight. Time crawled by second by second as she wordlessly jotted down the last of my statement.

"And what of Miss Adeline Hartwell?"

My eyes snapped back in her direction. "What about her?"

"What can you tell us about her employment with the company? Anything will help."

"Um," I rubbed the back of my neck and laughed a little to myself, "well... Adeline had been dating Noah, but I don't see how that is relevant to his death."

Taylor held my gaze for a brief moment before returning to her notes.

"What?"

"Miss Hartwell is currently in custody," she explained. "So, as I said, any information you have may be helpful in this case. What can you tell me about Miss Adeline Hartwell's employment with the company and her relationship with Noah Hernandez?"

Question after question, I breathlessly explained her role within the company and the whirlwind romance she'd been swept up in soon after signing her contract. A relationship none of them had ever seen coming. The unruly physical therapist who thrived in cheap thrills and crowded rooms, and the gentle ballerina who seemed more at peace with herself than anyone else. Some say opposites attract, but I can't say I'm one of them.

Officer Taylor asked her final question, then handed me a business card with a reminder to contact her if I remember anything that could be helpful. Once she was far enough away, I pulled up the Delten County Sheriff's Office on my phone and typed in Adeline Elise Hartwell into the search bar. Two clicks later, I came face-to-face with a sight I never thought I would see.

Adeline's mugshot.

Chapter Seven

Adeline

Sometimes the only place to go is inward, retreating to the safety of my mind as my body succumbs to the passage of time. The cost of giving in was normally far greater than the reward, but as the next seventy-two hours went by in a blur, it was my subconscious that constructed thick, impenetrable walls to protect me in my most vulnerable state.

From being pinned to the group in a familiar manner that had flashes of Noah blurring out my vision, to having any sense of autonomy stripped away during the booking process, and lastly, to the confines of my holding cell that robbed me of the last of my dignity.

For three days, my mind protected me for once.

That's not to say there weren't weaknesses in my defense. In one of the rare moments I was taken from my cell, I was forced to strip bare in a cool metal room accompanied by a handful of other inmates. Each layer of clothing revealed a kaleidoscope of bruised skin ranging from the deepest shade of plum to blistering red. It didn't matter how raw I rubbed my skin with the cheap lavender soap; it wasn't enough to wash away my sins. The blood was long gone, but I could still feel it seeping between my fingers as I clutched his gushing wound. Memories, as sharp as the blade I drove through his gut, invaded my mind, and every wall I'd strategically built came crumbling down.

Curled up on the bathroom floor, an officer had to toe me in the ribs for me to gain back any sense of control. Piece by piece, I picked myself up and started rebuilding those walls with each passing day. I was more than content with living within the confines of my fabricated sense of safety, until someone threw open my cell with my name on their lips, beckoning me forward with the promise of freedom.

Life was finally starting to come back into focus after three miserably lonely days. The weight of what couldn't be undone sat heavily on my chest as I was warned how failure to comply with bail conditions would result in it being revoked. With each of my belongings returned to me, it felt like the pieces of my past were fitting back together. It was easy to shrink into myself under the right conditions, but standing at a bus stop with a dead cell phone and hardly enough money to get home, that was no longer the case. Those fragile pieces of myself were being held together by the thinnest of threads. The entire bus ride home, I desperately clung to them, not wanting to lose myself surrounded by strangers. It was only the promise of crawling into bed any minute now and not emerging for days prior that kept me from falling apart.

I stepped out of the elevator, rounded the corner, and stopped short.

Two stacks of boxes lined the hallway, and leaning up against them was a navy-blue suitcase with a purple ribbon tied to the handle. A thread snapped as I rushed for the boxes and started rifling through them, confirming what I feared. A heart-beat later, I shoved the key into the lock and confirmed the other.

"Andy," I said, pounding on the door. "Let me in."

The old wood groaned under the weight of each step, giving him away.

"I know you're home! I can hear you."

I was about to knock again when the door was thrown open —well, as far as the chain would allow it. Light trickled in from the hallway, shrouding his features in odd shadows that seemed to shift with each breath. The apartment was nearly pitch black, except for the blinding glow of the television bleeding in from the living room and the crackle of what sounded like sitcom laughter. All that separated us was a flimsy chain, and I couldn't help thinking as he loomed over me, it wasn't enough of a barrier.

"Andy," I protested, forcing my spine to straighten.

"What the fuck do you want?"

"Did you seriously change the locks on me?" I gestured toward the door. "You can't do that, it's illegal."

Andy leaned in, making the shadow slither over the top half of his face, highlighting the puffiness of his skin and the redness blotching out the whites of his eyes. "Take your shit and get out of here."

"You can't just kick me out."

"Oh, really? The last time I checked, the only names on the lease are mine and Noah's. I have every right to do what I want when, on paper, you were never a tenant here. Either leave or I'm calling the cops." He peered down at me like something stuck to the bottom of his shoes. "And I doubt you'd want me to call them, seeing the mess you already got yourself into, Adeline."

"Fine. Just let me get the rest of my stuff from—"

Andy slammed the door in my face.

Holding onto that final thread felt like a badge of honor— the last shred of dignity I could cling to as I confronted every-thing all at once. I blinked several times, watching the twisted grains of wood go in and out of focus, reality not yet catching up with me. That's when I felt the final snap that shook me to my core. A sob slowly crawled its way up my throat, and I slapped my hand over my mouth the moment it tore free. Having lost so much already, I wasn't sure I had it in me to walk away. If begging on my hands and knees was what it could take, then so be it. I wasn't leaving until he let me in.

I was about to rap my knuckle on the door when Andy beat me to it, hammering his fist on the other side hard enough to splinter the wood. "I'm calling the police," he shouted.

Andy was likely bluffing, but I didn't stick around to find out.

It took three trips to get all my belongings downstairs. It might have taken a fourth had Albert, the doorman, not stepped in to offer his assistance. As we rode down the elevator in utter silence, I couldn't bring myself to look him in the eyes as I thanked him.

I'd assumed all my luck for the day had dried up until Albert offered me a place to charge my phone behind his desk and a moment to rest while I sorted out my situation, but as I stared blankly at my screen, I knew my options were bleak. All my friendships in the city were deeply intertwined with my relationship with Noah, and I suspected they would give me as much of a warm welcome as Andy did. In a cruel twist of fate, the one person I longed to be with felt the most out of reach. Halle, despite never truly knowing what happened behind closed doors, always managed to put a smile on my face. It felt like she could always sense when I needed a reason to feel something other than heartache.

But as my finger hovered over her contact number, I was well aware that simply wishing something could be true didn't mean I deserved it.

There was a chance I could get a hotel for a few nights, but that wasn't a long-term solution and would drain my bank account until I found a more permanent living situation, as I always hoped. Realistically, my options were either that, sleep on the street, or return to the theater. The mere thought of which made the back of my throat sting like little claws were shredding through the lining of my esophagus, and if I didn't think of something else right this instance, I might never breathe properly again.

I was about to set down my phone when it buzzed. Nearly the entirety of the screen was veiled in spiderweb cracks, but between the shattered pieces, I could barely make out a name I didn't have the liberty of ignoring.

"Hello," I said softly.

"*Bonjour, mon étoile,*" Blanchet answered in a thick French accent. "I was calling to make sure you made it home safely, but it seems I've answered my own question."

"It's nice to hear from you, Mr. Blanchet—"

"Charles," he corrected.

"Sorry. Charles. I'm doing well," I answered, my tongue thick in my mouth. I switched the phone from one ear to the other. "I—I just wanted to thank you for all of this. I'm not sure how I'll ever be able to repay you for something like this."

"That's a problem for tomorrow, *mon étoile.* It's important that you focus on taking care of yourself and resting these next few days. I expect you back in rehearsals by Monday. Can you do that for me, Hartwell?" he asked. "The opening show is six and a half weeks away, and I need my star back and ready as ever."

I clutched my phone a little tighter as my eyes darted to the stack of boxes.

"Adeline?"

"Yes, sorry. I'm still here. Actually...I'm not sure why I told you I was doing well. That couldn't be further from the truth right now."

"I doubt anyone in your position would be."

"It's not just that..."

"Tell me."

"I have nowhere to sleep tonight. My roommate kicked me out; he is—was a good friend of Noah's. I know you've already done so much for me, and I don't expect anything more, but I was curious if you know anyone who might have a room available. I hate to ask, but I have money to pay, and it would only be temporary."

"Where are you now? Your old apartment?"

"Yes."

"Send me your address. I'll have a car pick you up in twenty minutes."

As promised, a black sedan with tinted windows pulled up outside my complex. A younger gentleman with hair cropped close to his scalp and raised scars lining the back of his wrist held the door open for me before loading my belongings in the trunk. By the vacant look in his empty eyes and impassive expression, I suspected this was the last thing he wanted to be doing at nine-thirty at night—he wasn't alone in that regard.

Music filtered through the speaker as we left behind the commotion of downtown and ventured toward the glitz and glam of the Upper East Side. Historic townhomes that predated the vast majority of the buildings in the city were butted up against rising skyscrapers that spoke to a different type of wealth. Mesmerized by the classic brownstones and designer stores, I wasn't able to piece together where we were going until he pulled over.

Charles Blanchet stood under the eave, hands in his pocket.

"*Mon étoile*," he greeted, holding the door open for me.

"Mr. Blanchet," I sputtered, then corrected myself.

"Charles. This wasn't what I meant when I asked for help. I would feel more comfortable getting a hotel rather than putting you out tonight."

"Why waste your money when we already have a guest room ready for you?"

Beneath the eave, it took us going back and forth several times for me to finally accept his generosity. As stubborn as I was being in the moment, at the end of the day, who was I to deny a warm bed and a fresh meal?

The driver set down a box in the foyer before leaving to fetch the others.

"Remind me, have you met my wife, Josephine?"

I shook my head, not recalling ever seeing her attend a show during the fall season. The woman I presumed to be his wife had her back to us, lounging on a sleek white couch that over-looked the sprawling cityscape—a sea of twinkling lights as far as my eyes could see. Our conversation carried through the foyer into the main living area, and I couldn't help noticing Josephine drain the remainder of her wine before deciding to join us. Introductions were quick and relatively painless. My first impression of the elusive member of the Blanchet family wasn't based on her striking appearance—a short blonde bob, hooked nose, and lengthy figure—but instead, it was the way she carried herself with such careless ease that made her slightly intim-idating.

Charles ran off to check on the driver, and Josephine took it upon herself to give me the tour. I would have given anything to curl up in bed and bring an end to this hellish day, but it didn't seem like I had much of a choice in the matter as Josephine dragged me from room to room, breathlessly explaining the inspiration and design for each. Pretending to act interested, I asked questions here and there to be nice, but by the time she led me into the master bedroom, I was convinced she'd only offered the tour because she liked the sound of her own voice.

"Charles wasn't sold on this design, but after months of going back and forth, I was able to wear him down. Something I like to rub in his face for doubting me—I've learned that's half of what being married is, arguing over silly things until no one's happy," she explained, aerating her sauvignon blanc.

"How long have you been married?"

"Almost a year and a half. Some would say we're still in the honeymoon phase."

"That's sweet. And how did you two meet?"

"Charles worked with my father in the Financial District," she answered dismissively.

Exiting the master bedroom, we were greeted by an enormous oil painting that consumed the entire wall, floor to ceiling. A horrific depiction of a gruesome battle stared back at me. I caught flashes of the blood splattered across the floor, and I forced myself to look away before I could make a mess of her imported tiles from the Ardéche region of southern France (I hated myself for remembering that tidbit from the tour).

Josephine stopped short and beheld its glory.

"*Sang pour sang*. Blood for blood," she translated, a hint of an accent licking her every word. "Charles won this piece in an auction last spring."

Charles walked into the hallway mid-conversation.

"I knew the moment my father's firm bid on it, I had to have it for myself."

"I believe Henri is still bitter over it," Charles added. "Hasn't spoken to me since."

"Serves him right for cutting me off after we started dating," she snorted. "Have you ever seen the original, Adeline? It's housed in the Gallery of Art downtown."

I shook my head, and Charles answered for her, "It's an

old *contes folkloriques*—a folk tale from the late fifteenth century depicting the end of a horrific war waged by a greedy seigneur mourning the loss of his lover. Death had started the war, and death had ended it as he gruesomely murdered his rival's lover in exchange for all the pain he'd caused. *Sang pour sang.*"

Curiosity eventually got the best of me. My gaze dragged up and over the mahogany frame, the muddy field, the blood-splattered swords locked in battle, and finally, the depiction of a soldier kneeling atop a woman's back, a pair of scissors splitting her spine down the middle.

I blinked, and the scissors vanished.

Not scissors. A dagger.

"Although nothing compares to the original," Josephine continued.

"I can only imagine," I rasped, struggling to control the rhythm of my heart.

To my relief, the tour did in fact have an end. After showing me all the amenities the guest room had to offer and assuring me there were plenty of blankets in case I got cold in the middle of the night, we finally parted ways. I practically ran to the adjoining bathroom to wash away the grime and cheap lavender soap coating my skin, but stopped short at the sight of my reflection staring back at me—it was nearly as horrific as *Sang pour sang.*

Thick purple lines cut across the underside of my jaw, the edges fading into the softest shade of yellowish green. Lifting a trembling hand, my fingertip grazed the outline of his thumb along the columns of my throat, and for a split second, I swore I felt a phantom of his touch.

"Oh, Noah," I huffed out. "Why?"

Something crashed on the other side of the wall, and I nearly jumped out of my skin. It wasn't long after that the shouting started. Bits and pieces of their conversation bleed through our shared wall.

"—send her to a damn hotel, for all I care."

"Patience, *mon chaton*," Charles shouted.

Josephine spoke too quickly, her words blending as one. And while her response was indistinguishable amongst the relentless shouting, there was no denying that I heard the words "charity case" leave her lips. I prayed that by the time I'd finished showering, the worst would be over, but that didn't seem to be the case for my *gracious* hosts. I wrapped myself in a mess of blankets, trying to drown out the vile words they spewed at one another, no closer to a resolution than when they started. I lay awake for hours, staring at the ceiling. A painfully familiar sense of emptiness chiseled at my soul little by little, until I was nothing more than a shell of my former self.

Perhaps it was why I picked up my phone without thinking.

I wish I had it in me to be strong for both of us, but instead of calling, I took the cowardly way out and texted to let her know I was thinking of her. Halle was mourning the loss of a friend, and I guess in a way, I was too when all I sent her were two little words.

I'm sorry.

Chapter Eight

Adeline

It was difficult to wrap my head around it—missing someone I wasn't sure I ever truly loved. To doubt myself after being convinced for quite some time that I was better off without him. Was it guilt dragging its claws over my flesh, making me bleed unrequited feelings of shame and self-preservation? Or something else entirely? The simple indecision of it all pulled me back and forth in an endless battle of wits, no closer to an answer than when I started. I wasn't sure how much more I could take...

Noah Hernandez was gone, but his presence somehow consumed me.

Every breath was a reminder that he had taken his last.

Every touch was a phantom of his own.

Every sight was dull in a world without him.

Noah was gone, but that couldn't be further from the truth.

He was everywhere.

With nowhere to hide, I allowed myself to feel everything all at once—not that I had much choice in the matter. I couldn't retreat inward as I once had, but instead, grief welcomed me with open arms and enveloped me in a suffocating darkness that seemed to take more than it ever gave. I was numb, but every conflicting emotion rocked through me with its feverish touch. If I did manage to get a little sleep after hours of tossing and turning, my own mind would turn against me, dragging me into a bottomless pit, where screaming for help was as feeble as trying to claw my way out. Even in my dreams, there was no escaping him.

By the third night, I'd given up entirely, only allowing myself a small increment of sleep that would ensure the nightmares couldn't reach me. I wrapped myself in a cocoon of blankets, hardly leaving unless need be. I felt like a caterpillar encased in a chrysalis, waiting for a transformation that would never come—instead of emerging as a beautiful butterfly, I entered the kitchen feeling like someone had chewed me up and spat me out.

Expecting to be alone, I was surprised to find Charles reading at the breakfast nook this late in the morning. Sprawled before him on the kitchen table was a steaming cup of black coffee and a plate piled high with food. There was a cigarette pressed between his lips—the stench of stale smoke lingered in the room.

"Morning," I somnolently said, walking to the fridge to fill up my water bottle.

Silence was his only answer. I turned around, thinking maybe he hadn't heard me, but over my shoulder, I found skies of blue through a trail of smoky haze. He studied me from head to toe through a thin trail dancing before his features. It had only begun to fade away when he finally said, "Make yourself a plate of food. I'm not sure I've seen you eat since you got here."

"Thank you, but—"

"You're already so skinny as is. You can mope around all you like, but you don't get to neglect yourself under my roof," he insisted. "You're a guest in my home, Hartwell. And I don't let my guests walk around my home as skin and bones. Plus, you'll need your strength for today."

Charles didn't wait for me to come up with another excuse before preparing a plate for me. Fried eggs with yolks already running down their sides, bacon so perfectly crispy it looked picturesque, and pain au chocolat that had been dusted with powdered sugar. My mouth was already salivating by the time he set down the plate before me.

"What's going on today?" I asked between bites.

"Josephine and the realtor are showing the apartment later this afternoon. We'll need to be gone for the next three hours."

"Oh—of course, that shouldn't be a problem. There's a café down the street..."

"No," he interjected. "You'll be coming with me down to the theater while Josephine shows the apartment. And before you give me an excuse, it will be well before rehearsals, so you'll have the studio to yourself. You've done enough sulking about my house. Dancing will be good for you. No one wants to watch you waste away like this."

I set down the pastry. "I'm not sure I'm ready to dance again."

"And how will you know if you don't try?"

My sister Melissa had been the miracle child of our family. A little bundle of joy—six pounds and nine ounces—that saved a dying marriage on the brink of a divorce. For her services, her every whim became my parents' every will. Whatever Melissa wanted, she got. Which meant that the winter she begged our parents for ballet lessons after watching The Nutcracker on a school field trip, it wasn't even a question that she found a pair of ballet slippers wrapped under the Christmas tree that year. Her infatuations were normally short-lived—flavors of the month that lived and died with her short attention span, but ballet lasted longer than any of us ever expected. Being the younger sister, I had little choice in the matter as my parents carted me around town for her lessons and recitals, and eventually, her infatuation had become my obsession.

Clothed in hand-me-down dance wear, I started lessons the following year after nearly begging on my hands and knees for my parents' permission. With a childhood full of noise, dance had been the only time my head was silent. Peace had found me at last, and I did everything in my power to maintain it. If it meant working odd jobs to afford classes, saving up birthday money to buy my first pair of pointe shoes, or volunteering at the studio to observe lessons, then I was more than prepared to do everything I could to keep dancing.

Ballet had consumed my life, and for the first time, I felt whole.

I would have given anything to dance again, but fear was the greatest enemy of hope. It had robbed me of the only constant I could cling to in a sea of trepidation. It was a means of healing that I wasn't prepared to face after six long days since setting foot in the theater. I wasn't ready to return, but with Charles by my side, I wanted to at least try.

The studio lights flickered to life, blanketing the room in a harsh white glow.

I'd surprised even myself by making it this far despite the overwhelming urge to turn back with each step. But I keep my eyes trained on the ground and powered through, making light conversation with Charles along the way to keep my mind distracted.

Opposite the door was a wall of mirrors—a dancer's greatest tool. The ultimate indication of body alignment, posture, and extension, helping us create seamless, elegant silhouettes from head to toe. After eighteen years of being strapped in a pair of pointe shoes, my eyes instantly gravitated toward my reflection after avoiding it for so long.

I caught a flash of purple, threw my dance bag on the ground, and looked away.

The studio was eerily still. Something about the stagnant air and preternatural silence was reminiscent of the last time I was here. Silence was the companion of penitence, and both greeted me with open arms as I stepped into third position after warming up. I attempted to drive away the silence as *La Bayadère—The Kingdom of the Shades* bled through the speakers.

I took a deep breath and steadied myself.

The music was my guide—my trusted leader, taking me far away from this hellscape. I bent my body into a penché, matching the slow and controlled nature of the nineteenth-century ballet. As the music intensified and percussion dominated to create grandeur and drive, I moved accordingly. Quick, swift moments contorted my body in a series of glissades, tendus, and pirouettes that had me starting to lose myself completely.

There was no room for chaos in my mind. There was only music.

The melody had me in its grasp. A loyal friend who was as dependable as it was constant. A systematic collection of harmonies that expressed so much without words. Music was the avenue and dance was the expression of—

On the third pirouette, there vows a subtle aching deep within my knee. I attempted to ignore the pain, but as constant as music was in my life, so were the recurring injuries hindering my career—irrefutable evidence that no matter how much I loved my craft, it would never last. Dance would only be a temporary solution. My future was bright as a dying star, any second from imploding.

I pushed off into a pirouette, the world spinning around me in a blur.

With proper care and rest, I would only prolong the inevitable. There was an expiration date on my career, and despite being unable to fathom that, it was Noah who would kiss my tears away and assure me everything would be all right. Aside from being my partner, he was my biggest supporter—the person who would cheer me on from the audience, then rush to my side the moment the curtains were drawn to tend to my knee. I trusted him to heal me—to prolong the inevitable for as long as possible.

The aching sweltered with each turn until it felt like the entire right side of my knee was on fire. The pain was but a fraction compared to the realization that he wasn't here to heal me anymore. Noah wasn't here to carry me in his arms when I couldn't keep myself upright. He wasn't here to leave a trail of kisses up my knee as he praised me for all my hard work.

He wasn't here, and it was all my fault.

I kept spinning, welcoming the way the pain throbbed through my limbs.

Maybe I deserved to never dance again.

"Adeline," someone shouted.

My leg nearly gave out as I abruptly stopped.

The world came back into focus, and so did the looming figure in the doorway. A pair of dark brown eyes, nearly as black as the wisps of his hair, bore into me from across the studio.

"Adeline," Jin repeated, a softness in his tone. "Are you all right?"

The artistic director watched me from afar, a swell of emotions I couldn't quite pinpoint resisting in his gaze. I thought the churning in my gut would lessen when his eyes left mine, but the sensation worsened as they lowered to my knee.

I placed my hands on my hips and heaved a breath. "I'm fine."

"It doesn't seem like it."

"Can I help you with something, Jin?" I snapped.

He cleared his throat. "Charles has been trying to call you for the last twenty minutes. He sent me down here to check on you and let you know he wants you to meet him in his office."

"Okay, thank you." I grabbed my bag and headed for the door.

I nearly made it out when he called my name, stopping me in my tracks.

Standing well over six feet, Jin had perhaps a good foot on me. The size difference might have been intimidating in such proximity, but I was more concerned with the tone of his voice than his stature.

His jaw worked before he asked, "Are you sure you're all right?" I opened my mouth to speak, but he cut me off. "And I'm not talking about your knee. No one could get hold of you. Anastasia went down to your apartment, and your roommate said you moved out."

I offered him a weak smile. "As I said already, I'm fine."

"Adeline."

"Expect me back at rehearsals tomorrow," was all I said before leaving.

Charles motioned for me to enter his office, a phone pressed against his ear.

"Oui, elle vient d'entrer dans mon bureau," he said, pressing a series of buttons on his landline in quick succession. "Adeline, this is Donovan Bell from Carson & Bell Law Associates."

"Hello, Miss Hartwell, it's a pleasure to finally meet," Donovan responded, his voice bleeding through the speaker. "Thank you for taking the time out of your busy schedule to sit down and talk with us. Before we begin, I want to ensure you understand that everything we discuss is protected by attorney-client privilege, meaning anything you say will remain confidential."

Charles hadn't mentioned anything about a meeting earlier today, and I couldn't help feeling a little blindsided stepping into his office. But I guess even if he had, nothing could have prepared me for the inevitable.

"Yes, I understand."

"Perfect, let's begin."

Donovan and his associates attempted to walk me through the basics, starting with some light questioning that forced me to recall the most minute details regarding the events leading up to March 11. Donovan, to his credit, kept everything quite professional, and the entire thing was relatively painless until he started asking about the nature of our relationship, past fights, previous incidents of violence, events leading to our altercation, and overall intent behind my actions. Each question slowly wore me down until simply speaking felt like driving a blade into a wound not yet healed. I started stumbling over my words, and the walls began to close in.

Overly complicated legal terms were being tossed around back and forth. I asked for clarification once, but quickly became bogged down by the sheer number of them as the conversation dragged on. My mind was reeling by the time Donovan started outlining the sequences of events moving forward: an arraignment, a pre-trial hearing in twenty days, a discovery phase—it meant nothing to me other than yet another hoop to jump through in order to prove myself to a room full of strangers—individuals who would be deciding my fate, evidence or not. What proof did I have when words weren't enough? Lack of evidence was brought up several times, and each time it was mentioned, it seemed to always be accompanied by the fact that there were no witnesses.

"If we can prove she acted in lawful self-defense, Adeline stands a chance."

"What evidence do we currently have that can prove this narrative?"

"Would Mr. Andy Crawford testify on Miss Hartwell's behalf?"

Their voices started to merge into one.

"Mr. Crawford is not at liberty to speak at this time."

It became harder to differentiate one voice from another.

"—if we could get access to the CCTV—"

"—justifiable homicide—"

"—a plea deal—"

I felt myself starting to shrink back, trying to wrap my head around this.

"—premeditated—"

"—burden of proof—"

"—mitigating circumstances—"

Andy wasn't home enough to see the majority of our fights, but he heard enough of the fighting to testify, perhaps. I wasn't sure asking him would work in my favor. He'd made it clear where his loyalty lay.

"—Adeline—"

If only I could go back to the apartment and talk to him.

"Adeline."

I would only need five minutes alone.

"Adeline," a voice snapped.

Charles was staring at me, eyebrows furrowed.

"Sorry," I said softly.

Donovan cleared his throat. "Like I was saying, a plea deal is off the table. Our only concern at the moment is if the prosecution argues that you were defending yourself but used excessive force or your actions weren't entirely justified, you could be charged with voluntary manslaughter."

"And how much jail time is voluntary manslaughter?" Charles asked.

"Unless we collect enough viable evidence, she could be looking at five to twenty years."

Chapter Nine

Jin

The sight alone was enough to churn the breakfast in my stomach.

In all my years of kickboxing, I'd never seen anything quite like it. Deep purple lines ran across the length of her neck with edges fading into a strange yellowish-green color —nearly the entire right side of her neck, from jaw to clavicle, was consumed by a kaleidoscope of different colors. It was one thing to see them online when the bruises were still forming; it was an entirely different beast to hear her wheeze with each word spoken. And as much as it likely pained her to speak, I couldn't help noticing she wasted all her strength lying to me.

She smiled, but it didn't quite reach her eyes. "As I said already, I'm fine."

Adeline Hartwell was one of the most dedicated and prominent dancers within the company—a rising star, a heartbeat away from seeing her dreams come to fruition. In all our months working together, I'd never seen her hide her weaknesses. Adeline was always willing to admit when she was having difficulty with her knee, so it took me by surprise when she lied to me not once, but twice.

"Adeline."

"Expect me back at rehearsals tomorrow."

As quickly as she appeared back in my life, she was gone, taking with her all the warmth in the room. I nearly called her back, but thought better of it as she stormed off. Adeline could lie to me to her heart's content, but what truly bothered me was that I wasn't entirely sure she knew she was lying to herself, too.

With only an hour to spare until my next meeting, I took the rare opportunity to walk to the nearest coffee shop and pick up my mobile order. I used the brief moment of peace to mindlessly scroll through my phone. Among the countless spam calls, unsolicited ads, and unread messages from friends and family, the missing call from my brother instantly stood out to me. It wasn't like him to call or text while on site, so I called him back before my mind could wander to a dark place.

"Caleb?"

"What are you doing next Thursday?"

"Jesus." I sighed in relief. "I can't box on Thursdays. I already told you."

The quaint little coffee shop was abuzz. The hissing of an espresso machine, the humming of chatter, and the rich scent of mocha greeted me as I entered.

"This isn't about boxing," he said. "Although..."

I rotated the cups on the counter, checking the names written in black marker.

"No, Caleb. I can't keep having the same conversation with you."

"Fine. I get it, you're too strong to fall for the mighty guilt trip," he said in a mocking tone. "Anyway, at work yesterday, I might have overheard the owner mention something about an executive director position. Okay. I was eavesdropping, but that's beside the point. The Lotte is looking for someone to fill the role before they finish construction. *And...*"

"And?"

"I set up an interview for you next Thursday at nine-thirty in the morning. All you have to do is meet him at the theater. You are so very welcome."

"Caleb," I sighed, situating myself on the outskirts of the café while I waited for my order. "I have work. I can't just drop everything for an interview."

Applying for Opéra Bastille had already taken so much out of me...

"You're supposed to be thanking me," he continued. "All you do is complain about your job, but you don't do shit about it. There's only so much more I can take before I go insane. Why don't you just make up an excuse to your boss—a doctor's appointment or something?"

"The spring season starts in six weeks. Things are hectic."

"Then you aren't allowed to complain when you spend the next decade of your life wasting away at a job that you're miserable at, but too scared to get out of your damn comfort zone. You can do whatever you want. It's your life, but I'm not going to say anything to Destler yet. At least give it a few days before you make a decision, and after that, if you still want to miss out on this *once-in-a-lifetime* opportunity, then I guess I'll just make up an excuse for you..." He sighed. "Even though I really stuck out my neck to get you this interview in the first place. The owner isn't exactly the easiest to get an audience with."

I didn't have time to unpack all of that as the barista called out my name.

"I really have to go."

"Jin," the barista repeated.

"Fine. I'll think about it. See you tonight."

"See, the guilt trip does—" I hung up on him before he could finish that thought and walked over to retrieve my flat white. Heading for the exit, I noticed a woman sitting near the window who was intently staring at me from afar. Something about her sharp features and bronzed skin felt like reaching toward a memory just out of arm's reach. I recognized her face, but couldn't remember why that was.

She rose from her seat. "Excuse me, are you Jin Collins?"

"Yes," I answered hesitantly.

"Bianca Riviera" —she extended her hand— "with the *Republic Press*. Do you have a moment to speak on the events that transpired on March 11 at the Republic City Opera House? It will only take a few minutes."

It all came rushing back to me.

"I'm sorry, no comment," I answered, slipping out of the front door. She followed, meeting me stride for stride. Ms. Riviera had written plenty of articles about the opera house over the years, but she never struck me as the type of reporter to bombard her interviewees.

"What do you know of Noah Hernandez's untimely death?"

"No comment," I bit out, weaving through the crowded street.

Republic Press was among the dozens of media outlets we'd personally invited to the exclusive showcase to build anticipation for the upcoming season. Charles would have my head on the butcher's block if he knew I'd been anything less than kind to one of their reporters, but as she peppered me with more and more questions, I was starting to lose my patience. She interrogated me until we eventually hit a red light. I considered crossing the road, but thought better of it when a semi-truck came barreling in our direction.

"Ms. Riviera, I'm sorry, but I don't have the time to—"

"What about Adeline Hartwell's involvement in his death?"

"What?"

"What can you tell me about Adeline Hartwell since she

joined the company? Were you aware of her relationship with Noah and his potential infidelity with another unnamed dancer?"

I cut her off before she could ask another ridiculous question.

"Tell me, have you seen the photo of her from that night?"

"Of course," she answered, taming a black strand of hair blowing in the breeze.

"Then you should know better than anyone that there's more to her story than the police have led us to believe," I said. "Miss Hartwell is by far the most compassionate dancer in my company, and there's no reality in which she would have done what she did unless Noah deserved it. She's innocent—the bruises lining her neck are proof enough. And instead of passing judgment without knowing her story, I suggest you do some real journalism and interview Noah's past lovers instead of harassing me."

The light finally changed to green, allowing me to escape. When I glanced over my shoulder, Ms. Riviera was standing at the edge of the crosswalk, frantically writing down every word.

The afternoon dragged on while simultaneously flying by. I met with the composer to finalize our rehearsal schedule, discussed arrangements for when one of the violinists went on maternity leave, and reviewed the music score and libretto to ensure everything was in line with my artistic vision. By the time we were nearly done, a notification popped up on my phone, reminding me that my meeting with the marketing team was starting in fifteen minutes. I bounced from meeting to meeting with only my flat white to keep me going.

I'd become accustomed to the chaos. I was constantly

drowning in the workload, barely treading enough to keep my head above water, let alone meet Blanchet's unrealistic expectations. Instead of doing the sensible thing and quitting, the moment I sensed burnout lurking around the corner, I foolishly doubled down. It wasn't easy to justify resigning when leaving meant giving up on a part of myself in the process. Republic City Opera House was always meant to be a stepping stone—a chapter in my life meant to propel me further, rather than trap me within the confines of the district. I wasn't sure how much longer I could do this to myself, but each application I submitted felt like a betrayal not only to myself but to the life I nearly had.

The executive director role was a far cry from working overseas, but I did wonder what the position might entail. What creative freedom would I be able to indulge in? What talented individuals would I be able to collaborate with to make my visions come to fruition? What type of virtues did Destler hold himself to in a district built on the backs of others?

By the time I was sitting in on rehearsals, it felt like a blessing to be in my corner of the studio, offering feedback when needed. Well, as much feedback as I could possibly give when we were short two and a half dancers. Halle was still out on bereavement leave, Adeline was gone for obvious reasons, and Tatiana was still trying and failing to prove she was healed.

Anastasia's voice echoed through the studio as she counted their steps.

For the remainder of the third act, I allowed myself to indulge in a reality in which life didn't beat me down as much as it built me up. I imagined what it might feel like to not stumble into my apartment well past eight o'clock, too exhausted to manage a social life outside of these theater walls. I fantasized about spending more time with my family and putting myself first for once. By the time I sent off my last email for the day, I had to admit, I was at least curious about the position. It felt like something worth exploring if it meant giving myself a future that didn't *thrive under pressure, not gratification.* That possibility echoed through my head as I walked through the halls of the empty theater, one last task to check off my list before I would head out and meet my brother.

A strange tingling sensation snaked its way down the back of my neck as I started down the aisle. It took another ten steps for me to realize why. I wasn't alone.

In the fourth row of the orchestra center was a lonesome figure had their feet propped up on the seat in front of them. A notebook rested in their lap; pages covered in hurried lines and smudged ink. Silver headphones rested atop their head, taming soft waves of black hair. In a space specifically designed to draw the eye toward the ornate gold-leaf designs that bracketed the stage, a glistening chandelier that blanketed the entire theater in a heavenly glow, or the seraphic figurines that loomed above, none of them compared to her, because I was already looking at the most beautiful woman I'd ever had the pleasure of laying my eyes on.

Adeline Hartwell.

Chapter Ten

Jin

Lost in her own little world, Adeline scribbled away. Compared to the broken woman I last encountered in the dance studio, she was an entirely different person. Swept away far from this place on lyrical melodies and ethereal tones barely audible through her headphones, something about the way she held herself spoke of true peace—a side of her I wasn't accustomed to seeing. The sight of her like this made my heart quicken, as it so often did. I dared a step closer to get a better look at her, knowing this was a fleeting moment and I was only being greedy by wanting more.

Adeline whipped her head around, slamming her hand against her chest.

Oops. Too close.

I threw up my hands in surrender, a few papers slipping free.

"Damn it, Jin. You nearly scared me half to death," she said, ripping off her headphones. Her mouth hung open for a moment, then snapped shut. "Sorry, poor choice of words."

"I didn't mean to scare you. I was dropping these off for the maestro," I said, holding up the music notes. Content with my answer, she went back to scribbling in her notebook, and I took that as my cue to leave. That strange tingling sensation returned, and when I glanced over my shoulder, I found a pair of hazel eyes watching me before quickly returning to her work.

A smile tugged at the corner of my lips as I walked back up the aisle.

"I'm about to lock up the theater. Do you want me to walk you out?"

"Oh. Um..." Something about her eyes reminded me of the hours following a devastating storm: while mostly gray, there was so much life and beauty that resided there. "It's all right. I'll see myself out and have Mr. Sinclair lock up after me, but thank you."

"Mr. Sinclair's granddaughter is running a fever. I told him I would lock up for him so he could take care of her." I cleared my throat. "Really, I don't mind. I could even give you a ride home if you like." Or wherever she was staying.

"I—" She chewed on her bottom lip. Those stunning hazel eyes of hers no longer resembled the aftermath of a storm, but instead were the storm itself. Her gaze frantically darted between her hands and me as she struggled for words.

"Adeline..."

A single tear spilled down her cheek. She quickly turned and wiped it away with a curse, only for it to be replaced by another. The storm raged on, and I did the only thing I could think of to ease whatever was troubling her. Although we sat several seats apart, I'd never felt closer. There was comfort in the silence we shared. When words didn't feel like enough, it was all—

"I was planning on sleeping in the theater tonight," she blurted out.

A beat passed.

"Ah, I see...and where exactly were you planning on sleeping?"

"It hardly matters."

"See, I beg to differ. There's only one right answer, and if you say anything other than what I'm thinking in my head, then you are doing a serious injustice to your lower back." Adeline gave me a sideways glance, tears still spilling free. "I'm being serious."

"And so am I."

"Then you must have had a plan," I shot back.

"I was planning on sleeping in the props department," she responded hesitantly.

I snorted a laugh. "That's a rookie move, Hartwell."

She tossed up her arms. "Well, it's a hell of a lot better than sharing a wall with Charles and his wife."

"You're staying with Blanchet?"

"Honestly, I don't even know why I'm here," Adeline groaned, dragging her hands over her face. "It was hard enough coming back today...I'm running on zero sleep and needed some rest so I could think straight."

There was another long pause that sucked up all the air between us.

"Is the theater where you really want to be, given all that has happened recently?"

"What other choice do I have?"

"Stay with me," I blurted out, instantly wanting to bash my head in after realizing what I had said. "I mean...I have an extra guest room that's collecting dust. You could rent the room if you need somewhere to stay. The walls are thick, and I'm a clean roommate, I promise."

"Thick walls, huh?"

"The thickest."

Bashing in my head wasn't enough. I was going to nose-dive

off the stage. It's been a nice thirty-two years—well, as nice as it could be while it lasted.

Adeline laughed, and there was a good chance it was out of pity, but a win was a win.

"I appreciate the offer, Jin…"

"But…?"

"Well…"

"It's all right, Hartwell. I've had enough rejection for one lifetime. I can handle one more."

The tears were gone, and a soft smile graced her lips.

"Charles has already done so much for me. It feels wrong leaving after everything."

Rising to my feet, I smoothed out my pants before rifling around in my pockets.

"Here, take it," I said, extending a small silver key to her. "The correct answer you were looking for was the couch in my office. Stay there as long as you need. The cleaning staff usually comes by around six in the morning, so as long as you head out before then, no one will bother you."

She stared down at the key. "You don't have to do that."

"It's a hell of a lot better than sleeping on a bed of foam props."

"Charles and Josephine were probably just having a bad night. Every couple fights from time to time," she said, snapping her notebook shut and stuffing it in her dance bag. "It's sweet of you to offer me a place to stay, but I think you're right, I'm not sure this is where I want to be alone with my thoughts. I'm going to head back to their apartment before anyone notices me missing."

I narrowed my eyes. "Is that what you truly want?"

"I think it's for the best. Would you mind walking me out, please?"

If I were keeping a tally, that would be lie number three.

"I'll make a deal with you, Adeline."

Now it was her turn to narrow her eyes at me.

"Technically speaking, according to the zoning laws for the city, no one is supposed to be living on the premises. I won't tell anyone I saw you here in case you change your mind, but you have to agree to take the key," I said, handing it over.

She pursed her lips. "Fine, but if you start noticing any missing snacks in the break room, you can't say anything either."

I turned an invisible key to my lips and tossed it over my shoulder.

When all was said and done, Adeline allowed me to walk her out but declined a ride to Blanchet's place. Before parting ways, I reminded her one last time that both my offers still stood if she ever changed her mind. And while Adeline was proving to be a little stubborn, I felt better knowing she was walking away with that key in her pocket.

Chapter Eleven

Jin

Distractions are only as good as they last. Part of me hoped that celebrating this next chapter in Sophia and Caleb's lives would be enough, but that couldn't have been further from the truth. As we broke bread and spilled wine with our closest friends, all anyone could talk about was the rumors regarding the theater spreading like wildfire. Each worse than the last. I did my best to shut them down, but as adamant as they were to learn of the *potential murder*, it wasn't the investigation on the forefront of my mind. It was the small silver key and the dancer who now had it in her possession.

When distractions weren't enough, and the wine finally ran dry, Sophia offered to drive to the corner store to pick up some more, and I leaped at the chance to get some fresh air. The neon sign outside was the only thing that felt remotely welcoming about the corner store. Between the aisles of imported whiskey and decorative bottles of tequila, our presence alone was enough to warrant a few glares in our direction. An older woman in her late seventies made it a point to roll her eyes at us, and my loving future sister-in-law returned the gesture by lifting a bottle of wine high up in the air and placing her other hand on her stomach.

"What are the odds she's going to the front counter right now?" Sophia goaded, watching the woman disappear behind a display of chips.

"Maybe you should pop the cork and give her a real show."

"I bet you twenty bucks that she's trying to convince him not to sell to us."

I peeked my head over the aisle and caught a glimpse of the woman leaning in to whisper to the cashier, who seemed more concerned with the teenagers laughing near the candy section than with us in the deepest corner of the store. "Too late. She's already told everyone what a terrible mother you are."

Sophia playfully smacked me on the arm. "Next time you need a ride, you can walk."

"You love me too much to let me walk around the city alone."

"Love is a strong word. Obligated is more like it."

With three or so dozen people waiting for us back at the apartment, it was more of an obligation on both of our ends. While I was gracious enough to host for the night, Caleb had been put in charge of snacks and refreshments. Dinner had turned into drinks, and while that normally wasn't a problem, what he failed to realize was that some of his work buddies were planning on bringing their partners too, doubling the number of people we were originally expecting.

"That's exactly how I feel every time you ask me for comp tickets," I said, knowing she'd been itching to ask since we announced the dates for the upcoming season.

"It's not as if you have a girlfriend to save them for," she retorted.

Sometimes it was difficult to wrap my head around Caleb and Sophia's relationship. With long ash-brown hair, high cheekbones dusted with dark freckles, and an oval face that gave her an effortless type of beauty, she looked at odds with my baby brother. I know when he finally worked up the courage to introduce me to the track star he met in his Intro to Philosophy class, he was reaching for the stars when he asked her out.

"Ha. Ha. How creative," I deadpanned, weaving through the aisle. "You should really do stand-up. No, I mean it. Nothing gets a crowd going like a low-hanging joke."

I dropped the case of beer on the counter with a thud, and the cashier huffed out a breath before scanning the various brightly colored bottles sprawled out before him. Disappointed with the cashier, the little old woman shook her head full of blue curls and made for the exit, clutching a plastic bag full of malt liquor.

"Cash or card," the cashier grumbled.

"Card," Sophia answered, fishing out her wallet before I could. Stuck to the worn-out leather was a yellow sticky note. "Here, use Caleb's card. It's his fault I had to leave my own party in the first place."

She scanned over the checklist one last time.

"Dang," she muttered to herself. "We forgot Charlotte's hard seltzers."

I didn't even have a chance to offer to get them before she was gone, swallowed up by the tall rows of shelves. A moment later, the group of teenagers approached the counter, arms full of candy and sugary energy drinks. I stepped aside to let them pay and pulled out my phone to check the time while I waited. Sandwiched between an apology text from Anastasia for being unable to make it tonight and a missed call from Caleb, there was an unread message that kicked my heart out of rhythm.

Hartwell: If you did rent out your room, how much would you charge?

Hartwell: Asking for a friend.

I had to read it twice to make sure I wasn't seeing things.

It had been hours since we parted ways, and yet there wasn't enough distraction in the world to keep me from reliving her tear-filled confession from earlier. The key was a step in the right direction, but it didn't feel like enough when her lies spoke so much to the truth.

Jin: And did this friend of yours finally have a change of heart?

Three little dots appeared on the screen, then disappeared.

Having had a few drinks before we left, I wasn't sober by any means—nor was I drunk either, but the moment that incoming call flashed across the screen, it was the most sobering sight imaginable. I forced a deep breath in before answering.

"Hello," I rasped, clutching the phone.

"You never answered my question, which makes me scared I can't afford it."

Her voice was as sweet as honey, smooth as can be, and only a spoonful could bring a smile to your face without even trying.

"Well...you didn't answer my question either. And I thought this was for a friend."

Adeline huffed out a breath. "This friend of mine can't sleep because Charles's wife came home belligerently drunk. She currently has her head in the toilet, and when she isn't throwing up, she's screaming at her husband. Charles isn't exactly helping the situation..."

I couldn't for the life of me understand why she would ever stay with Blanchet. Something about that didn't sit right with me. Neither did the little tremble laced in her every word.

A beat passed. "Adeline?"

"I don't—I don't exactly feel comfortable being around them right now."

Sophia returned with the six-pack of seltzers, but not alone. It must have been someone she knew from work because they were chit-chatting about an upcoming case. While they caught up with one another, I gestured to my phone and then the door to let her know I was just stepping out for only a moment.

"I'm sorry," she huffed out a breathy laugh. "I didn't know who to call."

"No need to be sorry. I think anyone in your situation would be feeling the same. I know the last person I want to hear fighting is my boss and his wife. I'm actually glad you called me. I was thinking about our conversation from earlier. My offer still stands if you need a quiet place to stay, but I can't help feeling like you are still a little hesitant. What's holding you back? Money?"

"The money is a factor, but truthfully...I don't exactly have the best track record with roommates. I only really know you in a professional setting, and...well, I guess what I'm trying to say is, the last time I jumped into a living situation too quickly, it didn't end well."

Through the glass panel door, I could just make out the silhouette of Sophia—all smiles and laughter. I knew without a doubt that Adeline would be far more comfortable with us than trapped in Blanchet's penthouse.

"I'll tell you what," I started. "I'm having a party at my apartment in the south end of the district—my brother and his fiancée learned the gender of their baby, and we're celebrating. You're welcome to come stay the night to get away from the fighting, and you have my permission to interrogate my friends and family while you're at it. Consider it a trial run."

"A trial run?"

"If the thick walls weren't enough of a selling point, wait until you see the view."

She cursed under her breath. "Okay, Collins. Let's do it."

Chapter Twelve

Adeline

Misconceptions are bred from twisted words and faulty reasoning, passed down from person to person until they're unrecognizable from the truth. People often believe courage is a trait only found in those who are impenetrable to fear, but it's quite the contrary. Some of the bravest people I know experience fear almost daily, and it's because they are determined to face it head-on that makes them so strong.

That's the funny thing about anxiety. You can know something to be true but still find a way to convince yourself that you're the exception, not the rule. The curse of being self-aware with the inability to change despite yourself. I should have been over the moon that I advocated for myself by reaching out to Jin, but as I examined the thick layer of makeup coating my neck in the elevator mirror, all I could think about was the fact that at the first sign of trouble, I ran.

I leaned in, elongating the column of my neck to get a better look. It took a bit of color correction, a pound of foundation, and a dash of contour to look halfway presentable, and even then, the makeup caked onto my skin wasn't enough to conceal the truth. Under the right lighting, it was so painfully clear I was trying and failing to hide something. Even the boots, transparent tights, and fitted skirt were all part of the deception.

"Jesus Christ," I said under my breath. "What am I doing?"

Sneaking out of Charles's apartment.

Calling Jin for help.

Thinking I could hide the truth with drugstore products.

All of this was a mistake.

And yet here I was, watching the floor ascend with each passing moment, bringing me closer to a party I wasn't even invited to. Maybe if I turned around now and texted him that I wasn't feeling well, we could all pretend this never happened. I could go back to the apartment before anyone missed me and—

The elevator doors pinged open, and standing there, looking at his phone, was Jin. A heartbeat later, our eyes met.

As artistic director, Jin had been a constant shadow in the chaos. A voice of reason when everyone was at odds. Until now, I had only known him in a professional setting, and I couldn't help noticing how strange it was to see him outside of work. Without the confines of the theater walls, Jin looked so much more at ease. Simply stripping off his tie and dress shoes was enough to put a smile on his face and a glimmer in his dark brown eyes.

"Hi."

"Hi," I shot back, feeling the effects of his contagious smile.

"You know, I was planning on meeting you downstairs."

"Maybe I wanted to check out the place on my own."

"Thoughts?"

I shifted from one foot to the other, scanning over the light green wallpaper and potted plants lining the length of the hallway. "Compared to the multi-million-dollar apartment I was staying in, I would say it's a bit of a downgrade, but it has charm."

Okay, new plan: use the party as a much-needed distraction, then when Jin is sleeping, I'll slip out of the apartment and return before the sun rises.

It was flawed, of course, but it would work for now.

It didn't account for the fact that I promised to be at rehearsals that very next day and would have to explain to Jin why I snuck out in the dead of night, but when had any of my plans worked out in the past?

"Low expectations are good," he said, offering to take my overnight bag off my hands. "It just means I get a chance to really impress you, Hartwell. Let me give you the tour?"

"Shoes off?" I asked, reaching down.

"Normally, yes," he answered. "But it's been a bit of a lost cause tonight."

Over the phone, Jin had mentioned something about a gender reveal party. I was under the assumption that the apartment would be decorated in a blue and pink decor. Maybe some festive balloons, or some kind of elaborate means of revealing the big secret, but when we stepped inside, I was surprised to find the apartment felt more reminiscent of a college party than a family affair. The living room, kitchen, and balcony were a mess of drunken friends, blaring music, and darkened shadows.

"I thought you said this was a gender reveal party."

"It is," Jin leaned in to shout over the music, then pointed to the lopsided banner strung up in the dining room that read: *It's a girl*. "My brother's the first of his friend group to have a kid, and none of them know how to act. Tonight was an excuse to get together and drink for them."

"Isn't she a little far along to have just been learning the gender of her baby?" I asked, eyeing the pregnant woman I presumed to be his future sister-in-law, deep in conversation with a redheaded woman.

"Well," he started, "they were originally going to wait, but the nurse accidentally let it slip at one of their ultrasound appointments. She was a little upset at first, but I secretly think they're happy they won't get stuck with a bunch of yellow baby gifts."

Jin led me toward a dimly lit hallway where the party was thinning out, and the music felt more distant with each step. He pointed out the amenities in the front room, the shared bathroom, the linen closet, and both bedrooms. The tour was short and sweet, fitting for a place in the city with little wiggle room between rising skyscrapers.

"—and it's a quick commute to work. Only ten minutes with traffic," he explained, rubbing the back of his neck. "I'm going to put your bag in my bedroom to keep it safe, if you don't mind. Caleb accidentally broke the lock on the guest room, and I haven't had a chance to get a repairman down here yet."

I followed him across the hall.

Perhaps I was more prone to falling for misconceptions than I thought because, based on the man I knew behind the clipboard, I was under the impression I had him all figured out. As I crossed the threshold into his bedroom, that couldn't have been further from the truth. Unlike his office, lifeless and bland, there was such life teeming between these four walls.

The bookcase brimming at the seams drew me in first. Worn creases lined the spines from multiple reads, potted plants draping their vines down the shelves like outstretched hands; knick-knacks were cramped into odd places, and picture frames haloed the back wall. Rising on my tippy-toes to get a better look, I studied a picture of Jin standing shoulder to shoulder with a man about his height with shaggy brown hair, a white gash running across his forearm, and a boyish smile. In the background was a vast cityscape that could have been taken in London, but I wasn't sure.

"If part of your interrogation process includes snooping, then be my guest."

"It was in the trial run contract," I tossed over my shoulder.

"Hmm, is that so?" He leaned up against the closest wall, arms crossed. "I must not have read the fine print."

"Rookie mistake, Collins," I said, using his own words against him.

Every picture offered a tiny glimpse into his life. Endless adventures abroad, celebrated seasons with cast and crew, groups of friends who seemed to absolutely adore him, boxing matches that left little to the imagination as he glistened with a thick sheen of sweat.

I averted my gaze, picking up a frame that served as a bookend to distract and divert from the shirtless photos of my boss.

Jin couldn't have been much older than four in the picture. Dressed in traditional Korean garb, he clutched a woman's hand, whom I can only presume was his mother, and flashed the biggest smile at the camera in front of a sprawling East Asian palace.

"That picture was taken in front of Gyeongbokgung on Seollal, the first day of the Korean lunisolar calendar," he explained, tapping the glass. "I want to say that it was taken maybe ten or so years before my mother and I moved to America."

"You were so stinking adorable." I bit my bottom lip then peered up at him. While his chubby cheeks had thinned out, there was a certain gleam in his eyes that had transcended time. "You have no idea how badly I want to snap a photo of this and make it your contact photo."

"Knock yourself out, Hartwell."

"I knew you grew up in South Korea, but I had no idea you moved to America so much later in life. That couldn't have been easy. I moved to the next town over when I was twelve and was a total mess when I started middle school."

"You have no—"

"Jin," someone shouted, and a heartbeat later, a man popped his head into the bedroom. His green eyes jutted back and forth between where Jin and I stood at the foot of the bed. "Sorry, didn't mean to interrupt."

"You weren't...no," I sputtered, instantly feeling heat creep up my neck.

"Adeline, this is my younger brother, Caleb. Caleb, this is Adeline."

"You look really familiar," he said, shaking my hand. "Are you a dancer?"

"Yes, I dance for the Republic City Opera House."

My eyes darted between the frame lining the wall, Caleb, and then Jin.

"The resemblance is uncanny, right?" Caleb chuckled, noticing me staring. "But I know what you're thinking. We have different dads."

"And mothers," Jin added. "We're stepbrothers."

"Not that you liked to admit that when we were younger—"

Jin cleared his throat. "Did you need something, Caleb?"

"Oh yeah, we're looking for someone else to play? Do you guys want to join?"

"I'm assuming it's a drinking game."

"It wouldn't be a gender reveal party without a few drinking games." Caleb beamed.

I wasn't one to drink much before or during the season, but the idea of having a drink made my shoulders relax a little. Alcohol wasn't necessarily the best coping mechanism—but it was the right one for tonight.

"What do you say, Hartwell? Want to be my partner?" Jin

looked to me for an answer, and I think I might have surprised both of us when I said yes.

The dining room table had been completely hijacked. All the chairs had been lined up against the closest wall, and four beer cans dotted each corner. As Caleb wrangled up the last few people we needed to play, Jin took the opportunity to introduce me to Sophia. I only got the chance to congratulate her before Caleb bellowed, "The goal of the game is to finish your beer first. You start by tossing your ping-pong ball at the opponent's drink. If you hit it—no bouncing—then you chug your drink until the other team can retrieve the ball, pass it between all players, then slam it down on the table. Then you have to stop, and the next player gets a chance to throw."

Jin leaned in, his shoulder brushing mine. "It's a stupid game he and his drunk college friends made up."

"A game you just so happen to suck at, Jin," Caleb snapped. "*Anyway*, here's the kicker: when you finish your beer, you have to turn it upside down over your head, and if even *one* drop lands on your head, you have to get a new beer and start over."

"Sounds like a disaster waiting to happen," I whispered.

"You have no idea." He smirked.

"Adeline, Charlotte, and Mateo are one team. Jin, Isabella, and Juan can be another."

And with that, we took our corners.

As a seasoned veteran of the game, Charlotte had been playing since she met Caleb at RCU while studying law, and was without a doubt the backbone of our team. She coached me through every missed shot, then hollered every time I hit my mark—not that I was targeting Jin by any means. Okay, I totally was. There was something so contagious about her competitive edge that only intensified as the other team scrambled to get the ball.

Sip by sip, I felt myself start to loosen up as everyone

cheered me on, and I reveled in that slice of normalcy. No one gaped at the hidden bruise along my neck. No one brought up a past I couldn't outrun. No one berated the conversation. It felt good to laugh—I couldn't remember the last time I did.

Jin threw his hands high up in the air, trying to distract me while I aimed my shot.

"Don't miss, Hartwell."

I shushed him.

"No pressure—"

The ping-pong ball clanked against the can, and I chugged the remainder of my beer. I was aware of the chaos all around me, but nothing mattered in those last few seconds as the opposing side slapped down their ball right as I flipped the can over my head.

The room fell silent.

A beat passed, then another.

Right as I was about to celebrate the win, a single drop hit the top of my head.

"There was a drip. I saw it." Isabella shouted, wagging a finger at me.

"All right. All right. Let me check," Jin responded, quieting the crowd of onlookers who all had vastly different interpretations of what they saw.

To his credit, Jin was taller than the average man—a towering figure that loomed over me as he closed the distance between us step by step. Even with boots on, he trumped me in stature. When we were finally toe to toe, he gently ran the tip of his index finger along my hair. His gaze snapped to mine, the flash of recognition undeniable.

My stomach flipped in response.

"They won," he announced, and the entire room erupted into a frenzy.

I blinked up at him several times, unsure if I heard him

correctly. Amongst the cheers and leers, I easily could have, but there was no denying it when he flashed me a wink, turned on his heels, and left.

The bastard let me win.

Charlotte, Mateo, and I advanced to the next round, a false win under our belt. As we took our corner once more, Jin slipped through the crowd and disappeared outside.

———

Haloed by a sprawling cityscape and twinkling lights, Jin seemed a million miles away as he leaned up against the balcony railing, unaware that I had slipped outside.

"Your brother has quite the competitive edge to him."

Jin took a quick sip of his beer before turning around. The gesture felt reminiscent of the first time I met Josephine, but unlike that encounter, something about his body language spoke to a nervous tic rather than annoyance.

"Was it that bad?"

"I don't even want to talk about it. It's embarrassing," I answered, joining him on the edge. "If I move in, should I expect a wild party every weekend?"

"Tonight is the exception, not the rule."

"Just like letting me win."

Jin shot me a look, then fixed his gaze back on the horizon. He attempted to hold back his smile for as long as possible by biting the inside of his cheek, but eventually he lost the good fight.

"Hmm, you caught that?"

"The wink might have given you away."

"I knew I would have to go up against Caleb if I won, so I let you have the honor of playing my little brother," he joked.

"Maybe it was for the best; it gave me a chance to talk to

your friends and family while we played another round. Despite being drunk, everyone had really nice things to say about you."

"Good. I slipped them a twenty before you came. I'm glad they stuck to their scripts."

"Caleb might have gone off script from time to time, but for the most part, he did well."

"Does that mean the trial run went well?"

Coming here tonight, I'd been pleasantly surprised, but as much of a distraction as it was, this hadn't been the first time I'd been deceived by first impressions.

"I don't make big decisions while I've been drinking." I pushed off the railing.

"Smart. I wish I did that more in college."

"I guess we'll find out. Good night, Collins."

"Night, Hartwell."

I wouldn't be tricked so easily again.

Chapter Thirteen

Jin

I woke up with a stiff headache and a bit of regret.

Curled up in a mess of blankets, a sliver of sunlight trickled into the bedroom, bringing with it a new day that I wasn't prepared for. It took two alarms and a gnawing deep within my gut to get me to roll out of bed, and even then, I was wildly underprepared for the day and contemplating why I'd drunk so much on a work night—well, that was a lie, I knew perfectly well why. It might have had something to do with the five-foot-one dancer who was currently sleeping across the hall from me.

I wasn't blackout drunk by any means, but when I drink, no matter the amount, the end of the night is always a little fuzzy. Fragments of conversation slowly came back into focus, one sentence at a time. The game. The balcony. The flirting.

"Goddamn it," I groaned, dragging my hands over my face.

Had I really been flirting with Adeline? No, of course not. I would never put one of my dancers in a position like that knowingly. Last night had been somewhere in that strange gray area that couldn't decide whether or not it was toeing the line.

And the wink...

Okay.

Who was I kidding? I was flirting with Adeline.

Despite our *relationship* being strictly professional, that didn't mean I hadn't admired her from afar. A rising star whose softhearted personality and unwavering beauty somehow outshone the talent that instantly drew me in from that very first audition. Since the name Hartwell came across my desk, I've been at odds with myself, questioning more than my sanity.

The first drink was only meant to settle my nerves—a way to bridge the gaps in our conversations as she explored my bedroom with such child-like wonder. It reminded me of the way I caught her gazing up to the heavens, trying to sneak a little peek at the sprawling fresco anytime we rehearsed on stage. Just as she lost herself in dance, art seemed to captivate her as easily.

And then Caleb invited us to play that damn game. Adeline was hesitant at first, surrounded by chaos on all fronts, but little by little, I saw her starting to open up. Each time she hit my beer can, that devastating smile of hers widened until it was the closest thing I'd seen to her first few weeks at the company.

She needed last night as badly as I did, and for that, I was grateful she called.

I groaned into my pillow.

Sue me. I had one too many and flirted with a beautiful woman who happens to be my coworker and potential room-mate. As long as it ended there, it wouldn't be a problem. All I would have to do is shove that silly little crush so far down it didn't ache anytime she stepped into a room—yeah, I could do that. It's not as if I hadn't been practicing for seven months now.

I tossed on a hoodie and made my way to the bathroom to freshen up.

Through the slim crack in the guest room door, all I could see was darkness. The door had been closed when I went to bed at midnight last night, and again when I got up to go to the restroom at two-thirty.

I lightly knocked on the doorframe. "Adeline?"

No answer.

I tried again. "Adeline? Are you up?"

Nothing.

Wanting to make sure everything was okay, I announced myself once more before popping my head in the bedroom. It took several long seconds for my eyes to adjust, and when they finally did, I found the sheets had been neatly folded at the foot of the bed and not a sign to be found of the dancer who had been here not six hours ago. I checked the bathroom next, then the living room, kitchen, and even the patio for good measure, but came up empty every time.

It had been that damn smile of hers—it gave me false hope.

I felt like a fool for assuming last night would be enough to convince her to stay when she never shied away from telling me why she was so hesitant to begin with. Ultimately, I would always respect her decision, but I couldn't help the way my stomach lurched in response.

I guess we'll find out. Good night, Collins.

While hope hadn't followed through on its promises, Adeline sure did.

I'll just clean it up tomorrow. Famous last words.

To my friends and family's credit, the apartment wasn't a total mess, but the entire place needed to be scrubbed and sanitized.

I disinfected the dining room counter, fighting a stubborn headache that hit me in waves, making me think the worst was over before smacking me upside the head again. The pungent chemical smell wasn't helping either.

A few rogue red cups had been left behind on the kitchen counter. I tossed them in the trash bag and tied it up tight, not loving the way the stale beer churned my queasy stomach. I couldn't get the damn thing down the garbage chute fast enough.

It shut with a heavy thud, drowning out the ping of the elevator and the sound of footfalls brushing the carpet.

It wasn't until I turned around that I saw the figure lingering down the length of the hallway like a ghost of my past. Standing there, looking so small, was Adeline.

"I thought you left," I said softly.

As if the white bag with grease starting to seep through the paper was enough of an answer, she lifted it. A beat passed, then another, before she explained. "There's a breakfast place down the block. I went to pick us up some food," she rasped, her eyes shifting around the room, avoiding me entirely. "I wasn't sure what to get you, so I took a shot in the dark. I would have asked, but when I went to knock on your door, all I heard was snoring. Thank god for those thick walls, right?"

"I only snore when I've been drinking. It's the sober nights you should be worried about; that's when I sleepwalk."

Words seemed to fail her—she tilted her head, mouth slightly open.

I shook my head and huffed out a breath. "I'm only messing with you, Adeline."

And there it was again—the tiniest hint of a smile, along with the tension in her shoulders easing up a little. It was a relief to see what effect humor had on her. Lucky for both of us, I had plenty more terrible jokes where that came from.

"Good," she said, crossing the threshold of the apartment as

I held the door open for her. "Or I was about to say I need a deadbolt for my room."

There was still something off about her, something so small about the way she held herself. It was as if the version of Adeline I saw a glimpse of last night was as hazy as my drunken memories—close but couldn't quite take shape.

She delicately laid out the contents of the bag on the island, preparing a spread of black coffee and perfectly wrapped bagel sandwiches for us. All while she worked, her gaze remained trained down low, avoiding my gaze.

I braced my elbows on the counter. "You were planning on leaving, weren't you?"

Her hand froze over a pile of napkins.

"What gave it away?"

"Well, for one, you took your overnight bag with you to get breakfast," I said, gesturing to the backpack at her feet.

She sighed. "Yes, I wasn't planning on being here when you woke up."

"But..."

"But I realized it was a mistake," she admitted. "I made it about one block before my legs stopped moving altogether. Luckily, there was a café nearby. I sat down for an entire hour in complete silence, poring over every detail of the night, trying to figure out why I couldn't make it any further than one block, until I remembered what happened after we said good night.

"I lay in bed, staring up at the ceiling, patiently waiting for everyone to leave so I could slip out, but when you said your final goodbye and all I could hear was your footsteps in the dark, I remembered what you said about there not being a lock on my door. That thought alone should have been enough to terrify me, but it didn't...it was only us alone in the apartment, and I felt safe knowing you were here." She barked out a nervous laugh. "I might have my reservations about living here, but...it was the first night in a long time I slept through the night. I'm sorry for leaving in the first place."

"You have nothing to apologize for, Adeline." I swallowed the lump in my throat. "I'm glad you came back."

"Me, too," she admitted, staring down at her breakfast for a long moment. "I'd like to move in...if you'll have me."

Safety might not have been guaranteed in the past, but the beauty of the future: it's still being written. Adeline would be safe here. I would make sure of it.

"Always."

As we enjoyed our breakfast, I started the tedious process of editing an old leasing contract from a few years back when I last had a roommate. Unlike the last contract I had drafted, this one was month-to-month, offering Adeline a little more flexibility with her living arrangements.

The future may be unwritten, but our actions have the capability of shaping it.

Chapter Fourteen

Adeline

Encased in bronze, three statues sat atop their perch on the pediment—angelic figures meant to enrich the historic building and provoke a connection between the heavens and earth. As the woman loomed high above, their presence felt more like a warning than a warm welcome home.

Jin had dropped me off so I wouldn't be late for rehearsal while he swung around the block to find a parking spot. I wasn't expected to be in the studio for another ten minutes, but I couldn't bring myself to move as I patiently waited for my heart to steady.

Resembling its namesake, Republic City Opera House mimicked the neo-Renaissance designs of the buildings surrounding it. Yet it seemed so out of place with the skyline, with its tall looming archways, pillars as mighty as an oak tree, and larger-than-life statues that appeared to be chipped away from the stone building itself. In a city as vast as it was corrupt, the Opera House felt like it didn't belong—perhaps that's why I was so drawn to it.

I sucked in a deep breath, then blew it out slowly.

I could do this.

I didn't need someone to hold my hand to enter a damn building.

Maybe I could be braver than the voices telling me otherwise.

Unlike yesterday, I forced myself to enter through the front entrance, where the same depiction of the women could be found throughout the lobby. Nemesis balancing her scales in pursuit of divine judgment, Persephone holding a bundle of narcissus, and Apate caressing the small box of her own deception.

Art was an imitation of life, and of all the beautiful pieces in the theater, I was especially drawn to the various oil paintings and statues of the goddess of spring. Her myth represented the nature cycle of life, and the idea that even after so much death and destruction, rebirth was possible.

Optimism wasn't something I was accustomed to when the thought of failure was far more likely than success, but this morning was the closest I'd gotten to it in ages. It felt like the first signs of snow thawing after an especially harsh winter. I couldn't quite put a name to it yet, but staying with Jin felt like the season might finally change at last.

I cut through the auditorium. Eyes trained on the goddess with the promise of allaying fear. It was a blessing to make it as far as I did, but stepping backstage threatened to ruin any progress I'd made.

It was clear who'd seen my name on the call list and who had been blindsided by my presence. Deeper into the belly of the beast, the whispers grew louder with each step—some more vocal about their disdain than others. Without a depiction of Persephone to guide me, I keep my eyes forward and mouth shut.

I was no stranger to the cutthroat world of theater, but it was one thing to see the blade being polished and an entirely different beast to feel its bite. Crossing that threshold into the dressing room meant being the willful lamb walking into the slaughterhouse. If I knew these women as well as I thought I did, the onslaught would be immediate. Whispers weren't their straightest edge.

Noah thrived on living to the very edge of his charm and behaved as outrageously as the world would allow him, as long as the people he spoke to left the conversation feeling as good about themselves as they did about him. It was electrifying to be in his presence, and for the cast and crew, there was no question whether he'd left his mark. But it wasn't the dancers as a whole I was concerned about. It was one in particular. It hadn't dawned on me until now that if she hadn't taken a leave of absence, we would come face to face once more.

My pace might have slowed as I digested that fact, but I never stopped.

Tatiana had a role in all of this, didn't she? She'd been as willful as the lamb and as cruel as the butcher, but was she as much to blame as the one who handed her the knife? With enough going on in my life, I didn't think I had the energy to waste on Tatiana despite her complacent actions.

I mentally prepared for the incursion into the dressing room, but was instead greeted by silence. Every conversation died on the tips of their tongues as I entered the room. It was several long seconds later before the crunching of pointe shoes and mindless chatter broke the deafening silence. My fellow dancers returned to their hushed conversation, and while none of them showed their teeth, an uncomfortable weight had settled over the room. The sensation worsened with each vanity I passed, building and building like a wave far too large to support the weight of its only magnitude. I didn't quite understand why everyone was acting so strange until I reached my vanity and the wave finally crashed over me.

Shards of broken glass lay sprawled across the counter. The remnants of what I recognized as a bottle of dye we specially used to color our pointe shoes, spread across the surface in red, thinning lines that met the edge of a newspaper clipping. A pair of familiar chocolate brown eyes stared back at me. Below the image reads as follows: *It is with a heavy heart that we announce the sudden passing of Noah Luis Hernandez, twenty-nine years young. Noah, a beloved physical therapist and cherished friend, passed away—*

They were giggling behind my back.

I ripped the obituary off the vanity, and the room plunged into silence once more. The cold dye dripped from my hand, marking each stair I climbed and each corner I turned. The trail followed me all the way up to the offices on the other side of the building, and by the time I was staring at his nameplate, I could hardly see straight. A heartbeat away from pounding my fist against his door, I caught sight of my hand. The dye had seeped into my skin so thoroughly that I feared no amount of scrubbing would wash it away. My vision blurred around the edges. I attempted to blink it away, but all I could see were flashes of that night. The blood coating my hands. The metallic taste of it in my mouth. The sensation of it cooling against my skin—

I burst through the door in a desperate attempt to drive away the past.

Charles was talking on the phone. He took one look at me, whispered a goodbye into the receiver, then hung up. "I'd been wondering where you'd run off to this morning."

"Someone," I croaked out, then sucked in a wet breath. "Someone left this on my vanity."

His gaze dropped to the bloodied image of Noah clutched in my hand.

It wasn't the principle of threat itself. It was the intent behind it.

Whoever had paid for the obituary had carefully selected an image of him standing on the edge of a cliff after a hiking trip with his clinical buddies as meticulously as the words below it. It was a means of spinning his narrative in a positive light, using flowery words and heartfelt goodbyes to set the precedent for who he was and how he would be remembered. And in a sense, it had done exactly what it had set out to do. Noah had thoroughly manipulated the people in his life so well while he was still breathing that even in death, he could still do no wrong.

I would always be the villain in their story.

From the paper to the floor, the dye landed with a soft, wet thud. I had to forcefully push down the bile creeping up my throat as each drip splattered across my white tennis shoes.

"I'm assuming you know who did this."

I shook my head. The dancers were more bark than bite, but logically, it had to be one of them or someone else who had access to our dressing rooms. It was only a matter of who was sick enough to pull a stunt like this.

Charles gestured for me to enter his office. A far cry from the modern monstrosity that was his apartment, the space was adorned with vibrant posters, picture frames bustling with memories, and mementos that likely weren't from this century.

As I took my seat, Charles rose from his and offered me three things: a paper towel that did little to remove the ink already staining my skin, a trash bin to rid myself of the damned newspaper clipping, and a finger length of whiskey.

"It's nine in the morning." I vacillated, glaring at the tumbler.

"Yes, and you're also shaking so violently that the chair beneath you has started to rattle," he said, raising an eyebrow. "Take it, or I will."

I took a small sip, welcoming the burn.

"More, Hartwell. I can see you still shaking."

Little by little, sip by sip, Charles patiently waited for the tremors to subside.

"For you, *mon étoile*," he finally said, "I'll make sure this gets taken care of. We might not have surveillance in the dressing rooms for obvious reasons, but I'll check the system and see what I can find. There are cameras all over this building."

The tremors stopped.

"If that's true, then does that mean you have footage of"— Noah bringing me so close to the brink of death that I had nearly given in for fear that he would never let go, I thought to say—"the night you found me."

"Yes, Donovan and I believe we've found something," Charles said, plucking a carton of cigarettes and a lighter from his suit pocket. "We're getting dinner tomorrow night to discuss the evidence and how it might help the case. It might be in your best interest to come so you can prepare for your preliminary hearing."

The real question was, was the evidence enough? Was the footage damning enough to prove my innocence, or had Noah done such a thorough job in this life that they would martyr him in death?

"I'll go."

"Good, we'll leave the apartment around six."

"If you want to give me the name of the restaurant, I can meet you there."

Charles watched me through the hazy smoke, wordlessly demanding an explanation. And I guess he did deserve one after I slipped out in the night without so much as a note to explain where I'd run off to.

"About that...you have to understand how appreciative I am for everything you've done for me so far, which is why it was so important for me to find somewhere more permanent to stay. You've already done so much for me. The last thing I want is to be taking up space. I was planning on collecting my things and returning the key after work today."

"Does this have anything to do with my wife? Because I would apologize for her behavior, but that would imply it won't happen again, and I unfortunately can't guarantee that."

"No. No," I sputtered. "This has nothing to do with Josephine."

She was only half the problem.

"I assumed when I didn't see you this morning for breakfast that you'd finally taken my advice and stopped sulking around the house—either that, or you were sick of Josephine."

If only you knew.

"Is she feeling better now?"

"As good as she can be," he explained, the words laced with smoke. "Josephine hasn't quite been the same since her younger brother passed away. Patrick is gone, and now I'm here picking up the pieces."

"I'm assuming she was close with her brother."

He smiled. "That's a story for another time, *mon étoile.* Run off to rehearsal and let me deal with this mess."

I didn't want to be where I wasn't wanted, but the alternative was letting them win. And I'd be damned if I let them take this away from me, too. Spring might be right around the corner; it was only a matter of surviving the last of winter.

Chapter Fifteen

Adeline

There was a strange sense of beauty that resided within utter chaos. Between rising melodies and fallen notes, something was to be said about how different mediums of art could blend the lines of reality—breathing new life into music composed during the late nineteenth century. While beauty was inherent, it was the odd sense of peace I found thriving within that organized chaos that breathed life into me. With so little in my control, there was nothing left for me to do other than return to rehearsals in time to warm up. Amongst the bedlam of other dancers and the dye coating my skin, I let Gnossiennes No. 1 (*Lent*) wash away over me.

I may not be wanted here, but I knew this was where I belonged.

Chaos could be found in every facet of my life, yet the chaos in music was something I craved. I found peace rehearsing act 1 of *Le Cœur Sauvage*—a fast-paced ballet that followed the perilous journey of a young maiden tasked with seducing a tyrannical king. Forcing myself to focus on the epic story filled with deception and lies, it was oddly calming to slip back into my role and clear my mind of anything other than my next move.

Act 2, scene 3 was adjusted to accommodate Halle's noticeable absence. The whimsical ballroom scene served as the final encounter between the young maiden, played by none other than Tatiana Antonenko, and the tyrannical king she was ordered to assassinate. It was an electrifying piece that built on itself with each rising note, climbing in tempo and speed as the protagonist swooped in on her unsuspecting prey, dagger strapped to her thigh. Though I couldn't help noticing she was favoring one foot over the other as the scene progressed.

Xavier and I got back into position, taking the scene from the top.

The corps de ballet descended onto the dance floor, sweeping the protagonist into a flurry of chaos. Weaving through the crowd with wide-eyed optimism, she approached the dais with a burning need to see things through. Her destiny was written for this moment, and if she didn't follow through on her scheme, there would be no life worth living outside of these palace walls. The protagonist broke through the crowd and—

The lift started as it always did. Xavier's hands were steady on my hips. I felt weightless in his arms for a heartbeat, but when my foot hit the ground, I went stumbling forward into another dancer. Had I not run into her, I would have landed face-first on the floor.

"Sorry," I muttered, my cheeks turning flush.

I whipped my head toward Xavier.

He shrugged. "It's not my fault you can't land properly."

Classically trained with years of rigorous studying at one of the most prestigious private youth academies on the West Coast and extensive repertoire in works like *Romeo and Juliet, Giselle,* and *Swan Lake,* I didn't make a mistake that could put myself or my fellow dancers in danger.

"Stop," Anastasia called out, breaking through the crowd, arms flailing. "Stop the music."

I braced my hands on my hips and blew out a breath as she approached.

"Adeline, do you mind telling me what the hell happened?"

"She didn't—" Xavier blurted out.

"I asked her, not you," she interjected, then turned to me.

"His hand was too high on my waist. We lost the lift."

Xavier rolled his eyes, assuming Anastasia was too preoccupied with our conversation to notice. But nothing got past her. The choreographer whipped her head around. It was quite the sight to see as he straightened in response. He was nearly twice her size, but he had never looked smaller than standing next to her.

"Tell me, if I look back at those tapes, what do you think I'll find?" She poked him square in the chest, then pointed at the tripod in the corner of the studio. "Because I can almost guarantee this has everything to do with your starting position, Xavier." She paused, massaging her temple. "Shit. I understand we are wildly understaffed for the foreseeable future, and it's showing. But we can't afford such sloppy mistakes this close to the opening show. You are both exceptional at what you do. I know you two can fix this."

Turning on her heels, she called out, "Check their alignment, Jin. Make sure they're starting in the right place while I handle Tatiana and James."

Then she was off, barking orders at the next pair of dancers.

It was odd—the stark contrast between the artistic director so engrossed in his work, that it took more effort than necessary to peel himself away from his laptop, compared to the version of Jin smiling down at me on the balcony last night. They felt like two entirely different people, and I much preferred the latter.

"Return to your marks. Find your lift position," Anastasia called from across the room.

Like a well-oiled machine, the room shifted into position, ready to recreate the moment the young maiden broke through the crowd. Xavier stood behind me, both hands resting on my waist. All it took was two long strides for Jin to reach us. And suddenly I was sandwiched between the two men.

He eclipsed the fluorescent lights hanging high above, engulfing me in an array of various shadows as he closed in. The movement felt eerily similar to last night, with alcohol coursing through my veins and his fingers in my hair.

"Your hand is resting too far forward," Jin rasped in a low tone.

Ever so gently, Jin guided his hand backward—the barest hint of his pinky skimming my waist as he adjusted Xavier's grip. As subtle as the touch was, the shiver that rocked my body was anything but. Beneath my leotard, a shiver coursed up my spine and snaked around my waist, where it settled in the swells of my breast. The two men went back and forth discussing the lift, but I hardly heard a word.

Xavier pulled away a heartbeat before Jin did, and for that split second, only Jin's touch graced my waist. It felt as if I'd been standing on a live wire, only for it to be ripped away as the warmth of his touch disappeared completely.

"Are you ready to try again, Adeline?" Jin asked in a gentle tone.

I nodded, desperately hoping my face wasn't giving me away.

It was the alcohol—it was the only common denominator between now and last night. I shook off the strange feeling and stepped back into the starting position, trying not to give this any gravitas. But when I glanced over my shoulder, Jin was still watching me from afar, his gaze burning into me—it was difficult not to wonder.

"From the top, arms go up," Anastasia shouted.

Xavier snaked his hand up my back, where it settled between my shoulder blades, pulling me flush against his chest. Inch by inch, his gaze slowly traveled over my bare arm before settling on our joined hands, red dye still visible on the back of my knuckles. He opened his mouth, but before he could speak, Kaiser-Walzer, Op. 437 erupted through the speakers.

The scene mimicked the steps and tempo of a waltz, blurring the lines between ballet and ballroom dance. We spun around the room, trapped within the hypnotic melody. There was such fluidity in each step, moving in time with the crowd. I stepped forward into a pivot, lifting my right leg with slow, controlled grace. Xavier supported my balance as we turned together, and he took the opportunity to lean in and whisper, "I can smell the liquor on your breath, Addie. What a dangerous game you are playing."

Before I could react, Xavier lifted me in a sweeping overhead lift, arms extended as I arched my back. I caught our reflections in the mirror, and for a split second, I swore I saw him smiling.

Instead of guiding my descent, Xavier released me entirely. The floor came rushing for me as I extended my leg outward, trying to catch myself, but the position was all wrong. I crumbled under the weight of my own body, and my leg slipped inward, causing the side of my bad knee to crack against the floor first. The pain was so intense, so all-consuming, it felt as if someone had struck me with a sledgehammer. I slapped a hand over my mouth to stifle a scream, praying that the worst was behind me as long as I breathed smooth, even breaths. But each wave of pain felt like another strike, keeping me heaving on the ground, fighting the dizziness that came with it.

Xavier knelt beside me, his back to the other dancers.

"That looks really bad, you should really get someone to check it—oh wait."

Chapter Sixteen

Adeline

Sinking my teeth into the flesh of my palm, I stifled a scream as another surge of pain pulsated through my knee. As if wading through deep waters, I fought against two fronts: the emotional undercurrent, threatening to pull me down, and the relentless waves of blistering pain, crashing into me one after another. There wasn't enough time to suck down a breath before another wave slammed into me. One after another, I braced my hands on the studio floor and heaved, preparing for the next. With no end in sight, I was starting to lose faith in my ability to rise once more.

Like scavengers circling their prey, my fellow dancers closed in around me, curious how long faith would hold out. There was a familiar haunting gleam in their eyes that spoke to their true nature—the last time I saw it was when Tatiana had fallen from her good grace.

A set of deep brown eyes broke through the crowd. Anastasia followed soon after.

The only shred of humility in a sea of avarice.

This is what they wanted. *This* was what they were pushing me toward.

There was still blood on my hands, and there was nothing they wanted more than for me to know it. Perceptions were everything—while they might view me as easy prey, I refused to lie there and take it as the vulture swooped in, prepared to strike. I would not give them the satisfaction of watching me wither away on this studio floor. So, I attempted to prevail once more.

"Easy, girl," she said, putting a hand on my shoulder as I rose on one leg.

The backs of my eyes stung, and my throat swelled, yet there wasn't a tear worth shedding in front of this group. Before giving them exactly what they wanted, I gingerly applied some weight to my other leg. I released a shaky breath as a wave of dizziness shot through me. The breath turned into an even shakier laugh when I realized how ridiculous this all was.

"Adeline," she barked.

"I'm fine. I'm fine."

Jin cursed under his breath. "We need to get your knee checked out."

"Adeline, please sit down," Anastasia begged.

Blinded by my own ambitions, it felt so foolish looking back at it now—to think I could walk back into this theater and expect dance to repair all that was broken. I was still in the dead of winter and had no one else to blame for thinking otherwise.

Not being able to stomach being around these people anymore, I carefully walked myself toward the exit, limping the entire way there. It was an uphill battle to put one foot before the other, but somewhere between the third or fourth step, I was confident enough that I could make it to the physical therapy room on my own.

The sounds of dress shoes clicking against marley flooring chased after me. I picked up the pace—well, as much as I possibly could—then turned down the hallway.

"Slow down. You're going to hurt yourself."

The damage had already been done. Didn't he see that? All it would take is one career-ending injury, and everything I'd worked toward would be gone in the blink of an eye. The only shred of happiness I regarded—gone.

"Adeline," he shouted, jogging after me.

Today could have very well been that day, but instead, it was yet another reminder that all of this was temporary. And they had tried to take that away from me.

"Stop!" he barked, his fingers skimming my arm.

"He dropped me." I turned so suddenly, a wave of nausea churned my gut. "Xavier dropped me on purpose, and even if I screamed it at the tops of my lungs, not a single person in that studio would ever believe me. I can't do this anymore. I can't keep pretending everything is okay when that couldn't be further from the truth."

"Adeline..."

"No," I snapped, running the heels of my palms over my eyes. "None of them will ever understand what I've sacrificed to be where I am today—what pieces of myself I'd lost in the process. The note wasn't enough to drive me away. Now they're trying to clip my wings, too. I'm barely holding on by a thread, and if I lose this"—I swallowed the lump in my throat—"if I lose dance, I have nothing. Do you understand that?"

Only the sound of my heaving breath filled the space between us. The longer the question went unanswered, the more aware I became of the words that had spilled from my lips. Words that I already regretted terribly.

Jin stared down at me, at a loss for words until he finally said, "What note?"

"It doesn't matter now." I shook my head, walking in the opposite direction of this conversation that I wanted no part of, unshed tears blurring my vision. "Ask Charles if you really care."

"Hey, look at me." His tone was commanding yet gentle. "Claiming Xavier dropped you is a serious offense, especially after everything we talked about during alignments. We've had problems with him in the past, but nothing like this. I promise that I'll personally comb through the rehearsal footage myself."

"You believe me?" My pace slowed as we turned the corner.

"Of course, I do. I trust your judgment more than—" His eyebrows furrowed. "What's the matter?"

A familiar blue door adorned with small prayer candles burned down to the wick, and flowers showing the first signs of wilting came into view over Jin's shoulder—the aftermath of a forgotten vigil. Defying any sense of logic, the sight alone whisked me away from this moment and thrust me back into the past. Like a siren's traitorous call, the sound of relentless banging beckoned me forward. No matter how much I willed my legs to stop moving toward it, there was no stopping what couldn't be undone. Tatiana and Noah's moans merged into one, becoming a symphony of agonizing pain that left flashes of that night blurring out my vision.

I forced myself to look away, but caught a glimpse of my stained hand. My mind couldn't make sense of the past and present as the dye thickened in my hands.

"I—" Bracing my hands on my hips, I snapped my eyes shut to banish the memories away, but instead made them more vibrant in my psyche. "I can't," I said, hardly a whisper. "I can't—"

A hand lightly grazed my back, attempting to coax me back into the present.

"Okay. Okay. I got you, Hartwell. Take a deep breath in for me." Jin ushered me into a nearby room and eased me down onto a folding chair. "Wait here, I'll be back in one minute. Keep breathing."

Each breath felt as if someone had poured a bag of sand into my lungs. The heaviness strained against my ribs as if there wasn't enough room for them within their cage, and what little oxygen I could get down was rough and grainy as if flecks of sand that hadn't coagulated at the bottom of the lungs were now grinding against the lining.

Jin rushed back into the room, arms full of supplies. He dropped down to one knee, and the image of him kneeling before me turned fuzzy.

"It—it hurts to breathe," I stammered, rubbing my chest to loosen the sand.

"I know, sweetheart."

"It hurts so much."

"Find something red."

"What?"

"Search for something red in the room, and every time you find something, I want you to say it aloud. Okay?" he explained, a little out of breath. "Tell me what you see, Adeline?"

Desperate to loosen the sand, I didn't feel like I was in a position to question him when every breath felt like it could be my last. My eyes jutted back and forth, searching the stage equipment lining the four walls. It felt like a lost cause searching amongst the projection equipment, control boards, and lighting, until my gaze finally snapped on the tiniest hint of red that peeked out between two boxes.

"A rope," I mumbled.

"Good, what else?"

Placing an ice pack on my knee, he gently started wrapping my knee with plastic wrap to keep it firmly in place.

"Rope," I repeated, then continued my search. "Latter... curtain...and chair."

"Again," he coached, applying more layers.

"Rope. Latter. Curtain. Chair." Each time I said the word aloud, my gaze danced about the room, identifying their location. I repeated the items as if some kind of incantation, willing myself to even my breath and steady my heart. After the fifth round, I shut my eyes and sucked in my first full breath in what felt like a lifetime. When I opened them, Jin was still kneeling before me, a sad smile gracing his lips.

"Better?"

"Much," I rasped.

"It's none of my business, and you don't have to answer if you don't want to, but...does this happen often?"

Not two months ago, Halle had asked me a similar question. Noah and his buddies were doing their annual winter bar crawl, which perfectly coincided with the dates Halle's mother was in town. Tension within the Benson household had been strained since she remarried, so for Halle, it meant the world to her to have quality time with her mother without her stepfather and half-brother pestering her about her career. I was honored when Halle invited me to join.

Somewhere between the third and fourth bar, Noah took it upon himself to call and check up on me. Neither of us bothered to look at our phones when we were more preoccupied with the wine in our glasses and the laughter filling the apartment. Noah didn't care to listen to any excuse when he was more concerned with accusing me of all kinds of nasty things that were more about his insecurities than mine. Besides having an entire life of my own that predated my move to Republic City, Noah had trouble wrapping his head around that simple fact and grew incredibly suspicious of me when he learned that one of my old flings periodically came to the city for work.

I never understood why he hadn't trusted me, but I guess I do now...

I had locked myself in Halle's bathroom for twenty minutes before she used a paper clip to pick the lock, then proceeded to sit on the floor with me for another hour until Noah's vile words weren't consuming my only thoughts.

"You should be with your mother," I hiccuped. *"I feel terrible."*

"She knows a thing or two about jealous men. As long as she has a bottle of wine, I promise you she'll be fine on her own for a little longer."

Jin patiently waited for me to respond. So much untapped emotion resided in those deep brown eyes of his. I felt entranced by them, perhaps that's why I felt compelled to answer after lying for so long—he'd put me under some kind of spell and made the words fall from my lips with no way to stop them, even if I tried.

"Sometimes..." I cleared my throat. "Yes. Music helps, but not always."

Jin nodded. His gaze was distant as if he were still digesting that confession.

"Well, the good news is I have plenty of red things in the apartment if you ever need them." Jin rose to his full height. "I think it's safe to say we're done for the day. Ice now, and when we get home, I'll wrap your knee properly. I know you were looking forward to getting your stuff from Charles's apartment, but I don't mind going for you so you can get some rest."

"It's fine, I can just go another time."

"Really, I don't mind. Let me help you."

I looked down at my knee, then back to the artistic director.

This man was so at odds with the rest of my life. Jin didn't owe me a damn thing, yet he'd gone out of his way time and time again to help me.

"I don't get it," I blurted out, eyes searching him for something words alone couldn't express. "We hardly know one another...why are you helping me?"

"We all go through tough times in life, and usually that's when it's easiest to forget to ask for help," he rasped, eyes locked with mine. "I guess I don't think it's fair that anyone should have to go through that alone."

Chapter Seventeen

Jin

Four boxes—that was it.

All Adeline Hartwell had to her name was four measly boxes, and it took tearing apart the bathroom and searching every dresser drawer to finally accept that fact. I wasn't sure what I was expecting when I made the trek across town and nearly had to beg Josephine to let me in despite vaguely remembering me from the Christmas party she hosted two years ago, but it sure as hell wasn't this.

Three of the boxes were brimming with an assortment of neatly-folded clothes, while the fourth box had a myriad of different things: beauty products, makeup, books, random charging cords, and jewelry. I took the first box to my car, careful not to break any of the glass products, then returned with a rolling cart from the lobby for the others.

Before the elevator doors could close, a shoe jutted out between them. A heartbeat later, Blanchet stepped inside the tight space. Surprised wasn't quite the right word to describe it; perhaps confused better encapsulated the way he eyed me head to toe. Besides the nod of recognition, we rode in complete silence, patiently waiting for the other residents to get off on their designated floor. It wasn't until the last of them exited the elevator, and it was just the two of us, that he broke the taut silence. "Was Miss Hartwell afraid I might convince her to stay if she came to collect her belongings on her own?"

"Only a little shaken up from this morning. So I offered to come help her."

"Ah, yes. The note."

"No," I said. "Adeline injured her knee at practice—nothing serious. She mentioned something about a note, but didn't elaborate any further than that."

Above the elevator door was a small LED panel that displayed the ascending numbers. As Charles explained the situation regarding the targeted threat left on her vanity and the emotional turmoil it put her through, all I could do was blankly stare at those damn numbers. Given all Adeline had confessed to me earlier, plus the threat, it was no wonder she hadn't broken down sooner. By the time the elevator door pinged open, I was seething.

"And why's this the first time I'm hearing about this?"

"Do I need to concern myself with telling you everything that happens in my theater?"

"You do when it involves someone threatening one of my dancers."

"Perhaps you should concern yourself more with the upcoming season, given how well the last went." There was a lightheartedness to his tone that suggested he was merely joking, but humor could be wielded as skillfully as the blade if done correctly. Wasn't there a little truth in every joke?

Last fall season proved to be our worst yet, and as humiliating as our sales were, I wasn't sure what he was expecting from his team when marketing had been slashed by a quarter of what it was the season prior. Yes, it was my responsibility to make up for it this season, but there was only so much I could work with when all he gave was scraps. Now, with the salary proposal being rejected, there were rumors of dancers seeking out other companies. He had done this to himself, yet somehow, we were all to blame.

Perhaps it was a good thing I hadn't cancelled my interview after all.

"That's beside the point. This is about protecting Adeline."

Charles stopped at the door, key poised.

"I thought this was about protecting your dancers, Collins? Which one is it?"

"Can't both be true at the same time?"

As Charles stared at me, he didn't appear to be at a loss for words, but instead chose them very carefully. The air grew thick between us, the tension palatable as his key hovered over the lock, no closer to letting me in. Eventually, a smile tugged on the corner of his lips.

"Don't forget what happened to the last man Adeline was close to."

If bravery is not measured in a singular moment of strength, but instead the ability to repeatedly face adversity in spite of fear, then Adeline was by far the bravest person I knew. Given all she'd overcome and the threats she'd faced, I'm not even sure I would have been able to muster up the courage to go to rehearsals if I were in her shoes. Better yet, still find a way to put a smile on my face at the end of the day.

Lingering in the doorway, I caught myself unable to look away from the sight of Adeline flipping through the photo album she had stolen off the bookshelf in the living room. It was the second time I'd stumbled across the young dancer in her element, and it was the second time I'd accidentally startled her.

Adeline snapped the album shut and ripped off her headphones. While she might have plastered on a smile once the initial shock wore off, there was no hiding the rise and fall of her chest.

"Did you find what you were looking for?" I asked, placing the box of breakables on the counter. "Because there's another album from the following summer somewhere on the same shelf and my old journal from middle school below that. That's where I keep all my juicy secrets from my childhood."

"As much as I would love to learn all your darkest secrets, luckily for you, I don't know how to read Korean," she retorted, shelving the album. Adeline hobbled over the couch and propped her leg up on the coffee table. "Sorry, I didn't mean to snoop. I was just curious—"

"Thoughts?" I interjected.

She dragged her teeth over her bottom lip. "I may have gotten the impression you were one of the college students who studied abroad for one semester and haven't stopped talking about it since."

"Well, I can't say you're wrong." I chucked. "My scholarship program through RCU was offering an international fellowship. I would have been stupid to pass on a free trip to work in France for a summer."

And an even bigger fool not to accept a full-time position after graduation.

She rolled her eyes, but the smile gracing her lips told me everything I needed to know.

"I'm glad I caught you snooping through my stuff, so now I can admit I may or may not have peeked into a few of your boxes."

Adeline raised an eyebrow. "Thoughts?"

"I think we need to go shopping. Only four boxes?"

"Try moving across the country. Less is more."

"I moved across the world," I countered.

Less was indeed more, but not out of convenience. It simply gave us a head start. It made me wonder if Adeline held the same sentiment, or if this was really about practicality.

"Okay, you got me there," she admitted. "Charles didn't give you any trouble, right?"

"Not any more than usual. I've dealt with the old bastard for ten whole years now—twenty minutes wasn't going to kill me."

A timer rang on Adeline's phone, and she removed the ice pack from her knee, tossed it back in the freezer, and started walking toward the stack of boxes. Before she could get her hands on it, I plucked it off the counter and shook my head.

"Absolutely not. You need to wrap your knee. I'll grab the boxes for you."

"Jin—"

"It's only a few boxes. I can manage."

And to my surprise, she let me.

Adeline sat on the edge of the bed and started fussing with an elastic bandage. Her brows furrowed as she awkwardly wrapped her knee, the bandage loose in some areas and too tight in others. I watched from across the room, fighting the urge to step in and help. Adeline cursed under her breath, frowning down at her knee. It was clear she was fighting a losing battle, and there was only so much more I could take from the sidelines.

"Here," I finally said, rounding the bed. "Let me."

Adeline hesitated for a heartbeat, but when her gaze met mine, the frustration softened in her hazel eyes. There was no easy way to do this besides getting down on my knees, and I'd already put myself through that torment once today, I didn't think I had it in me to do it again.

Pulling out a chair from the desk, I motioned for her to prop her leg on the edge of the seat. Clothed in a pair of cotton pajama shorts and an oversized T-shirt that looked like she'd purchased it from a souvenir stand in one of the touristy spots of the city, it didn't take long to realize I'd made a grave mistake.

If kneeling before her was my own personal brand of torment, then whatever the hell this was would be my undoing. Succumbing to my own weaknesses would mean letting my eyes feast upon her bare flesh as they traveled up her legs toward the peaks of her nipples barely visible through the material of her thin shirt. If the call to temptation wasn't loud enough, part of me would give anything to drink in the sight of her without a lick of makeup on, hair still damp on the ends. She was breathtaking, and being this close to her was utterly intoxicating.

"It's all in the tension," I explained, my finger accidentally brushing the underside of her knee. I kept my eyes focused on my work, and while I'd robbed myself of one sense, the others sparked to life in such close proximity.

"So, artistic director *and* medic. Quite the resume."

"Caleb got me into kickboxing a few years back—not that I really have time to go anymore. But it was something I had to learn on the job or pay for it later," I explained. "Plus, working at the theater, it comes in handy from time to time."

"As competitive as your brother is at drinking games, I can only imagine what he's like stepping into a boxing ring."

"I've had a few bruised ribs that could confirm that. My little brother has always been a fighter, at least this way he'll get into less trouble."

Adeline's footing started to slip on the chair cushion. Before she could adjust her placement, the barest hint of her foot graced the innermost part of my thigh. I nearly groaned, realizing how starved I was for her touch—Jesus Christ, I need to get a grip.

I kept wrapping her knee, knowing that if I didn't focus on

doing this correctly, it could cause swelling and mess up her recovery time.

"I think it's nice you and your brother have something to bond over," she said, completely unfazed by the slip-up. "I thought that would be ballet for my older sister and me, but I was wrong."

"Are you two not very close?"

"Not at all. Melissa never really appreciated me following in her footsteps growing up, and I didn't appreciate the way she turned my parents against me for following my passions. Our childhood was constantly a competition in her eyes when it never had to be, had we chosen to support one another rather than fight."

"Caleb and I used to hate each other pretty much our entire childhood. When my mother married his father, we were both thrown into a blended family neither of us ever asked for. It wasn't until we were both adults that the relationship changed. I guess what I'm trying to say is, it's never too late."

"What changed between you two?"

"About thirteen years ago, when Caleb had a little bit too much fun during his senior year of high school, he eventually got into some trouble. He thought going to our parents for help would only make matters worse, so he called me out of pure desperation, even though it had been years since we last spoke. Long story short, it ended up being a false positive, and he had nothing to worry about, but something fundamentally shifted in our relationship when we reconnected. We'd spent so much time fighting this connection that we didn't know any different, but I guess I didn't realize at the time I needed him then as much as he needed me."

It occurred to me that I should probably stop touching her. The job was done, and I had no reason to anymore. Adeline rose to her feet and tested out my handiwork by pacing the room in short, slow strides.

"I'm not sure Melissa and I have anything like that written in the stars for us, but I'm happy that you two found one another after your rough childhood," she said, starting to rummage through the boxes once she was confident with the wrappings. "Whatever you helped him with must have done the trick, because he seems like he's doing well for himself. He and Sophia seem really happy together."

"You should really be elevating it instead of unpacking right now."

"In a moment," she mumbled. I gave her a look that did little to deter her as she pointed across the room. "Will you grab the jewelry box from that box, please, and hand it over? If you help me, I'll be able to elevate quicker."

What started as one single jewelry box turned into a full-blown assembly line. Working in tandem, I would unload the contents of each box on the bed, Adeline would sort them, then find them a permanent home. It was astounding how easy the conversation flowed between us. I, telling her about my first year in America and the struggles that came with assimilation, while leaving out some of the messy bits. Adeline, asking questions along the way before sharing her interest in travel and the dream to perform overseas. I soaked up every moment of her time, knowing the box was nearly empty. There would soon come a point when I wouldn't have an excuse to steal anymore of her time, so to prolong the inevitable, I slowed my pace.

"He mellowed out after college, but things weren't easy for them when they first started dating. Sophia had this terrible ex-boyfriend who was still trying to contact her," I started to explain while handing her a stack of books. "Simply blocking his number wasn't enough to keep him away. He started finding creative ways to reach out, like snail mail, fax, and even her work email."

"That is both terrifying and impressive. I didn't realize people even knew how to use a fax machine anymore."

"Exactly," I said. "It got really scary for a second, and when Caleb found out, he wanted to take matters into his own hands. The bastard didn't want to go alone and...well, let's just say, it was arguably the most difficult thing they had to overcome together, but eventually, when they did, they could finally focus on themselves and their happiness.

"Caleb took over his father's business after he retired, Sophia has her new job working at her firm, and now they're about to start a family, which is unreal to think about sometimes. Everything really worked out for them, and that makes me really happy to be a part of it."

"I think I met a few of her friends from the firm last night. Isabella, right?"

"Yeah, and Charlotte."

"They're both beautiful. I'm surprised Sophia hasn't tried to set you up on a date with either one of them."

"She has. Multiple times." I picked up a pile of sweaters and something hard and plastic flipped from the folds. The disposable camera was the run-of-the-mill model you could find at any drugstore, with twenty-five photos left. "Sophia said, and I quote, 'We're all starting to get worried about you, and Caleb is taking bets. If you don't start going out more, you'll leave me no other choice but to set you up on a blind date,'" I said, walking toward the closet, camera poised.

Adeline looked like the most stunning creature, standing on her tiptoes, trying to arrange a stack of jeans on the shelf. I leaned up against the doorframe.

"It sounds like she's looking out for you," she said loudly, her voice echoing in the small walk-in closet. "Though I doubt you really need any help from your sister-in-law, I'm sure you do just fine on your own."

"So, you think I'm good-looking?"

Adeline whirled around, the darkest shade of pink already staining her cheeks. And in that moment, I choose to snap a photo of her and all her blushing glory.

"Did you take my photo?"

"How else am I going to remember the day you officially moved in?"

The color leeched from her face, making her skin turn sickly. She couldn't even look me in the eyes when she gently took the camera from my hand and turned away, clearing her throat.

"Thank you for helping," she said in a small voice. "You're right, I think it's time I elevated my leg."

"Sorry, did I overstep?"

"No. No," she said, looking down at her feet, then back at me. "It's getting late, and I should start getting ready for bed. Thank you for helping me today, Jin. For everything. I'm not sure how I'm going to repay you."

"If I did something nice for someone and expected to be repaid in full, then it was never a nice gesture to begin with. I did what I did because I wanted to—because we're living together, and that's what roommates do for each other."

She still looked white as a blanket, but as the softest smile graced her lips. Life was slowly starting to return to her features as she stared down at the camera for a long moment. Then, before I could push off the doorframe, she snapped a photo of me in the doorway.

"What was that for?"

"You said it best, to remember the start of something new."

Chapter Eighteen

Jin

Rising from the ashes of a past worth forgetting, The Lotte stood proud on its corner of the district—mighty as ever. The brick exterior had spared the building from one fate and destined it for another. The intimate opera house-turned-cabaret was deemed a historic building a few years back and joined the ranks with the other world-renowned venues that dotted the ten-block radius.

And thanks to my brother, it was still with us today.

For reasons that aren't quite clear, the theater nearly burned down in a devastating fire that claimed four lives on that faithful night. A year and a half later, Collins Construction Co. had seemingly turned back time and made her anew. Caleb poured himself into every crystal chandelier winking down at me. Every Doric column stretched as high as a mighty oak to support the building's old bones. Every gold-leafed design made it impossible to commit every ornate detail to memory.

I strolled through the lobby, taking in as much as I possibly could.

Along the underside of the grand staircase was a plaque as Caleb had promised. A roadmap, as he once described it, to restore the theater to its former glory. With a few minutes to spare, I studied the black and white photo, my eyes jutting back and forth between past and present. It was remarkable what his people were capable of doing in such a short amount of time.

There was movement out of the corner of my eye. Shadows clung to the figure like a living beast, shifting and stretching as they approached, a slight limp with each step. The shadows retreated as he entered the lobby, but it was clear they were more at home reveling in his presence than lurking in the darkest corners of the room.

"Mr. Destler. Thank you for having me." I broke the distance between us, hand extended. "I'm Hyun-jin Collins, but please call me Jin."

"I like to go by either Erick or Destler."

While the district owner looked fairly young—perhaps in his early thirties—a lifetime of heartache was marred upon his skin. The nasty white gash that cut through his eyebrow and down his cheek was raised upon his light brown skin. The scarring was old and had signs of improper care. Although his right eye had a softness residing in the flecks of amber surrounding his irises, the left eye—narrowly missed by whatever had cut him—seemed to lack such warmth despite them being nearly identical.

"You should be thanking Caleb instead of me," he continued. "If your brother hadn't been as persistent as he was, I'm not sure this interview would have ever happened," he said, taking my hand.

After a week of relentlessly pestering me to go, I couldn't give him all the credit for my being here. It hadn't been Caleb who put the final nail in the coffin—that was all Charles.

"Sorry, I know he can be a bit much at times."

"Your brother is the least of my concerns right now," Destler said.

"Regardless—"

"It's you," he deadpanned.

"Excuse me?"

"Your brother isn't the problem right now, you are."

"Yeah, I heard you. I don't understand why."

He pulled out a folded piece of paper from his suit pocket, and my eyes skimmed over the first line of the document. It was the same show I'd performed a hundred times before, along with countless rejections that soon followed. Like a carefully orchestrated dance, I recited the words I'd memorized to heart. "While the gap in my resume may—"

"No," he interjected in a stern tone. "I don't care about that. I'd much rather prefer it if you told me, why, of all the theaters to choose from, you picked the *competition?*"

There was something effortless about the way he presented himself, but these few short moments talking to him were enough to know every word was perfectly calculated with the expectation of an equally calculated response. I choose my next few words nearly as carefully.

"I'll admit, I never really understood the rivalry between the theaters. The Lotte and Republic City Opera House have two entirely different clientele, neither of them is stepping on the other's toes," I explained. "Nor is any of this about me stepping on yours, for that matter."

"This is about history," he said, eyes boring into me, "and regardless of whether you're privy to that history or not, it doesn't explain why you would want to leave?"

With dozens of failed interviews under my belt, I had a perfectly curated response ready to go that highlighted my creative ambitions, subtle frustrations woven in with the highest praise for the theater, and my disappointment with certain limitations holding me back under Blanchet's supervision. The implication was professional but opened the conversation for further discussion if they wished to explore that avenue. It was the truth, but not the whole truth, and maybe if Destler wasn't willing to speak his truth, then neither should I.

Perhaps I might have held my ground, had Destler not said what he did next.

"Caleb says you are losing yourself. Is that true?"

The trust wasn't always warranted. It was something earned through merit and time, not handed out without rhythm or reason. Destler didn't necessarily deserve the truth of my struggles, but he did earn Caleb's trust, and that was apparently enough for me to speak mine.

"My fellowship in Paris was meant to turn into a full-time position after college but it unexpectedly fell through, and Blanchet took me under his wing"—I cleared my throat—"and while I am eternally grateful for the opportunities this job has provided me with, there's only so much more I can stomach when I've poured my heart and soul into this company year after year. Despite how loyal I've been, somehow, I am still at fault for his own shortcomings. No matter what I do, it will never be enough in his eyes.

"He's driving away his own people for his own personal gain, and anytime we try to express our concerns, we're shot down. I don't want to work for someone who prioritizes exploiting his dancers rather than celebrating them."

Destler studied me for a long moment, then walked away.

"Wait, where are you going?"

I followed him up the sprawling staircase lined with rich velvet carpet, his scarred hand tracing up the gilded railing as he tried and failed to hide what toll each step cost him in exchange.

"Mr. Destler. Wait."

The owner turned on his heels. "If what you say about Charles exploiting his dancers is true, then what have you done to stop him?"

"I've…"

"Nothing?" he asked, gripping the railing. "You know what Blanchet is capable of, and yet when faced with injustice, you ran to your younger brother and whined about it while you and the people you work with are being manipulated by a man who sees you more as a means to an end than an equal. You bitched about it instead of making a difference," he said. While his words cut deep, his tone was eerily calm. "I don't have the time, nor the energy to work with someone who isn't going to stand up against someone like that."

I took the first step. "You said it yourself. Charles is manipulating me, too. I don't know what I'm supposed to do to help."

"You have an impressive resume, Jin. The Lotte would be lucky to have someone like you, but I promise you, there's so much more you could be doing. Find me when you're ready to get off your ass and do something about it."

Chapter Nineteen

Adeline

It wasn't like me to be running late. Nor was dining with a district owner, but today was proving to be a rare exception. With only a few minutes to spare before my rideshare would whisk me across town to meet with Charles and Donovan to discuss the hearing, I dusted on a bit of blush and finished the look off with a red lip.

Jin was leaning over the kitchen counter, typing away on his cellphone. The sound of my bare feet padding against the wood made his eyes snap up in my direction.

There was nothing like it—the exhilarating feeling of being pinned beneath his gaze. During rehearsal, the behavior was warranted—even encouraged, when alignments were so important to honing our craft—but standing before him like this, clothed in so little, it was evident the quickening of my heart wasn't a fluke. It wasn't something I could simply blame on the rigorous nature of rehearsals anymore as his eyes dragged over me from head to toe. While his focus was zeroed in on my wrapped knee, it inched upward, settling on the hem of my short cocktail dress, then daring to trace the curves of my figure with his dark brown eyes. The dress was the deepest shade of midnight blue that made the faintest hint of freckles on my arms and legs look like constellations plotting the sky. And the way he seemed to count those stars made my cheeks heat.

Definitely not a fluke.

"I'm going downtown to grab a bite to eat with some friends. I was about to ask you if you want to go, but it looks like you already have plans."

"I appreciate the invite, but yes, I have plans for the night."

"A date?"

"No. No," I sputtered, then choked out a laugh. Not that it was anyone's business if and when I ever start dating again, but at this point in time, it was the least of my concerns. Dating was a luxury I didn't have the privilege of, nor could I make any promises of a future when so many uncertainties hung over me. It was better off this way. "I'm meeting Charles and the lawyers for dinner to discuss the preliminary hearing stuff—what was that look for?"

"What look?"

"Jin Collins"—I wagged my finger at him at the slight crinkle between his manicured brows—"don't you dare play dumb with me. I saw that look on your face when I said his name."

If the nervous laugh wasn't enough of a dead giveaway, Jin straightened, rubbing the back of his neck. I wasn't sure I was going to like anything he said next on the matter, but knowing he was incapable of lying only confirmed I'd made the right choice moving in with him. I liked that he couldn't hide behind his words like others once had.

"I guess I'm just a little confused why Blanchet is meeting with your lawyers."

A notification flashed across my screen. *Your driver is nearby.*

"Well, they're his lawyers, too," I said, collecting my keys from the bowl. "Shit, sorry. I have to go, or I'm going to be late. Have fun tonight. Be safe."

I followed waves of chestnut brown hair as the hostess led me through the labyrinth of linen-draped tables. Conversation filled the restaurant almost as gently as the soft twinkling tea light candles encased in amber crystal dotting each corner of the room.

Labeled the hidden gem of the Culinary District, Maestro Steakhouse wasn't the well-kept secret it had once been, now that it was plastered on the front page of every magazine in the city, raving about its authentic French cuisine.

Charles and Donovan were seated in a rounded booth toward the back of the restaurant, secluded in their own little world. Customary to his culture, Charles kissed either side of my cheek in greeting. The roughness of his five o'clock shadow ground against my skin. Donovan, on the other hand, opted for a handshake as I slid into the booth and sandwiched myself between the two men.

"Miss Hartwell, a pleasure to see you again," Donovan said, opening up his laptop.

"Good to see you, too. I wish it were under better circumstances."

"I'd argue quite the opposite."

"Donovan may cost a pretty penny, but he doesn't lose his trials," Charles interjected.

"Not in a decade." The lawyer smiled to himself, an inflated sense of pride slipping through the cracks of professionalism. "As you know, Miss Hartwell, the preliminary hearing was scheduled twenty days after your release. The purpose of the preliminary hearing is for the prosecution to show that there's enough evidence to proceed with the trial. If the judge finds sufficient evidence, they'll make the call to move forward. All we need from you is to be present, but not much will be required of you until the actual trial."

"Are you still confident we have enough evidence for the judge?" I asked.

Is there enough to prove my innocence, I meant to say.

"If I thought there was any chance I might lose this case, then I wouldn't be sitting here today," he answered, straightening his spine a bit.

"Well, what about—"

The word died on the tip of my tongue, and a lengthy waiter in his mid-twenties approached the table. He welcomed us to the steakhouse, explained the specials for the evening, then presented a bottle of pinot noir nearly twice my age to the table, claiming it was taken care of. Charles's eyes lit up as someone across the room lifted his glass in our direction. He excused himself and made his way across the room toward a gentleman and his far younger companion. Perhaps his daughter? Or maybe an escort? It was difficult to tell with the age difference.

As Donovan rambled on about the preliminary hearing and what would be expected of me, I couldn't tear my eyes away from the two men reuniting. Their conversation carried across the room, and with each bellowing laugh, I was struggling to pin down why he looked familiar. Something about his youthful blue eyes in stark contrast to his tawny skin, salt and pepper hair, and thick beard itched a part of my memory I couldn't quite piece together.

Not five minutes later, Charles returned, and I finally got my answer.

The mystery man was Sebastian Gonzalez, owner of the Starling Dance Company, a prestigious touring group celebrated for their diverse ensemble of dancers and fresh interruption of classical ballet. Apparently, the two went way back, and Sebastian was here celebrating the last leg of their tour.

I hadn't realized it at first, but when he rose from his seat and took his lover's hands in his, it finally hit me where I knew him from. It wasn't his credentials nor the lasting legacy of his dancers; it was the boxy silhouette of his frame that I had last seen from the shadows of the mezzanine the day Tatiana fell. He had been there the day of Noah's death.

Charles reached across me, handing Donovan something small and red.

"Ah, perfect," he said, sticking the flash drive in his laptop.

I thought to ask what was on the flash drive, but as I watched the cursor drag from file to file—deep down, I already knew.

The rim of the wine glass paused at my lips as a video titled March 11 filled the screen, bright and imposing. While time slowed for me in the present, the past sped by in a blur. The timestamp in the corner screen flew by until two figures walked into view, hand in hand. I should have been relieved that there was physical proof of Noah and Tatiana's infidelity, but...the sight of them clawing at each other's clothes made the wine sour in my stomach.

"My team is still personally combing through the raw footage, and while there's a possibility it might not be completed in time for the preliminary hearing, we could use this late-discovered evidence to our advantage come the trial," Donovan explained.

They disappeared out of shot, and bile stung the back of my throat. The past merged with the present as the horrors of that night unfolded before my very eyes. I snapped my them shut as that version of myself tiptoed toward the door, lured to my unexpected damnation.

I couldn't watch this. I couldn't live through this again.

"Adeline"—Charles's breath was hot on my cheek—"open your eyes. You have to see it. You'll have to watch this in court."

My eyes opened against my will.

Noah and I were screaming at each other now. While the footage was silent, I could still hear his voice ringing in my ear.

You have no idea what I sacrificed for you.

Noah encroached, taking with him every ounce of progress I'd made to leave.

You aren't listening.

Charles was right—I would have to watch this countless times before a jury of my peers. I forced myself to stomach what little I could, blinking rapidly, if only to escape the horrors for but a second.

You need to listen, Adeline. Listen to me.

Noah tackled me against the wall—

"Excuse me," I quavered. "I need to go to the restroom."

And while I managed to escape one reminder of that fateful night, the horrors followed after me as I slid from the booth and cut across the restaurant. It took what little strength I had to keep from falling apart in the middle of the labyrinth, but the moment I broke free and locked myself behind a closed door, there was no containing the rush of pain that shook my bones and sank me to my knees. A spine-tingling sob broke through, echoing off the tiled walls. It took several gulps of air before I felt as if I wasn't drowning on solid land.

Music. I needed music.

Fumbling through my purse was pointless. I dumped it out and lunged for my phone the moment it hit the tile.

"Fuck," I hissed, trying and failing to unlock the still-shattered screen.

A text message flashed across the screen along with several other unread messages that blurred in and out as unshed tears swarmed my vision.

Jin: My brother is convinced you owe him a drink for not coming out tonight.

My finger hovered over the screen.

Jin: It's an old tradition he started up a few years ago after I was constantly bailing on him because of work. I can't even tell you how many rounds I've bought over the years.

Clear as day, his voice echoed in my head. *Search for something red in the room, and every time you find something, I want you to say it aloud.*

"Find something red," I repeated to myself, eyes frantically searching.

Pristine black marble corner tops. Gilded scones. Mix-and-matched picture frames of different historical French landmarks. I was trapped in a modern monstrosity without a hint of red to be found. The walls started to close in almost as quickly as my lungs constricted in on themselves.

A flashing light on the ceiling caught my attention through the mirror.

"Smoke detector," I murmured. The relief was almost instantaneous, like the panic had been leeched from my veins. It took time for it to dwindle, but that small flashing light gave me enough clarity to find the most obvious red item of all. My fingertips brushed over the cool surface, tracing the seams of my mouth. "Lipstick."

The thrumming of my heart slowed as I shut my eyes, leaned my head against the back wall, and repeated the two items until I lost count.

The concept of overcoming a panic attack rather than shoving down those emotions one atop of the other until I was too weak to hold them down anymore was foreign to me. Slowly but surely, my heart steadied, and for the first time, I felt in control.

Tears spilled down my cheek as I sucked in my first full breath.

There was only so long I could hide in the bathroom before someone would notice. Especially when there was probably a glass of wine and a steak au poivre waiting for me at the table, but I needed a moment to gather myself.

Adeline: Technically, it isn't bailing if I never agreed to go in the first place.

The three dots appeared, disappeared, then appeared again.

Jin: Don't you have a fancy dinner to be at?

Adeline: Don't you have friends you should be enjoying your time with?

Jin: And why would I do that when I could be talking to you?

I dragged my teeth over my bottom lip, fighting back a smile.

Coming up short with a response, I considered three different options. The truth: I wish I had gone with you tonight instead of coming to this meeting. The vulnerable: At dinner, the lawyer showed me footage from that night. I don't think I could have overcome it without your advice. Thank you for helping when I was at my lowest. I don't think I could have done it without you. The lie: I'll talk to you later, have fun with your friends, and I'll see you back at the apartment.

He texted me back before I could settle on one.

Jin: I wish you were here, Adeline.

Before I could think better of it, I responded.

Adeline: Send me the address.

Eventually, I returned to the table, made polite conversation, and finished my meal. With the promise of something to look forward to, I managed to stomach the remainder of the night. The moment I was free, I called for a rideshare and sped off across town, knowing there was nowhere else I wanted to be than with Jin.

This section of the Entertainment District was a tapestry of sin and temptation, luring its prey with the promise of cheap thrills and good times. Patrons queued outside the nightclub, blanketed in a red, dreamy haze. Their excitement was palatable, nearly drowning out the hypnotic buzz of the neon sign that loomed above. Like a siren's call, it swore promises of its own that drove more and more people to dare to peek behind the curtain and see what thrills Don Juan offered.

I texted Jin, letting him know I was outside.

Jin: Go to the front of the line and give them your name.

I garnered a few glances at the front of the line from people who looked like they'd been waiting all night. My name tumbled from my lips, and I was whisked away into darkened hallways with various colored light spilling in from the other end and the drumming of a bass as infectious as it was deafening. Further down the rabbit hole I went, emerging into a sprawling expanse of the room where the music hit its crescendo and temptation was the loudest. The sunken dance floor beckoned anyone close enough to indulge. Bodies ground against one another, completely lost to the music and flickering neon lights. Beyond that was a bar backlit by glowing lights that turned each bottle on the back shelf into its own kaleidoscope of liquid gold.

Caleb was chatting up the bartender, deep in conversation, while Jin was leaning up against the counter next to him, the harsh glow of his cellphone illuminating the soft features of his face. I shot him a text, letting him know that I was finally here.

Those features shifted from a look of indifference to a devastating smile that only widened as he craned his neck, trying to find me in the crowd. Our eyes clashed from across the room, and I was suddenly closing the distance between us, wholly aware that the smile on my face was a mirror of his own.

Jin didn't wait for me to find him—no, he cut through the crowd and met me halfway. Had he been anyone else, I would have thrown my arms around him in a crushing embrace, but I thought better of it when I realized that might not be an appropriate response for our newfound friendship.

"This is *not* what I expected when you said you were hanging out with friends."

"Me neither. I have to be at the theater in less than..." He glanced down at his watch. "...twelve hours, and yet I somehow let my little brother drag me to a club on a work night. It's probably for the best. I promised myself this season I would make more of an effort to spend time with my friends and family rather than locking myself in the theater all night. Well, at the very least, I'm trying."

It was most definitely the wine talking, but Jin had outdone himself tonight. Dark gray pants hugged the muscles of his toned thighs before tapering off into polished dress shoes. The cream-colored button-up he wore had a few buttons undone, exposing a sliver of smooth skin. It was just enough to tease what he was hiding beneath without coming off too flashy or vain.

I looked away, realizing I needed to fill the silence.

"He's not even my brother, and I somehow got roped into it, too," I said, smoothing over the rings decorating my fingers.

A beat passed, then Jin gestured over his shoulder. "Should we..."

"Yeah. Yes. Please."

We walked toward the percussion of cheers. Caleb raised a

shot high into the air before downing it in one gulp. I'd forgotten how intoxicating it was to be in his presence as he swept me into a crushing hug that was quickly followed by a much gentler one from Sophia. A few other familiar faces broke through the crowd as we reunited with Jin's friends at the bar.

"I came to pay my debt. What do you want to drink?" I asked Caleb, fishing out my wallet.

He swatted the card away. "Technically, you showed up, so you don't owe me a thing. Having you here is the reward itself. I mean, come on"—he gestured to my dress—"where the hell did you come from, a date? You look amazing, and I would keep complimenting you, but I think my fiancée might get suspicious if I do. Jin, isn't it your job to compliment her, not me?"

Caleb flashed his brother a smirk, and Jin took a long sip of his beer in response.

"No," I said, ignoring the way he watched me over the rim as if he didn't quite believe me when I answered the same question back in the apartment. "I had dinner with my boss, so I definitely need a drink after that."

"Yikes. And I thought I needed a drink after spending the entire night with my older brother." He turned toward Jin. "I'm only kidding. It was a miracle you came out in the first place, I'm grateful."

Then he set his sights back on me. "I swear, when I told him he could invite you, I'd never seen his eyes light up like that before. Looks like I need to bring you along more often; it might be the only way to get the bastard to leave the house."

"Caleb," Jin warned.

"You're no fun," he groaned. "Come on, Adeline, let's get you something?"

Other than the dance floor, the bar was arguably the most crowded part of the club. Bartenders buzzed around the small sliver of space like little worker bees. We patiently waited for one of the four employees to notice us.

"Let me buy you a drink," Jin said, leaning in to shout over the music.

I pulled away, hoping to lessen the way my stomach flipped in our proximity.

"Yes, but with one expectation. You can't complain when I'm sloppy tomorrow at rehearsal."

"Oh, come on! One drink isn't going to make you sloppy." He chuckled.

I chewed on my bottom lip, and his gaze instantly fell to the movement.

"I might have nervously chugged a glass of wine at dinner." A beat passed. "Okay, maybe two."

"Why were you nervous?"

"Buy me a drink, and maybe you'll find out. I've been known to overshare."

The group migrated from one side of the club to the other and snagged a booth right as another group left. With room for only six, the rest of the party stood close by. Sophia grabbed me by the wrist and pulled me into the booth before I could decide where to go, and Caleb followed after, draping his arm over her shoulder.

It didn't take long for him to hijack the conversation with tales of his restoration project. While I couldn't find the support beams he was pointing to in the darkened room, I did find Jin watching me from afar. He gave me a knowing smile, and all I could do was shrug in response as his brother rambled on about rebar and framing.

"—madhouse. The damn place should have been nothing more than ashes," Caleb continued telling his story, but his voice was swept away by the music as I lost focus.

Jin whispered something in the girl's ear sitting next to me, then switched spots with her.

"For someone who claims to overshare when she's drinking, you've been awfully quiet since we sat down," he said, leaning back on the cushion.

His knee accidentally brushed against mine. I'd grown so accustomed to the ache in my limbs that it was strange to feel a tingling along my skin, and even stranger was the fact that it didn't lessen even when he pulled away, an apology on his lips.

I leaned in to say, "I can hardly get a word in between Caleb's stories. We should be taking a sip every time he mentions the fire or mezzanine."

"I might have to toss you over my shoulder and carry you home if you do." Jin took a long sip of his drink, allowing me a second to imagine how that might play out. "Would it make you feel better if I overshared first?"

"Um. Maybe."

"Well...I've been thinking about leaving the theater," he said, then polished off his beer. "It's been about four months since I first started applying to other positions. The furthest I've gotten is a second round of interviews, but nothing to show for it. So, it's mostly been a lot of daydreaming and not much else."

Jin was the beating heart of our company. The show lived and died under his supervision, and there was no denying how instrumental his efforts were in running a smooth show. If you had asked me a week ago to describe our artistic director, I would have likely regurgitated some rhetoric about willful spirits and unwavering loyalty, but knowing what I knew now about the man behind the clipboard, I wondered how much of it was a mask hiding his exhaustion this whole time. The theater was my salvation, and it hurt me more than I cared to admit that Jin might not find safety between its walls as I did.

"I think the theater would go up in flames if you left."

"Don't worry." He huffed out a laugh. "I'm not leaving anytime soon. Can't get rid of me that easily."

A beat passed.

"If you were to leave," I started, "what do you see yourself doing?"

"I guess there was always a version of myself that dreamt of working overseas. My internship in Paris opened a lot of doors, but for the same reasons why I couldn't stay, I need to be here for my family. In a perfect world, I'll find something within the district, and I can have the best of both worlds."

Thinking back to the dozens of picture frames dotting his bedroom wall, I guessed there was always a part of Jin that yearned for more. It was hard to imagine someone giving all that up.

"I understand how tempting it sounds to drop everything and move somewhere new with the promise of a fresh start."

"Temptation can be hard to resist." For a split second, I could have sworn his eyes dropped to my lips, but it was hard to be certain in the low lighting.

"I thought the district could be that place for me. Or at least I used to," I explained, deep in reverie, but it was Jin's silky, smooth voice that drew me back to the present.

"Not many people are brave enough to try. You should be proud of yourself, Adeline."

"You can call me Addie, if you like. I'm fine with either."

"Addie," he said aloud, testing the sound of it. "I like it, too."

A truth for a truth was a fair price, and now that Jin had admitted something, it was my turn to pay up. Going at my own pace, I explained the events of the night leading up to the surveillance footage. The fact that I attempted to stay as long as possible to prove to myself that I could watch this over and over again in court, but ultimately failed when a panic attack struck me like a bolt of lightning right to the chest, and the only way to resuscitate me was his little trick. The truth wasn't always pretty, but maybe holding in the messy bits of my life was how I'd gotten into this mess to begin with.

"I'm glad I could help you even if I wasn't there."

I smiled. "Me too, Jin."

"So...Charles is really helping you with the trial."

"Charles was there that night," I vaguely explained. While telling Jin a fraction of that truth felt liberating, there was little I wanted to relive of that night with him. "He—he offered me his hand in my darkest hour, and part of that support includes his legal team. Everything about the aftermath of that night has been incredibly overwhelming, and I'm grateful I don't have to do it alone."

Jin's attention was focused on his lap. He mindlessly starched off the wet label of his empty beer bottle, seeming to be lost in his own thoughts. The reason I recognized it so clearly was that it mirrored my own anxious tendencies.

"His legal team is good, but they cost an arm and a leg," he finally said.

"We haven't really sat down to discuss it, but he implied it would be taken care of. Charles mentioned it as an investment in the future of his theater. He said the price was worth not losing my talent. It all seems too good to be true, but I'm not in a position to question it."

"Maybe you should."

"What's that supposed to mean?"

His nail vigorously worked the edges of the label. Once he had the corner, he started to shred the thing to bits and stuffed it into the empty bottle.

"I only say this because—well, I care about you, Adeline, but I don't think Charles is the most trustworthy person. The fact that he has already explicitly said he's only helping you for the theater's benefit is telling enough. I would hate to see you get stuck with the bill if Charles decides he doesn't want to be as forgiving, or god forbid, you get injured, and he takes his help away completely."

If this were true and his motives were coming from a place of selfishness, then I would be a fool not to capitalize on it, when the only thing separating me from jail time was Donovan and his team. I couldn't afford any lawyer worth a damn, and any one the state would provide me simply wouldn't be enough. Charles may not be the best choice, but what other options did I have when so much was at stake?

I gently put my hand over his, and our eyes clashed.

"I appreciate your concern, and I've thought about those things too, but—but they said if I lose this case, I could be facing between five and twenty years. If taking this leap means my only chance to prove my innocence, then I have to take it."

Jin nodded like he understood but didn't necessarily agree with my decision.

If this was my best chance to prove my innocence, then I had to take it.

For once, I would choose me.

Because if I didn't, who else would?

Chapter Twenty

Jin

Cupping my hands under the faucet, I let the ice-cold water trace the veins down my forearms as it spilled over my hands. The shock to the system did little to steel whatever part of my confidence unraveled when I was near her. Alcohol helped, but it wasn't a viable everyday option—if anything, it opened me up to plenty more opportunities to stumble over my words, forget my train of thought completely, or even open my big mouth about the lawyer situation.

I guess Adeline wasn't the only one prone to oversharing when she drank.

It all seems too good to be true, but I'm not in a position to question it.

Maybe you should.

I was kicking myself for even bringing it up when I wasn't in a position to question her decision, nor did I have any real evidence to support that lingering feeling deep within my gut.

Putting reservations aside, what other option did she have? She was underpaid and overworked—I knew exactly how little ballerinas made, which was exactly why we'd been advocating so aggressively for salary adjustments. Even if she could afford a reputable lawyer, who was to say they would be good enough to win? Charles's team was her best chance, but something about the *selfless* act didn't sit right with me.

I almost told her as much, then she put her hand atop mine...

It wasn't like me to lose myself completely when I was near her, but tonight—I needed a moment to collect myself if I planned to endure another agonizing moment where chivalry balanced a knife's edge. Where every second in her presence was a constant battle not to give in to the urge to run my hand up her bare thigh just to see if the slightest touch of our knees accidentally brushing up against one another drove her as crazy as it did for me.

Had it been anyone else, I wouldn't have stopped myself.

I wouldn't have thought twice about giving in to that burning need for her.

"Christ," I muttered to myself, then splashed more water in my face. Maybe if I did it enough times, I could wash away the sinful thoughts.

Adeline deserved better than that. I had no right—

Two men were standing directly behind me, their looming figures taking up most of the arched mirror. The one on the left took a step forward once he had me pinned beneath his piercing gaze. Other than the three of us, the bathroom was empty, and I didn't particularly like those odds. His buddy with a broken nose followed in suit, and in that moment, I knew I was either going to get jumped or robbed while sporting a partial erection —what an all-time low.

"Destler wants to speak to you," Broken Nose said.

That sobered me up real fast.

"Um, yeah. Sure." I swallowed.

Erection long forgotten, I followed Broken Nose out the bathroom door while Tall, Dark, and Mysterious stayed two paces behind. We weaved through the crowd, making our way to the other side of the club, where a staircase led us to the balcony overlooking everything. Destler leaned over the railing, an unlit joint between his lips. His posture reminded me of an old black and white photo Caleb had shown me of Don Juan when it was a jazz club in its heyday. Dozens of patrons leaned over the edge, eager to catch a glimpse of the lively music below. Not much had changed in the hundred years since.

I cleared my throat. "You wanted to talk to me."

"No, I have something to show you," Destler said, brushing past me on his way to the small bar butted up against the wall. He plucked a small rectangular box off the counter and then handed it over.

"Okay," I said tentatively, my fingers tracing the edges of the velvet surface.

"Open it."

A pair of earrings twinkled back at me as a flash of red light sped across the club. Diamonds lined the center of a gold band, where it dripped into a crystal teardrop. The piece of jewelry was delicate in nature but bold in its wealth. With more questions than answers, I peeled off the white envelope taped on the bottom of the box, hoping it might explain why Destler had sought me out.

Promises are rarely kept, but the ones I whisper to you, I swear by.

— Patrick

I looked to Destler for answers. "I don't understand what I'm looking at."

"It's a message from beyond the grave," he responded, sparking his lighter. "What do you remember of the fires?"

Anastasia had called me in a panic, freaking out that she couldn't get a hold of me. Around that time in my career, I was staying well past closing time nearly every night, preparing for the upcoming season, and she assumed I was still in the district when the fire caught. By the time I turned on the news, my screen was filled with choking flames, pleas for citizens to save the historic buildings drowned out the relentless humming of sirens, and the seemingly righteous condemning the district as a place of sin that deserved to be brought down by the flames. The fires rocked the very foundation of the Entertainment District, stripping it apart brick by brick. And yet, despite any petty rivalries between owners, it brought together a community in its darkest hours.

"Well...the fire started in The Lotte late that night, then inevitably spread to Don Juan. Given how old the building was, they assumed it was an electrical fire at first, but it was later proven there was some kind of accelerant—"

"Wrong."

"What?"

"You're wrong," he said, a smile tugging at the corner of his lips. "You were about to give me a long-winded answer about how they still don't know how the first started today, despite suspecting foul play. And by the look on your face, I have a funny feeling you aren't used to being told you're wrong, am I right, Collins?"

I wasn't sure if I should be impressed or terrified of him yet.

"I was there the night of the fires," he said. "I know what started it."

My eyes dropped to his leg, and he nodded.

Destler had simply been there that night. He'd survived it.

"That was a year and a half ago. I'm confused why you

haven't told the police what actually happened if you were there."

He smiled again, but this time it lacked any of the willful spirit from before.

"You've been working in the Entertainment District for a while now. I'm going to go out on a limb and say you know how it was established."

I nodded, well aware of its dark history. There was money in show business, but it was nothing compared to bootlegging. The Entertainment District was merely a speck on the map before the Eighteenth Amendment. Those who evaded prohibition laws built their empires, making and selling alcohol in the various speakeasies scattered around town, but with money came power, and with power came competition. The cutthroat rivalries that emerged during an era that had no problem crumbling empires and spilling blood, leaving only a few families on top. After the ratification of the Twenty-First Amendment in 1933, the owners had to find new means of assuming power, which typically meant sex and/or drugs.

"During your interview, you told me you didn't understand the rivalry between the district owners today, and I told you it was about history, but that isn't necessarily the full truth. Rivalries are ever-changing beasts, starting as one thing and evolving simply because they're a burden passed down upon us. Growing up, it didn't take long to realize what my father expected of me, but that didn't mean I had to participate in it simply because I was conditioned to. I didn't have to be the one to decimate my own community because that's how it had always been. Charles, on the other hand, took the empire his father had strengthened and used it for his own personal gain rather than expanding it further."

Historically, ballet had been known to have a dangerous backstage culture that exploited young dancers for favors and funding. For *abbonés*, wealthy men who subscribed to the theater in the nineteenth century, backstage was a sort of men's club that normalized a hyper-sexualized atmosphere. And while those practices weren't in place today, I always resented the environment Charles created for his Financial District buddies that felt eerily reminiscent through a business and funding perspective.

"And while that was all fine and good," he continued, "Charles tried to take something away from me—something that nearly cost me the life of the person I love the most. Charles started that fire because he wanted to do what his father couldn't. This box"—he snapped it shut—"was a gift intended for *my* fiancée, a matching set to the necklace she was given a year and a half ago. Patrick was a sick bastard, too wrapped up in his narcissism to realize we both had him in our crosshairs until it was too late. Charles tricked both of us that night and set the fire in the theater to kill two birds with one stone—little did he know I wasn't so easy to get rid of."

"Patrick Martin?" I asked, brows furrowed. He nodded.

Of the four lives, Blanchet's brother-in-law was among those who perished in the fire. A tragic death that shook the very foundation of their family and echoed in the theater for months after. I knew the name all too well because I had attended his wake out of respect for Charles. If I concentrated hard enough, I could still hear his mother's bellowing cries echoing off the church's vaulted ceiling.

"Charles might exploit his workers, but he isn't a—"

"Murderer?" he interjected. "Regardless of what you assume he is or isn't capable of, that doesn't change the past. That doesn't diminish what hell he put my family through over a silly rivalry and bad blood.

"I was planning on being patient and waiting for you to come to your senses, but I don't have that luxury anymore. We made the official announcement this morning that The Lotte will reopen in six months, and not two hours later, this box was left at my fiancée's dance studio from her dead lover. Charles ran away with his tail between his legs, and now, a year and a half later, he's ready to finish what he started."

I couldn't help myself as I laughed. How ridiculous this all sounded as my mind slowly processed it all. "I have nothing to do with this rivalry," I tittered. "Why the hell are you even telling me this?"

Destler puffed out a cloud of smoke, the thin, hazy trails dancing about his features.

"You're wrong. Again."

He smirked, getting some kind of sick enjoyment out of it.

"You told me yourself; you're tired of Blanchet walking all over you and everyone else. And yet, you've been complacent—" I opened my mouth to speak, but Destler raised a hand to stop me. "Doing nothing makes you just as complacent. Well, here's your chance to make a difference before anyone gets hurt. I have a score to settle with Blanchet, but I can't do it alone."

"And what exactly do you want me to do?"

"It's simple." He beamed. "I need information."

With every intent to sully his offer, refusing to sell what was left of my tattered soul, I surprised even myself with what came out of my mouth next.

"I'll consider it."

<hr>

As the taxi sped through the empty streets, Adeline was fighting a losing battle. One that promised the end of a terribly long day. What little strength she had withered away until she eventually gave in, resting her head against my shoulder and falling asleep. For those brief moments we passed under a streetlamp, I would be blessed with the sight of her curled up next to me, making my heart swell each time.

Fate has a funny way of spinning its intricate webs. An endless string of possibilities that are all intertwined, regardless of whether or not we have the foresight to see the path being laid down before us. From the moment Adeline Hartwell walked into auditions, I knew another web had been spun without fully understanding the implications of what that truly meant for me yet. For a time, I prayed it meant a reality in which our fates would be connected, but as the months rolled by and seasons changed, that glimmer of optimism dwindled along with my spirit.

Adeline had tangled herself up in a mess of webs, and although she'd freed herself of one, countless others kept her trapped. Fate was a cruel temptress who took little pity on those who asked. And while there may have been a time when I wished we'd be woven together, perhaps I was right, just not in the sense I intended it to be.

Fate had brought us together for a reason.

If Destler came back with a counteroffer, I knew in my heart that I would say yes for her sake. I would agree to help him if it meant protecting her.

Chapter Twenty-One

Jin

Bile crept its way up my throat, lining my esophagus with an acidic burn that my morning coffee couldn't wash away as Xavier and Adeline took their starting positions. As I watched the old footage, the only thing stopping me from launching the computer monitor across the screen was digging my fingernails so hard into the flesh of my thigh that I feared they might split down the middle before breaking skin.

"Son of a bitch," I muttered to myself, unable to look away as the black and white image of Adeline tumbled to the ground, her fellow dancers closing in on her.

The video looped back to the beginning of the rehearsal footage. My cursor inched along the screen frame by frame as I studied the lift in agonizing detail. Alignments were checked, dancers were reassured, and yet when it came to the moment Xavier was expected to lift Adeline, there was the slightest shift in his grip.

Xavier was classically trained with a similar competitive edge and willful drive, so it wasn't even a question who Adeline would be paired with when she first joined the company, seeing that he was the only one who could truly let her shine. There was absolutely no reason, given his expertise and dedicated years of training, that he should have ever made such a foolish mistake, nor was there any reason she should have fallen as hard as she did.

Adeline was right. He pushed her.

Which made me wonder what else Adeline was right about that others were quick to condemn her for.

My cursor hovered over the main menu of the surveillance software. In the upper right corner was a file labeled achieved footage. The date March 11 roared in my ears.

As I was about to click it, there was a knock at my door.

Xavier popped his head inside. "You wanted to speak with me?"

"Come in." I gestured to the empty seat. "And close the door behind you."

If anger was indeed for the willful spirit that clutched hot coals with the hope of throwing them at others, only to burn themselves, then being near Xavier proved I was more than willing to let us both burn. As I retrieved the rehearsal footage, I let him wallow in the taut silence. Xavier tapped his shoes and craned his neck to get a better look at the clock hanging on the back of the wall, while I took my time.

"Rehearsal's starting soon. Is this going to take long?"

"Don't worry, this will be quick."

Xavier's expression fell as I rotated the monitor. His gaze jutted back and forth between me and the footage. It wasn't enough to simply watch the moment unfold. I wanted to revel in his consternation, so I flipped through the footage frame by frame until stopping on the one where his fingers splayed across her waist. Then I circled the desk, grabbed hold of the back of his chair, and leaned in over him to point out the sloppy alignment.

"If I remember correctly, you told Ms. Hartwell, 'It's not

your fault you can't land properly.' Well, that doesn't seem to be the case, now does it?"

"I never said that," he interjected.

"Should we rewind the footage and find out for ourselves?" I said, and Xavier snorted. "Or should I fast forward to the part where she crashes to the ground a little harder than she should have?"

That shut him up real fast.

He ran the heel of his palm over his eyes and let out an exhausted breath. "Tracy tore her ACL last spring. I didn't see you accusing James of purposely hurting another dancer. This is bullshit, and we both know it."

"That might be true, but"—I leaned in closer—"I didn't find surveillance footage of James giving a newspaper to Tatiana the same morning a bloodied note was left on Ms. Hartwell's vanity."

"Let me get this right," he chided, "you called me down here to accuse me of some kind of elaborate plan to attack Hartwell?"

Even if I couldn't fully prove it was Xavier who orchestrated the threat or if he was working in cahoots with Tatiana, I did have the rehearsal footage. And that was enough for me.

"Your contract with Republic City Opera has been terminated immediately. Collect—"

Xavier shot up, the legs of the chair screeching against the wood floor.

"You're firing me? Are you kidding me, Jin? I gave Tatiana the newspaper because Noah's obituary was in it with the time and date for his funeral. I didn't do shit to her vanity."

"Collect your belongings and leave the premises. Security will escort you out."

"So that's it? I give you seven years of my career, and this is *all* I get in return. Let me guess, Hartwell still gets to dance with this company." He seethed, daring a step forward.

"We aren't talking about Hartwell right now."

"This is ridiculous. Adeline murders someone—she murdered my friend," he amended, "in cold blood, and yet she gets to dance as if nothing ever happened without facing the consequences of her actions. Noah's blood is still on her hands. You're a goddamn hypocrite for letting her dance."

I took a step forward, peering down at his nose.

"I am not the judge nor the jury, and neither are you," I said with unnerving calmness. "You have no right to blame Adeline when you don't know what happened that night—none of us do. And you especially don't have the right to hurt one of *my* dancers."

"Do you even hear what you are saying right now?" He huffed out a hysterical laugh. "You sound absolutely insane defending a literal murderer."

"Get the fuck out of my theater, Xavier," I snarled down at him.

The tension was thick enough to choke on— slowly strangling us each the longer Xavier stood within arm's reach. Luckily for both of us, he eventually inched away, shaking his head as he made for the exit. Before he could leave, I called his name one last time.

"Don't forget to send in Tatiana next."

With the music as my guide, I chase after the sounds of "Mariage d'amour" echoing through the halls. Suddenly, all eyes were on me as I stumbled into rehearsals fashionably late. And yet in a crowded room, she was always the first person I found.

Anastasia shouted at the dancers to stay focused as she scampered in my direction. The gleaming smile plastered on her face dropped the instant she turned her back to the corps de ballet. "Jin, they didn't show up for practice. I have no idea where Xavier or—"

I lightly grabbed her by the elbow, dragging her out of earshot of the other dancers.

"I fired them," I whispered.

"You what?" She blinked up at me slowly.

"I fired both of them."

Anastasia stumbled back two steps before catching herself, hands fisted in her hair.

"Please tell me you're joking," she said, huffing out a nervous laugh.

I shook my head, and all she could do was stare up at me blankly. It took a moment for her to process what had happened, but when she did, she lunged for me, grabbing me by the lapel like a madman. My dress shoes screeched across the flooring as I attempted to catch myself. I could feel them all staring at us in our corner of the studio.

"Are you trying to give me a brain aneurysm, Jin? What the hell do you mean you fired two of my best dancers a few weeks before the opening show?"

I gently grabbed her by the wrists and attempted to pry her off me. "I'm going to need you to trust me, An. How about we go into the hall and talk about what happened?"

Somehow, I managed to coax her outside to keep our conversation private. Anastasia was uncharacteristically quiet the entire time, hanging on to my every word as I breathlessly explained Xavier's tort along with Tatiana's tearful confession. While refusing to have played a role in the vanity fiasco, Tatiana revealed plenty about her *whirlwind* romance with Noah that had been going on for months prior. Grief had dug its claws in so deeply that it threatened to never let her go, and while she swore to make amends and apologize to the people she hurt with her actions, I had little remorse for those who begged for forgiveness only after being caught.

Tatiana and Xavier were both complicit in their roles.

And both of their contracts had been terminated.

"Jin, I don't understand what you expect me to do about this," Anastasia said gently. All the fight left in her had withered away. "I'm down a soloist. Halle is still out, grieving this entire mess. And Adeline no longer has a partner. She's one of my strongest dancers...Blanchet is already breathing down our necks. Without the salary adjustments, my family is already struggling financially—I can't lose this job."

"I've already spoken to Halle, and she'll be returning at the end of next week. And for the other two problems, I think you already answered your own question."

There was no other choice, and we both knew it.

"She isn't ready."

"Let her determine that."

"Have you already spoken to Charles?" I shook my head, and she cursed under her breath. "If we are doing this, then we'll need to start today to prepare in time. Call him. Now."

Anastasia stood nearby, pacing in short, meaningful strides as I patiently waited for him to answer. It was about to go to voicemail when his rough accent bled through the line.

"Why did you log into the surveillance software?"

"Hello to you, too, Charles."

"Jin," he warned.

Because it's already been two days, and you haven't done anything about it.

I explained the situation regarding Tatiana and Xavier, and before he could get a word in, I proposed our only alternative, twisting it in a way that shaped her youth and inexperience into a means of ensuring the future of the theater. Using his own words against him regarding why he bailed her out in the first place.

It took some back and forth, but eventually, he said, "If she fails, then this is on you, Collins. You have one season to prove me wrong." Then he hung up.

Failure was the only guarantee in show business. It was the inevitable beast that was meant to teach individuals from their mistakes and allow them the opportunity to grow in spite of them, but failure wasn't an option in this instant—Charles made that much clear. And perhaps I should have been scared that failure meant the possibility of a final season without something to fall back on, but as I walked back into the studio and found her amongst the other dancers, I knew I had put my faith in the right person. I knew what wonderful thing she was capable of if only given the chance.

"Circle up," Anastasia barked.

The dancers approached, creating a small semi-circle around us. The last time I'd spoken to them like this, I had broken the news of Noah's untimely death. They watched me wearily as if the other shoe might drop.

"Starting today, Xavier Becker and Tatiana Antonenko will no longer be with this company," I announced. "And while this may come as a shock to you all, I assure you this decision was not made lightly, and their actions were grounds for termina-tion." I ignored the gasps and whispers from the crowd. "As well as the decision regarding who will replace Tatiana as soloist for this season."

"Did we finally get a guest principal?" someone asked.

Finding a guest principal was the least of our problems right now.

"No," I said. "Until further notice, the role of Carlotta will go to Hartwell."

If news of Xavier and Tatiana being fired was cause for

whispers, then the announcement of Adeline's promotion came as quite the surprise when the room fell silent. Adeline Hartwell was destined for this role; the company was too wrapped up in their own disappointment to see that now.

Adeline dropped her head, then ran her palm over her chest in soft, soothing motions. I nearly cut across the room, recognizing the signs from the day Xavier had dropped her, but before I could take that first step, she lifted her head. Our eyes met, and suddenly, the most devastatingly beautiful smile was gleaming back at me.

That smile fractured something deep within me.

And I would do anything to keep her smiling like that.

Some of the younger apprentices swept in, stealing her attention to congratulate her. I took the opportunity to approach James, who was standing off on the sidelines. I leaned in close and whispered, "If you drop her, I will make sure you never work in this city again."

He balked, staring at me with wide green eyes. "I—I wouldn't dream of it."

I patted him on the shoulder. "Good answer, James."

It was extraordinary to watch Adeline slipping into her role almost seamlessly. It was as if she had me under a spell—transfixed by every pirouette and fouetté that further confirmed her place was front and center on that stage. Her only downfall was her youth and inexperience, but pure determination had set her leaps and bounds above her peers. I could have sat there all day, committing her every smile to memory and basking in the light that returned to her hazel eyes. There was a type of weightlessness about the way she carried herself that was reminiscent of the time I pulled her aside after the second-round auditions and offered her the role of a lifetime—a version of who she was before Noah stole the light away from her.

I prayed this version of her was here to stay.

I spent the entirety of rehearsal daydreaming about how I might keep that smile on her face and almost missed my next meeting because of it. Emmanuel, our stage manager, had to call me twice before the trance was broken. The rest of the afternoon, I pored over messy budget reports, stressed over upcoming ticket sales, and consulted with the marketing team to ensure the season went off without a hitch.

As strenuous as the work was, I did enjoy the creative aspect of the theater and the promise of a beautiful performance to show for it. Art and music had always been a language I was fluent in, allowing me opportunities I never thought possible when my mother and I moved to America with nothing more than a dream and the money in our pockets. It paid for my schooling, sent me overseas to explore my passions, and made me feel whole when at a time when the mere idea of finding a reason to smile felt impossible. Republic City Opera House had given me a home when no one else would. It was an opportunity for a fresh start that I had desperately longed for. I took my first steps here, growing and adapting with the weight of my responsibility and resilience to overcome the trials and tribulations of a theater in shambles.

It had given me everything, yet it wasn't enough.

I rapped my knuckles against the doorframe and waited for her soothing voice to beckon me inside the empty dressing room. In a sea full of vanities, hers was the only one occupied. It was well past closing time, and everyone else had gone home. The sight of her scribbling in her journal, feet propped up on another chair, was a sight to behold.

Adeline tossed her notebook on the stained vanity, and a heartbeat later, she was throwing her arms around me. I stumbled back a step, hardly registering what had happened, but instinct kicked in, and I wrapped her in my arms. The warmth of her body enveloped me in the rich scent of her lavender shampoo, which invaded my senses.

"It still hasn't hit me yet. I'm a soloist." She beamed, releasing a breathy laugh.

There wasn't a single flower I could think of to compare to her beauty, but if I had to try, I would say being near her was like lying in a field of wildflowers. There was such warmth in her proximity, so many variations of vibrant colors that bloomed without the aid of others. Resilient and beautiful. Adeline was my little wildflower.

"I can. It was only a matter of time," I said, taking a step back when I realized I was still clutching onto her. "In all my years working here, I've never seen someone quite as talented as you."

She opened her mouth, then abruptly closed it.

"What?"

"Um, I guess I always imagined between the two of us, it would have been Halle. After everything she's sacrificed to get where she is now...I was always rooting for her."

"I imagine Halle would be proud of you if she were here."

"I'd hope so."

And that's when I noticed it. Sitting on the corner of her vanity was a bouquet of red carnations wrapped in brown paper, a little note tucked between its petals.

"Do you have a secret admirer?" I teased, plucking the note.

"No." She snorted. "Those are from Charles."

I know a star when I see one. One step closer to principal, mon étoile.

—Charles

Mon étoile. My star.

Not four hours ago, Charles was berating me for selecting someone so young and inexperienced, and now...it seemed as if he were riding the coattails of said decision. For Adeline's sake, I tried my best to slap on a smile for the rest of the night and celebrate her accomplishments, but it proved to be especially difficult when a text came through hours later.

Unknown: Don Juan. Thursday at 5 p.m.

Chapter Twenty-Two

Adeline

Ballet had always been an intriguing part of my childhood. It had been the stepping stones of my adolescence and a determining factor of my future success, but I hadn't always wanted to pursue a career as a dancer. My obsession with ballet had taken hold while sulking in the corner of the studio, forced to watch my sister perform; however, it wasn't until I saw *The Nutcracker* that I realized such a career was possible. I always assumed my passion for the arts would only go as far as my parents were willing to pay for it. That night, passion and obsession turned into stubborn determination and a longing for more. That performance lit a fire under me that never stopped burning.

And now I was one step closer.

I'd give anything to wrap my younger self in my arms and tell her what could be possible for both of us. She deserved this as much as I did. While I was well aware I was only rewarded this position on a technicality, that didn't diminish the fact that I beat out all my peers who are years ahead of me. It was an opportunity to prove my worth and rightfully earn all that was to follow. This was my chance to pour myself into what little I could control and focus on this sliver of happiness.

No matter how hard I tried, I couldn't wipe the smile off my face.

"If you'll follow me this way." The hostess did that strange customer service thing where she bobbed and weaved through the restaurant, slightly turned toward us to ask about our day. "Are we celebrating anything tonight? Birthday? Anniversary?"

"We're celebrating a promotion," Jin answered.

"Wonderful, I'll let your waiter know to bring out some tempura ice cream so you two can properly celebrate. Congratulations!"

Nova Sushi was a trendy Japanese restaurant on the west side of the district, featuring a rich blend of tradition and modern flair—a dimly lit, intimate space that glowed a reddish haze from the neon lights hidden beneath the sushi bar. Top hits played over the quiet hum of conversation and familiar ring of laughter. The space was effortless, and all it took was one look at someone's sushi platter to know why Jin came here often—often enough that one of the waiters greeted him by name as we worked our way toward the back.

The already narrow path shrank to nearly half its size as we walked alongside the sushi bar. Jin slowed his pace, allowing me to trail behind the hostess. I made it two steps before a man, completely oblivious to his surroundings, shot out of his chair. Thanks to my quick reflexes, I stopped before I could collide with the chair, but Jin, on the other hand, must not have been paying attention because a second later, we collided. A powerful arm hooked around my torso as we stumbled a few steps forward before finding our balance.

"Fuck," Jin grumbled close to my ear, sending a shiver down my spine. "Are you okay, Addie?"

"Oh, sorry," the man muttered, pushing in his chair.

Jin kept me in his arms for a heartbeat, our bodies melting as one. The swell of my ass pressed firmly against his upper thigh. The cool bite of his belt buckle cut into my lower back. A feverous sensation slithered under my skin as he gently released me from his cage, his fingertips trailing a path from hip to hip.

"Yeah. I'm fine."

I most certainly wasn't.

Suddenly, I was eternally grateful for the low lighting and the ability to mask my face in the soft glow of neon lights, burning as red hot as my face. By the time we reached our table, I thought I'd gotten out of the embarrassment scot-free, but something about the way he watched me over the top of his menu had me thinking otherwise.

"Hyun-jin!" An older Japanese gentleman approached with a smile that brightened the room and creased the corners of his eyes slightly. "Welcome back. Glad to see you finally found a date instead of being the odd man out with Caleb and Sophia," he said, a thick accent licking his every word.

Oh no, they're both staring at me now. If I hold up my menu any higher, would it be obvious that I'm trying to hide?

"Akira, this is Addie. She's my roommate and coworker."

"Ah, I see. It is lovely to meet you, Addie." He reached over the table and shook my hand. "And if that's the case, do you happen to have any single friends that might be interested in—"

"Akira," Jin warned, then cleared his throat. "Can we start with some water? Four, please—Caleb and Sophia will be here soon."

It was so endearing how their little family dynamic worked. The willingness to drop everything to celebrate one another, and somehow, I'd been dragged in. Listening to Jin on the car speaker earlier, gushing about my promotion to Sophia over the phone, warmed an icy part of my heart that I thought could never be thawed. I'd become so accustomed to the burden of begging the people around me to celebrate the little moments in life that I had given up entirely. It hadn't occurred to me that someone would willingly go out of their way to make this night even more special than it already was. I guess it never was a burden after all, I was just asking the wrong people to be a part of those moments.

"Yes, of course." As Akira backed away from the table, he winked at me. I tried my best to bite my lip to keep from laughing, but I eventually lost the good fight.

"What just happened?" I giggled, fanning myself with the laminated menu.

Jin groaned, "He likes to meddle in other people's lives, which is why he tries to play matchmaker with whoever walks into his restaurant who's remotely the same age as me."

"I think it's kind of sweet," I admitted. "It seems like he cares about you."

"He's just putting on a show because he still thinks he can make us work."

"And how do you know that?"

Jin silently pointed to the sushi bar where Akira was blatantly staring, two thumbs up, the biggest smile on his face.

"If he brings us a sashimi platter in the shape of a heart, we're in trouble."

"I'm guessing this has happened before," I chuckled.

"Twice...and if it happens for a third time, he's losing a regular."

The entire table vibrated as Jin's phone lit up, drawing his attention elsewhere. I studied the way his brows furrowed and his eyes darkened as he read the notification flashing across the screen.

"Caleb texted me, but all it says is 'love you.'"

As if on cue, Akira reappeared with our tray of drinks. A glass of water for each of us and an ochoko set for the table.

"Caleb called earlier," he grinned, "and he said he owes both of you a drink. Enjoy."

We both stared down at the ochoko set for a long moment before Jin cursed under his breath. "The bastard isn't coming. I know we were supposed to celebrate together, but if you want to go somewhere else, I—"

"We can stay. I don't mind," I blurted out, eyeing the sake. "Plus, I'm not sure how much longer I can wait to eat. I'm starving."

Famished from the day we started with the spicy edamame, making light conversation about the theater between sips of sake, blatantly ignoring the elephant in the room. While Akira didn't bring us a heart-shaped sashimi platter, we did order a ridiculous sushi boat laden with delicate sashimi, rolled maki, and thin slices of nigiri, each piece a delicious burst of color nestled between ginger and wasabi.

I dipped my dragon roll in a concoction of wasabi and soy sauce as the conversation lulled to its natural end. Silence was all that followed, and the elephant in the room became more difficult to ignore.

"Okay, I have to ask you something a little awkward," I said, biting my bottom lip. "Does—does it feel like we've been set up, or am I going crazy? This feels like a date, right?"

The soft music. The dim lighting. The intimate space. The ploy to get us alone.

Jin's chopstick slipped, and his bluefin tuna flopped on his plate.

"I—" Jin laughed, then shook his head. "I can't help feeling like that is exactly what Caleb and Sophia wanted when they bailed on us. You aren't crazy, but no...this feels nothing like a date to me."

My heart stalled, and my laugh wobbled.

"I was only joking." Maybe if I slid out of this booth, disappeared under the table, and crawled out of this restaurant on my hands and knees, we could pretend I didn't just say what I did. We could go back to our normal lives and be better off for it.

"Adeline, you didn't let me finish," he said, raising an eyebrow at me. "This feels nothing like a date because...if this were a real one, I would have done a hell of a lot better to impress you."

Oh.

Oh.

"Okay, then let's hear it, Collins," I said, trying and failing to play coy. "How would you wine and dine me?"

Ever so slightly, Jin dragged his tongue over the seam of his lips, releasing a breathy laugh. The sound burrowed itself deep into my mind, making me wonder what it might be like to have his breath hot against my ear with his hands splayed across my hips, like earlier when he caught me. My stomach hollowed out as the thought took shape.

"Hmm," he hummed, deep in thought. The sound alone electrified my every sense. "It's hard to say when I'm being put on the spot like this, but all I know for certain is it wouldn't be enough to take you to dinner and call it a night. Someone like you deserves something special."

"Give me a break." I rolled my eyes.

"Okay. Okay, you caught me"—he raised his hands in surrender—"I know exactly what I would plan, but I don't want to give away any of my good ideas. What I will say is, if all went well, I would have found an excuse to take you out on the balcony at the end of the night."

I raised an eyebrow. "The balcony?"

"The balcony," he repeated, so sure of himself.

"I've already been on your balcony."

"No, not like this—not after a date to ruin all future dates."

"And how often does that work for you?" I asked, sipping my sake.

Jin leaned in, elbows braced on the table. "I couldn't tell you. I've been holding off on the right date for that one. Maybe we'll see how this fake date goes, and I can let you know."

Then the bastard winked at me—maybe it wasn't too late to crawl out of here.

I scoffed. "Give me a break."

He flashed me a knowing smile. "What?"

"A good-looking guy like you must get plenty of dates. *Maybe* some ballerinas?"

"I'm not going to lie; I may or may not have a thing for ballerinas...but no. I think you've forgotten the part of the night where Akira tried to set me up with you, not once but twice. There isn't much time to date while running a theater, and what little free time I have, I want to spend it with my family."

My heart ached for Jin—for the man hiding behind the easy smile and witty jokes. He might brush off the comments, but there was no hiding the fact that he was putting excuses before his own needs. Jin Collins was a proud man with a youthful ethos, a well-endowed career, and looks that would have any woman on her knees. Yet he had already written himself off, given up looking despite the longing in his voice. He was lonely; everyone around him knew it, but maybe that proud spirit of his was preventing him from realizing it.

Loneliness had become an epidemic—a plague upon our minds that thrived on keeping us down and numb to reality, in which it could never get better. Part of me could sympathize with Jin in that regard. I was also lonely, maybe not in the same way, though one struggle did not diminish the other. He was in desperate need of someone to call his own to fill that void, but my loneliness couldn't be fixed by the right person stumbling into my life—that burden was mine to bear, and mine alone.

But maybe tonight neither of us had to be alone.

Accomplishments were typically regarded as an afterthought in my household growing up. An excuse to throw together something last-minute to only serve the purpose of throwing it back in my face when I accused them of treating Melissa and me differently. There are only so many times you can be told you're being ungrateful for what you have until you start to wonder if you are the common dominator in all of this. It becomes easier to celebrate in silence rather than burden others with your woes.

And when you're accustomed to that way of life, effort doesn't go unnoticed.

Jin's effort didn't go unnoticed.

An hour later, we were back at the apartment. The evening proved to be quite the little celebration with good food and even better company—even if it was all an elaborate setup. It felt refreshing to celebrate the rare but wonderful things going on in my life amongst the chaos. In a long-winded effort to distract and avoid the recent events in my life, I had another win under my belt.

"Seeing that the fake date went so well..." I turned on my heels, feeling a bit braver than usual, thanks to the sake. "Did I earn the balcony?"

Jin opened his mouth, closed it, then smiled. "I'll tell you what, head out to the balcony and I'll meet you there in a second, all right?"

The backdrop of the city resembled the missing stars in the sky. A symphony of distant sirens, honking horns, and chatter melted into one as the city hummed with relentless energy. As I braced my hands on the railing, all it took was one look to know why Jin loved this place so much. And it was a shame I hadn't taken the time to appreciate it the last time I was here—I guess I was distracted by something far more mesmerizing.

The sliding glass door swooshed open, then Jin appeared next to me, a knitted blanket draped over his arms.

"So..."

"So," he rasped.

"You take this mystery girl on the date of her dreams to ruin all future men for her and bring her to your balcony. Then what?"

"In theory, the reason why the balcony strategy works so well is that it gets so cold up here, I have an excuse to curl up on the couch with a blanket to stay warm."

"Smooth," I praised.

"Thank you." He beamed. "Then I would do anything humanely possible to steal as much of their time. We would talk about anything and everything if it meant getting to be with them. Or at least until they decide to leave."

"And if she doesn't want to leave?"

Jin shook his head. "That's the thing, I don't kiss on the first date. I'm saving myself for the right one."

"Oh, of course. How presumptuous of me. Sorry." I laughed.

"I'm quite the catch. I don't just give it out for free," he said, puffing out his chest a little.

When the laughter eventually died, I took the opportunity to cut across the balcony. Jin stood along the railing, watching me intently as I sat down on the couch. He didn't dare move a muscle until I patted the cushion next to me. The silence between us was comfortable, like I could have basked in it forever as long as I was near him, but despite that, I found myself wanting to fill the silence, if only to hear the sound of his smooth voice.

"It still blows me away that someone like you hasn't been

taken already. You're just—you're a great guy, and you deserve to be happy."

Jin stared at me for a long moment, then said, "I promise you it isn't for lack of trying, it's just…"

"It never works out," I guessed.

"Yes," he replied. "The problem was either we weren't compatible because Sophia randomly set us up for the sake of getting me out of the house, or when I did find someone I cared about, it never ended well. My last relationship was about two years ago—fuck—it just really hurt when it ended."

There was pain still simmering below the surface.

"It was mutual. I couldn't give her the relationship she deserved because of the theater. I would tell myself that I should be grateful, that if I put my head down and made the most of the position I was given, it could mean everything I went through would have been worth a damn in the end. I could have the family. The home. The life I always wished for if I only worked harder, but I was only lying to myself…"

He cleared his throat.

"I expected it to hurt when she left me, but I felt numb more than anything else. Then it dawned on me that I was more upset with the fact that I might not be able to give anyone the love they deserved because I was trapped in this career more than the actual relationship ending—" His gaze fell to my fingers, mindlessly stroking the thick threads of the woven blanket. "Are you all right?"

"Yeah."

"If I didn't know any better, I would say you're trying to unravel my blanket fiber by fiber."

"I'm sorry—"

I was about to regurgitate some bullshit excuse when his hand engulfed mine.

"It's all right, you have nothing to be sorry for. What's on your mind, Addie?"

"It's just—"

Jin's attention was solely focused on my every word, but the gentle stroke of his thumb over the back of my hand made me lose my train of thought completely.

"I know it isn't quite the same." I had to start slowly, or I might lose myself again. "But...something you said reminded me of my past—when you mentioned expecting it to hurt, but when it did end, feeling something entirely different."

"And what did you feel when it ended?"

"Like I was finally free."

Jin squeezed my hand. "It sounds like that relationship ended a long time ago."

"I guess it did." I blew out a breath, then turned toward the skyline, finding it might be easier to say what I need to say next if I wasn't looking at him. "Noah was cheating on me...I should have known, but...When I walked in on them, I knew what I was supposed to feel. It should have been the single most devastating thing to ever happen to us, but all I could think about was the fact that I could turn around and leave, and that would be it —I would be free. It was my only chance to run away and let someone else fall for his lies. I tried. I really did."

I needed a moment to collect myself. I kept my gaze fixed on the horizon, attempting to steady my breath. Jin didn't say a word as the minutes ticked by; he only held my hands and offered me the thing I needed the most—reassurance that I wasn't alone, at least for tonight.

"Jin," I rasped.

"Yes."

"They'll never believe me..." I swallowed down the lump rising in my throat. "Noah was too good at what he did. I will always be the *jealous* girlfriend who walked in on something she was never meant to see. I can't help thinking he's still haunting me, even though he isn't here anymore. I should finally be free, but..."

"People didn't see Noah for who he was. In life, he was everything to them, and in death, he's now somehow become their martyr."

I turned back to him. "And how did you see him?"

"Noah somehow had everyone wrapped around his finger. He manipulated the people around him by using his charm and good looks to create a mask that allowed him to get away with whatever the hell he wanted, and he didn't care who he hurt along the way. From the moment he started working for the theater, he slept and lied his way through the entire ensemble until somehow catching you in his snare.

"I never blamed him for falling for you—there wasn't a single man in that theater who wasn't completely bewitched by you on and off the stage. And I never blamed you for falling for him either. I had hoped that by choosing you, maybe something might fundamentally change for Noah. That he would push aside his old ways and change for the better, because he would finally realize how fucking lucky he was to have you in his life."

Jin frowned, his gaze fixed on our connected hands.

"I wish I could turn back time and warn you instead of... instead of sitting back and watching him do what he did best. You deserved better, and I'm sorry for not saying anything, Addie."

A phantom pain constricted my throat. Without thinking, I rubbed the faded bruise, nearly gone now. Jin's eyes lingered there for a beat.

"You deserved better," he repeated softly, his hand rising to my neck. When he was within a few inches, he paused, and his eyes found mine, silently waiting for any indication to stop. And when I didn't give him one, he gently dragged the back of his knuckle down the column of my neck. "You deserve someone to take care of you."

One touch, and I felt myself slowly start to slip away. Imagine a reality in which the concept of turning back time wasn't so far-fetched. Where lies weren't so easily heard, and I had led by instinct rather than fear and desire. As his touch consumed me, I shut my eyes, leaned in, and lost myself in a version of the past that could never be.

A version where it might have been us.

"Don't you think, Adeline?" he mumbled, his voice closer.

My eyes flew open, his burning gaze clashing with mine.

What the hell was I doing?

It killed me to see the light dwindle from his eyes as I pulled away, but it was nothing compared to watching him sit there as I folded up the blanket, draped it over my arm, and put even more distance between us.

"Adeline," he said, pushing to his feet, "if I overstepped—"

"You didn't." I forced a smile. "Don't worry, you didn't do anything wrong. I haven't spoken much about what happened with Noah, and I think I might have pushed myself a little too much—too many fresh wounds. Thank you for tonight, it meant more to me than you'll ever understand. And thank you for the wonderful fake date, the balcony was well worth the wait." As if I wasn't full of enough bad ideas, I rose onto my tippy-toes and pressed a kiss on his cheek, if only to keep my rejection from stinging any more than it already had. "Good night, Jin."

Simply putting distance between us wasn't enough to outrun all I had nearly given in to, but I sure as hell tried. I made it halfway through the living room before he was calling me back, his footfalls not far behind. Against my better judgment, the next time he called my name, I turned on my heel, completely unprepared for the man standing in the doorway. There was something a little disheveled about the way he gripped the frame, his chest rising and falling in quick successions as he stared back at me.

"L—let me take you on a real one," he sputtered.

"Jin," I warned.

"You don't have to answer now, but I hope you'd at least consider." He sucked in a deep breath. "Please."

The answer was right there. All I had to do was open my mouth and tell him no. This entire mess would be put to rest, and we could pretend none of it ever happened. Jin was the type of man who would honor my rejection and not hold it against me as others had. All I had to do was open my mouth—but when I did, something else entirely came out.

"I've said before, I don't make big decisions after I drink. Good night, Jin."

Chapter Twenty-Three

Adeline

Indecision was the killer of joy. A means of keeping us trapped between two places. Our minds would much rather dissect each decision to the point of beating a dead horse than deal with the ramifications of picking the wrong one. As I stared up at the ceiling, no closer to falling asleep than when I lay down an hour ago, I waited to be consumed by spiraling thoughts that served no purpose other than to pull me every which way and confuse reality with fiction. But instead of being trapped in that dark place between decisions, I saw the tiniest glimmer of light—a choice I couldn't so easily let go.

One that meant tiptoeing across the hall, knocking on his door, and giving in to this inherent pull that couldn't separate us.

It was selfish to even consider.

Everything about this was wrong.

I had no right to feed into this little fantasy when Jin deserved someone who could pluck the stars from the heavens if it meant giving him a fraction of the light he brought to others. How could I possibly make him happy if I couldn't even guarantee there would be a tomorrow?

Sleep did eventually find me in the wee hours of the night. I dreamt of Noah. Having successfully kept the memory of him at bay thanks to Jin's trick, he'd found new and creative ways to invade my psyche. Blood seeped through the drain, filling the tub. No matter how much I willed my limbs to move, there was little I could do as blood rose. With my last gasping breath, a hand closed around my neck and forced me under. The blood was too thick to peer through, but the familiarity of his touch I knew all too well.

I startled awake, covered in sweat, and panting. Once I was up, I had no desire to try to fall back asleep for fear of being betrayed by my own mind. I lay there for another thirty minutes before the roar of the coffee machine dragged me out of bed.

Stuck to the empty mug on the kitchen island was a yellow sticky note that read: *Last night only confirmed what I'd been lying to myself about for a long time now. And I have a funny feeling I'm not the only one.* There was another note stuck to the counter. *I have to drive up north to meet with a potential donor for the theater. Call me if you need anything.*

The note found its way into my journal, squished in between cursive lines and mindless doodles. The messy personification of my deepest thoughts dotted on each line. On the subway ride to work, I attempted to make sense of what couldn't so easily be explained, but no matter what collection of words found themselves between those pages, it seemed I couldn't unravel who was lying.

In typical preseason fashion, I arrived well before call time, letting myself in with the key Jin lent me. With mere weeks separating us from the showcase, I took it upon myself to bridge whatever gaps were needed to step into this role flawlessly, and truthfully, I wanted an opportunity to practice without any distractions.

I grabbed a new pair of pointe shoes off my vanity and ventured toward the stage.

There was no other rush like taking center stage and basking in the sensation of being part of something much bigger than yourself. To feel so small in a space so grandiose—it was as if it were an extension of the heavens themselves. It was what I imagined peasants groveling in the slums during the medieval era must have felt like when they first set foot in a European basilica and beheld such ornate wealth. It was the closest thing to reaching God.

To be one with—

At first, I thought I was hearing things again. The old bones of the theater groaned and creaked from time to time, and I'd learned to ignore the way the building shifted in the dead of the night, but when the unmistakable sound of a male voice cut through the silence, there was no denying it. The first word struck me like an arrow through the chest, and although I instantly recognized the cadence of his voice, it was several long moments before I could be certain that I was safe.

"—absolutely not," Charles said firmly.

"I wish I were, but that's what they want," another voice replied.

From my vantage point behind the curtain, I was only privy to the sight of Charles. Standing tall beneath the stage lights, he could have very well been the lead in one of our ballets with his consuming presence and powerful voice. Slipping seamlessly into his role, he huffed out a dry laugh and encroached on the man out of sight.

"They know that you need them, and when people know you're desperate, they take advantage of that," the other man continued.

"I can't keep throwing money at this blindly. Look at this

place—everything's falling apart," Charles said, voice tight as he gestured to the theater.

I inched forward, curious to see how this performance would play out.

"I don't know what to tell you other than to figure it out. Because until you do, we can't move forward."

"No, I'm stuck."

"Same difference."

One more step forward—

Charles's gaze snapped in my direction as a floorboard creaked beneath my heel. The heated nature of their conversation sizzled out instantaneously as his expression softened and a small smile tugged at his lips.

"*Mon étoile*," he said gently.

"I—I'm sorry. I didn't mean to eavesdrop. I heard arguing..." I replied, stepping from the shadows.

The man Charles has been speaking to stood an inch or so shorter than him. With blonde hair showing the first signs of graying and a hooked nose, his deep green eyes spoke to a sense of youthful spirit that hadn't withered away over the years. He bore a striking resemblance to Charles's wife.

Charles leaned in to whisper something into his ear before they reluctantly shook hands and parted ways. The hooked-nose man flashed me a smile before disappearing backstage.

"Was that Josephine's father?" I asked once he was gone.

"What are you doing here, Adeline?" he snapped.

"The stage," I sputtered, hating the way my entire face felt like it was on fire. Charles raised an eyebrow. "It needs the most work compared to the rest of the theater, so if you're going to focus on repairs after the season wraps up, you should start with the stage. Tatiana tripped a few weeks ago, and I think that's why, and I nearly tripped the other day, too."

"I thought you said you weren't eavesdropping."

As majestic as the century-old building was, time had been its greatest weakness. There was no hiding those inherent flaws that spoke of its withering bones and peeling wallpaper. Republic City Opera House was in desperate need of a facelift, and from the whispers I'd heard in passing, it had been years since repairs had been made. It made me happy to hear Charles was taking that into consideration and potentially restoring her to her former glory.

I shrugged. "Jin's younger brother owns a construction company. I'm sure if you spoke to him, he might be about to work something out for you after he finishes his current project. He's currently renovating another district theater, but maybe he can squeeze you in."

He stared down at me for a long moment as if truly seeing me for the first time.

"You care for this theater, don't you?" I nodded. His eyes rose to the painted ceiling and dazzling chandelier as he spoke. "Thirty years after its construction, the Austro-Hungarian immigrant who built this theater got into some legal trouble. His choices were either to stay and deal with the consequences or flee the country—he chose the latter. My grandfather had been working beneath him for years, and he sold it to him for dirt cheap before running in 1916. Republic City Opera House has been with the Blanchet family ever since.

"I grew up playing hide-and-seek in the orchestra pit, running through these halls during rehearsals, and stealing faux weapons from the prop department to have sword fights with my friends." Lost in reverie, it took him a moment to return to the present. "This theater is more than a building—it is a legacy, one that has been passed down to my father, then to me, and my future son or daughter will inherit all I built for them. And when that day comes, I want to give them more than was ever given to me—I want them to thrive. Each season is a scorn on my legacy, for better or worse, which is why you have such an important role to fill, being as young as you are."

I tilt my chin up a little higher. "I understand the concern about switching leads so close to the opening show, but I can assure you, I'm taking this role seriously and doing all I can to prepare in time for the showcase. It's why I am here so early today, so I can practice."

"I don't take chances on risks I don't see paying out," he replied. "What we do need is good publicity. I've scheduled an interview for you and the *Republic Press* for the week of the showcase. Bianca Riviera has been persistent about this story."

"Isn't that the purpose of the showcase? Is the interview really necessary?"

In the weeks following the incident, I did my best to avoid the tabloids. Other than his obituary, I wasn't even sure if Noah's death had been mentioned to the public, and I refused to find out, for fear of spiraling into a dark place if I found some kind of regurgitated lie about what happened that fateful night. While the showcase would of course put a spotlight on me, I had no desire to single myself out and allow for any opportunities to be questioned without a lawyer present. Even if Bianca Riviera swore to keep her questions focused on the upcoming season, what kind of journalist would she be if she didn't ask the hard-hitting questions that would get people to pick up her newspaper, rather than the competition's?

"I was under the impression you cared about this theater, Adeline," he said, a slight tick in his jaw. "Am I wrong?"

"I—"

"Ms. Riviera will be emailing you shortly. I suggest you consider what this means for you," he said, not willing to hear whatever excuse I was trying to piece together. Charles uncere-moniously walked off stage.

The email came several hours later during rehearsals. And like the text from Jin warning me that Halle was returning tomorrow, both went unanswered.

Chapter Twenty-Four

Jin

U**nknown:** Don Juan. Thursday at 5 p.m.

The trip up north proved to be worth the long drive. With limited funding and donors backing out at the last minute due to a less-than-profitable fall season, it was refreshing to be surrounded by like-minded individuals who saw the theater for what it was. Despite my reservations, I genuinely cared about the theater and wanted it to reach its full potential. Though the actions of others would always be its greatest downfall, it had always been up to me to bridge those gaps.

Between the luncheon and potential traffic, Charles wasn't expecting me to be back at the theater today, but with a little luck and easy persuasion, I reached the outskirts of the city well before five o'clock.

I stared down at the text for a long moment while I leaned up against the side of my car, waiting for the gas tank to fill. Had it been any other day, I might have ignored the text from Destler altogether, but call it a gut feeling, I knew this had happened for a reason. Betting on blind hope and the obligation to right these wrongs, I sped off to the district, ready to make a deal.

Or at least try.

The darkened alleyway swallowed up any light from the evening sun. Pinned between two rising brick exteriors, I made my way down the dingy path, following the soft glow of a lit cigarette toward the side entrance of Don Juan.

"Damn," Broken Nose said, crushing his cigarette beneath his heel. "I owe Damon forty bucks. I was sure you weren't going to show up."

"And why's that?"

"You put on a brave face when you walked out of here the other day, but I could see the look in your eyes, you were scared shitless," he said with an easy smile, then extended his hand outward. "I'm Antonio, Erick's cousin."

I had been scared, but not for the reason he thought.

"Jin," I replied, shaking his hand. "I can't say I see the resemblance."

"I know. He lacks any of my natural charm, but don't worry, give it some time, and he'll warm up to you." Antonio held the door open for me, then led me through the back of the house. "Just don't tell him I said that," he shot over his shoulder.

"Depending on how this meeting goes, no promises."

Antonio barked a laugh that echoed through the empty club.

The air in Don Juan felt stagnant this early in the evening. It felt as if the building was holding its breath, patiently waiting for the lights to dim and the bass to shake the foundation of the century-old building. We cut through the dance floor and ventured down a familiar hallway. The air grew thicker as we approached a fork in the road: a set of stairs leading to two different paths. Antonio picked the path not yet traveled, and we descended into the unknown.

With a few taps on the pin pad, the metal door groaned

open. No, it wasn't the door groaning—it was too muffled to have been that.

Stepping over the threshold, my understanding of time and space altered in the blink of an eye—decades gone in a flash. Hidden beneath the nightclub was a lounge that resembled the glitz and glam of the turn of the century—a speakeasy, by the looks of it. Having an appreciation for architecture thanks to my little brother, I might have taken the time to admire the art decor flair and vibrant shades of emerald that had been dipped in liquid gold, had the moans not grown louder, more ravenous.

Breaking off the lounge was a long concrete tunnel, the mouth of which was lined with plastic that covered the walls and floor. The only speck of color in the darkened passageway was splattered red paint that led to a man doubled over on his hands and knees. Little by little, he dragged his bruised and battered body farther into the awaiting darkness. My mind was slow to process the horrific scene unfolding before me. To realize the splattered paint wasn't paint at all. And there was more than darkness lurking in the shadows...

I whipped my head around in time to see the large metal door click shut, locking us both inside. Antonio flashed me a toothy smile, then motioned for me to turn around with a twirl of his finger.

"Time is ticking," a familiar, smooth voice lilted.

The shadows parted, and Erick emerged from their suffocating embrace. The silence that fell over the room was thick and heavy on my shoulders; it made each sickening scrap of flesh against plastic painfully louder as the bleeding man frantically tried to get away to no avail.

With exasperated effort, Erick squatted down before him, blocking his only path to freedom. The bleeding man seemed to sense it, too, because when Erick took the tip of his blade and balanced it under his chin, all the fight he had left was gone in the blink of an eye. Staring down the neck of a dagger, the man choked down what little air he could, tears brimming in his eyes. The blade inched closer, but no matter how much he willed himself to speak, fear had crippled his speech.

"Come on, Reed," Erick continued, the cheerful gleam in his tone, sending goose bumps rushing down my arms and legs. "Let's not play this game again."

With a posture as rigid as a board to keep the blade from finding a new home, Reed ever so gently dragged his gaze across the room, only stopping when he found me frozen in place. Where words had failed him, it was the look in his bloodshot eyes that called to me—the last chance at hope that someone might put an end to this hell. I couldn't stand by and watch this happen. I had to—

Antonio slung his arm over my shoulder as I was about to take my first step. He leaned in close to say, "I wouldn't feel too bad for him. Another threat was delivered to the dance studio, but this time, one of the dancers caught our buddy Reed driving away."

Reed's agonizing screams echoed off the concrete walls like a wave lapping on the shore. One replaced the other as Erick dug the tip of his blade into the underside of his jaw. A stream of blood trailed down the columns of his neck, mixing old blood with new.

Whatever pull I felt toward him snapped like a taut line meeting its end. No matter how much I willed my legs to move, I couldn't bring myself to stop the horrors unfolding before me as Erick shoved him to the ground and kicked him relentlessly. The harrowing snap of his ribs reverberated in my own bones. I couldn't bring myself to rush to his aid when Antonio's words still rang in my ears.

As Reed sobbed for someone to help him, I imagined being

in Erick's shoes—imagined what I would have done to Xavier if I had the chance.

Erick had every right to protect the woman he loved.

But that didn't mean I had to watch.

Amongst the brightly colored bottles lining the back of the bar was a bottle of whiskey adorned with a wax seal—the only spot of red, other than Reed's blood. I kept my eyes trained on the back wall until the screams withered away.

"Jin," Erick called. "Hand me the box on the table over there."

Perfectly curating every word spoken, Erick was intentional in everything he did. He could have very well asked his cousin to retrieve the box, but no, he asked me with clear intent. Hidden behind his silky voice and willful charm, I saw this for what it truly was, and I only had a split second to decide if I would oblige. Would I be complacent in his crimes and stand by his side as he toppled Charles's reign, or turn my back on him forever? This wasn't about obeisance; this was about loyalty, and it didn't take a fool to recognize this for what it was.

I cut across the lounge and retrieved the familiar velvet box.

Blood wasn't enough of a payment for Erick. I soon learned that this was more about sending a message for what he had done to his fiancée than revenge itself. Antonio grabbed both sides of Reed's face, holding him in place as Erick's blade met its mark, piercing through his earlobes. The oddly shaped incisions were just big enough to shove the diamond earrings into the bleeding wounds. Reed's pleas came out as a bubbling mess as he fought for words. He used what little strength he possessed to thrash within Antonio's hold, only making Erick butcher his handiwork.

Pleased with the incision, Erick rose to his full height, letting the blade fall to the floor with a deafening clink. Antonio stepped away and let Reed crumble back to the ground.

"Last chance, Reed."

He smiled down at him with predatorial delight.

"Three."

Erick removed a gun from his waistband in one swift motion, then pointed it between his eyes. I lunged forward on instinct to stop him, but Antonio had me by the shoulders before my heel touched the ground.

"Two."

Click.

Reed sputtered, "Go to hell."

Erick never did reach the end of his countdown. The sound of gunfire splintered the air and rocked the very foundation beneath my feet at such close range. The shot still rang in my ears, but the deafening sound was nothing compared to the way Reed's lifeless body flopped in a heap at my feet—flesh sliding against plastic. The bullet wound between his brows was nearly as vacant as his dark brown eyes staring up toward the ceiling.

I lifted a shaky hand to my mouth, unable to look away as blood pooled all around me.

Man was not meant to play God. What right did anyone have to play judge, jury, and executioner when life was so precious and redemption was always possible? It was clear this wasn't the first time blood had been on Erick's hands, and by the way he looked death in the eyes without fear of retaliation, it wouldn't likely be his last.

Erick saw himself fit to determine who lived and who died, and I didn't quite know how to process that yet.

"Antonio," Erick said, pulling a small silver key fob from Reed's pocket. "Search his car and see what you can find using his navigation system. When you have an idea of where he was before the studio, take the car to Cooper's shop and dump his body somewhere Charles will find it."

"Not the theater," I blurted out, and suddenly all eyes were on me. "Anywhere else. Someone recently died there, and if anyone finds Reed's body before Charles does..."

Don't give them a reason to point the finger at Adeline.

"Not the theater then," Erick assured me. "We—"

Both of their cellphones buzzed simultaneously, and their entire demeanor changed in the blink of an eye. It was funny, in a dark sort of way, how one singular text could cause such a visceral reaction, yet the man bleeding out at their feet did little to faze them. I wondered how many bodies you had to see in one lifetime to grow so accustomed to death constantly lurking in the shadows.

"Find Damon and get the damn body out through The Lotte," Erick said to his cousin, then turned toward me. "Jin, you're coming with me."

Silently, I followed Erick out from the depths of hell and into a sprawling nightclub once more. I could still feel the reverberation of the shot vibrating through my bones, but despite the quickening of my heart and sweat licking down my spine, I felt a strange sense of calmness wash over me with each step. Or perhaps I was still in a state of shock, because when the hallway spit us out into the main seating area of the lounge, I didn't blanch at the sight of the silver badge gleaming back at me or the police officer who wore it.

Erick stepped in front of me, hands tucked in his pocket.

"Sanderson, this Jin Collins, one of my new associates."

"Pleasure to meet you, son. I'm Officer Sanderson."

Sanderson was a sight for sore eyes. Balding head glistening off the lights high above, protruding waistline hanging over his belt, and cologne that did little to mask what couldn't be so easily hidden.

"Nice to meet you, too," I said, struggling to keep my voice steady, but as I extended my hand, all I could think about was the dead body somewhere beneath our feet.

And that's when I saw it.

Two specks of Reed's blood splattered across my knuckle.

Sanderson shook my hand a millisecond later, leaving me no other choice but to whisper a small prayer to myself that he didn't look down. My heartbeat roared in my ears with each second that ticked by. And in some kind of sick joke from the universe, it turned out Sanderson was the type of man who would shake for longer than necessary in some kind of weird pissing match. I cut my losses and shoved my hands in my pockets before I lost more than his respect.

Curtain. Cocktail straws. Bottle of whiskey.

I repeated the items over and over again.

Sanderson turned to Erick, his expression falling. "If you have one more mouth to feed, then it's going to cost you," he said in a dry tone.

Erick retrieved a money bag from behind the bar and pulled out a wad of cash.

"Seventeen hundred more," Erick offered.

Sanderson flashed him a bored look. "You know, it's been a while since RCPU came down here to do a routine check since the fire," he retorted.

"Two thousand and let me know if someone named Reed Hackett is reported missing."

Pleased with the counteroffer, Sanderson snatched the cash out of his hand and sauntered out of the room. "Pleasure doing business with you. See you next month."

As quickly as he came, he was gone, making me question more than just my sanity. Maybe I was hallucinating from witnessing such a horrific death. Yup, that was it. This was the beginning of my slow descent into madness.

As soon as he disappeared out of view, I bowed over, hands braced on my knees. The way I struggled to suck down a single breath, it felt more like I'd finished a marathon rather than survived a one-minute conversation.

"Jesus Christ, Erick. What the fuck was that?"

"What? Never seen a dead man before?" he teased, and I felt all the blood leech from my face, drip by drip.

"Goddamnit," I choked out, voice high and scratchy. "Sanderson. Reed. Everything. I don't know what the hell's going on here, but this isn't what I signed up for when I came down here to talk to you."

"Jin," Erick drawled, eyeing me from head to toe. "Two months ago, the dance studio my fiancée works at held a community fundraiser that later made the front page of the *Republic Press*. Someone deliberately took that photo of her, drew red *X*'s over her eyes, then stuffed the clipping in the studio's mailbox so she would find it. Someone threatened *my* family. You told me you wanted change, didn't you? Well, I hate to break it to you, but this is how we get it. *This* is how we fight back—this is how we send a message."

"I—I want to help, Erick." I hated myself for tripping over my words in front of him. Suddenly, I was thirteen again, struggling to make sense of the English language and adjusting to my new life in America. "But not like this."

The corner of his lips twitched in a ghost of a smile. "Sanderson was coming today regardless of whether you showed up or not. Don't worry, I don't plan to drag you here every time I need to interrogate one of Blanchet's men. I just had to be certain you were someone I could trust."

I scoffed. "This was all some bullshit test to see whether or not I would sell you out?"

"Good job, took you long enough," he said.

"You're a sick bastard."

"And you should be proud of yourself. You passed with flying colors."

"This is ridiculous. I'm leaving."

I made it all but ten feet before Erick was calling me back.

"What!" I threw my arms up.

"I need you," he said without hesitation.

"It didn't look like you did—"

"I *need* you," he repeated, jaw tight. "The truth is, I can't do this without you, and given how close you are to Blanchet, I needed to know for certain you wouldn't turn on me. Charles has threatened my family not once but twice since the fire, and I'm certain that if I don't act fast, something is going to happen to the only woman I've ever truly loved. I won't ask you to do anything you aren't comfortable doing, but I need someone on the inside who can help me stay one step ahead. I need someone who can help me protect my family."

Having only spoken to Destler a handful of times, it wasn't the cadence of his voice that took me by surprise; it was the look in his deep brown eyes that spoke of such vulnerability and hopelessness. Erick was scared, and the reason I recognized it was that it was a mirror to my own.

A heavy silence fell between us.

We were two desperate men, searching for an ounce of faith to cling to. Praying that one might help the other. But could I trust a man who liked to play God? The answer would always be no, but Erick had intentionally shown his hand, and now I was ready to play mine.

"You can offer protection, can you not?"

He nodded. "I know what I am asking of you comes at a massive risk. When all is said and done, the executive director position is yours and I'll ensure you're taken care of."

"And," I interjected, Erick's eyebrows furrowed as if he wasn't sure if he should be concerned or impressed, "in addition to my protection, you agree to look over one of my dancers. I need to make sure she's safe."

"That isn't how this works."

"You said—"

"Everything has a cost in this city, Jin. Does it not?" He raised an eyebrow, waiting for an answer that would never come. "And should you want more, just know, Antonio started as a club manager at Don Juan and Damon as head of security before starting to take on a more *serious* role beneath me. Maybe you should consider your options before you bite off more than you can chew."

Erick was desperate, but not desperate enough to take the bait.

Accepting a salary position was one thing; giving myself over to Destler like that was an entirely different beast. I wasn't sure if Antonio and Damon were here on their own accord, but I couldn't stomach the idea of selling what was left of my tattered soul to someone like that—someone who took pleasure in pain and thrived in chaos.

I would simply have to find another means of securing Adeline's safety.

Leaving the district, I was more than content with my decision, even proud of myself for not giving myself over entirely to him. There was honor in forbearance, for Adeline didn't deserve any version of myself that couldn't give her that wasn't earnest in nature—nor did I deserve to actively harm myself after everything I'd been through. However, a few hours later, I received a text that almost made me go back on everything I'd said.

Adeline: It happened again...

Chapter Twenty-Five

Adeline

The brittle snap of rosin crunched beneath my toes. The amber substance turned to a fine powder as I ground my pointe shoes against the floor, looking for traction. Another crack echoed through my bones as I stepped on a chunk of unused rosin, the sound nearly drowning out the groan of the studio door.

The entire corps de ballet turned in time to see Halle step inside.

Our eyes meet from across the room for a single heartbeat. Halle looked away and didn't look at me again for the remainder of rehearsal.

Taking a razor blade and a tube of super glue, I got to work deconstructing a brand-new pair of pointe shoes, mending and snapping them to perfection. The process was tedious and a bit redundant, but necessary every few days. I loved the simplistic and repetitive nature of it, allowing me to shut off my brain for but a moment and focus on the beauty of destruction. Though there is only so much you can do to soften the shank before you run out of distraction. That felt especially true this evening.

The preliminary hearing, showcase, and opening night all coincided in the same month. One happening after the other. A hefty load to bear all on my own, and fortunately for me, I didn't have to. Donovan, I'd grown to learn, liked to view the world through his rose-colored glasses. He was convinced that as much of an opportunity as this was to prove we had a case worth fighting, it was a chance to spin the narrative in our favor and gain the momentum needed for the actual trial. Navigating the legal process felt like trying to learn a foreign language the night before the final exam—but my attorney's confidence echoed into my own uncertainty. Having Donovan by my side was a blessing, but that didn't mean I wasn't nervously counting down the days till the trial. One shank at a time.

"Can I please borrow some glue?" a familiar voice rasped.

Halle, of all people, stood in the doorway, holding a bag of unopened pointe shoes. There was something so small about the way she carried herself. The sight of her crooked posture, tired eyes, and turned-down smile was reminiscent of a child creeping into their parents' bedroom in the dead of the night, still clutching a piece of their nightmare with them.

Every missed step at rehearsal.

Every curse spoken under her breath.

Every blatant attempt to avoid me.

It was clear there was some kind of nightmare she couldn't let go, and because I knew that feeling all too well, I set down the tube of glue on the empty vanity to my right and watched her slowly inch closer out of the corner of my eyes. My heart lodged in my throat.

"Thanks," she mumbled, taking the seat next to me.

The two of us got to work, sharing the tools spread out between us as we had so many times before. There was a sense of familiarity in the silence that had once been a comfort to be a part of, but unlike those other times, the various crunches and snaps of our shoes only highlighted how little there was to say between us. In all the days since the accident, we had never been physically closer, but I couldn't help feeling like a chasm separated us in more ways than one.

And because Halle wasn't particularly a fan of sitting with her discomfort, she was the first to attempt to break it. "I was surprised to hear you'd been promoted to soloist. I was sure it would go to—"

"Halle," I said, cutting her off. "I thought you didn't want to speak to me."

"It's complicated," she admitted, and while her work never wavered, her voice sounded raw and broken. "Really fucking complicated. And messy. And—" Her razor blade hovered over the leather sole as she shut her eyes, collecting herself. "You have no idea how incredibly difficult it is to be back at the theater after what happened—trying to move on without him here."

I wasn't sure whether to laugh or cry—maybe both.

"Halle, I..." *I watched the life drain from his eyes as he bled out in my arms. If I closed my eyes and concentrated hard enough, I could still feel his blood seeping through my fingers. You know nothing of the pain I bear every day, yet suppress for fear of how giving in might fracture what is left of my soul,* I thought to say.

I sucked in a deep breath and steadied my wandering thoughts. We both carried our own pain; one did not diminish the other, I reminded myself. It wasn't fair of me to compare, and because I wanted to give her the benefit of the doubt and assume the comment was coming from a place of hurt rather than malice, the next thing that came out of my mouth was what

I wish someone would have told me the first time I stepped foot back in the theater.

"If dance didn't mean as much as it did to me, I don't think there would have ever been a reality in which I came back. The memories of him here are still too fresh..." I started fidgeting with the satin lining of my shoes. "Nothing about coming back will ever be easy, but...I guess what I'm trying to say is, you should give yourself some credit. You came back for a reason, and you're brave for doing so."

Something in Halle's forest-green eyes spoke to the type of grief that feasted on souls and preyed on happy memories. Those wounds were still far too fresh to return, but despite knowing that, she had taken the needle and thread and attempted to stitch herself back together without the means of doing so. There are only so many jagged lines and broken stitches we can endure before we realize it's in our best interest to hand over the needle and thread and let someone else mend us back together. As much as I wished I could listen to my own advice, I wanted to be that person for Halle. I wanted to help.

"Addie," she choked out. "I—I've been trying to wrap my head around this, and I still don't understand what I walked into that night. I don't understand—"

The razor blade landed with a thud as Halle burrowed her face in her hands. The strangled sob that came from her splintered something deep within my chest, and I wrapped Halle in my arms, desperate to soothe the tears away. When her arms snaked around my torso, I lost myself completely, turning into a sniffling mess, clutching onto her for dear life as a sob rocked through me.

"Jesus, Adeline. It hurts so much."

"I know."

"Life just feels so empty without him. When he left, he took a piece of me with him. I—" she hiccuped, finger nails digging into my spine. "I don't know how I can move on without him."

"Ouch, Halle," I mumbled, but she wasn't listening.

"Just thinking about him hurts so much."

"Hal..."

Each finger nail was wedged between a different vertebra. The tighter she held on, the more it felt like she was attempting to pluck out my spine. I attempted to pull away. Her nails dragged across my bare flesh, over my shoulder blades, then settled on the flesh on my upper arms when I couldn't take it anymore. She peered up at me, unshed tears trapped in her long, dark eyelashes, reluctant to let me go.

"Why did you do this to me?"

"What?"

"Why," she shuddered, shaking me with the word, "did you do this to me?"

"I—"

"Why did you take him away from me?" she reiterated. Her words were slow and methodical, as if it were the first time she had spoken them aloud.

"Halle," I breathed. "You have to understand, I—I didn't want this. I never meant to hurt him that night. He wouldn't stop."

"Clearly, I don't," she spat out, then tore her hands away like the mere thought of touching me was beyond her.

You killed him.

Tell her.

Tell her you killed him.

Tell her.

Tell her.

Tell—

"No," I yelped.

Halle was pinning me down with her gaze, confused and a

little taken aback. I huffed out a frustrated breath, dragged my blunt nail over my bare thighs enough time to leave faint parallel marks in its place, before I found the courage to speak again.

The truth was rarely spoken, tangled up in a mess of lies that felt impossible to free myself from. Halle didn't understand, nor would she ever if she wasn't privy to all that was left unspoken. She would never understand if she truly believed me to be the monster when, in reality, the monster had always been the one hiding right beneath her nose.

"Do you remember the night we went out for Noah's birthday and someone spilled a drink on him?" She nodded, eyeing me wearily. "The bouncer had to pry him off the poor guy, and when all the boys got kicked out, no one could find me for thirty minutes."

It was a blessing that security hadn't called the police on us, despite the threats, but that didn't deter Noah from trying to start a fight outside of the bar when the man agreed to leave, too. One drunk misstep had led to another, where logic had been thrown out the window, and emotions ran high.

"A few nights before his birthday, Noah and I got into a bad fight. Things got out of hand and—" He had grabbed me by the shoulder, shoved me against the wall with such force the stars dotting my vision were as bright as the night sky, then proceeded to scream at me until his voice went hoarse from overuse—but I couldn't bring myself to say all that. "He took me to bed and kissed me senseless as if the only way he could stomach apologizing to me was in the cover of darkness, where his promises were sweeter, and I couldn't see through his lies so easily. Each kiss came with its own promise that it would never happen again. That if we could overcome this test of our relationship, we would only grow stronger because of it...and I believed him."

A fly caught in a web will always struggle, but if the spider can somehow whisper in the fly's ear and convince them that the web is there to protect them rather than trap them, it will always be easier for the spider's fangs to hit their mark when the prey capitulates.

I loved Noah—at least I thought I did—and that *love* had been a blight on my soul.

"The night of his birthday," I rasped, "when he wrapped his hand around the man's neck and slammed him into the corner of the bar...it felt like my ribs were closing in so tight, I was scared they might puncture a lung. I couldn't bear the sight of it. I locked myself in the bathroom and prayed he was too drunk to find me. It reminded me of what he was truly capable of and how fragile all his promises were."

"What you're implying..." She looked away for a beat, jaw tight. "He would never."

"Halle." I sighed. "Multiple times."

"No."

"You were his friend, you should know better than anyone the part of himself he hid from the rest of the world. The aggression was only the tip of the iceberg."

Halle shoved to her feet, chair grinding against the floor.

"Don't you dare," she said, sucking in a sharp breath. "Don't you dare try to accuse a man who can't defend himself. Noah wasn't the type of man who would hurt the people he cared about. He never hurt—he just wouldn't."

Too stricken by grief, her heart was her greatest enemy. Even if I had the surveillance footage playing before her eyes, I don't think she would believe me...

In a fit of rage, Halle shouldered her dance bag and made for the door.

"I was leaving him," I said, stopping her in her tracks. Only when she glanced at me over her shoulder did I continue. "After

I caught him with Tatiana, I had finally made up my mind. Noah—he wasn't happy with that decision...and while he isn't here to tell his side of the story, I am. After spending so long being terrified that if I spoke up I would only make things worse; it isn't fair that I have to hide this too because you aren't willing to hear the truth."

"And what if the truth—"

"The truth is," I snapped, "Noah attacked me, and I defended myself. End of story."

"Addie—"

"No, I'm done hiding the truth to keep the peace between us. If you truly are my friend, then I need you to trust me—just this once."

I'm done protecting your feelings at the expense of mine.

Halle steepled her hands and pressed them against her forehead.

Her breaths came in short and uneven successions as she collected herself.

"I want to believe you. I really do," she said, her voice thick. "I think I came back sooner than I should have, but if I don't pay my loan this month, it will only cause more issues for my mom, and my bereavement leave was running out." She sighed. "If what you say is true, then I can't even imagine the pain you've been in. You *are* my friend, and I want to be there for you. I just —I need more time to process this all. I'm sorry."

"I want to be there for you, too."

"All I'm asking for is time. Please."

Time was meant to mend all wounds, though the construct of time could be slippery. I wasn't sure if our friendship could be repaired after what I had done, which made me consider that it was time that would ultimately fail us or the clock itself. Halle left with the promise to return when she was ready to have a more in-depth conversation, leaving me to consider if the hands of the clock might ever move again—for the sake of our friendship, I prayed they would.

I sat in that silence for a long while, considering.

Thinking. Dissecting. Worrying.

When I had had my fill and was fed up with the sound of my own voice in my head, I stuffed my belongings in my dance bag, ready to put an end to this trying day. The only thing louder than the inner critic relentlessly shouting at me for retribution was the odd crunching sound that came from beneath my sweater.

I paused.

The navy-blue fabric stared back at me, patiently waiting; for what, I wasn't sure. Once I had found the courage, I peeled back the layer one after the other to reveal a crisp white envelope below, the bottom right-hand corner of which was soaking wet. Everything below it was stained red. I might have cursed the damn thing for ruining my clothes had its contents not stolen the breath from my lungs.

Stuffed inside were three pieces of paper folded in smooth, flat lines. The first: an old photo of Noah and me sitting on a fire escape on a sweltering fall day with both of our eyes dotted out with red ink. The second: a thin, crinkly piece of paper titled "Office of the Court Medical Examiners: Report of Investigation by County Medical Examiner," with the name Noah Hernandez dotting the top line. The paper was filled with rushed notes and small doodles that outlined the trauma to his body on a blank silhouette of a man. The third and final page: a blank autopsy report—well, blank other than a single name etched across the top line.

Adeline Elise Hartwell.

Chapter Twenty-Six

Jin

An autopsy report.

Someone had threatened her with a fucking autopsy report.

As if she hadn't already been through enough—now this.

After leaving Don Juan, I somehow ended up back at the theater, clinging to any sense of normalcy I possibly could. Or perhaps it was guilt that drove me here instead.

Strange how the construct of a lie can weave itself so thoroughly with the truth that it's difficult to tell how long I'd been lying to myself. Happiness always felt just out of reach, one opportunity away from being in my grasp. One more application. One more chance and I could have it all. If I only put my nose to the grindstone and stayed out of trouble, I would be rewarded for my endeavors. That's what I'd been telling myself for the last decade as I withered away on the steps of the theater, and now...

When all is said and done, the executive director position is yours, and I'll ensure you're taken care of.

The job was mine, and yet, the lie I'd been feeding myself for years wasn't enough to fill me with blind hope and a jagged sense of optimism as it once had. The role meant nothing if I couldn't ensure Adeline's protection as I had secured my own.

I was more than prepared to collapse on the small leather couch in my office out of pure mental exhaustion when my phone rang a quarter to midnight.

"I didn't know who else to go to," she said, voice thick. "I thought about calling you earlier, but I didn't want to bother you while you were at your meeting."

"I'm coming to you," I replied. "Are you at the apartment?"

"Really, it's okay. You don't need to come home because of me," she insisted.

"I don't have to do anything, but I want to be there for you."

"It's late. I'm probably going to bed soon anyway. I just thought someone from the theater should know."

There was a time and place to be upset, and now wasn't the time *nor* the place when Adeline's well-being took priority above all else. Though I could see it simmering just below the surface as I sped through the empty theater.

"Even if you fall asleep, would it make you feel better if I were there?"

There was a long pause.

"Yes," she finally breathed.

Little did she know, I could be on the other side of the world, and I would drop everything if she needed me. Hell, I'd already signed part of my soul to the devil himself to ensure she wasn't trapped in a bargain she didn't have the means to escape. Adeline didn't know it yet, but she had me wrapped around her little finger.

All she had to do was ask, and I'd be there.

It took several blinks for my eyes to adjust to the darkness. Then a few more to realize the shadow in the kitchen belonged to Adeline. The stove light was on its way out and only provided enough light to illuminate the hissing tea kettle she was tending to.

The curtain billowed as a breeze cut through the apartment and rustled the cotton pajama shorts and thin camisole she wore.

"What are you doing"—I glanced down at my watch—"up so late? I thought you said you were going to bed."

"I couldn't sleep," she said, hooking her headphones around her neck, "so I was making myself some tea. Would you like some?"

Beaten down by the day, both mentally and physically, I couldn't think of a better way to spend my night—well, early morning. As the clock struck midnight, I propped my hip against the counter and watched her dance around the kitchen with a sense of familiarity that made my heart tighten in response. There was something so domestic about sharing the space, stealing her time, and watching how comfortable she was living here. There wasn't a doubt in my mind that this was where she was always meant to be.

"You're getting home pretty late," she pointed out, pouring a dash of milk in my tea.

"I got tied up at the theater." Not technically a lie, but far from the full truth.

With secrets yet to be spoken aloud and intentions buried beneath crumbling alliances, against my better judgment, I hadn't worked up the courage to tell Adeline about my deal with Destler yet. I'd already tried to warn her about Blanchet once, but without any physical evidence to back up my claim, despondence would always surpass suspicion.

If taking this leap means my only chance to prove my innocence, then I have to take it.

Adeline deserved the truth, but until I could prove Blanchet would cross her, there was no point in worrying her when everything else in life was weighing heavily on her heart. I would shoulder this burden until I knew for certain.

"Well, I have my excuse, what's yours?"

Adeline hopped up onto the island, mere feet from where I was leaning over the marble counter, hands wrapped around a steaming cup of tea. Another breeze cut through the apartment, and I welcomed the way it caressed my flushed skin.

"If I were better at lying, I would tell you it's because of the showcase, but"—she studied her finger tracing the rim of her mug—"I can't stop thinking about that damn note they left in my dance bag. It feels like no matter what I do or think, it's constantly at the forefront of my mind."

"Do you want to talk about it?"

Please talk to me, sweetheart. The show. The report. The hearing. Anything.

"Not particularly," she said with a soft smile. "I'm perfectly aware whoever is doing this is just trying to spook me, but my anxiety loves to fill my head with nonsense and create scenarios that will never happen. It's exhausting to constantly be at the beck and call of my own mind. I was lying in bed for so long, staring up at the ceiling, I figured making a cup of tea and listening to music was a better use of my time."

This wasn't the time nor the place, I reminded myself. The threats would be dealt with, but for now, my concern was Adeline's well-being and nothing else.

"And what kind of music does this kind of night call for?"

Adeline peeled the headphones off her neck and gently placed them atop my head. With a tap of her screen, a symphony erupted in my ears. I recognized "Reflections" almost instantly by its heartbreaking melody.

"Is classical music the only thing that helps when you're feeling anxious?" I asked, taking the phone from her hand, then disconnecting the headphones so we could both enjoy the music together.

"Funny enough, I used to hate classical music." She giggled. "I didn't understand how anyone could enjoy music without any words. It wasn't until I started dancing that I was able to tolerate it." She chewed on her bottom lip. "Growing up in my household, there was constant noise—I guess that's the best way to describe it. My parents were co-owners of a business, but neither of them knew how to leave work where it belonged. Working together and starting a family took a huge toll on their relationship, and they didn't exactly hide it well. If it wasn't my parents fighting, then it was Melissa throwing a fit in order to be the center of attention again. Listening to music gave me an escape from that noise—little stolen moments all to myself, as fleeting as they were."

"When I first moved to America, I really struggled at first," I explained. "The borough I moved to wasn't very diverse, and I hardly spoke a lick of English, to make matters worse. It was terrifying to move across the world with just me and my mother, but music felt like I could bring the tiniest pieces of home with me. I didn't know it then, but music was a language everyone could speak, and before long, I was starting to make friends with kids who also loved music. After feeling alone for so long, it was comforting." I took another sip of tea. "I'm assuming journaling helped with the *noise*, too."

"Actually, I didn't start journaling until later in life," she said, a set of hazel eyes peering at me over the rim of her mug. "Another dancer at my last company used to journal—"

Those devastating, beautiful eyes of hers widened the tiniest bit.

"I'm sorry." She choked out a laugh. "I can't get over how uncomfortable you look wearing that tie. It's stressing me out, and I'm not even the one wearing it. Aren't you even uncomfortable?"

I straightened the navy-blue tie. "I was only trying to make a good impression."

"No, you look ridiculous." She set down her mug. "Come here. Let me help you."

Sitting atop the counter, Adeline and I were relatively the same height. It was hard to decide what was more distracting, drinking in the sight of her under the cover of moonlight or the way she gently tugged me forward by my tie like a dog on a leash. Her bare knee grazed my upper thigh, and I sent a small prayer up to anyone who was listening that she didn't accidentally brush up any higher.

Adeline diligently worked loosening the tie. Silence fell between us as thick as fog rolling through a coastal town in the wee hours of the morning. And I soaked up every second of her attention.

When she finished, I swallowed the lump in my throat and attempted to back away.

But Adeline didn't let go of my tie.

"The note wasn't the only reason I was up," she said, staring down at her hands.

"Is that so?" The words felt raw, sliding against my throat.

"I'd been thinking about what you'd asked me the other night. And I'd come up with a hundred different reasons why it's a bad idea. One hundred and one," she corrected herself, and my heart dropped like a bag of bricks, "if you count the fact that we live together."

Asking her for a chance had come as easily as breathing it, but that didn't mean I wasn't kicking myself for opening my big mouth in the first place. I had no right to ask that of her. Nor did I have any right to pray every night that her silence meant there was still hope for us.

And now...it was time to deal with the consequences of my own actions.

"Or how selfish it would be for me to not be able to give you the relationship you deserve when I can hardly manage everything going on in my life," she continued. "Or the fact that this reality can all be taken away in the blink of an eye if a jury of my peers says so."

I attempted to step back again, but she held tight.

"Tell me why," she rasped, a little out of breath, "I can't say no when you're standing right in front of me after already making up my mind."

Those hazel eyes of hers were normally the closest thing to being home for me, mesmerizing and easy to get lost in, but when she suddenly pinned me beneath her gaze, there was something so oddly unsettling about the way she looked at me—there was a type of hunger that couldn't be so easily fed. And because I recognized the hunger so furiously, I didn't think twice as I took a half step forward and wedged myself between her spread thighs. Every movement was slow and calculated. I monitored her every breath, searching her eyes for any sign to stop, though she never gave me one.

"I know exactly why, but I'm not sure you'll like the answer," I mumbled.

"Try me," she said softly, tugging on the tie the barest hint.

"Because no matter how much you try to convince yourself we can't be"—as my hand inched up her waist, I leaned forward and breathed the next words against her skin, placing a feather-like kiss on her bare shoulder—"you can't ignore the pull toward each other anymore. Isn't that right, Addie?"

I inched closer up her shoulder, leaving a trail of kisses in my wake.

The pad of my thumb lazily stroked her ribs like a musician

strumming a harp, listening to the beautiful music we made together with each panted breath.

"It's easier for you to shove those feelings away like some kind of dirty little secret rather than speak them into existence," I said, dragging my bottom lip, savoring the way she burned beneath me with each stolen kiss, "but you're curious. I see it when you try to hide the way you blush during our conversations. Or the way you save that beautiful smile of yours for my eyes only. Or even when I catch you staring at me during rehearsals and you don't think I notice. Do you want to know how I know that?"

I placed another kiss on the spot where her shoulder met the base of her neck. A shiver ran through Adeline. She sucked in a breath, clawing my bicep for stability.

"Because I'm watching you, too. I haven't been able to take my damn eyes off you since your audition." Her heartbeat raced beneath my touch as I skimmed over the columns of her neck. "You can't say no because you know deep down it would be a mistake not to try this once. Isn't that right?"

I didn't consider myself a particularly religious man by any means, but as I pulled away and beheld the sight of Adeline so disheveled before me, it was the closest thing to a religious experience in my thirty-two years of life. Beneath her thin camisole, her nipples were barely visible, drenched in moonlight spilling into the darkened apartment. For a wonderful heartbeat, I considered what it would be like to take them between my teeth and worship her properly. What beautiful little moans she would make if she finally accepted this divine fate.

"I asked you a question, Addie," I said with a smirk.

A beat passed, then Adeline shook her head and huffed out a laugh. If I were a betting man, which I wasn't, I would put all my money down that if I flipped on the overhead lights, her cheeks would be stained the deepest shade of pink.

"What was the question again?"

"A little distracted, huh?" I drawled, biting the inside of my cheek. "That's how I feel anytime I'm in the same room as you."

I stepped back, and her smile slowly faded.

"Thank you for the tea," I said. "Good night, Addie. Get some rest."

The call to temptation was the loudest when I was near her. It was one thing to listen, but it was an entirely different beast to give in. We could very well choose the latter and finally explore these hidden truths between us, but it was never about sex when it came to Adeline. And until she explicitly told me so, I didn't think I could offer that piece of myself to her without giving her everything else. It pained me to walk away, but temptation wasn't worth the heartache that would soon follow.

"Okay," she called from the kitchen.

I turned on my heels. "Okay?"

"I will go on a date with you under one condition, but you might not like it."

Anything. Name it.

"Try me," I shot back.

"We will wait until after the hearing next week. Let me worry about one thing at a time."

If I told her how long I was willing to wait for a chance to be with her, I might scare her away. Adeline Hartwell was well worth it.

I nodded. "It's a date, sweetheart."

Chapter Twenty-Seven

Adeline

The passage of time went by in a blur, each day bleeding into the other. The only measure of time was the nightmares building in strength and frequency with each passing night. There was hardly a moment to think, let alone rest, with so much riding on this performance.

Before long, I found myself present before the court commissioner like a lonesome marionette doll, the strings of which were being pulled by Donovan and his team. If he said to introduce myself, I croaked my name aloud. If he said to smile, I obliged. If he said to sit there and look pretty, I folded my hands in my lap and was the picture of innocence.

The half hour I spent at the regional court center, I felt entirely numb from head to toe. It felt as if I wasn't wholly in control of my own body, simply going through the motions. Donovan would pull his string, and I would dance without a second thought, because if his team was adamant about one thing, it was the fact that I didn't look like a killer, and he knew we could use that to our advantage. So, I played my role, danced my dance, and before I knew it, we were dismissed. With enough viable evidence to support my case without the help of the footage that was still being reviewed at the time of our hearing, my trial was scheduled six months from now.

Six months to prepare for battle.

Six months to dance to my heart's content.

Six months to savor the last of my freedom.

Six months was all that stood in my way from the rest of my life, and in the meantime, it was the responsibility of Donovan and his team to strengthen their case and polish that image of the innocent ballerina they wanted me to be so badly.

As promised, Jin was true to his word. Like the gentleman he was, he allowed me time to process the hearing on my own terms and untangle myself from one mess before I willingly put myself through another. While he was patient in that regard, his promise did nothing to stop the stolen glances from across the room, or how he purposely went out of his way to drag his knuckles across the back of my hand in passing during rehearsals, or even the scattered sticky notes that somehow found their way to my dance bag, lining the frame of the bathroom mirror, and stuck to the cup of coffee he made me each morning.

Despite whatever promises we'd made to each other, what little strength I had was wavering. It had come to a point where simply being in the same room as him was excruciating. The memory of his lips caressing my skin had permanently scorched my flesh, and each time his gaze purposely lingered there, it burned brighter.

Even in the dead of the night when the mere thought of him lying in the bed across the hall kept me up late, tossing and turning all night, those memories felt like drenching those burns in pure alcohol—raw and too fresh not to tend to. If I closed my eyes, ran my fingers between the innermost point of my thighs, I could almost imagine a reality in which we didn't stop—one where I worked up the nerve to cross the hallway, crawl between his sheets, and finish what we had started, rather than give myself over to the nightmares once more.

To admit to what we'd both been lying to ourselves for so long.

It was the reason I'd gone back on everything I'd said...

It was the reason I had given him this one chance.

Jin felt like an enigma in my life; a fraction of reality that didn't quite feel like it belonged. A shred of happiness penetrating through the darkest night. A tendril of hope when I'd given up long before. Everything about who he was and how he'd stumbled into my life felt like a well-orchestrated dance that had started long before the first note.

And now that he had taken my hand and started this dance, I wasn't sure I could stop.

I wasn't surprised when Jin refused to tell me where we were going, only to keep in mind that we'd be outdoors for the majority of the evening. Spring in the city was notorious for beautifully bright days and chilly nights. I tore apart my closet until I finally settled on an outfit that felt fitting for our date yet would keep me warm. Jin, on the other hand, opted for a pair of black jeans, white sneakers, and a forest green shirt—simple in nature but accentuating his greatest assets. The outfit must have been part of an elaborate plan to distract me, because instead of trying to guess where he was taking me the entire drive there, I was more concerned with stealing glances at his arms, shaped by years of kickboxing.

We hit a pocket of traffic on the outskirts of town. Twenty minutes later, a man at the entrance of a dirt lot flagged us down with the promise of ten-dollar parking. Couples and young families piled out of their cars with an assortment of blankets and variations of picnic baskets. I hated myself for how long it took to realize where we were going, but as we rolled by the Riverview Park sign on the edge of the dirt lot, it finally clicked.

I whipped my head around. "Jin! Is this what I think it is?"

He shifted the car into park. "That depends. What do you think it is?"

"Republic City Philharmonic Orchestra in the park?"

Actions were known to speak louder than words, which is probably why Jin reached behind the passenger seat, pulled out a tote bag stuffed with beach towels, then plopped it in my lap with little more than a smile to answer for. There was an odd fluttering feeling deep within my gut that only worsened as Jin rounded the hood of the car and held the door open for me.

Oh, I'm in trouble. Big trouble.

The Riverview amphitheater was a sprawling half dome with seating for about a hundred or so people closest to the stage. Beyond that was an endless sea of blankets and lawn chairs taking up real estate on the grassy knolls. Jin and I found an empty spot toward the back, and despite the obstructed views, nothing could wipe the smile off my face.

In my journal, I kept a running list of activities I wanted to try since moving to the city, and seeing the Republic City Philharmonic Orchestra in the park was number four on that very long list. With limited tickets being sold and unusual hours at the theater, I'd never had the opportunity to go before now. Nor had anyone cared to take me.

The setting sun had dipped beyond the horizon, shifting the sky into hues of fiery red. Using the last of the dying light, Jin diligently worked, arranging the different containers before us. Artisan crackers paired with an assortment of foreign cheeses, fruit so fresh it could have been picked earlier this morning, and not one, but two flavors of hummus to dip our vegetables in. The attention to detail hadn't gone unnoticed, and the more thought I put behind it, the more traction the gesture held.

It was no longer a small fluttering deep within my stomach;

it was a collection of hundreds of butterflies all frantically flapping their wings at once.

"What's this?" I asked, unscrewing the lid of the canteen.

"In case you want a little something special," he answered, taking a swing of what I assumed to be sangria. "I told you I could do much better than a sushi restaurant."

"To be fair, you could have taken me to a food stall in the park instead of a concert, and I'm sure we would have had a great time," I retorted, stealing it right back.

"I'll keep that in mind for next time."

"Bold of you to assume there will be a second date."

"Bold of you to assume I don't already have it planned," he shot back, eyes narrowed, playfully.

A single note pierced the evening air. The strings, brass, and woodwinds joined in, one after the other—all hitting the A note in unison. A chaotic hum bouncing off the grassy knolls signaled the beginning of the show. I couldn't set my sights on the horizon where hues of orange faded into black quickly enough, and yet, with so much demanding my attention elsewhere, I couldn't help noticing the way he watched me. His gaze scorched my flesh with a painfully familiar burn. There may have been a time in the past when I was ashamed by the redness in my face, but now, I welcomed it, knowing he couldn't take his eyes off me.

On cue, the noise faded into nothingness. Musicians shifted in their seats, tightening their bows, poised for the night. A hush fell over the crowd, and the conductor stepped forward, baton raised. With one swift motion, Beethoven's Symphony No. 6 (*Pastoral*) echoed through the park. One song faded into the next, time marching to its own beat as we indulged ourselves on good food, lively music, and even better company.

The end of each song brought with it a small twinge of disappointment, knowing there would inevitably come an end to the night. Refusing to let this moment slip through my fingers, I inched closer to Jin and rested my head against his shoulder. The kiss atop my temple and strong arm wrapped around my waist grounded me to the present, and I was reminded what spring might feel like after all.

"Thank you for this, Jin," I rasped, nestling myself in more closely. "I mean it. I can't get over how incredibly thoughtful this all was."

"As long as it puts a smile on your face, it was worth it."

Jin had once opened up to me and told me music was a language everyone could speak. It was the means of connecting with others when more than borders divided us. He could have very well taken me here on our first date because of my love and appreciation for the arts, but I wasn't lost on the fact that from a young age, music had made Jin feel like he belonged, and I was honored to be sharing this experience with him.

A burst of light caught my eye. A picture of Sophia and Caleb smiling flashed across Jin's screen from its place between us. He ignored the incoming call, and not two seconds after it went to voicemail, it started ringing again.

With a reluctant sigh, Jin peeled himself away from me, offering a grumbled apology before answering it.

"Sophia," he whispered, "I'm—"

He paused, listening to the roar of conversation barely audible through the phone.

"Okay." His jaw tightened. "Okay."

The call was short and sweet, but his expression afterward was anything but.

"Is everything okay?"

"Fuck," he cursed, running his fingers through his hair. "Sophia was calling me from the hospital. It kills me to do this to you...But I need to be there for them. I'm so sorry."

"She isn't having the baby already?"

"No," he said, starting to package up the uneaten snacks. "Something happened to Caleb, but I don't know what the hell is going on. She was hysterical, and I could barely make out a word over the phone. I'll drop you off at the apartment if you like, or you can stay here—"

"I'm coming with you."

"You don't have to do that."

"Too late. I'm coming."

———

Grim faces and hushed whispers filled the empty waiting room. Jin sat bent over, elbows braced on his knees, mindlessly staring at the speckled floor. Neither of us had dared to breathe a word since arriving as we waited for the ongoing tests to finish, and even if I had, I wasn't sure there was anything I could say to comfort him in such a time of perpetual uncertainty. Words would never be enough when empty promises couldn't be kept, so I offered him a different type of comfort by sliding my hands into his.

Jin bowed his head and released a long exhale before pressing his lips to my knuckles. There we remained for quite some time, his thumb painting lazy circles on my flesh.

Hanging high above the plastic fiddle leaf fig nestled in a woven basket was a boxed television that looked like it had been placed there decades before. Silently, I watched the news segment flashing on the screen to a backdrop of odd coughs and hushed conversations.

Jin must have felt me tense up because he squeezed my hand and asked, "What's the matter, sweetheart?" His voice was rough and grainy.

I tipped my chin toward the corner of the room where the news ticker read: *Missing person.* "That man—Reed Hackett," I corrected myself as his name appeared below a picture of him sitting on the beach. "I—" I shook my head, trying to wrap my head around it. "I saw him only a few short weeks ago. Gosh, I wonder what happened to him?"

"Adeline"—a beat passed—"how do you know that man?"

"He's a driver for Blanchet. Reed picked me up from my old apartment and drove me across town."

Jin opened his mouth, then closed it. "Did—"

"For Caleb Collins," a nurse called out, and Jin jumped to his feet.

"We're putting a pin in this conversation," he said, dragging me toward the awaiting nurse. Through the pristine white hallways that reeked of antiseptic and cleaning products, we followed the nurses, Jin never letting go of my hand.

"Room 435"—she pointed in said direction—"second door on the left."

The door swung open, and Sophia shot to her feet. The sound of her chair grinding against the floor made Caleb jerk in his sleep. Or so I thought. His face was so swollen I couldn't tell the difference. Caleb's face was nearly unrecognizable under the harsh glow of the fluorescent lights. The entire left side had swelled up so profusely that it had begun to sag under the weight of his own skin.

I did my best not to blanch at the sight of her fiancé lying in a heap of crisp white blankets, but promises were often hard to keep. That felt especially difficult as I took in the long leg splints, extending down both of his legs.

"Jesus Christ, what happened?"

Caleb tilted his head, those swollen eyes of his instantly finding our interlocked hands.

"Look who made it," Caleb slurred. "The happy couple."

Sophia ambushed Jin, wrapping him around in a much-needed embrace. "Ignore him, he's on so many painkillers right now, I'm not even sure he knows what day of the week it is."

"I think it's the day you finally tell me what's going on between you two," Caleb continued, blood still visible along the lining of his gums and between his teeth.

Jin pulled away, taking her by the shoulder, eyes assessing her from head to toe before turning toward his brother. "Well, seeing that you interrupted our first date and no one's telling me what happened, I'm getting a little upset."

"Ha. I told you," Caleb shouted, sticking out his hand towards Sophia. "You owe me ten bucks. I knew there was something between them."

I shifted from one foot to the other, standing on the outskirts of the conversation.

"Sophia," Jin said. "Please."

A sob bubbled up her throat, her eyes fixed on her fiancé. Words failed her every time she tried.

"I got a few good punches in," Caleb answered in such a lighthearted tone, given all that had happened. Whatever the doctor gave him must have been strong. "Must have given the bastard a black eye."

"Well, seeing that you have two, this isn't really looking good for you," Jin retorted, surprisingly calm despite the state of his brother. "Come on, Soph. Let's talk outside."

"Okay," she sniffled, letting her brother-in-law guide her outside.

Not ten seconds after the door closed behind them, Caleb was already calling my name, beckoning me to his bedside. "So, how was it? The date."

"What do you think?" I sank into the closest chair. "It was Jin, of course, it was perfect."

Caleb smiled up at the ceiling. "And Sophia called me an idiot for bailing on sushi."

There wasn't a doubt in my mind that Jin would have stayed the night had Sophia not kicked us out around ten-thirty. With a little persuasion—and a lot of guilt tripping—she managed to get him out of the hospital door with the promise to return bright and early tomorrow.

While faced with adversity, I discovered there were two versions of Jin. The forward-facing one that presented itself with a level of professionalism that excelled when people were relying on him the most—the version I'd grown to appreciate from afar within the confines of the theater. And there was the other version, the one that rarely let himself crumble.

For his brother's and Sophia's sake, he refused to let the latter show and instead attempted to keep a level head through the entire visit. It wasn't until the door clicked behind him that I noticed the toll it was taking on him to keep that facade firmly in place. He refused to let his guard down all at once. It was like a fracture in a dam—at first, the damage was minimal, a few leaks here and there that manifest themselves as the occasional sigh or odd shift in mannerisms. But that's the thing about a fracture: the longer they go without being fixed, the more likely they are to spread.

The entire drive home, I could see him slowly starting to tear at the seams, barely holding onto that thread. The more desperate he was to hold on, the more he grappled without purchase. By some miracle, we made it home before he lost himself completely.

Jin roughly tossed his keys on the kitchen counter. They slid off the edge and landed with a thud before the apartment fell silent once more. I flinched. The fractures spread, and all Jin could do was slap his hands on the counter, bow his head, and brace for impact as it all came rushing forward.

Run, Adeline. Run.

The little voice was back.

Run. Before it's too late.

I'd seen what came from the fractures. I'd willingly put myself before the dam and swore it would never hurt me again before being washed away when it finally burst.

Again.

And again.

And—

What sounded like a strangled sob cut through the silence.

Was he crying?

I took a tentative step forward, convinced I was hearing things. A heartbeat later, Jin's back shook as another sob rocked through him, confirming exactly what I feared. Before I knew what I was doing, I had my arms wrapped around his middle. The sobbing worsened as all he'd been holding in for the last few hours came pouring out in one fatal blow. I held onto him for dear life, letting him know I was there for him.

The storm eventually subsided.

Cries turned to labored breaths.

Heartbeats found their rhythm once more.

When Jin found it in himself to face me, he turned in my hold and rested his chin atop my head. We remained there for what felt like forever, wrapped in the other's embrace.

There were apologies whispered in the dark.

And kisses atop my head as appreciation.

An echo of a past written in empty promises and blatant lies. It pained me that my first instinct was to suspect the worst, to collate. To run and cower in a corner at the first sign of trouble. It wasn't fair to either of us for me to constantly be assuming the worst when it came to the men in my life. Comparison may be the theft of joy, but what if I couldn't help it...

But what if I can't separate the two?

"Sophia told me that Caleb was ambushed after work by two men," he rasped, breaking the silence. "They shattered his kneecap with a baseball bat, and Caleb is a lucky bastard that the damage isn't bad enough for surgery. It might be eight to twelve weeks before he even walks..."

"I don't understand—" I cursed under my breath. "Were they trying to rob him?"

"No"—he sucked in a breath—"don't let Sophia know I told you this, but they attacked him because he's working at The Lotte. They not only threatened his life if he doesn't stop construction, but Sophia and the baby. Adeline," he choked, "I— I don't know what to do. I feel so damn helpless in all of this, and I don't know how to protect the people I love anymore."

The way my chest splintered felt like the branches of a lightning bolt, spreading every which way and threatening to strike me down. As foolish as it was to stand in the middle of the storm after being hurt so many times before, the truth struck me with such clarity that it was a blessing rather than a curse.

"Jin, I need you to look at me."

Taking either side of his face, I forced myself to meet his glossy eyes and come to terms with the truth: Jin was not Noah, and it wasn't fair that I kept treating him like he was. Noah never cried in front of me, confessed his deepest insecurities, or put the needs of the people in his life before his own.

Jin was not Noah, I repeated.

"The worst is over," I said, forcing a smile. "Caleb, Sophia, and the baby are all safe, and we'll make sure it stays that way. Right now, we need to let the police do their job and find the men who hurt him. I promise, you are not helpless. Your brother needs you more than ever right now. I have never met anyone with a bigger heart than you, and I know without a doubt, you're going to do everything in your power to take care of him. Everything is going to be all right, okay?"

Jin leaned into my hand, eyes shut as he whispered, "Okay."

"Okay," I repeated, voice slippery. "It's been a long day, and we have another one ahead of us. It's about time we go to bed."

Whatever fight he had left in him vanished as I dragged him down the hall toward the bathroom. With only one bathroom in the apartment, I insisted he go first while I waited outside, seeing that he could barely keep himself upright. The muffled sound of running water and shutting cabinets was a symphony of his exhaustion. Several minutes later, it was my turn, but instead of moving my feet, I couldn't take my eyes off Jin carrying himself across the hall, one misstep away from crumbling into a million pieces.

The door closed behind him, and I stood frozen in place. Though I didn't understand the hesitation at first, after finishing up my nighttime routine, it dawned on me how desperate I was to pick up those pieces. Rather than walking to my bedroom, I cut across the hallway and gently rapped my knuckles on the wood. Jin's soft voice called from the other side, and I cracked the door open to find a shiftless Jin sitting in his boxers on the edge of the bed, a sliver of moonlight drenching him in a haunting glow.

"I—I was just checking on you. I wasn't sure if you wanted to be alone right now."

"Please," was all he said as I let myself in and crawled into his bed before I thought better of it. Jin was there a second later, wrapping his arm around my middle and dragging me flush against his skin. "I don't want to be alone right now, and I don't think you want to either."

"No," I breathed, tucking my head against his chest.

"Thank you, Adeline," was all he said before we both fell asleep.

Chapter Twenty-Eight

Adeline

Pulled from a dreamless sleep, my mind woke long before the tingling in my limbs was realized. It took several long moments to remember where I was when darkness clung to me as tightly as the arm wound around my torso. To remember whose flesh scorched my skin everywhere we were connected as one. Whose breath gently tussled my hair.

Mind and body finally as one, I became painfully aware of what unspoken truths pass between us—what lines were inevitably crossed. As I lay curled up in Jin's bed, restless beneath his heavy limbs, I couldn't for the life of me regret crossing it in the first place.

Jin needed me last night.

And a part of me needed him as well.

I squirmed under the sheets, attempting to break free.

"No," he groaned, his voice gravelly and rough against my skin as he pulled me flush against him. The small soft sliver of my lower back brushed against the hardest parts of him. I sucked in a breath, and he blew one out against the back of my neck.

"Unless you want me to pee the bed," I mumbled, "I suggest you let me go."

Another groan, then all his warmth left me. "Come back. Please."

Attempting to rub away the sleep from my eyes, I padded across the hallway and relieved myself. Not without taking a moment to brush my teeth and rinse the stale taste out of my mouth with some mouthwash. Still a little wobbly on my feet, I returned to his bedroom once I was done. It felt like second nature to slip back between the sheets, drape my leg across his, and tuck my head against his bare chest. Even more so when he started drawing lazy circles along my back. The soothing motions lulled me back to sleep as my eyes grew nearly as heavy as my heart. There we remained for quite some time, enveloped in one another.

"I wish last night hadn't ended the way it did," he said, his voice gently pulling me from the cusp of sleep. "I wish I could have given you the night you deserved."

"Jin"—with a little stretch and a big yawn, I attempted to right myself—"please don't beat yourself up about last night. There's only so much we can control in uncontrollable circumstances. I know you put a lot of time and effort into the night, and it didn't quite pan out as we'd hoped, but I promise you, the thought alone made the night what it was."

"Not by a long shot." Jin snorted.

"Would it make you feel better to know it was more than anyone had cared to do for me before?"

He pulled away to look down at me, then frowned. "Not particularly."

"Let's just say, you can only beg someone to put in the effort so many times before you realize if they truly cared, you wouldn't have to ask in the first place. Eventually, you stop asking altogether," I replied, my fingertip mindlessly skimming his bare chest, not wanting to meet his eyes. "So yes, regardless of how the night ended, it meant more to me than you'll ever understand."

A beat passed. "I'd like to make up for last night, if you'd let me."

"Hmm. Would that technically count as date number two or a restart on the first?"

"I think we both deserve a fresh start," Jin said.

"Does that mean you'll tell me what you had planned for last night?"

Jin laughed, and my head shook with his chest. "Absolutely not, if we're redoing last night, then I might steal some of those ideas. I had quite the night planned for us."

"Please."

He sucked air between his teeth, contemplating.

I flipped up on my stomach and propped forearms on his broad chest.

"Please," I repeated, elongating my vowels.

His hand instantly found the small of my back, and for a moment, I think we both forgot how to breathe. I raised an eyebrow, and he mumbled a curse to himself.

"Fine," he said, biting back a smile. "But you can't complain if the next one can't top it."

I traced my finger across my chest in the shape of an X.

"Orchestra in the park was only the beginning of the night. If you were feeling up to it after the show, I wanted to drive us to one of those historic jazz clubs on the outskirts of the Entertainment District. It would have taken a few drinks to work up the courage, but eventually, I would have asked you to dance with me."

I snorted a laugh.

"What?" His smile was a mirror to my own. "At the company holiday party, I remember Halle having to physically drag you off the dance floor to get you to stop. To this day, it still bothers me that she did that because I'd never seen you happier. I always promised myself that if I got the chance, I'd let you dance to your heart's content," he explained. "After that, I imagine we would have had a drink or two, and I would have suggested we walk home instead of getting a cab so I had an excuse to take the long way home and steal more of your time."

"How very chivalrous of you," I teased, glued to his every word. "Then what?"

"On Thirty-Fourth Street, there's a small botanical garden that cuts through the park. I'm not in the habit of getting my hopes up, but if it were up to me, I would have taken you to the gardens and kissed you senseless."

"I thought you didn't kiss on the first date," I said, using his own words against him.

"Adeline," he chuckled, "you're the exception to every rule. I'm a weak man when I'm near you, which is why coming home after all that and not inviting you into my bedroom would have been even more difficult than it already is on a daily basis."

"Well, I did technically end up in bed with you..."

"Details. Details."

"What if I had said yes?"

Both of our smiles fell, and his hand stilled on my back. We stared at one another for a long moment. As I realized I had said those words aloud, Jin was most likely wondering if he'd heard me correctly.

"What—what if everything had gone as planned? The orchestra in the park. Dancing together in the district. Even the kiss in the gardens. What would you have done had you realized we were both fighting a losing battle and asked anyway?"

If battles were meant to be fought with honor and dignity, then I had all but raised the white flag. Jin may claim to be a weak man, but had he asked, I wasn't sure I had it in me to deny him.

"I wouldn't have put you in that position."

"You're telling me if I jumped into your arms and begged you to take me to bed, you would have said no based on *principle?*"

"I thought we already established that I'm a weak man when it comes to you."

"Then you should have no problem telling me what you think would have happened."

There was still much I'd yet to learn about the artistic director. Each day with him was another stitch in a tapestry not yet woven—a picture still revealing itself. Despite not being able to see him in full, there was something so alluring about taking one of those loose threads and pulling just to see what he might do when it all started to unravel. Toying with Jin was a dangerous game, forcing each of us to walk a fine line. I knew what I was doing when I started us down this path—though I never imagined I wouldn't be the only player in the game. While I'd asked the question to watch him squirm, he answered so I might unravel with him.

"That's the thing, Adeline. If I'm going to fantasize about what could have been, then I'd much rather think about the other night in the kitchen." As slow and methodical as his words, he flipped me onto my back and crawled atop me. The weight of that statement was as punishing as his body pressing me into the mattress. "All the things I would have done to you had I not walked away."

A small prayer spilled from my lips as easily as his name did. Jin inched closer and closer, hovering his lips between the columns of my neck. Silently asking for permission as he mumbled my name in return—his own form of adoration.

"I think about that day a lot," he breathed.

I tipped my head back, nails digging into his side.

"I would have worshipped you." Reminiscent of our tryst in the kitchen, his lips traced over the hard edges of my collarbone, leaving goose bumps in their wake. Unlike that night, he didn't stop as he skimmed over the swells of my breast. "I would worship every inch of you if you'd let me, Addie."

Thread by thread, Jin slowly started to unravel me.

The farther south he traveled, the more the edges of reality started to blur—losing myself to his touch made me fear every kiss hidden by the darkness—every whisper a figment of my imagination. The farther he traveled, the more I feared this was too good to be true. That I was still fast asleep in my own bed, dreaming of him settling himself between my thighs as he reached the hem of my tank top.

"Is that what you want? For me to worship you?" he asked, hand bracing my hip bone to keep me in place as the length of him brushed the innermost part of my thigh.

Dreams were meant to be the manifestation of our wants, desires, and greatest fears. Little bits and pieces of our day that shape themselves into reality, not yet imagined. It hadn't been the first time I'd dreamt about me and Jin together, but they were few and scarce when the nightmares always found a way to slip between the cracks. If desire was a match, then it had been struck long ago. The flames should have smothered themselves out by now, but the longer we stoked the flames, the more they threatened to burn us both alive.

Rather than torment me with his lips, Jin took my right nipple between his teeth and lightly pulled, forcing me to endure an entirely different type of torture.

This couldn't be real.

Any minute now, I would wake up in a heap of sweaty sheets, flushed and out of breath.

The tip of my nipple caught between his front teeth, and

waves of pain and pleasure mingled as one. A sharp hiss turned into a breathy moan, and in that moment, I knew this couldn't possibly be a dream. Jin pulled away, an apology on his lips, but before he could remove himself, I wedged my hand between us and ground my palm against the length of his cock, begging him not to stop.

Unable to contain himself, Jin bit down harder.

"Is that what you want, sweetheart?"

Over his boxer briefs, I took my time exploring the shape of him.

"Only if I get to return the favor," I moaned.

And with that, the final thread snapped. He yanked down my shirt and hooked the hem under my breasts. Jin took a second to admire the sight before he cursed under his breath, brought his lips to my burning flesh, and branded me his. He was gentle with some areas and rough with others: kissing, biting, sucking the sensitive skin until my breasts were swollen and I ached for more.

More.

I needed more.

I continued to stroke him so I might never wake up from this dream. Shifting my hand forward, I gently caressed his balls before running my hand up the length of him again. Jin jerked forward, resting his forehead against my chest, completely at my mercy as he rode the waves of pleasure coursing through him.

"Adeline," he moaned. "What are you doing to me?"

"I need more," I panted. "I need you."

The sound of an alarm startled me.

This was it. The moment I'd been dreading all along. The ever-fleeting nature of the dream and the potential to be ripped away at any moment when the edges of reality and fantasy blended as one.

A chill slithered down my spine as his weight left me. I

opened my eyes, expecting to be lying in my bedroom, but there he was, kneeling between my thighs, phone in hand. Jin shut off the alarm and tossed it aside in the mess of sheets. His chest rose and fell in quick succession. The veil of our lust had been lifted, and neither of us was sure what to do next. All we could do was stare at one another, not daring to break this connection. Jin looked nearly as hungry as I, his gaze lingering on my exposed breasts still moist from his lips.

"Adeline—" he sighed.

"We'll be late for work if you keep looking at me like that."

Jin smirked. "I don't see the problem here."

And that's where he was wrong.

There was a sense of familiarity to how the rest of the morning played out. The lonesome coffee cup waiting for me on the island when I finished getting ready for the day. The drive through the city, where neither of us spoke and instead listened to the radio because we preferred the quiet this early in the day. The way we parted ways backstage, with a reluctant smile and a heavy heart.

He was wrong because there are consequences to every action, and despite pretending everything could go back to normal, we couldn't hide our sins between ruffled sheets and the cover of darkness. There were consequences to every action, and sooner or later, they would come for us both.

Chapter Twenty-Nine

Jin

Touched by the grace of God, Adeline Hartwell was a blessing I'd been convinced would never be. An answer to a prayer nearly forgotten in the wind. A shred of happiness too bright that I refused to let it be as fleeting as this moment.

The door closed behind Adeline, and for a second, I had to collect myself.

Prove that she'd really been here—that this wasn't some sick joke.

The taste of her still lingering on my lips was proof enough, but there were other signs scattered across the room. The wrinkled sheets from when she curled up against me in the dead of night, like she also knew if she didn't hold on tight enough, this might all fade away. The sight of her lip balm pressed against the rim of the glass on my nightstand when she woke up in a fret, desperate for water. The piercing feeling deep within my gut that only Adeline herself could stir within me.

She'd been here—it hadn't been a dream.

Doubt was fickle—an unseeable force, desperate to convince

me to question more than my sanity when I impulsively asked her something I thought I would never have the strength to do.

That kernel of doubt, as small as it was, had the power to wedge itself between every stolen glance when I couldn't bear the thought of taking my eyes off her, every memory of her failing to hide her blush-stained cheeks, and every glimmer of light slowly returning to her eyes.

I had somehow convinced myself that maybe, just maybe, she had only said yes out of pity and all of this was one big mistake.

That was until this morning.

Doubt may be fickle, but the question of desire was anything but.

As Adeline and I parted ways backstage, my phone buzzed in my pocket. Reality slowly started to slip back into place, my smile slowly fading along with it. Dozens of unread messages and missed calls from both Sophia and Caleb filled my screen. The two were completely at odds with one another on whether or not I should be there so Sophia could go home and rest. Two-thirds of the way through the message, I had already come to terms with the fact that, despite already being at the theater, I was going to call out sick before anyone saw me and blew my cover.

Instead of driving straight to the hospital, I took a quick detour through the city for a much more pressing matter.

Beneath the midmorning sun, the glow of the sign outside of Don Juan dulled in comparison to the vibrant reddish hue that blanketed the city street at night. With little to offer this early in the day, this portion of the district felt like a ghost town. Which felt especially true as Damon, silent as ever, led me through the empty club with such preternatural grace, he easily could have been mistaken for a residual haunting of the place. Like specters drifting in the breeze, I followed him toward the main bar where Erick was sitting.

I clenched and unclenched my fist.

With his back turned toward us, he seemed much more preoccupied with whatever he was working on rather than the sound of footfalls quickly approaching, but with a reluctant sigh, he peeled himself away from his laptop to greet us.

"Collins," he said, shoving to his feet.

The next heartbeat, I sent us both careening into the closest wall. The back of his head cracked against the dry wall with such a resounding smack that it rattled my teeth on impact. Erick flinched beneath me, but solely based on the wicked gleam in his brown eyes and the unnerving smile tugging at the corner of his lips, it was likely from surprise rather than actual fear or pain.

Damon, several paces away, rushed for us. It felt as if I was standing on a train track, my foot caught beneath the iron beams. There was nothing I could do but watch as a 10,000-ton freight train came barreling toward me. I shut my eyes and braced for impact, knowing if I didn't relinquish my hold right that second, I might very well be sharing a hospital room with my brother tonight. If it were me versus a freight train, the freight train would always win.

The high-pitched screech of rubber against wood echoed through the building. I opened my eyes to find Erick's hand raised in Damon's direction, his smile unwavering. Unable to sign with both hands, Erick mouthed whatever he was trying to say to his right-hand man, and though I wasn't certain, I was convinced he said, "Let's see how this plays out."

I rammed my forearm harder against his throat, determined

to wipe that damn smile off his face. "Did you know?" I asked, gritting my teeth as I applied more pressure.

"Ah, there he is. I was waiting."

"Did you *fucking* know my brother is in the hospital because of you?"

"Sounds like you're mad at the wrong person"—his voice was tight but level—"I'm not the one who broke his kneecaps."

"But he wouldn't be in the mess to begin with if it weren't for you. Charles wouldn't be targeting my family and the people I love if it weren't for *you* and this damn theater."

"Are you mad at me, or are you mad at yourself for not stopping it from happening in the first place...?"

The question ate the space between us. Sucking up all the breathable air and making me feel like I was drowning on dry land. I must have eased up against his throat without realizing it because Erick managed to squirm out of my hold, shove me in the chest, and send me stumbling back a few steps.

Erick sucked air between his teeth. "Looks like I hit a bit of a sore spot."

"You aren't—"

"I'm not what?" He took a step forward. "Listening to you? Understanding? Sympathetic? All of the fucking above? I hate to break it to you, but you aren't the only one scared shitless that Blanchet is going to hurt the people we care about the most. For months," he seethed, "I've had my fiancée's every move followed, so I have some kind of shred of hope to cling to that she's safe. And even then, I can't look her in the eyes and guarantee her safety...we might have drawn the first blood, Collins, but who's to say he won't be the last."

His words sliced through the air, clawing through my deepest insecurity. Layer by layer, word by word, I felt the implication of Blanchet's actions rub me raw and vulnerable until the back of my throat stung and my fingers shook. There was no alternative to failing, because to fail meant to lose everything.

"Be upset," he added. "But don't be upset at me when I'm trying to help you."

"I'm upset"—I roughly combed my finger through my hair—"because no matter what I do, it is never enough. Because I have no idea what I'm doing."

Erick knew so little of my situation—the reason I'd agreed to this entire mess. Perhaps I was tired of being weighed down by this burden, or the mere thought of not having to do this alone after being the sole provider of my family for decades, I couldn't refuse the lifeline he was offering me. Everything came spilling out. The assault on my brother and the threats directed at his family. The mess of legal trouble Adeline was wrapped up in. The pressure of fixing it all on my own.

Once I started, it was hard to stop. Erick was silently listening, arms crossed, nodding as I went on. And when I finished, I felt a little lighter, but sometimes saying it aloud isn't enough to banish those demons.

"She refuses to tell me the entire story, but...I know it was self-defense."

Erick tilted his head.

"The Blanchet family comes from old money, and they have plenty of resources in the city to make something like that disappear if he wanted to. You're probably right about him having some kind of alternative motive for going the long way around this. Charles likes to play games, and as hard as this might be to hear, she might be another pawn to him."

I drummed my fingernails absently on the table.

"Have you told her yet?"

My eyes met his.

"No," I admitted. "I tried to warn her about him, but she responded by saying she had no other choice—it was either this or jail. Nothing's happened yet, and I have nothing to prove that Charles is working in bad faith, which is why I haven't worked up the nerve to bring it up again. I didn't want to scare her when she has enough to deal with right now."

"Take it from me," Erick said, holding my gaze, "secrets only benefit those who keep them. When she inevitably finds out, which she will, she might not be as forgiving if you told her now."

I nodded, needing a moment to unpack that.

"Come, I need to show you something." I followed the owner into his office, where two items sat atop his desk, both wildly out of place in the renovated space. "Do you recognize these?"

Turning over the red bottle, I read the worn-out label, peeling at the corners.

Maquillage pointe. Color: Claret Rouge.

"This is the brand of dye we use at the theater for the pointe shoes."

Erick pulled out a newspaper clipped from his desk drawer. An image of a young blonde woman, I could only presume to be his fiancée, looked back at me. Her eyes dotted out by red X's in the shade *Claret Rouge*. An identical match of the photos found with the autopsy report...

Tatiana had done everything besides get down on her hands and knees to beg me to keep her position as soloist, swearing she played no part in the vicious threats meant to scare Adeline from the theater after Noah's death. There was motive, probable cause, and video footage of Tatiana and Xavier passing hands. But what if I made a mistake? What if it hadn't been her after all? With too many similarities to be a mere coincidence, that left me with the most haunting question of all: if Hartwell was indeed his rising star, then what would Charles gain by threatening her?

"Antonio and Damon searched Reed's belongings. The car was clean besides the bottle of dye that had rolled under the passenger seat, and these stuffed in his glove box," he said, handing me the stack of small square papers. "Parking stubs from the structure across the street from the Opera House."

March 2 at 7:35 a.m.

March 10 at 7:15 a.m.

March 11 at 7:22 p.m.

March 22 at 10:12 p.m.

March 26 at 7:05 a.m.

March 30 at 6:00 a.m.

April 3 at 1:10 a.m.

April 4 at 9:34 p.m.

The list went on without so much as a rhyme or reason other than the dates coinciding one after the other. Early morning, late nights, these stubs placed Reed at the theater at times I most certainly would have seen him, though I couldn't say our paths ever crossed.

"Reed isn't who we're looking for," I said, testing the words aloud. "He isn't the one who executed the threat, but he knew who did. Adeline mentioned something about Reed picking her up and driving her on Blanchet's behalf when she saw his missing person's report on the news last night. What if Reed isn't the one threatening both Krissy and Adeline, but he is the one driving them to and fro? What if these parking stubs are a clue to who is?"

"If Blanchet is targeting the grand reopening of The Lotte, then looking into these dates might give us a clue into learning what he has planned. Do you have access to the theater's surveillance system as the artistic director?"

"Yes and no." I rubbed the back of my neck. "I have access to the system, but Charles keeps a close eye on who logs in. The last time I did, after the first threat, he questioned me within minutes of logging in. If I tried again, he'd be too suspicious."

"Collins," he deadpanned, "if I gave up every time that I hit a dead-end, I wouldn't be standing here today. Plausible does not mean impossible; we're just missing something we aren't seeing yet. And I'd be damned if we missed a chance to protect the women we love. We're figuring it out, even if it takes us all night."

I thought to correct him the moment the word went tumbling from his lips—to claim it was too early, that whatever entanglement Adeline and I had fallen into wasn't anything more. But my mother didn't raise me to be a liar.

The sticky note caught my eye the moment I stepped into the apartment. The pop of highlighter yellow was a stark contrast to the dimly lit space. There was enough light filtering in from the hallway to see the elegant cursive filling the square edge-to-edge and the slightly lopsided smiley face below it.

I hope you had a great day.

The day had been far from it, but as my finger glided over the ink, I had a funny feeling things might turn around now that I was home from the hospital.

The sound of short, labored breaths and tearing led me down the hallway, where I found Adeline sitting on the bedroom floor, hard at work. Spread out before her was a pair of scissors, a small clear tube of superglue, a utility knife, my hammer (which I had no idea how she found), and a needle and thread. If you didn't know any better, you might think you'd stumbled across a crime scene.

The leather shank was stubborn, but so was Adeline. She gave it two more goes then nearly launched it across the room, only stopping when she noticed me leaning up against the door-frame. Her face turned the softest shade of rose.

"Want some help?" I drawled.

Slowly, she lowered her arm and then patted the space to her right.

"Here, hold this for me," I said, placing the note on her knee as I lowered myself to the ground. Her face went from the softest shade of pink to beet red, and there was no other feeling like knowing I was the reason why.

"Well, did you?" she asked bashfully. "Have a good day…"

I managed to get the shank free from the shoe, then handed it over.

"It's better now, and that's all that matters." Caleb was in good spirits and far less sedated than before; though I knew my brother well enough to know, vulnerability was seen more as a weakness than a strength in his eyes. If he was putting on a brave face, which I knew he was, he was doing it for Sophia's sake, instead of mine. "And you?"

The last time I'd seen Adeline, she was sprawled out on my bed, panting and bare-chested. I hadn't seen her since we parted ways this morning, and other than the stain on her cheeks, it didn't seem like either of us was going to address it.

"Hand me the knife, please." I obliged, watching her painstakingly break in her new shoes. Each dancer had their own method to the madness, and I loved to watch Adeline get lost in her craft. These in particular had a special day ahead of them, and it was clear she had that in mind as she scored the tips for traction. "I'm not ignoring you, I promise. I'm just thinking of some suggestions of where you might vacation if you wanted to use up the rest of your PTO, you know, seeing that we all did so well at rehearsal without you," she said, voice dripping with sarcasm.

"That bad?"

"It wasn't all bad," she answered with a sigh, then a reluctant smile. "Charles gave me the keys to the dressing room, which was exciting, but part of me wishes he hadn't..."

"But you've earned it."

"I have, but..." She chewed on her bottom lip. "There are already enough eyes on me right now between the other dancers and the threats. I feel like giving me the dressing room without being principal only added fuel to the fire."

The threats were meant to instill fear, gain insight into some kind of fight or flight within Adeline, and tarnish her career. Other than the two she'd received, there hadn't been a peep since, but I was wary of the silence, determined to see things through before they struck again—

Erick's voice pierced through pure stubbornness.

Take it from me, secrets only benefit those who keep them. I didn't believe my secrets were in bad faith, but it wasn't the keeper's responsibility to determine that.

"I actually wanted to talk to you about the threats," I said carefully, not missing the way her knife faltered. "I'd been meaning to tell you that I decided to work with someone to help me figure out who has been leaving them. I'm not getting the support I need at the theater, and I want to make sure that you're safe."

Her gaze met mine, searching. "Do you still think it was Tatiana and Xavier?"

"No, not anymore," I admitted. "And before you ask, no, they aren't coming back. Even if they weren't the ones leaving the threats, they're far from innocent." She was at a loss for words as she blankly stared at me, seeming to dissect that statement line by line. I would have given anything to take one measly peek inside her mind and see the inner workings of her deepest thoughts—to ease whatever troubled her that she couldn't speak aloud. "I wish I had more answers about what's going on—but your safety is my biggest priority, and I promise I'm doing all with what little I have. But I need you to do a big favor for me in return."

"Okay."

"Please don't tell Charles that I'm getting help elsewhere." Those hazel eyes of hers narrowed in my direction, prompting me to explain further. "I know if he found out that I went behind his back and worked with someone he didn't care for, it might blow up in my face."

"I promise," she rasped, holding out her pinky finger.

I followed suit, but when she tried to hook them together, I pulled back.

"And...promise me that you won't let the other dancer ruin this moment for you. *You* deserve to enjoy the showcase without caring what others think. I know that's easier said than done, but you deserve to be happy. Just at least try to savor it."

She stared down at my hand for a beat. Adeline was prone to turning over thoughts in her head like a chef searing a tender steak to rich perfection. It was the nervous shift of her eyes or the fidgeting of her chiffon skirt during rehearsal that gave her away. She never quite felt sure of herself, which is why it surprised me when she hooked her pinky with mine and kissed the pad of her thumb with such certainty.

"I'll try," was all she offered.

Promises seemed to be all we had. And while Adeline swore to keep my secret and do something kind for herself, as I kissed my thumb and followed suit, I made a different silent promise to Adeline that I intended to keep.

Chapter Thirty

Adeline

World-renowned ballerina Vivienne Duret was known for her technical brilliance and expressive dancing during her reign in the late 1920s, one of the first greats to walk this stage. Well aware of her lasting legacy, it was an honor to dance where she once did, in addition to the hundreds of others that had once called the Republic City Opera House home.

Vivienne was credited with starting the long-standing tradition of signing your name inside the wardrobe located in the main dressing room to signal the start of a new season. I hadn't quite worked up the nerve to do it yet, feeling as if I hadn't truly earned the right compared to my predecessors, who were given their positions based on merit rather than circumstance. Though the idea wasn't lost on me—especially after last night.

You deserve to enjoy the showcase without caring what others think. I know that's easier said than done, but you deserve to be happy.

The inability to change and truly embrace happiness wasn't for lack of trying. Clear as the tip of an arrow being driven into a heart, I knew what change I was striving for when I dropped everything and moved here to be part of one of the most prestigious dance companies in the country. Despite being one step closer to seeing those dreams come to fruition, external factors were slowly deteriorating the internal ones. Deep down, I knew I deserved to sign my name as much as anyone else who has come before me, but in the midst of everything going on around me, it didn't feel as sweet as it should.

Just at least try to savor it.

The promise weighed heavily on my heart.

The concept of instilling change felt foreign to me when change was typically met with failure. I didn't know how to move forward when fear was the only constant in that regard, and yet, it was in spite of this fear that I still wanted to see the seasons change. Not because of some silly pinky promise I made to Jin, but for myself.

The nature of a showcase was to build anticipation, generate press, and work out the kinks before opening night with an audience that was predominantly made up of media outlets and special guests. That didn't make the pre-showing any less stressful.

One step backstage, and that was evident.

Light technicians strung the lights on stage, fitting thick blackout curtains between each row of lights before hoisting them high into the air. A costume designer weaved through the crowd with rolling clothing racks bustling with sparkling outfits, nearly hitting a props coordinator whose head was peeking out over a tower of boxes stacked in his shaky arms. There was a certain type of hum in the air that was music to my ear as anticipation grew with each step.

Amongst the faces I recognized and the few I didn't, Anastasia seemed to appear out of thin air.

"Hi—"

The choreographer hooked her arm in mine and yanked me

in the opposite direction before I could make sense of what was happening. For a woman with such short legs, she moved surprisingly fast, and I had to match her stride for stride to keep up.

"Should I be concerned? Seeing that you are kidnapping me and all."

"Shh," she hissed. "I'm doing you a favor."

"I might be more appreciative if I knew what the favor was."

She didn't dare speak another word until we were standing outside my dressing room.

"Adeline, I say this not because I don't think you can't handle it, but because you need to be focused for tonight."

"Okay," I said wearily.

"The press isn't supposed to be invited backstage until after the showing, for whatever reason, someone thought it was a good idea to let a few of them in. Or maybe they snuck in. I don't know. This performance is important for both of our careers, and I don't want some damn journalist distracting you. I can handle any questions about the article, and"—she reached around me for the doorknob, then playfully pushed me into the dressing room—"in the meantime, I need you to get ready."

"What article are you even talking about?"

She blinked once—twice—then cursed under her breath, attempting to shove me back into the dressing room. "Forget I said anything. It is the least of your concerns, right—"

"Anastasia," I warned.

"Don't argue with me on this. If I can get a two-year-old having an all-out temper tantrum dressed in the morning, then a whiny twenty-two-year-old is nothing."

The constant back and forth was pointless when there was no winning with Anastasia. Frankly, she wouldn't be where she is today if she had simply rolled over someone who raised their voice at her. Those qualities were admirable for her position, but right now, I didn't particularly like them.

So instead of wasting another breath, I obliged, giving her the impression that I would play nice. It was only when left to my own devices that I snuck out of the theater, walked up to the newsstand on the corner of Hudson and Fifth, and bought a copy of the *Republic Press*.

On the fourth page, there it was, an article written by Bianca Riviera that made my heart stop.

"Killer Ballerina."

Chapter Thirty-One

Adeline

The newspaper article filled up two long columns of text with a tiny photo of the theater squished between them. And no matter how hard I tried, I couldn't bring myself to read beyond the title blotted in thick black ink. "Killer Ballerina." The name taunted me, rattling around inside my mind with such vigor that each time I heard the voice whisper it back to me, it felt like a migraine colliding against a fractured skull.

Over.

And over.

And over again.

With the newspaper tucked away in my coat pocket, I returned to the theater in time to start my preshow ritual. With too much riding on tonight's performance, I would be doing a disservice to not only myself but my peers by obsessing over the article—I had a promise that I intended to keep, after all. But my mind had another plan...

Each step.

Killer ballerina.

Each breath.

Killer ballerina.

Every plié.

Sullied by my own self-worth and the harrowing words of another, the article was at the forefront of my mind the entirety of warm-ups, burrowing itself so deeply into my brain that it was hard to differentiate her words from mine.

They all know.

The whispers were back and louder than ever.

Killer ballerina.

They're talking about you.

Killer ballerina.

They know what you did.

Killer.

Killer.

Killer.

Killer.

Killer.

Killer.

Killer.

I couldn't shake the word loose.

Killer.

Killer.

Killer.

Killer.

Killer.

Killer.

You killed Noah. And no one will ever believe you.

One promise.

I'd made one fucking promise to myself, and I couldn't even keep it.

It wasn't fair.

This performance was meant to be a fresh start. The chance to sign my name amongst the greats. An opportunity to prove my worth atop a stage that had always been my home when the concept was foreign.

I'll take one step on that stage, and they will all know.

Killer ballerina.

There was a knock at the dressing room door.

Long, angry streaks ran down my cheeks, smudging my foundation. I grabbed the closest brush and attempted to add a bit of blush to fix the problem, but it only made matters worse. If the puffy eyes weren't a dead ringer, then the empty smile would likely give me away if someone looked closely enough.

"Come in," I called over my shoulder.

Through the vanity mirror, I watched Jin peek his head inside the dressing room. It wasn't the bloodshot eyes or the poor attempt to hide it that caught his attention first; it was the dozens of bouquets cramped into the small room, each sent by various companies, partners, and nonprofits I had no idea knew my name, let alone would go out of their way to send me flowers for my *big night*.

"I guess I wasn't the only one with the same idea," Jin said, clutching a bouquet to his chest as he stepped inside.

"Are those for me?" I asked, lowering the brush to the vanity.

"I know it's only a showcase, but I figured..."

Delicately wrapped in brown kraft paper, the bundle of purple and white wildflowers branched out every which way. An explosion of heavenly scents and different textures all bound together in one heartwarming gesture.

"Thank you, Jin. They're beautiful," I said, setting them aside.

"I'm glad you like them. Caleb also bought you an apology

drink for missing your performance, but I figured you didn't want a warm beer—oh, it's okay, you can read that later," he croaked as I reached for the pink note hiding behind some lavender. "Really, you don't have to."

But I didn't listen, flipping open the small rectangular card.

Wildflowers are resilient. No matter the location, temperature, or lack of rainfall, they find a way to bloom. I know you've been through a lot this year, and sometimes it feels like you don't have the right conditions to keep growing, but whether you know it or not, you have always been a wildflower.

—Jin

My gaze slid from the card to a red-faced artistic director who was suddenly far more interested in staring at the ceiling than me, gawking up at him.

"Jin..." I breathed, then forced myself to reread the note.

Resilience was saved for those who earned it. It implied the capability to withstand immense amounts of pressure and still find a way to blossom. It suggested a strength I simply didn't possess. For years, I'd been worn down, beaten, chewed up, and spat out. I wasn't growing, no matter how hard I tried to reach for the sun—I was wilting.

Wasn't I?

A childhood filled with noise.

But you silenced it with dance.

A crumbling marriage that made you feel like it was your job to repair it.

But you moved away.

A broken sibling relationship that shamed you for being yourself.

But you cut her out of your life.

A dance partner who attempted to sabotage your career.

But you got right back up again.

A series of threats that wanted to take the only thing you've loved away.

But you danced harder.

A boyfriend who beat you verbally nearly as much as he did physically.

But you were trying to leave.

I kneaded the note between my fingers.

You have always been a wildflower.

Jin believed me to be, so why couldn't I do the same? Why must I put myself down every chance I got when, in reality, every time I had been shoved to the ground, I got right back up again? I was so focused on the fear and anxiety I felt during each circumstance that I'd been completely blind to my actions afterward.

Maybe that's what being resilient was after all.

"Jin," I mumbled. "Could you do me a favor? Please."

"Anything."

"Read this." I snatched the newspaper off the table. "The *Republic Press* wrote an article about me, and I'm too scared to do it myself, but the anxiety is distracting me so badly to the point that I don't think I can dance my best tonight without knowing what it says. I don't think it will make me feel much better, but if I just knew—"

"You don't have to explain yourself." We both paused. "You never have to with me."

"Okay," I rasped.

The subtle way his eyes shifted, widening at certain parts, made my stomach churn. I crossed my arms and began to pace, knowing that conditions didn't have to be right, but I couldn't stop growing. I had to do this for myself because I was allowed to be scared, but I was never allowed to give up—I just didn't have to look at him while he did it.

A hand landed on my back, and my eyes shot up.

"How bad is it?"

He held out the newspaper.

"I—"

"Trust me. You want to read it, sweetheart."

And because I trusted him more than anyone else who had stumbled in my life, I took the newspaper, flipped to the fourth page, and attempted to do what I couldn't bring myself to do all morning: I read past the words "Killer Ballerina."

"'The National Domestic Hotline reports,'" I read aloud, finding comfort that the words didn't have to live in my head if I expelled them as quickly as I read them, "'that one in four women over the age of eighteen in the United States have been a victim of physical violence by an intimate partner in their life-time—a stark contrast to one and seven men who will experi-ence the same. This unsettling statistic speaks to a reality in which women are in constant fear of being harmed by someone they love. In this disturbing context, twenty-two-year-old balle-rina Adeline Hartwell is under investigation for the death of her partner—'"

The mention of my name struck me in my chest with such force, I had to tilt my head back, shut my eyes, and take in breaths to the count of ten until I found it in myself to continue. His hand started moving in small circles along my back, grounding me to each breath taken.

"You can do this," he mumbled, leaning into me.

With one last count of ten, I opened my eyes and made the active choice to be the wildflower.

"'In this disturbing context,'" I tried again, "'twenty-two-year-old ballerina Adeline Hartwell is under investigation for the death of her partner, twenty-nine-year-old physical therapist

Noah Hernandez. Hartwell has gone on record, saying she acted in self-defense, but public opinion is vastly divided. Some condemn Hartwell for her alleged crime of passion, while others understand the troubling reality women face in this country.'"

His hand remained in place, as constant as his presence.

"'Artistic director of the Republic City Opera House, Jin Collins'"—my eyes shot to his and that heartbeat he held my gaze felt like a lifetime, it was only when he gave me a small nod, that I found it in myself to keep going—"'defended Hartwell, saying, "Miss Hartwell is by far the most compassionate dancer in my company and there's no reality she would have done what she did unless Noah deserved it. She's innocent—the bruises lining her neck are proof enough." A former partner of Hernandez, who wished to remain anonymous at this time, recalled his "violent outburst" and explained, "Noah never laid a hand on me, but I was always terrified of his bad temper, especially when he'd been drinking."

"'As her court date quickly approaches, one question remains: Is Hartwell yet another victim among the 500,000 women assaulted by an intimate partner each year? As the public eagerly watches this case, only time will tell whether or not Hartwell is a cold-blooded killer or a survivor finally speaking her truth,'" I finished, lowering the paper.

"You—" I released a shaky breath, then tried again. "When did she interview you?"

"She cornered me in a café the day you came back to work."

I huffed out a laugh, completely at odds with myself. "That was weeks ago. I hadn't even told you what had happened that night. And even now...you know next to nothing."

Trapped within his gaze with no hope of escape, he said, "You weren't part of my life as you are now, but that doesn't mean I didn't know the worth of your character."

Jin dared a step forward, taking the paper from my trembling hands.

"Since the moment you stepped into that audition and took my breath away, I've known exactly the woman you are, and every day I've been lucky enough to be part of your life has only confirmed what I already knew."

Another step, bringing us toe to toe now.

"I don't blame them for assuming the worst. The narrative being spun about that night doesn't paint me in the best light. I have so many regrets when it comes to being with Noah, but..." I huffed out a breath, turning away, hands on my hips. "Why did I have to fall for him when I knew it was wrong? Why was I so blind to the fact when I had every intention—" I couldn't bring myself to face him, but I sensed him tense up out of the corner of my eye. "The night of my audition, I went back to my hotel, as nervous as I was, and I couldn't stop thinking about the way your gaze burned into me. It felt like you had struck a match and smoothed its embers all over my flesh. Anastasia and the others were taking notes the entire audition, but I don't remember you picking up your pen once."

"I couldn't bring myself to write down a single note if it meant taking my eyes off you for one second."

"I couldn't get you out of my mind the entire time I packed up my belongings and moved across the country to pursue my dreams," I confessed, slightly raising my voice, frustrated as the past came rushing back all at once. "Then Noah somehow stumbled into my life. I—I don't know how it happened. I was constantly in his office and—before I knew what was happening, I was trapped. I'd become dependent on him for every aspect of my life. From my physical health, to my living arrangements, to my financial security. Leaving him and the theater meant losing it all."

I turned on my heels, the movement matching my growing frustration.

"I regret so much," I said, voice clipped.

A seawall can only endure so much of the storm. Each truth that tumbled from my lips felt like another lash of the sea, threatening to crumble the very foundation of my refuge. As I stood before Jin, breathless, stripped down to my barest vulnerability, I watched the last crack splinter the wall.

"I wish it were you..."

Jin opened his mouth, then shut it.

"I—" There was something so small and boyish about the way he took me in. He swallowed the lump in his throat and tried again. "We can't change the past, but I hope you know there could be a future for us despite everything that has happened in our lives."

I nearly laughed in his face, the deranged type of laughter that felt there was nothing I could do to stop it as it bubbled up my throat.

Addressing the past felt like standing in a rose garden, surrounded on all fronts. Each traumatic beginning manifested itself into a mess of thorns. If such a reality existed where escape was possible, it would mean wading through the roses, enduring each individual thorn that caught my skin and sliced me open to break free.

It meant reliving *everything* with each tickle of blood. Every open wound. Over and over again until either the rose bush prevailed, swallowing me whole in its labyrinth of branches, or I emerged on the other side with no guarantee I wouldn't succumb to the blood loss. It's hard enough to subjugate yourself to that level of torment...it was an entirely different beast to ask someone to willingly join.

"Is that the future you want, Jin?"

Do you want me, thorns and all, I nearly asked.

Beyond these dressing room walls was a world hell-bent on tearing us down. A myriad of uncontrollable circumstances had tangled us in a mess of lost faith. Despite that, in a world full of noise, I had finally found my silence.

The chatter backstage faded away like the tide lapping the shore before being pulled out to sea once more. The hiss of machinery came to a standstill. The relentless hum of music hit its final note as Jin trapped me in his gaze. Nothing beyond these walls mattered other than the small nod of his head and the way he breathlessly said, "I want everything."

Putting one foot in front of the other, I imagined parting through the rose bushes—thorns slashing across my raw skin. Blood soaking me bone deep. Putting my hand in his and making it out on the other side like I'd been dreaming of for far longer than I can remember.

As I closed the distance between us, I grabbed both sides of his face and crashed my lips against his, knowing I wanted whatever *everything* entailed.

As if he'd been anticipating me for a lifetime, there wasn't a moment of hesitation. He couldn't thread his finger through the hair lining the nape of my neck quickly enough, as if he didn't hold on tight enough, I might slip through his fingers.

Jin was as starved as I was famished.

Each nip of his front teeth along my bottom lip.

Each moan he breathed in.

Each bite of his nails.

It only fueled my hunger instead of satisfying it.

Desire was a curse I didn't know could be broken—the willful slaughter of joy in pursuit of wronged dignity. I assumed feeding into this inherent need would break me in the process, but I couldn't have been more wrong. Jin could shatter me into a thousand pieces, and I would thank him for it because to be starved meant to *feel* for the first time in more than half a year.

Not daring to break our connection, Jin lifted me by the backs of my thighs, and I instinctively wrapped my legs around his hips. The memory of him pressed against me was a familiar yet odd sensation that no midnight fantasy could anticipate. I'd only dreamt of his touch, and now that I could slip my tongue past the seam of his lips, I could finally make him unravel as badly as I had each night I had slid my fingers down my stomach to the mere thought of him across the hall.

Jin plopped me down on the vanity counter, making the cosmetics clatter against one another. My tutu awkwardly squished between our bodies. Desperate for more, Jin leaned forward, deepening our kiss. His erection brushed against my inner thighs.

I broke free, sucking in a sharp breath. The tights were thin enough that when he ground himself against the apex of my thighs, I could feel every inch of him.

He groaned. "I'm two seconds away from ripping these damn tights and fucking you."

"Jin," I moaned.

"Is that what you want, sweetheart? For me to make you come before you go on stage so you can dance in front of hundreds of people still aching for me."

The tutu made it impossible to watch the length of him grind against my sex. Instead, I watched Jin's brown eyes fill with wonder as he brushed his thumb over my clit. The sensation was a mere suggestion of what might be if he followed through on his threat and split my tights down the middle.

"Is that what you want, Adeline?"

"No." I leaned in, dragging my teeth over his bottom lip. "I want you to bend me over this vanity at the end of the night and tell me how good I did on stage."

"Get on your knees. I'm not sure I can wait until then."

I slid off the vanity and fell to Jin's feet.

There was a sort of frantic, feverous need embedded in his deep brown eyes as he attempted to unbuckle his belt. As his gaze slid to mine, he froze, sucked in a sharp breath, and the gravity of our situation settled in.

Reaching out a tentative hand, he caressed my cheek with his knuckle as if he were trying to commit the moment to memory.

"You're the most beautiful thing in my life," he sputtered.

Sitting on the back of my heels, I traced my hands up either thigh—never breaking his gaze the entire time.

"I need you, Jin," I rasped, my hands tracing up the planes of his muscular legs. Any sense of hesitation was gone in the blink of an eye as my fingers wrapped around his belt buckle.

"Stick out your tongue, sweetheart."

Despite being the one on my knees, it seemed I had all the power. Jin melted for me, turning into a trembling mess as he freed himself from his slacks and grasped the base of his shaft. In slow, leisurely motions, he stroked himself, completely bewitched by the sight of me, mouth open, ready for him.

"Good girl." Jin slapped the tip of his cock on the flat of my tongue, and I squeezed my thighs together, searching for the slightest sense of relief. I couldn't—

There was a knock at the door. "Five minutes to showtime."

We both froze, breathless.

Suddenly, the world around us came rushing back into focus.

I slowly pulled away, letting my tongue lap over the crown of his cock.

"Five minutes isn't enough time with you—not by a long shot. I want to take my time with you." Jin shut his eyes, took a big, deep breath in, then shook his head. "I'm sorry—I let things get out of control."

As much as I hated to admit it, Jin had a point. Reluctant to walk away from this when we were just getting started, I rose onto my tippy-toes and pressed a gentle kiss to his cheek. Jin only let me get a step away before pulling me back in for a kiss so amorous it made me nearly go back on everything we'd agreed to.

"Find me after the show," was all I said before exiting the dressing room and making my way backstage, knowing if I didn't, I might not make it on stage tonight.

Chapter Thirty-Two

Jin

The corps de ballet scurried to the edges of the stage, and the auditorium descended into total darkness. The soft pitter-patter of vamp against wood matched the racing of my heart as the darkness attempted to claw its way backstage. The rushed snap of the string of a violin splintered the air, cueing a single light center stage to banish the darkness away, bringing with it the light so painfully absent from the opening of act one.

It wasn't the small ornate crystal sewn to her bodice that made her dazzle, nor the spreading phlox spun into her ebony hair; it was that glowing smile of hers that radiated such warmth; it was an honor to be in her presence. I was utterly bewitched by her beauty, and by the way the crowd subtly leaned in closer to the stage, I knew they were under her spell, too—though she had trapped me long before.

The truth didn't always have the privilege of being known, but what a privilege it was to finally speak them aloud. To confess to Adeline that I'd been spellbound since the first moment she set foot in my studio.

And it seems I wasn't alone in that regard.

I wish it were you...

The past is woven in a manner that can never be unraveled, no matter how hard we try. The lord knows, there's nothing I wanted more than to tear apart the tattered stitches Noah left to rewrite our history—to create a tapestry of our own after that first audition, but life didn't work that way. All we can do in spite of the past is take that needle and thread in hand and see what beautiful art we create together.

To create a future not yet stitched together.

From my place beyond the velvet curtain, I could have spent a lifetime watching Adeline steal the hearts of her audience—the lord knows, she'd stolen mine. There was something so magical about watching her captivate the room one pirouette at a time, which was exactly why I had to leave.

Haloed by the fresco hanging high above, box five was close enough to kiss the heavens they depicted. I imagined it was why Blanchet chose the box each performance, if not to wine and dine his closest confidants, then for the arrogance of someone who found themselves worthy enough to be at home with these depictions—if you viewed box five at just the right angle, it appeared he was one with the painting itself.

Perhaps it was why he thought he was the exception and not the rule—why he let others take the blame for his actions. Blanchet saw himself as a god among men, but I saw him for what he truly was—a heretic.

I gave box five one final glance before slipping into the shadows.

Exclusive performances lived and died by the whim of the press. Legacies could be fortified with one article, then sworn to infamy by another. By intermission, the chatter that echoed off the lobby's high ceiling was always a good indication which way the pendulum would swing. Charles expected me to be his eyes and ears, then report back with my findings. Little did he know, while he may have my left, someone else was whispering into my right ear.

I assumed position on the outskirts of the lobby, Erick's instructions echoing in my head as I patiently waited for the doors to open and the press to file out.

Time isn't on our side. If this is our only chance to get answers, we'll have to bend time so it is.

Posed like little toy soldiers ready for battle, the ushers rushed for the five double doors lining the auditorium. At the stroke of seven, the doors opened. The roar of conversation filled the lobby as guests thumbed through their programs in passing; the name Adeline Hartwell seemed to be all anyone could be talking about. Stunning. Sensational. Exquisite. Ethereal. There weren't enough adjectives in the dictionary to encompass the raw talent Adeline possessed and how bright a future she had at her fingertips. I wished I could bottle up this moment and use it to banish every bad thought she'd ever uttered to herself when she thought I wasn't listening.

I would have loved to revel in it all had Lincoln Schutte not walked past me.

The *Daily Gazette* reporter strutted toward a group of old friends. One of whom playfully tugged on the graying strip in his beard. Lincoln lightly clasped him on the shoulder, tilted his head back, and laughed. All smiles and mirth compared to the last time he set foot in my theater.

Charles might have been the one to throw his invitation in the trash when I suggested inviting him after what had happened last season, but I was the one who fished it out.

The guests appeared before me like chess pieces moving across the board. I stood on the outskirts of the lobby identifying my pawns, rooks, bishops, knights, and king, calculating how each would bring me closer to victory. A particular guest I didn't recognize caught my attention as he walked in front of a rook I knew didn't stand a chance against Schutte. He moved with purpose, a glass of wine fisted in each hand as he cut across the lobby toward a woman he had his sights set on. Anticipating his next step, I kicked off the wall and met him where I needed him to be. With a slight bump of my shoulder, his plastic glasses went tumbling from his hands and collided with the carpet below, sending a spray of red wine splattering on Schutte's light gray suit.

Heads turned, and conversations stopped mid-sentence.

Those who were close enough to Schutte seemed to hold their breath as the reporter stared down at his stained suit, the look of shock bleeding into horror.

"You've got to be kidding me..."

"I—I'm sorry. It was an accident. Someone bumped into me," the man sputtered.

And for exactly the reason Schutte hadn't been invited for the fall season, he exploded. Apologies weren't enough to reverse whatever damage my little pawn had caused in Schutte's eyes. He continued pouring his frustrations out as the pawn struggled to utter another apology loud enough to be heard over the shouting. The pawn continued with no prevail, taking a step backward in defeat, but Schutte saw it as an opportunity to advance.

"Do you have any idea how much this suit costs?" he seethed.

"No. It was an accident. I swear."

Another step forward.

I hopped on the radio and called security and the custodian in one breath. If time was indeed not on our side, then we would simply have to kill two birds with one stone.

Mary, our lead custodian, answered the call first. The cart bustling with supplies jolted to a stop as she took in the reason

I'd called her. Her eyes darted between the red wine soaking the carpet and the two men trotting around in it.

"Give me one minute, I'll get this taken care of." I leaned in to speak over the shouting.

"Thank you, Mr. Collins."

A heartbeat later, two security guards burst out of the side door. While Mary's attention was drawn toward the commotion, I took the opportunity to unhook the keycard from her belt loop and slipped into the crowd forming around the pawn and the queen.

Each step further away felt like uttering a small prayer that putting my faith in Schutte hadn't been a mistake. Once I reached the side door, I ran. If this truly was our only opportunity to get answers, then there wasn't a moment to waste.

The adjoining hallway branching off from the lobby was a small, narrow space that, despite being well-lit by hanging fluorescent lights, felt dark and desolate. The walls started to close in on me as I followed the bend in the path, slamming my shoulder as I took the corner too quickly, nearly missing the security room altogether as I attempted to right myself.

"Fuck," I mumbled to myself as I frantically swiped the keycard. "Fuck. Fuck."

Another string of colorful curses left my lips as I shoved my way into the broom-closet-turned-security-room and found neither of the two monitors was logged into the surveillance system. The pop-up screen taunted me from afar as I tore apart what little there was in the room for any sign of a forgotten password. Searching the leaflets tacked to the bulletin board and scattered sticky notes tucked away in odd places proved to be a waste of time; each dead-end was another reminder of how little time there was.

My phone rang. I hit the speaker bottom, tossed it on the desk, and continued searching.

"March 2 at 7:35 a.m."

"Wait."

"March 10 at 7:15 a.m. March 11 at—"

"Erick," I barked, throwing open a drawer. "Give me a damn moment. I don't have the footage yet."

"And is there any particular reason why that is?" Erick bit out.

"Oh, you know, I just love wasting precious time," I shot back. "This is exactly what I want to be doing right now, searching like an idiot for something that might not even exist." The laugh that left my throat was robbed of all mirth, dry and strained, but the one that quickly followed was breathy and elated. Tucked beneath the discolored mousepad was a lonesome strip of paper smudged from years of use. "Shit. Okay. I found it."

K8DFH8c@PfvogB2

I typed in the password, the artistic director in me reeling at how easy it was to find from a safety standpoint. A few clicks later, I had the archived footage pulled up and ready to go.

"Give me the first date again."

"March 2," he paused, allowing me the chance to pull up the file, "7:35 a.m."

"7:25. 7:30," I muttered to myself as I dragged the cursor across the progress bar. "7:3—"

"What's the matter?"

"Nothing. Just—give me a second. Please," I fretted, watching the footage jump seventy-three minutes without an explanation. Thinking it must be a fluke, I called out, "What's the next date?"

"March 10 at 7:15 a.m."

And for whatever reason, the footage skipped forty-six minutes.

March 11 at 7:22 p.m.

Gone.

March 22 at 10:12 p.m.

Gone.

March 26.

Gone.

March 30.

April 3.

April 4.

All of it. Gone.

I reared back, fingers tugging at the roots of my hair.

As disappointing as the lost footage may be, it did prove one thing: we were on the right track. Someone had deliberately sliced the footage to keep whatever Reed and Charles were doing hidden. While we didn't have the answers we were looking for, it didn't mean there wasn't another means of discovering the truth.

It made me wonder what else had been scrubbed from the servers.

Clicking on the live footage tab, I toggled to the small square screen labeled lobby. One security guard had cornered Schutte near the entrance while a RCPD officer jotted down notes. My pawn sat on the foot of the stairs, an ice pack pressed to his cheek. There was one security guard, but where was the other? Bouncing from screen to screen, I found him passing the concession stand, nearing the side door.

"Erick," I rasped. "I have to go."

I hit the end call button, and not two seconds later, he was calling me back. I let my phone go to voicemail along with the other dozen or so unread messages. With time actively working against me, I used the last few minutes I could spare to do as someone had done before me and erase any footage of me entering the security room.

The guard threw open the door and stepped down the hallway on heavy feet.

The cursor hovered over the log out button, but the date March 11 roared in my ear.

Time ticked by at an impossible rate. The laws of physics were forgotten as I clicked back into the achieved footage and retrieved last month's folder. My eyes darted back and forth from the video to the live feed, showing the security guard approach the bend in the hallway. Rehearsal sped by in a blur, dancers left for home, and the theater was finally still. A small silhouette of a shadow popped on the corner of the screen at 9:35 p.m, and—

"Damn it," I muttered, exiting the video before I could get an answer.

The security guard turned the corner out of view, only giving me a few heartbeats to log out of the system, tuck the passcode back into place, and step out of the broom closet without notice. I called Erick back, if only to do something with my hands as our paths crossed.

"What the fuck do you think you're doing?" Erick answered as a way of greeting.

I kept my eyes trained forward.

"Mr. Robinson, I'm afraid there's nothing I can do about finding you seats for the upcoming opening. As of this moment, they're all gone, but perhaps if something comes up, you'll be the first one I call," I said. There was a long pause on the line, but eventually he was able to piece it together.

He cursed. "All of it?"

"Every last one."

Erick began rambling on about our next move and potential leads. An active mind is solemnly put to rest. I didn't hear a single word of it as I passed the security guard.

And his fading black eye.

Chapter Thirty-Three

Adeline

Every so often in life, we are blessed with a dash of introspection. The ability to be wholly present in a moment, yet have the foresight to understand the role this catalyst might play henceforth in our lives. The production of *Le Cœur Sauvage* sped by in a blur, the ballet so ingrained in my bones that it was second nature to slip into the beautifully tragic role of Carlotta and her lover. It wasn't until James took his hand in mine behind the velvet curtain that the weight of this moment finally sank in.

A roar of applause shook the foundation of the century-old building as we walked hand in hand on stage. A swell of emotions blossomed within my chest, and had I not been clutching James, I might have collapsed under the weight of my trembling legs. The winsome nature of it all was overwhelming in the best way possible. The cheers echoed off the painted ceilings, stretching to every corner of the room as James and I took a bow before an adoring crowd. I shut my eyes and savored the way the moment touched my every sense. The reassuring squeeze of his hand in mine. The bellowing applause of a job well done. The cool drip of sweat down my spine. The sweet aroma of bouquets being tossed at our feet.

It all spoke to a future I wanted so badly, more happy memories to cling to—the freedom to take a step forward instead of two steps back. I wanted to be the one to curate that future instead of sitting on the sidelines, desperately waiting for a miracle to take shape.

In pursuit of yet another happy memory for the night, I sought out Jin the moment I stepped off stage, expecting him to be right there waiting for me as promised, but he was nowhere to be found. Rising to my tippy-toes, I kept searching amongst all the smiling faces for the only one that mattered.

"Congrats," a soft voice said to my right.

As easily as slipping on a perfectly curated mask, I forced a smile and turned to congratulate Halle on a job well done. There was a slight rise and fall to her chest that suggested her post-show jitters had yet to wear off. Both of us were still buzzing from the thrill of performing center stage, yet despite that, there was little to say in return. A beat of silence passed between us; her eyes roaming over her pointe shoes as she chewed her lower lip.

"My mother—"

"Oh."

Halle sucked on her teeth. "She really wanted to make it, but a last-minute flight was pretty expensive. She told me to tell you that she wishes she were here to see us both and promises to come another time when money isn't tight."

"That's very sweet of her. I hope she's doing well."

The silence persisted.

"I was thinking..."

"Yes," I urged.

"We never did get that drink that you promised me," she

said, mindlessly picking at her nails. "Seeing that we have something to celebrate, I was thinking now might be the best time."

It was unclear what would repair the tattered edges of our friendship, but a night out might be exactly what we needed. Or at the very least, the alcohol would break some of the lingering tension we couldn't seem to shake off.

"I would really enjoy that, Hal," I said, offering her a genuine smile.

"Me too, Addie. I've really missed you."

"Ladies," a voice boomed, the single word laced with a strong accent.

Charles plucked the cigar from his lips and then planted a kiss on either cheek, the rough prickle of his scruff grinding against my skin. A cough bubbled in my throat as the crude smoke churned in my lungs.

"*Sensationnelle*," he praised in his native tongue. "I've never seen anything quite like it, *mon étoile*. You're going to make me a very wealthy man if you keep dancing like that on my stage."

"Thank you, Charles. You're too kind."

"No, I should be thanking you," he snorted.

With his attention zeroed on me, Halle tensed up on the outskirts of our conversation. Her eyes shifted from side to side in quick succession, as if she was searching for the perfect moment to slip away without notice.

"Really, I couldn't have done it without the rest of the dancers. We all put in such hard work to make the show what it is, right, Halle?"

"Without a doubt." She nodded, a little life returning to her eyes.

"I'd be more inclined to agree if the corps de ballet hadn't butchered the second half of the ballroom scene when Carlotta attempts to stab the king," Charles said, placing a hand on her shoulder. "Nothing Collins and Anastasia can't fix, right?"

She bit the inside of her cheek. "Yes, Mr. Blanchet."

"Speaking of Jin, have you seen him? I can't find him anywhere," I cut in.

"He's running around here somewhere. Why don't you two come with me while we wait for him to finish up? Jin will come find you when he can." He gestured to his right. "Come, *mon étoile*. I need to introduce you to some sponsors; they've been dying to meet you."

Inclined to keep searching for my artistic director, I decided to send him a quick text about my whereabouts instead, then followed Charles into the depths of the backstage area. If the price of stardom was shaking a few hands and faking a smile or two, then so be it.

Halle and I walked a few paces behind Charles. I lightly bumped my shoulder into her and leaned in to whisper, mimicking a terrible French accent, "I thought you were *sensationnelle*."

"Oh god," she groaned, rolling her eyes. "Not this again."

"I'm serious. You were incredible tonight, and I'm so freaking proud of you. Don't let him get under your skin like that."

The edges of reality blurred as Halle shot me a look that seemed reminiscent of the first time, I insisted she not let management get the best of her. And all the times after...

Noah had been spending Christmas with his family out of state, and neither Halle nor I could afford to fly home for the holidays. Opting to make the most of the off-season, we decided to spend the time together in the city. What should have been an incredibly lonely time of the year proved to be a fundamental shift in our friendship that I hadn't foreseen.

Halle swayed on the top step like a sailor standing on a ship's bow during a raging storm. I lunged forward, catching her before she could roll down the stairwell.

"I'm okay." She swatted my hand away. "I just need a moment."

The distant hum of "All I Want for Christmas" was barely audible. Halle leaned her head back against the cool concrete wall, shut her eyes, and hummed the tune.

"I want to go back to the company party. I was having fun."

"I love you, but I refuse to clean up your throw-up like last time," I said.

"I'm—I won't throw up," she slurred, cracking open one eye. "Promise."

"I don't think you want management to see you like this, Hal..."

"Or what? They won't promote me to soloist? Oh, wait, they already did that."

She slid down the wall, then curled her knees into her chest. I took a seat next to her on the step below.

"Hal—"

"No," she sniffled, swiping the back of her hand over her cheek. I'd never seen her cry before and was a little taken aback by the way she shuddered. Not sure how else to soothe her, I ran my hand up and down her arm to let her know I was here. "I feel like I keep failing her over and over again."

"Failing who? Yourself?"

"My mom." She laughed, but it was robbed of all mirth. "She gave up everything so I could move to the district and chase my dreams. I promised to pay her back, but she told me it was okay. That if one of us was going to achieve our dreams, she wanted it to be me. I—" She cursed under her breath. The single word bounced off the tall concrete walls. "I wouldn't have taken it had I known how bad things had gotten with her and my stepfather. She never told me—we told each other everything."

"Do you want to talk about it?" I asked gently. "Talking sometimes helps."

She exhaled. "My little brother called me last week and told me he overheard her calling a divorce lawyer while Steven was at work. I guess she can't afford to leave him, and now she is more than content with suffering in silence if it means seeing my dreams come to fruition. I feel like the worst person ever. I can't pay her back because I already spent all the money moving here. Adeline—it just doesn't feel like enough when each season passes by, and I'm still stuck in the same role."

Any advice I could offer didn't feel earnest when I hardly knew how to help myself, let alone another, but I tried, nonetheless.

"You shouldn't blame yourself for the decisions of others. Those were her choices, not yours, Hal." Her eyes darted back and forth as if she were trying to keep the tears from spilling free. "Your mother is actively choosing to make a sacrifice for her children because she loves you. And while you might not be able to change what's already been done, there are ways you can be there for her while you figure out your next step moving forward. One day, management will see how amazing you are—"

Halle shot me a look, not entirely convinced.

"—and you'll be able to help her in whatever ways she needs to leave your stepfather, but until then, stop beating yourself up for this."

"Easier said than done," she huffed out.

"Doesn't make it any less true."

I blinked several times, banishing the memory.

It took the last of her energy to muster up a smile, but when she finally did, it was the brightest thing I'd seen in quite some time. From then on, it seemed impossible to wipe it off her face as we shouldered our way through the narrow hallway teeming with staff celebrating the show.

There was a certain thrum pulsating in the air, a tantalizing sense of energy that lulled me into submission. Department leads lifted their red cups to a backdrop of sharp whistles and drunken cheers. Laughter bounced off the brick walls as bottles were passed between friends. Halle got dragged into a toast by another dancer she was close with, leaving me behind. After weeks of heartache and loss, everyone seemed desperate to cling to any sense of normalcy that could potentially numb their pain. Despite tonight only being the beginning of our upcoming season, everyone celebrated as if it were our last.

Charles turned the corner and led us toward the greenroom.

Reserved primarily for guest performers, the room had been repurposed for the night's festivities. Dancer and staff alike piled into the room, rubbing shoulders with men dressed in their finest suits who partook in cheap thrills that came in a variety of different flavors. Some picked their vices carefully, sampling the brightly colored bottles stacked on the rolling utility cart, some tried their luck with the dancers who caught their eye, while others spread their vices into thin white lines atop polished mirrors, not caring who saw.

Some seemed to be at home in the chaos. I, on the other hand, had enough chaos going on in my head at any given point that I didn't care about creating more of it. Before I could even begin to think up an excuse to leave, a flute of champagne materialized before me.

"Every time our paths cross, you seem to be offering me a drink," Charles chuckled, accepting the glass. "Careful, or I might get used to it."

"Most people wouldn't complain about that," the older gentleman replied.

"Adeline, you remember Sebastian Gonzalez, owner of the Starling Dance Company."

"Yes, of course," I said, accepting the drink to be nice. "How could I not? I think the bottle of wine you sent us might have ruined all other wines for me in the future."

"A good bottle of wine could never be wasted on a star like you, Ms. Hartwell."

Charles clasped a hand on his shoulder. "If you'll both excuse me for a moment."

The crowd swallowed him up. The only sign that he was still there was the roar of laughter and cheers that soon followed, leaving Sebastian and me to our own devices. I took a tentative sip of champagne, if only to do something with my hands.

"I must say, you were exceptional tonight. I couldn't take my eyes off you," Sebastian praised. "If Charles isn't careful, I might steal you right out from under his nose. Talent like yours doesn't come around very often. I see principal in your future one day, Adeline."

"Oh, thank you so much, but I'm still very young and have much to learn. I'm sure in time I'll prove myself to take on such an important role within this company."

Someone shrieked with laughter as a man in a suit dragged one of the dancers into his lap. She slapped her hand on his chest playfully, but made no effort to remove herself. I shifted from one foot to the other, trying to drown out the noise.

"Talented and humble," he snorted, taking a long sip of his drink. "A rare trait to find in a place like this."

"What do you mean by that?"

"Perhaps you've heard the rumors about the Financial District," he started, then gestured toward the men congregating around their vices. "Well, I guess they aren't quite rumors. Charles has always loved to surround himself with important people who gorge themselves on cheap thrills. They're much easier to manipulate that way, aren't they?"

I wasn't sure what he was implying, but he continued speaking as if I did.

"They stuff themselves into their overpriced suits, fill up on tiny hors d'oeuvres, and suffer through a two- to three-hour show with something else in mind to make it all worth it. It never truly is about the love for the arts, wouldn't you say?" he continued, gazing out at the very men he had berated. "I can't even begin to tell you how many business deals have lived and died between these walls, but that's the secret, Adeline, someone is much more likely to say yes when the person you have in your crosshairs isn't seeing you through sober eyes. The sneaky bastard knows what he wants; it's just a matter of waiting until he can get his chance to strike."

I followed his line of sight. Charles was shaking hands and trading business cards.

"I thought you and Charles were friends?"

"Friend is a strong word—associate might be more fitting."

"Then why are you here if you aren't so fond of his business methods, Mr. Gonzalez?"

"Just because I don't like to partake, it doesn't mean I can't indulge a little fun." He smiled down at me.

A burst of movements sped by out of the corner of my eye. The shadow raced by too quickly down the hall for any form to take shape. Rubber shrieked across linoleum flooring, then a heartbeat later, I got my answer.

Jin appeared in the doorway, slicking a rogue hair back into place.

Our eyes clashed from across the room. It was as if I were stepping back on stage, the trajectory of my heart rate skyrocketing, sweat licking down my spine, something akin to being drenched in the glow of a spotlight warmed me down to the bones. There was no other thrill like being pinned beneath Jin's stare, not even performing before a sold-out theater.

"I'm sorry. Please excuse me," I said to Sebastian, never taking my eyes off Jin.

Relief swept me off my feet and dragged me right into his arms. Not caring that we had an audience, I threw my arms around his neck and felt weightless as he spun us in a small circle.

"I don't even have words to describe it, Adeline," he breathed into my neck, gently lowering me to the ground.

"I know." I was back on solid ground, but I made no effort to let go of him. "It was exhilarating. I don't think I've ever danced like that in my entire career."

"I'm so damn proud of you—" Jin's attention flickered over my shoulder, the soft edges of his smile faltering. I turned, following his line of sight. Charles watched us from across the room with an expression I couldn't put a name to. Those piercing blue eyes of his were robbed of any light, a stark contrast to the room, which was bustling with joy and laughter. The shape of his silhouette resembled that of a tenebrism painting, highlighting how intently he studied our interaction.

An intern cut in front of me, obscuring my view.

When the path was cleared, Charles was offering a lighter to a colleague with a cigar pressed between his lips, making me wonder if I was seeing things again. The colleague presented himself in a far more casual manner than the rest. Suit jacket long forgotten, buttons undone on his cornflower blue dress shirt. There was a carefree spirit about him that, like the breeze cutting through a field of wheat.

Much more relaxed compared to the last time our paths crossed on stage.

The man I presumed to be Josephine's father clung to Charles as they moved about the room, greeting men who were borderline feverous to shake his hand. Each interaction was straightforward, brief, and uneventful. It was the way the businessmen left that interaction to find their polished mirrors or pile into the adjoining bathroom that had me questioning the nature of their business.

"You know, I'd heard stories," I said, peering out to the

crowd, filling their carnal desire, "about backstage parties, but I never imagined it would be anything like this. I figured most of them were rumors."

Jin signed, drawing his attention back to me. "It's part of the reason I've been wanting to leave for so long. I've always hated how he insisted on securing sponsorships, and I sure as hell don't appreciate the way his *friends* treat the dancers."

Desire came in many forms, and it appeared the guests from the Financial District weren't the only ones having their fill. The corps de ballet was just as guilty, whispering in the ears of the men stuffing Charles's pockets, sneaking off to darkened corners of the theater, or partaking out in the open for anyone to see.

Vickie, a new dancer to the company, was sandwiched between two men on the velvet couch. Crawling over one of them, she brought an older gentleman's knuckles to her nose and snorted whatever substance dusted his skin. I looked away as the man she had crawled over took the opportunity to drag her more firmly into his awaiting lap. Vickie seemed to be enjoying herself, but the entire interaction rubbed me the wrong way—especially if she wasn't of sound mind. When I mouthed the words *are you okay?* She nodded her head and smiled, but I made a mental note to ask Jin if we could give her a ride home regardless, to make sure she made it home safely.

"I had no idea it was like this," I admitted.

"As much as I hated Noah, the only good thing he ever did for you was keep you away from this side of the company. I'm assuming he always made you get dressed and leave as soon as the show was over." I nodded. "Even if it was probably because he was a jealous bastard, he was protecting you from this."

"Perhaps that was the only good thing to come out of that relationship," I said, toying with the rim of my glass. "He would call me a cab right after the show only to stay himself...it makes me wonder how many others there were before Tatiana."

"Addie," he said in such a gentle tone that it made my heart quicken.

"Yes."

"You and I both know, this isn't how you want to be spending your special night. So, tell me, if you could be anywhere else, where would you want to be right now?"

"Take me home."

Distant memories clung to me, such as shadows stretching at high noon, impossible to outrun and constantly nipping at my heels. Darkness was their greatest confidant, hiding in plain sight until they lashed out when you least expected it, like demonic entities taking possession of a soul. Jin, despite not having any shadows that I was aware of, seemed to understand how they drained me. He simply took my hand and led me back to the dressing rooms to collect my belongings to keep the shadows at bay.

The more distance between me and that greenroom, the easier it was to breathe. By the time I was pointing out Jin's car in the structure to Vickie, a twinge of pride had settled deep within my chest for keeping the past exactly where it belonged —behind me.

Vickie lived several blocks past our complex. We dropped her off, tucked her into bed with the help of her roommate, then backtracked home.

Republic City was a vibrant cityscape that breathed with life—a melting pot of different people and cultures. With millions calling this place home, there was no shortage of noise to fill the cool night air. Yet when we stepped into the apartment, it was eerily still. There was no relentless hum of traffic, distant honking accompanied by the wail of sirens, or even the thunderous backfire of an old car echoing off the skyscrapers. The outside world felt a million miles away as the door clicked behind us.

"I have champagne, or if you're feeling adventurous, Caleb's warm beer is still up for grabs."

"Um, champagne is fine," I said, placing my dance bag on the tiled floor.

The pop reverberated through the air. Jin made quick work in the kitchen; the sound of him shuffling about was drowned out by the cascade of running water. As I waited for it to warm up, I tossed over my shoulder, "I'm just going to take a quick shower."

"I can see that," Jin said, his silky voice dangerously close. I whipped my head around, and there stood Jin in all his glory, leaning up against the doorframe, a flute in each hand.

Neither of us had dared to breathe a word of the dressing room, painfully going about our night, dissecting the performance act by act as if Jin hadn't laid his cock on the flat of my tongue with every intention to choke down every inch of him mere moments before I danced on stage.

Oh, god. What was I doing to myself?

"Hi."

He smirked. "Hi."

My heart fluttered out of rhythm.

This was pure torture—agonizing, relentless torture of voluntary exposure. I had no other but myself to blame when I'd starved myself of him for so long, blatantly denying this feverous attraction only to feed off whatever scraps of his affection I could in order to take pleasure into my own hand, only to deepen this need beyond recognition. How could I ignore this any longer, knowing firsthand how empowering it was to get down on my knees and see him melt for me?

Ever so gently, I plucked the flutes from his hands, took a long sip as the bubbles tickled my nose, then prayed it was enough to give me the courage needed for what was to come next.

"Champagne wasn't exactly how I imagined celebrating tonight," I rasped.

Jin stepped forward, eating away at the space between us. The bathroom was already tiny as it is, but with him encroaching on my space, I felt like we were being crammed into a dollhouse half our size.

"And what exactly did you have in mind?" he asked in a low, gravelly voice that seemed to slither itself over each individual goosebump prickling my flushed skin.

"You never found me after the show."

He dragged his teeth over his bottom lip in an attempt to bite back a smile, but failed terribly when a breathy laugh crawled up his throat like he was both a little taken aback and impressed by my boldness.

"Technically speaking, I did find you in the greenroom after the show, but..."

The language of touch had always been lost on us—a forbidden sense of longing that took shape in alignment and accidental run-ins, always wishing there was more. Jin ate the distance between us and brushed the back of his knuckles along the underside of my jaw. We were finally able to give in to this compulsion, and I didn't think I would ever tire of the way his touch felt against my skin. "There were too many people around to properly congratulate you like I intended to."

"Tell me how good I was tonight," I commanded softly.

Hooking his index finger under my chin, he leaned in to meet me halfway. His every word was a featherlike touch against my lips. "Adeline," he said in a tone that resembled the desperate nature of a suppressed groan, "I considered quitting my job right there on the spot so I could spend every waking moment of the rest of my life sitting front row and watching you grace that stage with your presence."

"If you did that, then how would I get to live out my fantasy of fucking my artistic director?" I mumbled against his lips. "It would be such a travesty—"

The words died on the tip of my tongue as Jin crashed his lips against mine. The rushed, desperate nature of the kiss was akin to sucking down the last sip of water on the brink of dehydration. It was desperate, calculated, and filled with such longing that I never imagined a time I would grow accustomed to how it felt to be his at last.

"What a filthy little mouth you have," he said, scraping his teeth over my bottom lip. "It's always the quiet ones with the dirtiest minds."

Words failed me as my mind went a little hazy. The edges of my confession were getting lost in the wind as Jin deepened the kiss. All I could do was wrap my arms around his neck, cling to him for dear life, and revel in the way his hand explored on its own accord, memorizing the shape of my spine as it arched into him.

"How many other little fantasies have you been hiding from me?"

I chuckled. "There's no way in hell I'm telling you that."

Hooking his hand around the back side of my waist, the other hand braced on my shoulder, Jin spun me so quickly it felt like being trapped in the tail end of a pirouette. My hip bones smacked against the sink counter in a delicious ripple of pain, the sensation echoing through my bones as Jin pinned me in place with his broad frame, then leaned in to move my loose curls off my shoulder.

"It's not your vanity but..." I could hear the smile in his voice as his lips caressed the side of my neck.

"As long as you promise—" I choked out a moan as he ground himself against the small of my back. "Just promise me someday."

"Soon, sweetheart," he promised with a trail of kisses down my neck, exploring the shape of my body with the familiarity of a lover. One hand slipped beneath my tank top, the other toying with the waistband of my leggings. It was as if, despite the few times we'd explored this forbidden side of our friendship, he knew what to do to bend me to his will. "Let's make a deal. Tell me all the little fantasies you've ever had about me, and I'll make sure to return the favor."

With sedulous effort, I took his wrist and guided him down my torso, inch by devastating inch. His reflection spoke of a man riddled by lust, practically shaking with need at the sight of his hand dipped between my thighs.

"Besides the fact that anyone can catch us in the act—" Though I couldn't bring myself to admit it, in the midst of a relationship I couldn't escape, daydreaming was sometimes the only means of doing so. I would imagine a reality in which Noah and I never were, and a certain artistic director found me alone in the dressing rooms, well past closing time. Desire, the temptress she was, knew this unspoken connection between us was a ticking clock—minute by minute, second by second, bringing us closer to the inevitable. Jin would bend me over that damn vanity and show me just how good a dancer I truly was. "—the entire allure of the vanity is that I get to watch."

"Do you like the idea of watching someone fuck you, Adeline?"

"Just you," I breathed, grinding my ass against his lap, desperate for friction. "I've imagined what it might be like for so long, I want to see it for myself when you finally make me come."

Jin proved me wrong a second later.

This fervent need hit its crescendo as his finger brushed against my aching clit. A look of relief struck his features as if he, too, had been holding his breath since the first day we met. I realized it wasn't my pleasure I was searching for; it was watching him unravel on my behalf.

"Fuck," I groaned, tipping my head back against his shoulder.

Steam clung to the air, making the edges of the mirror nearly as foggy as my head. The steam slowly worked its way toward the center of the mirror, leaving a small sliver of space that showed our shared reflection with such clarity it felt as if I was glimpsing into our future.

All that could be between us if we simply gave in.

"Such a good fucking girl," he purred, hot against my ear.

"Jin," I begged, squirming in his hold as my legs began to tremble.

"You can handle it, sweetheart. Can you do that for me?"

Pleasure and pain married as one as his hands worked in tandem. I slapped my hands on the counter to keep steady as another tremor rocked through me. Before I was even aware that my middle finger had hit the glass, the first champagne flute collided with the other, falling like a row of dominoes. A sharp click silenced us both—Jin was quick but not quick enough, as the second champagne flute rolled off the edge of the counter and exploded at our feet.

"Goddamn it," a familiar voice echoed.

"I—I didn't mean to. I'm sorry," I shuddered.

Shattered glass littered the kitchen floor.

What had once been an apology from an argument long forgotten now sprawled before me in a heap of wilting limo-

niums and tattered roses. Careful not to slice my already aching knees, I lowered myself to the wood floor and started the strenuous process of cleaning up yet another one of Noah's messes.

"Don't move," the voice snapped.

It seemed like lately, I was constantly picking up the pieces between us. Grappling at the tiny shards of glass all while frantically trying to mend them back together, salvaging what little I could. It didn't take long after moving in six months ago to learn that burden was mine, and mine alone.

What Noah and I had was something akin to a dying flame—

A pair of hands grabbed my face.

"Adeline."

The edges of my vision snapped back into focus. Jin stared down at me with eyes so dilated they looked like a bottomless pit. I blinked rapidly, trying to piece together why Jin was here, kneeling on my kitchen floor.

"You're bleeding," I rasped, reaching out to where he knelt in the glass.

"Don't worry about me," he said in a gentle but firm tone. "I need to make sure you're okay."

It took several blinks to make sense of my reality—to remember where the past and present lived. My vision turned hazy as I attempted to pull out of his hold. Jin, refusing to let go, pulled me closer, wrapping his arms around me in a crushing embrace.

"It—" I hiccuped against his chest. "I couldn't make sense of what was happening. It felt like I was back with him. I thought—"

Every muscle in my body stiffened as the footfalls grew closer. Trapped in the corner of the kitchen, there was little I could do as Noah approached me from behind, snaked his arms around my middle, and gently burrowed his face in my neck.

"It's time to come to bed, love," he whispered, dragging his chapped lips along my skin. *"Please, Adeline."*

"Take a deep breath," Jin said, mimicking the actions.

I sucked in a breath to his count, then released it.

"Good," he coached.

It took several deep breaths to return to baseline, and when I did, Jin was there to lighten the mood and offer a shoulder to cry on. Jin was there by my side as I banished the past away to make room for the future.

Once I managed to regain control of my emotions, Jin left me to shower as he disposed of the broken glass. When I finished washing the grime of the show off my body, I emerged into the living room to find him sitting on the couch, waiting for me amongst a heap of blankets, bubbling champagne, and an ice pack for my knee. I spent the rest of the night curled up next to Jin on the couch until we fell asleep in each other's arms.

I was grateful that for the rest of the night, the past stayed where it belonged.

Chapter Thirty-Four

Jin

Over the course of the last few years, life had felt like standing in an undercurrent—swept away with no egress. Unable to see it for what it truly was, I thought the current was doing me a favor, taking me from point A to Point B with little fuss. But that's the thing about the current, it never truly feels like a threat until suddenly your head is underwater. Part of me had come to terms with the fact that I might not have the strength to fight it any longer, then a certain ballerina stumbled into my life, and I was suddenly determined to make it back to shore.

The sound of sizzling bacon and clanking pans woke me up. With no recollection of how I ended up in the living room, memories of last night slowly started to piece themselves together until I could make sense of why I was curled up on the couch with only a small knitted blanket to keep me warm.

Another bang echoed in the kitchen, followed by a mumbled curse. I peeked my head over the cushion, rubbing the sleep from my eyes. The blurry silhouette of a figure danced about the kitchen, clothed in a heather gray branded hoodie from my boxing studio—which I had tossed on the floor in the middle of the night—and a pair of pink cotton shorts. Adeline was already glowing with the rising sun, but as she noticed me peeking over the couch, I had no idea how she could be any more stunning. The smile that radiated from her made me want to take the knife right out of her hands, carve out my heart, and hand it over to her, because there was no reality in which it wasn't already hers.

"I hope you're hungry," she said, flipping a lopsided pancake.

With a big stretch and a shaky yawn, I patted over on bare feet to Adeline, wrapped my arms around her middle, and placed my chin atop her head. "Morning," I said groggily.

"You're distracting me," she said, squirming in my hold. "I'm going to burn them."

"I think they might already be ruined."

Adeline choked out a wounded scoff, then playfully smacked me with the spatula.

"Go sit down, or you aren't getting a plate. And I made some damn good homemade orange juice."

Choosing the most honorable choice of the two—not because the slices of oranges on the cutting board looked divine —I took a seat at the island and watched Adeline get to work. The antithesis between Adeline's craft of dance and her cooking was striking. While dance required precision and discipline, the way she moved about the kitchen was insouciant.

"Did you see Anastasia's message on Teams?" she shot over her shoulder.

"Yeah, she must really be struggling this morning if she pushed back rehearsal."

"Well, the last time I saw her, her husband was trying to trade her bottle of champagne for a glass of water, so..." Adeline said, depositing a plate teeming with crispy applewood-smoked bacon, cheesy scrambled eggs, and one lumpy pancake in front of me.

"Thank you. It looks delicious," I said, unable to control myself as I grabbed her by the waist and pulled her into my lap. I kissed her temple, and she melted into me as she had on the couch last night. "Now that we're pushing back rehearsals, today might be the perfect time for our do-over. What do you think?"

"My lawyer scheduled a video call with me in thirty minutes. If you don't mind waiting—I have no idea how long it will be—then yes, I would love to."

"Not a problem, take all the time you need," I said, planting another kiss. "I think you underestimate just how long I've been waiting for this. I can be patient for a little while longer."

The meeting had taken something from her in return. It had chewed her up and spat her out two and a half hours later when she emerged from her bedroom with exhaustion written all over her face. Adeline attempted to collect herself, slapping on her bravest face for the evening.

"We don't have to go," I'd said.

"Please, I need this. I don't want it to ruin my day."

And with that, we sped off uptown with the promise that what I had in store would be enough to turn her day around—or so I hoped.

Delten Botanical Gardens was divided into different subsections that showcased the various flora and fauna from around the world: one hundred and thirty acres with sixteen gardens to walk through hand in hand. From the perfectly curated bonsai courtyards of the Japanese gardens, to the colorful Koi fish disappearing beneath lily pads, to the replicas of ancient Greek statues erected in the rose garden, we soaked up every square inch of the space. Yet in a world designed to awe its audience with vibrant colors and rich culture, Adeline was still the most stunning creature I'd ever laid my eyes on.

Little by little, I noticed her start to perk up. However, it took wandering around several gardens and an overpriced iced coffee to get a hint of a smile on her face, and even then, it didn't feel like enough.

Between the rose garden and visitor center sat a massive, domed conservatory. The glass double doors, which had been blocked by a metal A-frame, read, "Temporarily Closed — Visit Again Soon!" Adeline hadn't dared to voice her disappointment each time we passed the building, but it was the subtle sweep of hazy eyes that spoke true. With only thirty minutes until closing time, I didn't have the heart to tell her it wasn't likely the greenhouse would be opening today. Though that didn't stop me from grabbing her hand and steering us toward the glass exterior.

"What are you doing?" she whispered, trying to keep up with me.

I shushed her. "Someone will hear us."

Beyond the large glass doors was like stepping into another world. Misty glass panels stretched up to the heavens, where a massive dome circled overhead. Tropical foliage covered every square inch in lively shades of greens and exotic-looking flowers. The humidity instantly clung to my skin as we stepped into the lush greenery.

Standing in the center of the conservatory, Adeline spun in a small circle, eyes roaming over the dome looming above. The hem of her black sundress lapped over her bare thighs.

"I think you might have outdone yourself." A smile tugged at the corner of her lips.

"Nothing says 'first date' like a little trespassing," I joked. While there was no harm in sneaking into a closed exhibit, that didn't stop me from taking a spare metal A-frame and placing it in front of the entrance to give us a warning in case anyone returned. "Next time, we can rob a bank or try our hand at espionage."

She paused.

"I'm not sure adding to my criminal record would be best." Adeline laughed, but it was the kind of laughter that tapered off far too quickly, nothing earnest about it.

"Is there something on your mind?"

She opened her mouth, then snapped it shut. I wasn't quite sure what was rattling around in her head, but by the look of it, it seemed as if she was waging a war with herself. I gave her a moment to search for whatever words were lost to her.

"I was thinking..."

"Yes?"

She huffed out a frustrated breath.

"I can't help thinking we shouldn't be doing this." She gestured between us. "We shouldn't be taking these chances."

"I'm sure all they'll do is give us a slap on the wrist for breaking into the greenhouse, but we can leave if you feel uncomfortable being here."

"No, I'm not talking about that," she interjected. "I'm talking about us."

"Us...?"

It would have been less painful had Adeline carved the single word into my flesh with a serrated blade. As easily as it might have been to lie there and take it as she broke skin, the shift in her demeanor was too sudden to have been a coincidence after all we'd shared. None of this made any sense.

Did the lawyers say something to get into her head, or was this about him...

"Us?" A laugh bubbled up my throat. "Okay."

"Jin..."

"If I did anything to make you think I wasn't taking us seriously, then I'm sorry. If I'm being honest with you, this was never about sex for me. What happened last night was—"

"No, Jin, it's not that," she interrupted. "It's—Um."

She took a moment to collect her thoughts, then said, "I'm terrified things might change after the trial...I'm scared you are going to finally realize how much of a mistake this was, and I don't want to put either of us in a position to get hurt when we are already dangerously toeing this line. Donovan, my lawyer, found out from a colleague at another firm that Noah's prosecutor pinned down a witness that might sway the entire trial."

"Adeline," I rasped. "Do you think some silly trial will change how I feel about you?"

Her silence was confirmation enough. It took everything not to close the distance between us and wrap her tight in my arms, but I didn't dare move an inch.

"Even if I'm found innocent, that doesn't erase the fact that I—that I killed a man." The confession sounded rough and gravelly coming from her lips, as if it had been the first time she'd spoken it into existence. I already suspected enough, but I needed to hear it from her lips to know for certain. Adeline Hartwell might have washed her hands clean of that night, but by the way she carried herself, I could tell there was still so much she was suppressing about that night.

"Do you feel guilty for what happened that night?"

"You don't understand, someone had to scrub his blood off me in a holding cell," she said, her eyes vacant, lost in that haunting memory. "I try not to think about that night. Noah didn't deserve that...I don't think anyone does..."

"And if you hadn't stopped him, then what?"

She stared at me, expression unmoving.

"Answer me truthfully: if you hadn't stopped him, would you be standing here today?" Again, silence told more of the truth than she wasn't wholly capable of saying aloud. "You may not believe it today, maybe not even tomorrow, but one day, you'll realize the truth. You'll realize Noah deserved everything that happened to him."

Her eyes slightly widened. "But—"

"People who are willing to hurt the people they claim to love over and over again aren't innocent, no matter how many times they beg for forgiveness. Truly, it breaks my heart to know you're carrying the burden of his death on your shoulders, and I wish more than anything you could see yourself as I do—as a survivor."

"I'm *not* a survivor," she scoffed.

Okay, we were finally doing this.

"And what was Noah doing to you before his death?"

She mumbled something under her breath that I couldn't make out.

"What?"

"Choking me," she snapped. "He was choking me, Jin."

"Adeline."

My gaze fell to her neck. The bruise was long forgotten, but not the memory of the shifting bruises wrapped around her throat like Noah still had her in his clutches.

Adeline noticed me staring. She wrapped herself in her arms and turned away.

"Sweetheart."

I shut my eyes and tried again. "I wasn't there, but the way you are explaining it sounds like it was either you or him. If you hadn't done what you did, do you truly think Noah would have let go?"

She exhaled. "It felt like I was drowning on dry land."

"I can't even begin to imagine what you've been through, and it breaks my heart that you are shouldering all this pain and guilt when what you did was incredibly brave.

I hate seeing Noah continue to take from you despite being gone."

"He's gone, and I still can't escape him," she admitted. "He's always there to remind me that I don't deserve to be happy whenever I'm near you. Right now, he's rotting in some gaudy coffin his mother probably picked out, and yet, when I finally get my chance to be happy, I get assaulted over and over again by the memory of him as if he were still here to lay his hands on me. I can't outrun it. I can't outrun *him*."

"It doesn't have to be this way, Adeline. You don't have to fight these battles alone; we can do it together. We can keep the memory of him at bay. You deserve so much more than you give yourself credit for, and all I wish more than anything is for you to believe it as much as I do. There's such a bright future ahead of you, and whether or not I'm a part of it, I want you to be happy."

"I want you to be a part of it so badly it hurts thinking about it." Her throat worked. "I just don't know what I can offer you at this point in my life. I see the way you look at me. You want *more*, and I can't bear the thought of you wasting your time waiting for me to heal from this. It could be years before I truly recover from the damage Noah left behind. It's not fair because you deserve to be happy."

Little did she know, I didn't know true happiness until she entered my life.

The pieces of Adeline's past were slowly taking shape. The little I knew painted a picture of mental coercion and manipulation tactics to keep her trapped within Noah's clutches.

Despite this all-consuming desire burning between us, I knew she wasn't in a position to jump into a new relationship with wounds this fresh—nor would I ever want to rush her into one when it was likely how she ended up with Noah mere weeks after moving to the city. Adeline needed the power of choice—the ability to feel in control after such a basic right had been stripped from her.

She deserved autonomy.

"What if we...had a trial run?" She raised an eyebrow. "I'm going to be frank with you. After what we did last night, I don't see a reality in which either of us can leave this greenhouse and saunter back into our normal lives as roommates and pretend nothing ever happened. It was already painful enough to be in the same room as you before I knew the feeling of your touch, and now...As I said, there's something between us. Something *strong*. What if we eased into whatever's forming between us with a trial run, kind of like before you decided to move in?"

Adeline snorted. "Isn't dating already a trial run of sorts?"

"Don't laugh. I'm being serious." I chuckled. "It will be all the fun of a relationship without any of the pressure. You'd have all the control over where we go from there."

"Still sounds like a lot of pressure to hold that much power over both of us. I think you forgot how this entire anxiety thing works," she said, chewing the inside of her cheek. "What happens if we start this *trial run* and realize down the road it wasn't the right choice? Then what?"

"Then I'll personally box up your belongings and take them to Caleb's apartment. You can stay there as long as you need, and you don't have to worry about things being awkward between us or being forced into an uncomfortable situation by staying with me."

"It could take a long time before I truly know what I want. Can you wait that long?"

"You can take your time with me. I sure as hell will when it comes to you."

The soft shade of pink staining her cheeks turned as bright as the red hibiscus haloing her black hair. It took her a moment to recover from the comment.

"Do we have a deal?" I extended my hand outward.

I expected the brief moment of hesitation, but that didn't make the heartbeat she stared down at my hand, turning over my words one by one in her head, any less agonizing.

His gaze lifted, zeroing in on me.

"It's a deal, Collins."

"Oh, thank god," was all I said before sweeping her into my arms.

Anytime I'm near Adeline, the sparks of our attraction simmered just below the surface. While nothing was truly capable of smothering out this desire, by preventing it from flourishing under the right conditions, you could keep it from at least spreading. I was wholly aware the spark we had was something special; I just never imagined the few times I'd managed to get my hands and lips on her would feel like dosing myself in kerosene and testing whether or not I could survive when the sparks ignited.

Adeline crashed her lips against mine, wrapping her legs around my waist. I cradled her underside to keep her supported and found she wasn't wearing any spandex or shorts under her sundress. My fingers dug into the swell of her ass sculpted from a lifetime of ballet, prompting Adeline to rake her fingers through my hair and part my lips with her tongue.

My little wildflower had taken the canister and dosed me from head to toe, and as our tongues met stroke for stroke, I was more than happy to be consumed by the flame.

This desire was beyond reason. It was carnal and needy, like every heartache was a rite of passage, so I might know how sweet it could be to have her in my life. Being with Adeline was all-consuming and downright overwhelming in the best way possible.

Adeline was light in my arms, but my legs suddenly became too weak to support us both. I sat down on a nearby metal bench, and she took advantage of the new position by straddling my lap, then starting to selfishly grind her sex against my jeans, searching for relief.

The flames of lust grew at a rate neither of us could control. We burned as bright as a wildfire ravaging a forest after the dry season. There was no stopping the flames from consuming us both.

The delicious moans spilling from her lips were met on the tail end of a short breath. I hooked my arm around her waist and helped guide her back and forth. The extra weight against my lap made the thin material of her panties soak through, and those breathy little moans of hers turned desperate. We were dauntless in our endeavors, as if we both knew we'd been waiting for this long enough.

"What happened to taking your time with me?" she mumbled against my lips.

"Not when someone could walk in at any moment and see you grinding your pussy all over me," I groaned, reveling in the way she burned my skin everywhere we touched.

"Good," she breathed, fumbling my belt buckle like she couldn't get the damn thing undone fast enough. "I'm done waiting."

The way she looked down at my cock was what a muse was to a painter—a strike of inspiration after years of failing to put brush to canvas. Awestruck by the sight of me, that need blossoming in her hazel eyes darkened as I dared, "Spit on it."

A second later, it hit the crown on my cock and dripped down the shaft. In slow, leisurely motions, Adeline took her hand and stroked my length, slightly twisting her hand toward the tip in a way that made my head go a little fuzzy each time she teased me. It was pure agonizing torture every second she spent zeroing her focus on the crown—edging me toward oblivion.

"Adeline," I moaned into her mouth.

"I like the way you moan my name," she retorted, dragging her thumb over the tip as she reached the crown again. I blew out a tight breath. "Did you know I've moaned your name before?" she asked, punctuating the sentence with another twist.

"Jesus Christ." I pressed my forehead against her, too overwhelmed by her touch to focus on two things at once. If we didn't slow down, I didn't think I would last much longer.

"I lost count of how many times your name has left my lips when I made myself come to the thought of you."

"At the apartment?"

Adeline stopped abruptly, locked her eyes with me, and said, "I would moan louder, hoping you might hear me."

"Show me," I demanded, hooking my pinky around her panties. "Show me what you would do to yourself while I was sleeping across the hallway, hoping I might catch you."

Lifting her sundress, Adeline bared herself to me.

She had always been slightly more reserved and kept to herself. The only place I'd truly seen her come out of her shell was on stage—well, until today. This darker side of her wasn't so easy to coax out, but now that I had her in my arms, there was no stopping her as she shifted her panties to the side and took pleasure in our wildest fantasies.

"Like this?"

"Yes," I said, bewitched by the way her finger circled the hood of her clit.

A delicious moan spilled from her lips. Something instinctively primal surged through me, and I bucked my hips without thinking. My cock brushed her wetness, and for a heartbeat she froze. I thought I might have crossed a line. An apology was on the tip of my tongue until she rasped, "Don't stop."

Adeline continued to stroke her clit, and the sight was magical. I bucked again, and she threw her head back, giving me her neck. I burrowed my face against her flushed skin, letting her know she was safe with each kiss I trailed down the column.

"Oh, Jin," she moaned. "I need you."

"I'm not sure I have a condom. Do you?"

"No." Adeline slowed her rocking.

"I've been tested recently, but…"

"I—" She pulled away slightly. "I'm not on birth control anymore. I didn't think there was any point when I hadn't been intimate with anyone for a while, but"—she sucked in a sharp breath when I nibbled the skin below her ear—"I'll go to the doctor and get a prescription as soon as I can."

"I can—" I attempted to catch my breath. "I will drive you."

I nibbled again, and Adeline shifted in my hold, bringing her flush against the base of my cock. Sex was out of the question—we both knew that—but that didn't stop her from fully grinding herself along the length of my cock, base to tip. It danced a dangerous line, but what of consequences when I never imagined something could feel so good.

"That's it, baby. Just like that."

Her nails bit into the nape of my neck for leverage. Lost to her own satisfaction, I don't think she realized how roughly she was carving into my skin, but the mix of pain and pleasure excited me in a way that had me thrusting my hips to meet her stroke for stroke. The hem of her dress was hiked up around her waist, giving me a clear view of how we came together as one.

"I—I can't—Jin." She trembled atop me.

"You can. Be a good girl for me."

Pleasure rocked through me, and Adeline chased her own soon after. I barely had enough time to lift my shirt before I made a mess of myself. Between the cum dripping down my stomach and Adeline's wetness on my lap, I was filthy.

We remained unmoving in each other's arms for quite some

time. All we could hear was the sound of our panting breaths—a sweet sympathy for our lasting decisions.

Eventually, she peered down between us and came to the same conclusion I did. I couldn't leave the greenhouse like this.

Adeline slid off my lap, brought her knees to the dirt, and dragged the flat of her tongue over my abs, cleaning the mess. Second by agonizing second, Adeline carved out a part of my memory that would go down as the single-handedly sexiest thing I'd ever laid my eyes on.

This woman was going to be the death of me.

Chapter Thirty-Five

Jin

Adeline Elise Hartwell underestimated the strength of a weak man.

If trust was the reward for a relationship built on patience, then I could gladly face whatever trials and tribulations were destined to come our way. In such a short amount of time, we'd already overcome so much. What was one more trial if it meant receiving the greatest reward of all—her trust.

Trauma in any form can resemble that of a parasitic creature, a growing and shifting beast that may appear dormant for a period of time, but in reality, it's slowly eating away at the soul piece by piece without the host even noticing. Then, with the most subtle of triggers, it can shred through skin and bone, opening old wounds you'd assumed were healed—I knew its venomous bite all too well. The beast residing within Adeline was still feasting on a fresh wound, and no matter how all-consuming the pull toward one another was, I had to give her the space she needed, or we'd be starting a relationship that would only be destined to fail.

If Adeline needed time to make sense of our situation, then so be it.

I would gladly wait a lifetime for her.

While nothing had fundamentally changed as I took her hand in mine and led her from the conservatory, stepping beyond those glass panels felt like her existence had breathed new life into me—a bright, more vibrant one where loving Adeline came so easily.

The following day, both of us were expected back at the theater. With a successful showcase behind us, there were pages of notes on my desk that needed to be smoothed over before the show one week from today. Returning to Republic City Opera House, we seamlessly slipped into our old roles: the rising star on the cusp of stardom and the pining artistic director, watching from his lonesome corner of the studio as he tried and failed to pore over his notes. The roles were all the same, though there wasn't a tingle of shame when I gawked openly in her direction. No more hiding when she caught me staring. My hand could linger during alignments, and I didn't have to fret about crossing any lines. I could soak in every moment of her attention I stole, and in return, I knew Adeline felt as strongly.

"Halle and Thomas," Anastasia barked out, silencing the music with a tap of her phone. "You two are moving ahead of the music—watch your count."

The ballroom scene was logistically the most complicated part of the entire ballet, and according to Anastasia's notes, it required the most attention prior to opening night. This was the fourth time we'd run through this particular scene, and it was starting to take its toll on the group. Anastasia bounced from dancer to dancer, offering her expertise. While the other dancers got the lashing of her tongue, I snuck up next to Adeline on the sidelines, arms crossed, and subtly jabbed my elbow into her arm.

Leaning in close, I whispered, "That first sequence was beautiful."

She peered up at me through dark lashes. Around the irises of her eyes was the softest shade of brown that tapered off into a striking hue that couldn't decide whether or not it was storm gray or seafoam green. I'd do anything to keep those beautiful eyes trained on me.

"Why, thank you, *Mr. Collins.*"

I ran my tongue over the tip of my canine.

"I'd love to hear you call me that in bed," I whispered.

While there was nothing left to hide, old habits seemed to die hard. Adeline averted her gaze, checking her appearance in one of the many mirrors that lined the studio, and the selfish bastard I was, I couldn't help myself as I turned to savor the sight of her blush—

A pair of green eyes stared back at me.

Halle's gaze flickered back and forth between me and my little wildflower's reflection. When our eyes locked, she turned away, pretending as if she'd been watching Anastasia the entire time. Though there was no mistaking the way her freckles stood out amongst the blotches of red spreading across her cheeks.

My phone buzzed in my pocket, and I excused myself from the studio. Instead of finding an email like I was expecting, it was a meeting invitation five minutes from now.

Meeting invitation from Charles Blanchet.

"Urgent."

Today at 11:30 *a.m.*

"Shit," I cursed under my breath, beelining it for the nearest stairwell. Built in the late 1800s, the theater was a marvel to look at and an integral part of the district's heritage sites, but whoever designed the interior must have been a sadist. It would be a miracle if I made it to the upstairs offices in less than five minutes, even if I took two steps at a time, but I tried nonetheless.

With seconds to spare, I somehow made it.

It didn't hit me until I was standing outside his door how strange the entire meeting invite was. I hadn't seen Charles since the showcase after the security—

Did he know what I'd done?

I faltered back a step.

No, that couldn't be true. Any video footage of that night had been scrubbed clean as thoroughly as the dates he wiped from the system—dates Destler and his team were now scrambling to uncover. As risky as it was to have done what we'd done, I took precautions to ensure it didn't come back to either of us. This couldn't be about the files. I was being paranoid.

Or was I? Shit.

The door swung open, and Charles eyed me from head to toe. "You're late."

"Yeah—"

"Come in, and close the door behind you."

Charles retreated behind his desk to continue whatever paperwork he was working on before I showed up. As I took a seat, I patiently waited for him to finish, crossing then uncrossing my legs. Silence would be wielded as skillfully as a weapon. Charles was, without a doubt, a craftsman in that regard. I sat in the stale silence for as long as I could bear it. Eventually, I cleared my throat to show he wasn't the only one who knew how to hone his craft.

"Charles, spare me the mental gymnastics. Can you tell me why you called this meeting already? I have a million things to do, and they need me at rehearsal."

He peered up at me, and the way the light seemed to be sucked right out of his blue eyes was predatory. "Forgive me for wasting your time. I thought I might return the favor."

"Excuse me?"

"Republic City Philharmonic Orchestra called. They were very eager to learn what kind of employee Hyun-jin Collins is and whether or not I would recommend him for the artistic director role at their company," he deadpanned, mindlessly tapping a red flash drive on the desk. "We are on the precipice of the most important season of my career, and my fucking artistic director has one foot out the door. You'd better have a good excuse because from where I'm sitting right now, it looks to me that you aren't as loyal to this company as I thought you were."

Each application felt like a silent plea to break free from the shackles of this company. A ray of sunlight peeking through the clouds. And for each rare opportunity that presented itself in the form of a job listing, I always made sure to double—no, triple—check that the small box, asking whether or not they had permission to contact your current employer, was ticked off. I wasn't sure how I could have made such a foolish mistake, but now, more than ever, my loyalty was being questioned for it.

Loyalty was not always written in ink; sometimes it was presented in messy lines and tattered pages. The potential fugacious nature of it made earning said loyalty that much more special. Charles had once had my faith when I had nowhere else to go. The devout little director I was, there was only so long I could hold onto that loyalty when he proved himself ignoble over the years. I could sense he knew I'd been slipping through his fingers, but with too much at play for him to be questioning me at a time like this, I had to revert to a version of myself I'd much rather prefer to keep in the past.

Erick needed answers, and I needed the truth.

If not for my sake, then Adeline's.

I crossed my arms over my chest. "Are you going to keep accusing me of something I didn't do, or can I explain myself?"

"By all means"—he jerked his hand—"I could very well drag any bastard off the street to sit in on rehearsals and ogle at my dancers for half your salary, and they'd probably give me a fraction of the trouble you're worth right now."

How did I ever find refuge with him?

"I've given this company a decade of my life. Have the years meant nothing?"

Charles smiled, and there was something slightly unhinged about it, but I couldn't quite put my finger on it. "Then go ahead, Jin, tell me what could have possibly compelled you to search for another job when I'd done so much to take you off the streets and offer you a chance no one else would."

It was because he made you dependent on him. The nature of the relationship always started symbiotic—something that both parties could benefit from, coming in many different forms, but ending all the same. It wasn't until it was too late that you realized how truly parasitic he could be. It was what he had done with me, and what he was attempting to do with Adeline now.

"And while I'm eternally grateful for everything Republic City Opera House has provided me, I was exploring my options and seeing if my salary was still competitive with the industry standard." The lie rolled off my tongue with such ease. "If I were to receive an offer from another company, I planned to use it as leverage to negotiate a higher salary."

"And had I said no, would you have left?"

Little did he know, I could be just as much of a leech.

"I've built too much here to abandon all I've worked for."

The response left us at a standstill—Charles too proud to admit he'd been bested, and me, too humble to add fuel to the fire while I was ahead. He dismissed me, and I returned to the dance studio to catch the final scene of *Le Cœur Sauvage*. From my corner of the room, I made a silent vow to myself to tread more lightly. There were precautions in place that I could and would fall back on once I left Republic City Opera House in the past where it belonged. Vowing not to take another risk, I opened up the job search application on my phone, ready to deactivate my account so no more pesky recruiters could message me, and I wouldn't be tempted by any new job listing in the meantime—after all, I had The Lotte to look forward to.

In the top right-hand corner, a flash red notification caught my eye. I clicked on it, not thinking much of it.

You have an unfinished application for the Republic City Philharmonic Orchestra. Your draft is saved—complete it now before the position fills.

It looks like both Charles and I showed our hands today.

Chapter Thirty-Six

Adeline

"Be a doll and turn the volume up, Adeline," Caleb said from the back seat. I wasn't privy to the sight of Sophia elbowing her fiancé in the gut, but I heard the whoosh of air leave his lungs before adding a please to his sentence.

Freshly discharged from the hospital, Caleb leaped at the chance to soak in his newfound freedom. What had started as a nice dinner for the four of us had somehow turned into a night out as we were crawling through district traffic in Caleb's work truck, the only vehicle that could accommodate his wheelchair.

Caleb was fortunate that his injuries hadn't required surgery. The recovery would be relatively straightforward but would require a lot of time, patience, and physical therapy. Based on the way he sprawled out in the back seat, singing painfully off-key, the youngest of the Collins boys appeared sanguine. It was the eldest I was worried about.

There was an underlying need that Jin constantly wanted to fill, a persistent hankering to be at the hospital for his brother. In the time since the accident, Sophia had to put her foot down several times because she knew that anytime he visited, he would be impossible to get rid of. Jin settled on sending the couple food and running errands for Sophia whenever he could. He already had so much on his plate, and I could tell the moment we rolled Caleb out of the hospital, an invisible weight had been lifted from him. Which was probably why he'd let Caleb convince him to go to the district for a drink or two to celebrate—the two brothers seemed at ease to be with each other again.

The ten-block radius that made up the Entertainment District was bustling with endless options, each accompanied by a glowing sign, trying to entice patrons toward sin and temptation. There was no shortage of trendy underground bars reminiscent of the district's heyday, nightclubs that thrived in the darkest corners, live music that spilled into the streets, and gentlemen's clubs that were considered the more unsavory side of this part of town. Each promised their own memorable night.

"Where do you want to go?" Jin asked, hand gripping the stirring wheel.

Caleb grabbed the back of the driver's seat and leaned forward. "Must you ask?"

Jin groaned, "We go there every time."

"By all means, find another place in the district where we are guaranteed free drinks and won't be forced to pay an outrageous cover charge," he challenged.

"We wouldn't have to pay a cover charge if we went into a normal bar for once."

"Jin, reason with me here. I think you fail to see my vision. That bastard owes me for taking the hit for him, and at the end of the day, it benefits all of you, too."

"Make a decision fast, the girls are trying to call a cab," Sophia called out, her ruby rose nail clanking against her cellphone screen.

"Is the only reason you care about free drinks because you owe me one?" I asked, turning in the passenger seat.

I didn't miss the way Jin smiled; eyes fixed on the red lights ahead. "Yeah, Caleb. I'm pretty sure you owe Adeline a drink for not going to her show."

"Hey, I—"

"And no, a warm beer doesn't count," Jin interjected.

"I was a little preoccupied at the time." Caleb gestured to his leg.

"Excuses. Excuses," I sing-sung.

The two brothers went back and forth, arguing about a slight technicality of their long-standing tradition as Jin made his way toward a parking structure that would place us in the heart of the district. There was something to be said about their relationship and how blessed they were to be this close. Admittedly, I was a bit jealous, knowing that Melissa and I could never have something like that, until I realized I didn't need to mourn one relationship when I'd gained three more. Jin, Caleb, and Sophia had welcomed me with open arms since the day of their gender reveal party. It really did warm my heart that this was here to stay.

With a bit of bribery and an open threat to wheel Caleb wherever the hell he wanted, Jin somehow convinced the group to start the night at an Irish pub called The Tavern with the promise that it would only be the first stop of the night.

With a tap of his credit card on the parking ticket dispenser, the arm rose.

I reached for my cellphone in the cupholder. There were a few unread messages.

Halle: Please send me the address again.

I copied and pasted the address into the text thread.

Halle: Thanks, Addie! See you soon.

I started typing out a response when a flash of red caught

my eye in the corner of the screen. "Damn it," I muttered under my breath. "Caleb, I think your cord is broken. My phone hasn't been charging this entire time."

Twenty-five percent. Lovely.

"Oh, yeah, that thing is a piece of shit."

"And why exactly do you still have it...?"

"Caleb doesn't know the definition of 'throwing it out,'" Sophia said with air quotes. "He still has a box full of old video games from his childhood that were collecting dust in our closet. I've tried to throw them out twice, but the fight we had after wasn't worth trying for a third."

"I'm going to laugh in your face when that box pays for our daughter's college."

The Tavern was a lively place adorned with mahogany wood that stretched to every corner of the long rectangular room. The only pop of color was green, white, and orange flags strung up across the ceiling like the loose strands of a spider's web caught in the wind. Stepping inside felt like being whisked away over land and sea. I'd never been here before, but I was instantly drawn to the energy vibrating through the space and the collection of one-dollar bills stapled to the ceiling and pillars. Each was stamped with a message or date from the patron who left it.

Charlotte and Isabella showed up soon after, christening their arrival with a round of shots. They'd been working on an especially difficult trial and claimed the alcohol was part of their recovery process. Sophia toasted them with her soda water, and Caleb, looking for an excuse to finally drink after getting off a particular medication, joined in. Seeing my window of opportunity closing, I slipped from the booth and followed after Jin at the bar.

"Caleb seems like he's doing well," I said, leaning up beside him.

"My brother cracks me up." He blew out a breath. "After being beaten up in the streets, forced to take a leave of absence from work, and unable to tend to his pregnant fiancée, any sane person would be stumbling over their feet. Not Caleb—still his old obnoxious self, but now he's on four wheels. As long as there is an elevator or a ramp, he's unstoppable."

"Caleb is...well, Caleb is Caleb." To put it simply.

The bartender returned with a vodka sprite and a Guinness. Before I could even get my wallet out of my purse, Jin had already handed over his credit card. I gave him a pointed look, and he shrugged.

"You didn't have to do that."

"Oh, yes, I did. It's one of the perks of being—"

"Complicated?" I cut him off. Now it was his turn to give me a look. "I heard you mention something to Caleb when you were loading his wheelchair into the bed of the truck earlier when he asked about us."

"I figured it was easier than explaining our little agreement to my brother," he said, taking a sip of his foamy beer.

"It's okay. Complicated is good. At least for right now." I smiled up at him.

"Complicated is good," he repeated the words as if testing them aloud. "I'd love to have that in writing."

I snatched the pen from the bill holder and started scribbling on the bill I was planning to pay with. When I was pleased with my work, I handed it to him and felt my stomach somersault as a smile graced his lips.

"Terribly complicated. J+A," he read aloud. "I like the heart next to my initials. It was a nice little touch. Now we need to find the perfect place to hang this."

"Wait. Don't you dare move a muscle until I get a picture of it," I squealed, pulling out a disposable camera from my purse.

"I liked what you said a while back about taking pictures of happy moments. I figured it was worth bringing tonight."

Jin leaned forward, tucking a strand of hair behind my ear, and said, "Sweetheart, one camera isn't going to be enough for what I have planned."

The way Jin looked into my eyes had me contemplating whether or not I should rip that damn dollar bill from his hand and tear it into a million pieces. Saying things were complicated was a lie, and a terrible one at that. This *trial* was a means of protecting myself, and I needed to be reminded that rushing into things was the reason I was in this mess to begin with.

"Oh, earth to Adeline." Caleb's voice carried across the bar, startling me. I whipped my head toward the booth, and by the look on his face, it seemed like this wasn't the first time he'd called my name.

Halle stood next to him, hands clasped in front of her shimmering black dress.

"Hey, you made it," I choked out.

It was a small blessing that the pub was shrouded in shadows, because I wasn't sure there was any hiding the redness in my face as I closed the space between us and wrapped Halle in a hug. It was four whole heartbeats before she returned the gesture.

"I did," she rasped. "It's been a long day. I need a drink. Badly."

Our time at The Tavern was short-lived—a whirlwind of shots and laughter that Caleb used as leverage to continue our trek through the district. Halle wasn't one for group settings unless she curated said group, but with each sip, I noticed her slowly starting to open up around Sophia and her friends. They made quick work to include her in their conversation and get to know her one intrusive question at a time. By the time we were bulldozing Caleb through the bustling district streets, there was hope this night might prove to mend a fraction of our relationship after all.

When we arrived at Don Juan, Caleb and Jin ventured off to the front of the line while the girls stood off on the sidelines, waiting to be let in.

Halle snuck up beside me and said, "You and Jin seem happy together."

"Oh," I sputtered. "We aren't together."

Terribly complicated didn't feel like an appropriate response, nor did I want to explain what all of that entailed.

A beat passed.

"Jesus," she muttered under her breath, the single word coming out rushed. "I'm not blind, Adeline. I saw the way you two were looking at each other at the pub, and I've seen the way you looked at each other for months. I just didn't think you had it in you."

Off in the distance, Caleb clasped hands with one of the bouncers. Their laughter carried past the queue of people lining up against the brick facade of the building.

"What do you mean by that?"

"Just forget I said anything." She shook her head, then walked toward the boy as they waved us over. Beyond the door was a narrow hallway leading into the club. I felt Jin's hand slip into mine, but I pushed forward to catch up to Halle toward the front instead.

I had her by the shoulder a second later.

She whipped around and said, "Adeline. Just drop it. Please. I want to have a fun night with you, okay?"

There was a version of myself that would have likely nodded her head, shut her mouth, and plastered a smile on her face for the sake of keeping the peace, but I'd bitten my tongue enough times to know I wasn't protecting myself by not speaking up; I was only enabling others. I was fed up with letting that timid version of myself win—it wasn't fair to me, nor did it solve anything.

As I pulled Halle aside at the entrance of the club, I noticed Jin watching me over the heads that separated us. I gave him a reassuring nod before turning back to Halle, prepared to leave that version of myself in the past, no matter how terrifying it may be.

"If something is bothering you, then I'd rather you say it than spare my feelings."

"It's hardly been more than a month, for Christ's sake," she bit out. "I thought I could do this—put on a brave face and pretend like everything is okay when that couldn't be further from the truth. I have far too much self-respect to put myself through this and be forced to see you disrespect Noah over and over again.

"We just laid his body to rest—did you know that? Of course, you didn't, because Noah's celebration of life was last week, and you didn't even bother to show up. At first, I tried to give you the benefit of the doubt. I assumed it might be awkward with his family there, but thanks for inviting me tonight, because you made things perfectly clear. While I was burying my best friend, you were off fucking our artistic director."

My molars ground together with such force that I was scared they would pop right out of my gums.

"I already told you. We aren't together, nor is it any of your business if we were," I said, trying to keep a level tone despite the stinging behind my eyes. "I'm starting to notice a trend here when I repeatedly tell you the same thing over and over, yet you refuse to believe me. It gets to a point where I just stop trying altogether."

"Maybe I would take your word if you didn't lie all the time."

"You want the truth. Okay." I snapped, shouting over the music. "I didn't know about Noah's celebration of life because no one bothered to tell me, but had I known, I would have never shown up because there's nothing worth celebrating. And while you waste your time grieving over someone who doesn't deserve a fraction of the love he received in life or death, for once in my goddamn life, I'm free—"

"Ad—"

"Don't interrupt me," I interjected. "For months, I'd been silently suffering with absolutely no way out, and I thought you might be the one person who could help me escape. I confided in you at the lowest point in my life, terrified that speaking up would only make matters worse. And you know what you did when I tried to explain what happened? You took the words of my abuser over those of your best friend. You believed a dead man over *me*."

"I don't want to hear this. Noah warned me that you would say something like this, but I didn't want to believe him." She tried to walk away, but I yanked her back by the strap of her purse.

"You don't get to walk away because you feel uncomfortable. I didn't get to walk away, and neither do you," I dared, white knuckling her purse. "Did you know the first time he hit me, he started limiting which of the other physical therapists could see me? I was getting injured often enough that he started working on me exclusively, so no one could report the bruises and get him fired. He manipulated every part of my life, kept me isolated, financially dependent on him, and used his charm and wits to keep me gaslighted and confused. Everything he did was to benefit himself. Noah was good at what he did, but I just didn't think you were stupid enough to fall for it, too."

Halle's throat worked. "No one is going to believe you in court."

"Why, because you're going to testify against me?"

A pregnant pause.

"I think we both know the answer to that..."

Then she walked away.

Grief may be the price we pay for love, but the absence of grief can be nearly as shocking. Those who choose to mourn the wicked may forever be set in their ways, glorifying a man who could do no wrong in their eyes, blind to the fact that they only ever saw a piece of his true character. While Halle wept for a man she'd convinced herself was a martyr, I patiently waited for the claws of grief to slice through my chest as I watched her disappear down the narrow hallway—leaving behind the shadows of our friendship.

An entire song came and went before I realized it would never come.

Sorrow had no place in my heart when the mere thought of grieving a friendship that had died long before now was over-shadowed by resounding frustration. Far too often, I had opened myself up to people undeserving of my compassion, who mistook my kindness for easy prey. Looking back at it now, Noah was quick to test the water between us, finding holes in my defense in order to easily manipulate me. Keeping me complacent in his lies and deception.

Halle may not have ever laid a hand on me, yet she was far from innocent. I hoped that without Noah whispering in her ears, she would come to realize that he had her manipulated just as easily.

As I made my way to the bar to settle my nerves, it was abundantly clear that to move forward, I had to let go of the past

—I had to say goodbye to the pieces that didn't fit into my new life.

Though understanding didn't always correlate with belief.

And that's when the whispers grew louder.

The right choice wasn't always the easy one, and despite knowing I had finally put myself first in this friendship for once, the inner critic latched onto Halle's every word and spun them into my own. The inner critic roared in my ear until I couldn't make sense of who said what, pulling me apart, insecurity by insecurity.

While I was burying my best friend, you were off fucking our artistic director.

One shot quickly turned into two in an attempt to drown out the voices. Our conversation had awoken a sleeping giant, and now that he had fuel, the only way to smother out the flames was to numb them.

It's hardly been more than a month, for Christ's sake.

God—it was infuriating to know you were in the right and still have your own mind actively working against you, trying to convince you that you are somehow at fault. I didn't want to be in this head anymore. I didn't want to be the craftsman of my own unhappiness.

Why did I have to be my own worst enemy?

When I returned to the table, there were, of course, questions from the group about Halle's whereabouts, but no one seemed to bat an eye when I told them she needed to get a good night's rest for rehearsals tomorrow. And with that, everyone went about their night, unaware of how much it ached to be stewing in my thoughts—everyone but Jin.

His hand felt like a brick atop my thigh. "Are you okay?"

"Yes," I lied, giving him a bright smile.

He returned the smile, but it lacked any of its normal warmth. I guess there was no hiding from Jin—he knew me too well. Unlike Noah, who would have dragged me to the corners of the club and screamed at me until I told him, or would flat out ignore me, Jin didn't push or pry for an answer. He simply leaned in to whisper that I could tell him when I was ready.

I made my best attempt to put on a brave face and salvage what was left of the night: indulging in shots with Charlotte and Isabella, sitting on the edge of my seat as Caleb recalled the story of him fighting off the two attackers who cornered him on the street outside of his office, and basking in the safety of Jin's presence.

By ten o'clock, the consequences of my actions were slowly catching up with me. And I reveled in the way my body sank into itself more firmly as the alcohol did its job. The inner critic was still whispering in my ear, but with each sip, that voice grew more distant.

Excusing myself from the group, there was a certain weight-lessness to my limbs as I carried myself across the club. Each step echoed through my bones. The entire room felt this weird balance of being more vibrant in nature yet muted at the same time.

Ice-cold water traced the love line of my palm as I held my hand under the faucet. The cooling sensation sobered me enough to thank the bathroom attendant without my words slurring together. Though it hadn't been enough to register where the buzzing along my ribs was coming from until I fished out my cell phone from my purse and realized someone was calling me.

It took several blinks for the letters on the screen to shift back into place.

"Shit," I cursed under my breath, swiping the screen. "Hello."

"Adeline, we need to talk." Charles's rich accent bled through the phone.

The door to the restroom burst open, and a group of friends laughing stepped inside.

"Okay, give me a minute," I said, exiting the bathroom in search of a quiet place to talk. A glowing exit sign cast the end of the hallway in a soft green hue. I propped my foot between the door and the jam, then stepped out into the dingy alleyway, butted up between the club and the business next door. "Sorry about that, Charles. I can speak now."

"I spent the last hour and a half on the phone with Donovan," he started. "I know he spoke to you about the witness testimony. How long were you waiting until you were going to tell me?"

"Charles—"

"You had one job, and you couldn't even do that correctly. I'm holding onto your freedom by a thread, and every misstep is bringing you closer and closer to losing everything. There's only so much I can do to defend you in court. If you don't fix this right now, you'll ruin everything."

"I—I'm not sure there's anything I can do to change her mind."

And I don't think I care to try.

If Halle had made up her mind about testifying, there would be no reasoning with her, and trying to do so might only make matters worse. She'd already seen his blood on my hands; I didn't need to give her any more of a reason to speak on Noah's behalf in a court of law.

"If you have any shred of dignity for your career, you'll make it happen. Then again, going out drinking on a night before rehearsal isn't exactly principal material either." I was about to speak, but he cut me off again. "I don't have time for excuses, Adeline. I can hear you struggling not to slur your words."

A beat passed.

"I'm not sure I can continue to take risks on someone who isn't dedicated to their craft."

"Sir." I white-knuckled the phone. "This is out of the norm for me, and I take what I do for this company very seriously. Jin's little brother was released from the hospital, and we were only getting a drink and dinner to celebrate."

"Where are you?"

"Um...a nightclub in the district."

"The name. What's the name of the club?"

"Don Juan."

The next few words he said were unrecognizable, muffled, and sharp, like a curse word meant more for his ears than mine.

"If you're truly loyal to this company, then prove it," he challenged, voice clear. "I am sending a car to pick you up. If you have an ounce of respect for yourself and your career, you'll get in it and leave."

Before I could get another word in, he hung up.

I snapped my eyes shut, pressed the cool metal against my forehead, and fought the urge not to chuck my phone against the nearest brick wall.

"No. No. No," I groaned, lightly tapping my phone against my forehead and—

The side door swung open with enough force to crack the brick along the back wall, taking me out with it. I stumbled back a step and might have been able to steady myself had a body not collided with me at full force a heartbeat later. The side of my knee slammed against the filthy alleyway floor first, next was my shoulder, which was a small blessing because it gave me a second to catch myself before my head could be next.

My scream echoed off the brick walls, drowning out their slurred apologies as he groaned on the floor next to me. My nails dug into the pavement as I bowed over in pain, hissing with each wave of nausea that washed over me.

A soft swish was my only warning as the door clicked shut behind me.

"Sorry. Shit. Are you okay?" the man slurred.

"No, I'm not *okay*," I snapped.

The worst of the pain was initial, burning off like dry kindling, hot and fast. I managed a few shaky breaths before I could stomach the idea of struggling to my feet and trying the door. Locked. Ignoring the sickening throbbing in my limbs and the steady trickle of blood down my shin, I grappled for my phone, Jin's contact blurring behind unshed tears.

"Hey, this is Hyun-jin Collins, please leave a message—"

I hung up and tried again. A notification flashed across the screen.

Low battery. 5% battery remaining.

"You're bleeding. Like a lot," the man continued, but I ignored him as he attempted to push up to his own two feet, but fell back on his ass.

"No. No. No. No," I chanted, frantically calling again. In the corner of my screen were two little bars that taunted me. My phone was roaming, sucking up more battery life with each failed attempt. When Jin didn't answer for a second time, I left a voicemail, then a text, before trying to call Sophia and Caleb with no luck.

"Answer your damn phone," I muttered to myself as it went to voicemail.

Accepting defeat, I hobbled through the alleyway, circled to the front of the building, and cornered the only doorman outside. A small fella with dark auburn hair and light freckles dusting his arms.

"Um, excuse me," I shouted over the music spilling through the door. "I was in the club a moment ago, and I got pushed out through the side exit leading into the alleyway." I gestured to the trail of blood spilling down my shin. "My phone is about to die, and I can't get a hold of my friends. Is there any chance I can peek my head in and find them?"

"I'm sorry, sweetheart. If your name isn't on the list and you don't have a handstamp, there's nothing I can do for you," he said gently. When he noticed my smile fade, he continued, "You can wait off on the side and try texting your friends again. If they don't answer, go to the diner down the block and see if they have anything to patch you up."

"Okay," I said, failing to hide the wobble in my voice.

Standing on the curb, I called them once more—nothing.

My cellphone was at three percent when a text from Charles came through, listing the make and model of the car coming for me. A wave of panic struck me like an arrow through the heart as the little number in the corner of my screen dropped to two percent.

Adeline: My phone is going to die. I'm standing outside the club.

A minute ticked by, but the text was still marked unread.

"Why did you run away? I was trying to help you." I whirled around. The man from the alleyway loomed over me, a slight sway to his tall stature. He was close enough to smell the sting of alcohol on his breath and the stench of cigarette smoke clinging to his clothes. Adding insult to injury, he sloppily fished out a pack from his pocket and lit another, not before offering me a smoke. "You need to get that cleaned up. It could get infected."

I ignored him, staring down at my phone, praying for a reply.

"Want a ride home? I can make sure you get taken care of. It's the least I could do after hurting you," he slurred.

"No, thank you," was all I said.

He stepped closer, and I stepped back. "I'm only trying to help."

"I already told you, no."

I glanced over my shoulder to the sound of shouting; two men were being pulled apart as they swung out into the open air. Their verbal altercation worsened as the single bouncer tried and failed to separate them. As the fight spilled into the street, I had to step back on the curb to make room. A hand brushed the small of my back.

"Don't touch me!" I snapped, heart galloping.

"No need to be a bitch about it, I was only trying to help."

The glowing white light of a rideshare pulled curbside, and as the man reached for the door handle, I used the distraction of the fight at our backs to slip into the shadows. The sound of shouting grew more distant the more space I put between the club and me.

I picked up the pace, frantically typing on my phone.

Adeline: Please meet me at the diner down the block.

But the footfalls chasing after me grew closer.

"Wait up," they called out.

The diner was several shops away, none of which were open. Each step closer felt like someone had taken a branding iron and was searing me bone deep. Blood pooled in my boots. My shoulder ached. I was choking down my own tears, trying to push myself harder, knowing this body had repeatedly failed me in the past.

"Come on, don't be like that."

His grimy fingers skimmed my bicep, and I cut left into the street, narrowly missing a black sedan. The car screeched to a stop and laid into the horn. The sound of rubber against asphalt was as harrowing as the slap of flesh against the hood of the car. The driver hung out of their open window, shouting at the man following me as they argued back and forth about who had the right of way, giving me the chance to hide behind a parked car.

When the sedan eventually drove off, I caught a glimpse of the last three digits of his license plate.

D5T.

"Fucking bitch," the man muttered to himself, crossing the road. "Where'd you go?"

Recognizing the blessing for what it was, I used the last percent of my battery life to double-check the license plate number Charles had sent me, sprint in the direction of where it had pulled off curbside in front of Don Juan, and climb inside.

I wasn't sure where the hell I was going, but I knew I was safe.

Chapter Thirty-Seven

Jin

The pungent stench of bile and stale beer lingered in the cramped stall. Caleb gripped the rim of the toilet bowl and heaved. I held onto the back of my brother's collar, making sure he didn't slip out of the wheelchair. It took two more heaving breaths until the contents of his stomach spilled free. An orchestra of horrendous smells and sounds merged as one.

I kept my eyes trained on the speckled ceiling and fought the urge to vomit.

Caleb slumped back in his seat and muttered, "Holy shit."

"Feeling better?"

"I would lie to you, but I don't think I have the strength." He wiped the sweat from his brow. "Okay, I think I'm good."

We made it halfway out of the handicap stall before another wave of nausea slammed into him again. Somehow, Caleb managed to make it to the toilet in time.

"I love you," he said, his words echoing into the bowl. "You're the best older brother, have I ever told you that?"

"I'm your only brother." I patted him on the back. "And ditto."

"Rude," he slurred. "I want to hear you say it aloud. You wouldn't say *ditto* to Adeline if she told you she loved you, would you?"

"She hasn't so..."

Caleb heaved again, panting to catch his breath.

"Does Adeline still love me after you told her about what I did?"

Something about us cramped in a gross bathroom stall while I held back his hair was oddly nostalgic. It was a small blessing that Caleb found it in himself to slow down the drinking after he and Sophia started seriously dating. And while this was the last place I wanted to be right now, I understand my brother needed tonight more than he let on.

"She adores you," he said, wheeling him away.

"Good. Good."

"I know right now isn't the best time to be asking this, but I was hoping I could take you and Sophia out to dinner next week and you two could help me talk to her about that."

Caleb whipped around in his chair. "You haven't told her."

"Goddamn it, don't look at me like that. There hasn't exactly been a great time to do it; she's been juggling everything going on in her life, the last thing she needs to do is worry about something that doesn't even matter anymore. Now that things are starting to get more serious between us, I figured it might be a good time to do so."

"I thought you said things were complicated."

"They are. *Complicatedly serious.* Whatever. Are you going to help or not?"

Sophia stood outside the bathroom, a cup of water in one hand and a handful of ibuprofen in the other. "What are we helping you with?"

"Jin hasn't told Adeline about Ethan yet."

"Jin," Sophia scoffed.

"I mean, I have, but not everything. Forget I asked." Pinching the bridge of my nose, I cursed under my breath. "I shouldn't have brought this up tonight. We'll talk about it when you're sober."

"Well, don't wait too long. I hate to see a perfectly good relationship go from complicatedly serious to just complicated," Caleb hiccuped.

"Okay, no more drinking for you—" I stopped short at our table. "Where's Addie?"

Isabella and Charlotte looked up from their phones long enough to take in their surroundings and the empty chair across from them.

"I don't know. I thought she was with you," Isabella answered.

"No, she went to the bathroom," Charlotte said. "But that was like ten or so minutes ago."

I pulled out my phone to check up on her, but found a whole slew of unread messages and missed calls staring back at me.

Missed call at 10:21 p.m.

Missed call at 10:22 p.m.

Adeline: Please answer your phone.

Adeline: Jin!

Missed call at 10:25 p.m.

Adeline: I'm locked out of the club, and I can't get a hold of anyone.

Adeline: My phone is going to die. I'm standing outside the club.

Adeline: Please meet me at the diner down the block.

I returned her call, but it went right to voicemail.

Panic has a funny way of creeping up on you. Crawling into our deepest thoughts like a spider inching its long, hairy legs over the parenchyma of your mind. It waits and watches from afar, only striking when the moment is right. There was nothing I could do as panic sank its fangs into me. The venom entered my bloodstream, moving through my body faster as my heart thrashed within my chest. The more it spread, the more it married with the alcohol in my veins.

I rushed out of the club, not thinking of anything other than reaching her.

The stench of stale coffee and fried eggs smacked me in the face as I burst into Lin's Diner. The few patrons eating this late at night swiveled in my direction, including the waitress, who was startled and dropped her pen.

The fangs struck again when I didn't see her hazel eyes amongst the lot.

"Have you seen a short woman? About five feet. Black hair," I asked the waitress breathlessly. "She's wearing a red dress."

"No, sweetheart," she answered. "Haven't seen anyone like that all night."

I could feel the venom curdling my blood and clotting in my veins as I sprinted back into the night, praying that my little wildflower was somewhere nearby and it was simply a matter of finding her. More than prepared to mindlessly wander the streets looking for her, I was sober enough now to know that was a terrible idea, so I set my sights on Don Juan.

Each second wasted was another strike of the fangs.

Over.

And over.

And over again.

"You aren't listening to me," I snapped. "I was in the club not five minutes ago."

"And how the hell would I know that?" the short fella shot back.

"Because you saw me. I told you I was coming back."

"And did you get your hand stamped like I told you to...?"

"It's a fucking stamp. Are you kidding me?"

"No handstamp. No entry."

Sophia wheeled Caleb down the narrow hallway. "What's going on?"

"This asshole won't let me in without a handstamp," I said, gesturing to security.

"Did you get your hand stamped?" Caleb asked.

"Well, no, but—"

"Jin, that defeats the entire integrity of the handstamp system."

"Exactly," the short fella chimed in.

Was I going crazy? I was going crazy.

"Jesus Christ. I'm going inside."

The short fella attempted to leap in front of me, shouting something into his earpiece. A heartbeat later, someone had me by the back of the collar and was yanking me back. I whirled, ready to swing, but found a familiar face smiling down at me.

"Are you causing trouble at my club?" Antonio clicked his tongue.

"Mr. Donati, he's trying to enter the club without a handstamp."

"If you mention a handstamp one more time, I'm not personally responsible for what happens to you next," I said, pulling away from Antonio to straighten my shirt.

"It's all right, Phill. They're with me," he said, then turned his attention to my brother. "I was actually looking for you. Erick wants to know when you'll be coming back to work. No offense, but your foreman is kind of a dick without you here."

"I'll be on crutches in a week or two. Then, I suppose," Caleb answered. "But I was planning on coming on Monday to check on the progress."

"You've got to be kidding me?" I swore.

"What?"

"You can't seriously be thinking about returning to work after what happened." If battery and assault weren't enough to deter him, then the threats alone to his family should have been enough to keep him well away from The Lotte. "Okay. This isn't what we are talking about, right now." I pivoted toward Antonio. "I can't find Adeline. She's missing."

"Hm, okay. Remind me what she looks like again."

With a few taps on my phone, I had a zoomed-in photo of Adeline from the company holiday party pulled up. Adorned with a beaming smile and a tacky snowman sweater, she shone as bright as the star atop the tree in the background.

"Hey. I just saw her."

All three of us snapped our necks toward Phill, peeking over our shoulders.

"Yeah, like twenty minutes ago. She lost her friends and was trying to find them. She didn't have a handstamp, so I told her to go to Lin's Diner to charge her phone in the meantime," he explained.

"She never made it to the diner."

Antonio whipped out his phone and, with a few clicks, had a surveillance application pulled up. The security guard coached him through the events of the night until eventually he had a still frame of Adeline standing on the street corner on his phone.

My heart crawled its way up my chest cavity and lodged itself in my throat as a man stumped out of the darkened alleyway and approached her from behind. I was choking down what little air I could, watching the horrors of their encounter unfold before me.

"I'm guessing that's her?" Antonio asked.

The shadowy figure advanced on Adeline, bringing himself

close enough to get his grimy hand on her. My little wildflower bolted in the opposite direction, moving out of frame. The twinge of hope blossoming in my chest fizzled away as the man followed after her.

I stood there, staring at the phone, unmoving, the timestamp in the corner sped by.

A single thrash of my heart beat was enough to know nothing good would come next. By the second heartbeat, I was well aware a panic attack was about to rock through my system so hard I might see stars. There was no amount of red that could save me from this one.

"What's going on?" Caleb said, craning his neck. "I can't see."

"Someone followed her—"

A black sedan rolled to a stop at the corner of the screen along with a small, shadowy figure. I snatched the phone out of Antonio's hand, stopping him mid-sentence as the shadow crept around the car and opened the side door. At first, I thought I was seeing things; however, after rewinding the footage a few times, I caught the tiniest hint of a black heel before it disappeared behind a closed door.

"She got into a cab." I choked a laugh. "She's safe."

Relief swelled within me. The edges of the panic attack slowly faded away as my heart found an even rhythm once more. We piled back into Caleb's work truck and sped through the district back home. I clung to that sentiment, knowing that shred of hope was all I could do to keep from falling apart. Adeline was back home at the apartment, safe, and it was only a matter of reaching her. The speed limit was suddenly a mere suggestion. Every yellow light was a test of horsepower. There was nothing that could keep me from getting back to her.

A text notification flashed across the CarPlay screen as I

threw the truck into park outside of our apartment complex. I lunged for my phone, swiped it open, and my heart dropped like a bag of bricks.

Adeline: I'm safe. But I will be staying with Charles tonight.

Chapter Thirty-Eight

Adeline

The district sped by in a blur—the symphony of buzzing neon signs and music spilling out into the streets, faded away as the ringing in my ear worsened. The bass from the club was still vibrating in my bones. All I could do to keep the tears lining my bottom lashes from spilling free was fixate on the way they buzzed beneath muscle and tissue.

Leaving behind the sin and temptation, the sedan weaved through the little boroughs that surrounded the ten-block radius. Each time we rolled to a stop, a wave of nausea coursed through me like someone attempting to balance on a buoy during a raging storm. It was a small blessing I didn't make a mess of the backseat before the driver shifted into park.

Charles was waiting for us in the lobby of his building. He placed his hand on my shoulder and said, "You did the right thing, *mon étoile.*"

My entire body felt numb.

I followed Charles to the elevator and rode the entire way up in heavy silence. It wasn't until we entered his apartment and the door shut behind us that I felt the events of the last hour start to bleed through the haze.

I fought as best as I could, but it was a losing battle.

Charles led the way to the kitchen, and the first thing I noticed was the way the silence clung to every empty corner of the apartment in an attempt to fill the void of the missing furniture and decor. He made quick work of pouring himself a glass of wine to pair nicely with the lit cigarette between his lips. As the gracious host he was, he offered me both, but I declined in lieu of a cup of water.

"Where's Jos—"

"Not here," he interrupted. "She's staying with a friend. Indefinitely."

"Oh. I'm sorry," I said, my voice swallowed up in the space between us.

"If I wanted your pity, I would have asked for it," he said with a somber smile.

The red wine sloshed around in his glass as he took a long sip.

"Yesterday was her late brother's birthday, and it seems the last place she wanted to spend it was here." A beat passed. "It's funny how someone can be gone yet still find a way to pull the strings of the living. Isn't that right, Adeline?"

I was far from sober, but the way he glared at me was the most sobering event of the night. "It—it's getting late, and I should be heading home. Jin is probably worried sick about me. If I could borrow a charger for a little while, I would get out of your hair."

"Sit," he said firmly, snatching the phone out of my hand and plugging it in across the kitchen. The quick burst of movement sent another wave of nausea slamming into me. "This will only take a moment. You can charge your phone in the meantime."

Fighting the subtle spin of the room, I had no other choice but to sit down and wait.

"You haven't been in the city for long enough to have been here during the fires, but a little theater in the heart of the district nearly burned to the ground. Tragic, really."

I nodded, unsure how this related to Josephine.

"Before the fire, the bank seized the property and decided to sell it to the highest bidder. The Martin family was the first to jump at the opportunity, pissing off a few other eager buyers in the process. Josephine and her brother took on the dying business for themselves and built it from the ground up. And while they were willing to play fair, others weren't as forgiving."

He plucked the cigarette from his lips and blew a trail of hazy smoke that ate up the distance between us before continuing his story.

"You have to understand, Destler had his own ambitions. The man was consumed by the idea of owning The Lotte, and didn't care who he hurt along the way. At first, it was nothing more than a few counterbids and silly intimidation tactics meant to scare us into submission, but that wasn't enough for him. He wanted to make sure there was no one left in his way."

A harsh white glow illuminated the kitchen backsplash as my phone lit up. I started toying with the rim of my cup as I watched the general outline of a notification flash on my screen, one after the other.

"That's when Destler set his sights on Krissy, the new leading lady of The Lotte," he said, voice dripping in pity. "Patrick was hopelessly in love with her, and Destler took advantage of that. On the night of my rehearsal dinner, he held us all at gunpoint and kidnapped her, demanding the deed to the theater in exchange for her safe return. Patrick, being the lovesick bastard he was, thought he could have it all: outsmart

Destler and save the girl. But he was blinded by his own ambitions, and it drove him right into Destler's trap."

"The fire...?" I rasped.

"When the smoke cleared, there was nothing left of him to bury. Josephine carried most of the burden of his death on her shoulders, and she hasn't quite been the same since. She always thought that if she hadn't pressured him to buy the theater, he would still be here with us today. Even their father, an old friend of mine, still struggles to make sense of it."

"I'm confused. Why was Destler never tried for murder?" I asked.

"There wasn't anything left of Patrick to help convict Destler of his crimes. He walked away a free man, and seeing that he's now engaged to Krissy, I've always suspected foul play," he admitted. "Which makes me really curious, why would Jin and his younger brother be friends with a monster like Destler?"

"Caleb's construction company is leading the restoration of the theater," I answered. Another flash of white light cast over the backsplash. "They only know one another in a professional sense."

"Adeline," he said, clicking his tongue. "Do you know why I brought you here?"

"You said over the phone—"

"You're far too trusting—it's what got you into this mess to begin with." I flinched, his words striking true. "You have too much potential on stage for me to actively sit back and watch you squander it. You survived one monster; you don't need to put yourself in a position to be near another, which is exactly why you need to be careful of the Collins family. There are things they aren't telling you—reasons why, despite countless job applications, Jin can't seem to land another artistic director role."

"What are you talking about, Charles?"

"That's a conversation you two need to have, not me," he said, standing up. "It's late. Let me show you to your room. Stay as long as you need."

Charles plucked the phone off the counter, his eyes falling to the background image of Jin standing in the rose garden, a pink begonia tucked behind his ear. The call eventually went to voicemail, and the image of our first date disappeared with it.

The phone continued to relentlessly buzz in my hand, one call or missed call after the other. It wasn't until I was behind closed doors that I allowed myself to sift through them. Each a horrific timeline of the last hour, taking me from the moment he realized I was missing to mere seconds ago, begging me to return his calls. My finger hovered over the call button...

There are things they aren't telling you.

The whispers seeped back into the subconscious, finding refuge.

Mere hours ago, I would have crumbled to my knees with relief to hear the sound of his voice, and now that he was only one tap away, I wasn't sure I could bring myself to do it. I wasn't sure I could add another voice ringing in my ear when Charles's words still rattled around in my skull.

You survived one monster—

I shot Jin a text letting him know I was safe.

—you don't need to put yourself in a position to be near another.

I was staring down at a picture of our first date again, wondering what could have possibly compelled Charles to have said what he did. Jin wasn't a monster, right? No, of course not. Jin was *not* a monster. This entire thing was ridiculous. I don't understand why Charles would even say such a thing.

But you didn't know Noah was a monster when you first met, the whisper said.

"Goddamn," I muttered to myself, eyes snapped shut.

What Charles was insinuating hinted at a version of Jin I wasn't even sure had the capability of existing. There were so few reasons that would automatically disqualify someone as experienced as Jin, and those that came to mind were horrific.

The screen went black. My reflection stared back at me, unmoving, leaving me with the hard truth that one of them was likely lying to me. But which one was it, Jin or Charles?

Jin: I'm on my way

Recognizing I tend to overthink before I have all the answers, much like the newspaper article, I decided to face this head-on and put this entire thing to rest before it escalated beyond reason. All this worrying would be for nothing, and I would have something to laugh about on the car ride home.

I typed his full name into the search bar. The first eight results of which were a few social media accounts he hadn't been active on in years, his bio on the Republic City Opera House website, and a college professor in Mississippi who happened to have the same name.

In my drunken haze, the memory of his ring-back tone echoed in my brain. Along with a conversation we had weeks ago. In lieu of going by his full name, Jin had always chosen to shorten it. Something he confided in me when he opened up about his struggles assimilating into life in America as a young boy. And while he personally went by Jin, no government documentation would recognize him by the shortened version.

I typed out Hyun-jin Collins, too curious to stop myself.

The first result stopped me in my tracks.

A smaller, more ambivalent voice whispered in my ear, telling me not to click on the link for the Delten County Sheriff's office, but that voice was quickly squandered by any self-preservation as compulsion gave in.

A pair of familiar dark eyes locked with mine.

I tossed the phone, and it slid across the floor like a rock being skipped on a lake before colliding with the underside of the sink, if only to escape their piercing glare.

"What the fuck." I slapped my hand against my chest, the thrumming of my own pulse echoing into my fingertips. "What the actual fuck."

The word "no" spilled from my lips like an incantation that, if spoken enough times, could make this all disappear, along with the glowing phone tucked under the underside of the counter.

As if approaching a startled animal, I crawled on my hands and knees toward the screen, craned my neck, and prayed that I hadn't seen what I had before hurdling my phone across the room.

Jin appeared to be at least a decade younger in the image, but the look in his dark eyes spoke to the type of hardship and pain that could only be accomplished by a lifetime of suffering. He was nearly unrecognizable.

Below the image read:

Name: Hyun-jin Collins

Charges: Aggravated Assault, Battery

Incident Description: Involved in a physical altercation on December 3, where multiple individuals attacked the victim, resulting in severe injuries.

Court Outcome: Pled guilty to reduced charges; sentenced to 1 year with 6 months served and probation.

The phone clattered to the floor, and I fell back on my heels. The sound rattled around in my brain over and over as I tucked my knees and heaved a sharp breath. It was several long seconds before I realized the pounding was coming from within the apartment, not my head.

The alcohol churned in my gut, setting fire to my internal organs. A stark contrast to the way my flesh wrapped around me too tightly, the more I attempted to make sense of what I had seen. It was as if my own skin was slowly suffocating me.

Bang. Bang. Bang.

I stumbled to my feet, moving on instinct rather than reason.

Charles burst out of his bedroom, wielding a wooden baseball bat.

"I—I think it's Jin outside," I said, hardly a whisper.

The muffled sound of his shouting punctuated each bang on the other side of the door.

Charles held his hand out. "Stay here."

The acoustics in the apartment amplified every creaking floorboard groaning beneath Charles's heel, the resounding snap of the lock turning out of place, the grating of the hinges swinging open. It made me feel as if I were standing next to Charles as he confronted Jin.

"Where is she?" Jin snapped.

"She doesn't want to see you, Collins. Go home."

The sound of his voice made the contents of my stomach churn more violently. Sweat licked down my spine as my back smacked against the wall. I hugged my arms around myself, tilted my head back, and was overcome by claws of panic. Each breath came out in an agonizing wheeze. It felt like any moment now my lungs would give out on me completely.

He scoffed. "I don't believe that for one second."

"You have exactly five seconds to get out of my house. Five."

"Charles, if you don't get out of my way—"

"Four."

"—right now, I'm going to take the bat from your hands and—"

"Three."

Jin started shouting my name; the last syllable of my name was wounded.

Sang Pour Sang, Josephine's beloved painting, loomed at the end of the hallway. The horrific depiction of a fictional battle taunting me from afar, asking something from me in return, I wasn't quite sure how to interrupt.

"Two."

And while I didn't have an answer, I was terrified that if I didn't step in and intervene by the time Charles finished his count, the living room would turn into a derivative interpretation of it. Despite how much it pained me to put one foot in front of the other, I emerged from the hallway, and our eyes instantly clashed from across the room. It seemed as if no matter the situation, he could always sense the invisible string that connected us. Making me wonder if he also sensed the line snap by the way his expression fell.

"Sweetheart, I've been looking every—"

"I think it's best if you leave," I interjected. "I'm going to stay here tonight. Maybe longer."

Charles released Jin's collar and then stood guard on the outskirts of our conversation, leaning up against his baseball bat much like a cane.

"I—I don't understand." His gaze shifted between Charles and me. "If this is about the club, Caleb was shit-faced. I had to take him to the restroom and make sure he didn't fall out of his wheelchair. By the time he was done throwing up, and I checked my phone, you were nowhere to be found. I was terrified. I couldn't find you. I couldn't get a hold of you. I'm so sorry. You know I would never intentionally mean to hurt you."

"No, you just lie instead, Hyun-jin."

"What's that supposed to mean?"

"I really don't want to do this right now, Jin," I rasped, eyes flicking to Charles, who intently watched me. "Can we please talk about this later?"

"This is all one big misunderstanding. Let's go home, and we can sit down and talk about it properly."

"I'm not leaving."

Jin cursed under his breath and stepped forward, and I stepped back.

Words could be twisted, manipulated, and shaped into entirely new narratives. I'd been on the receiving end of far too many flipped narratives to know; all it would take is a "let's sit down to have a conversation" for lies to take shape. Staying with Charles was the last thing I wanted to do, but I would take this scenario over leaving with a man I hardly recognized anymore.

"Whatever this is between us doesn't work if we don't communicate. I want to fix whatever's the matter, but we can't start to make things better until I know what's going on. Will you please tell me what happened?" he asked, failing to keep his voice even.

"Who's Ethan Bennett?"

Jin's entire body flinched as if I struck him.

"Here's your chance. Clear the air while you still can."

"You have to understand. I wanted to tell you—"

"Aggravated assault and battery," I snapped. "Are you kidding me, Jin? Seriously? After everything that I've been through, it didn't once cross your mind to tell me?"

From a very young age, I was told that I was the easy child. The pleasant, soft-spoken younger sister who rarely got in trouble or raised her voice. I was praised for my compliance, and what was seen as an attribute was actually conditioning me to slip deeper into these inherent weaknesses. I always had a lot to say; I just never had the voice to say it aloud. A younger version of myself would have shoved all her emotions in a bottle and sealed them up, convinced it was better to stay quiet rather than insist on confrontation, but for once, I wanted to toss the glass bottle on the floor and see what came spilling out. I deserved that much after Jin might as well have taken one of those shards of glass and shoved it into my heart.

"Every day," he bit out, startling me in the process. "The thought has crossed my mind every single waking moment you've been in my life because for the last ten years, there hasn't been a single day that hasn't gone by when I'm not reminded of what I did, and the opportunities I lost because of it. You have to know I'm not ashamed of what I had to do to protect the people in my life; I'm disgusted with myself for being too much of a coward to tell you about my past.

"It doesn't even matter that I was planning on taking you to dinner with Sophia and Caleb to sit you down and have a proper conversation about it, because that's just another excuse to prolong the inevitable. I had no right to keep the truth from you this long, and I'm fully prepared to deal with the consequences of my actions."

You had all this time, and yet you didn't.

"Tell me," I challenged, wanting to see what other lies he might tell.

"Do you remember when I told you the story about Sophia's ex-boyfriend?" I nodded. "Ethan Bennett refused to believe that he'd lost Sophia for good and was determined to win her back. So, when Caleb came into the picture, things turned more aggressive—borderline violent. He would sit in his car outside of her work and watch her, leave bouquets of roses on her doorstep with threatening notes, and harass her online. When she finally broke down and told Caleb what was going on, it was too late.

"Ethan had anonymously mailed explicit photos to her athletic director, and—" He blew out a breath. "There were rumors that she might lose her track scholarship because of it. Sophia begged him not to do anything and let it work itself out, but Caleb had too much pride to sit back and watch her suffer. I was in the process of packing up everything to return to Paris the week after graduation when my brother broke down and told me everything. He wanted to take matters into his own hands, and—I couldn't let him go alone. Neither of us could have ever imagined that confronting him after work would have turned out the way it did. Ethan had a knife—and well, at the moment it was either him or us."

Our eyes met, and something resembling understanding washed over his features.

"Ethan's grandfather worked for some fancy law firm, and with all of our fingerprints on the knife and no other evidence, it was hard to prove who started it. Caleb and I were facing one year in jail for defending Sophia, but we pleaded guilty to lower our sentence, knowing we didn't stand a chance compared to the resources at Ethan's disposal. I don't remember much of those six months—I blacked out a lot of it—but knowing Caleb and I were stuck in that cell while Sophia still wasn't safe was absolutely terrifying. I started having panic attacks nearly every day. I felt so hopeless...

"I did what I had to do to protect both Sophia and Caleb. While I don't regret the messy parts of my past, I will never forgive myself for choosing to protect the peace rather than tell you the truth. Some part of me thought that by prolonging the inevitable, I could give you a chance to understand why I would do such a thing. I wanted you to love me for my worth before defining me by my past. I don't expect you to forgive me, but if you choose to, know that I am willing to work through anything that comes our way."

"I'm not in a position to forgive you right now."

His throat worked. "I understand."

"I hope you know you can't protect everyone, Jin," I said softly. "I'm going to stay here for a little bit. I need some time to think."

"I'm sorry, Adeline. I never meant to hurt you."

Charles put his hand on Jin's shoulder and shoved him back. As the door shut in Jin's face, all I said was, "Noah used to tell me the same thing after every time he hurt me, too."

Chapter Thirty-Nine

Jin

Clutching a backpack twice my size, I remember having to adjust my strap every few steps to keep up with my mother after she gently shook me awake in the dead of the night with the promise that if I stayed quiet, I would get *gamjajeon* for breakfast. It was that special time of the day when the sky couldn't quite decide if it was night or day. The golden rays of the sun danced on the horizon as we drove westbound. Keeping true to my promise, I didn't dare breathe a word aloud, not even when I noticed a pair of headlights following us.

There's so little I remember of that day, such minute details that didn't make sense why I'd clung onto them for so long. Perhaps it was my brain's way of protecting itself. Like the cool air biting my round, chubby cheeks as I leaped from the cab. Or the crossing guard blowing their whistle at a car attempting to park in a loading zone. I couldn't recall a single thing my father said to my mother as he confronted her on that harrowing winter morning, but his parting words were forever seared into my mind as my mom physically tore me from his arms, never to see him again.

I didn't think anything could hurt more than being forced to flee home with my mom and losing my dad all in the same day. That type of pain was reserved for once in a lifetime—or so I thought.

Charles shoved me back, using his full force to send me stumbling into the hallway. My eyes never left her with each faltering step. I needed her to see I meant this. I need her to understand it was never meant for things to end like this for us.

I didn't want to lose someone I loved again.

"I'm sorry, Adeline. I never meant to hurt you," I groveled, swearing by every word.

As a child, I was naive enough to believe goodbye wasn't forever. That my father would make good on his promise and visit our new home in Busan or even find me in America when we moved again years later. I was a fool then, and I was a fool now for thinking words alone could heal all that was broken. While they might not heal, they could very well tear us apart.

Adeline didn't dare break my gaze as she said, "Noah used to tell me the exact same thing after every time he hurt me, too."

I was well aware that I might have lost her before she was ever truly mine.

That haunting truth was constantly at the forefront of my mind. Following me around like a shadow, nipping at my heels. Much like a real shadow, they would bend and grow over the course of the day, adapting to my mental whims. Lengthening beyond reason as the next three days flew by in a hazy blur. Only in the dead of the night would they appear to recede, giving me a moment's rest before crawling over my duvet and settling themselves atop my chest on the cusp of a dream. It felt like bricks were being stacked atop my chest, one on top of the other, forcing my internal organs to shift around in order to breathe properly.

Without fail, at some point in the night, I would wake up in a gasp and lunge for my phone, praying she might have texted me back.

Jin: I know you don't want to talk to me right now, and I want to respect that, but please don't stay there if you don't feel safe. Here's Sophia's number in case you don't feel comfortable there. They will take you in, no questions asked.

Jin: I'm ready to talk about this whenever you are.

Jin: I respect whatever decision you choose. If you want to end our trial, that's okay. I just want you to be happy at the end of the day.

Jin: I miss you so much.

They went unanswered. Every last one of them.

Excuses were saved for those willing to justify their mistakes rather than take accountability. And as I had before a jury of my peers, I admitted that I was guilty in this regard. I had actively chosen to lie by omission, and despite having every intention to sit down and tell her with the help of Sophia and Caleb by my side, it was far too late for that. After everything she'd been through, Adeline should have been privy to that information long before she ever signed her name on that dotted line.

I had fucked up.

And I had no one else to blame but myself.

If the mere suggestion of love insinuated the possibility of losing it all, then I deserved to wallow in the heartache that would soon follow. The fraction of love and support she showed me wasn't earned. I deserved to miss her so much it threatened to split my heart into two and leave me a tattered, sniveling mess every time I was forced to sit in on rehearsal and bear witness to the lengths she went to ignore me—and boy, was she creative, all right.

Love was not bound to arbitrary reasons, and the abundance of love meant there had to be a part of me prepared to lose it all, even if it was unrequited forevermore. I was more than prepared to spend a lifetime pining for what could have been, had she not slipped during act two. The fall didn't result in any serious injuries, but the way her eyes caught mine from across the room after blatantly ignoring me for days proved there was still a part of her that wanted to turn to me in times of need.

There was still trust that I would catch her if she fell. It was the reason I was back at Charles's apartment complex, and all the motivation I needed to believe there was still a fighting chance for us. I'd be damned not to try.

Charles opened the door a quarter of the way, realized who was standing on the other side, and attempted to slam it in my face. I only had a split second to shove my shoe between the frame and the door before it snapped shut.

"I only need a moment," I said, placing my hand on the door for extra leverage.

"Desperate isn't a good look on you, Collins."

"I'm not here to cause problems. I need to give her something, then I'll leave."

"She isn't here."

"I don't mind waiting until she comes back."

Between the door and the jamb, he studied me with those piercing blue eyes of his. A hint of a smile, curling the corner of his lip.

"Adeline hasn't been here since Monday. I figured you two had kissed and made up," gibed Charles as he swung the door open. "Be my guest if you don't believe me."

And because I wasn't known for making particularly sound decisions lately, I didn't think twice before barging into his apartment and scouring the place for any sign of her. My heart wedged itself deep within my throat as I desperately searched for a wayward hair tie, her dance bag bursting at the seams with clothes she fought to take out, or even a balled-up journal entry she failed to make in the waste basket. Anything.

Though each room yielded the same conclusion: Adeline wasn't here.

If Adeline hadn't been here in two nights, and she wasn't with Sophia. That could only mean one thing...

"I have to go," I said, attempting to shoulder past him. Before I could make it by, a hand shot out in front of me. Charles and I stood side by side, our gazes locked.

"Remember what I told you the last time you were here: don't forget what happened to the last person she loved."

The culture surrounding theater was deeply rooted in superstition. Plays, productions, and ballets lived and died by the rituals and curses ingrained in every performer's brain. While I didn't consider myself a believer, it had become a habit to check the ghost light on my way out if I was the last to leave. With the sole purpose of providing light for any ghosts or ghouls that called this building home, the floor lamp positioned center stage had likely seen its fair share since the opening of the theater's doors. With one confirmed death in my lifetime, I couldn't say I was surprised when I stepped into the auditorium and found the light switched off. Whether she believed in the superstition or not, I didn't imagine she wanted to invite any spirits from beyond the grave.

Adeline had been right where I'd found her all those weeks ago. It was as if I'd been suddenly transported through time and space, bringing me back to the exact moment I stumbled across her, feet propped up in the third row, frantically jotting down her thoughts as quickly as they popped into her head. The dreamer in me desperately wished I had somehow stepped through time—a chance to do it all over again without the constructs of fear and negligent decisions shaping my path forward.

And although this wasn't a second chance, it might very well be a last hope.

Jin: Look up.

It gave me exactly twenty seconds to mentally prepare myself at the top of the aisle before she realized I was lurking in the shadows.

As she had in the studio earlier today, Adeline's stormy hazel eyes found mine. So much emotion resided within the soft shades of brown that tapered off into a striking hue that I couldn't decide whether or not it was gray or seafoam green. I wasn't sure she was aware of how much her eyes gave away. All it took was one look to get lost.

I ventured down the aisle and cut through row two to give us some space.

"You told Charles you were staying with me," I said, leaning against the back of a seat so I was facing her, arms crossed. "How long were you planning on staying here before someone noticed?"

Adeline shoved the sleeve of her dusty pink cardigan up and looked down at her wrist, pretending to read a watch that wasn't there. "I guess all it takes is two nights before someone notices I'm missing. Again."

Draped in shadows, there was something small about the way she was curled up in the seat, like the shadows were right at home tracing the contours of her turned lips and bloodshot eyes.

"You told me you needed your space, and I was trying to give it to you. I had no idea you would resort to staying at the theater again. Sweetheart—" I sighed. "Adeline, I understand you'd rather be anywhere else than staying with me right now, which is why I came to let you know that Caleb cleared out the guest room for you, and you can move in tonight, if you like."

"I'm fine staying here...at least for a little while longer."

"You can't sleep in the props department, avoiding me forever."

"One"—she held up a finger—"I still have the key you lent me, so I'm not sleeping in the props department anymore. And two"—another finger—"I'm not trying to avoid you *forever*, Jin. I — I just need time to wrap my head around this. It's a lot to deal with on top of everything else going on in my life. And frankly, I'm upset with you."

"And you have every right to be upset. I intentionally left out the messy bits of my past because I was scared to admit that side of me to you. Be upset. Scream at me. Curse me out until you're blue in the face. Do anything besides shut me out."

Please, wildflower. Give me something.

"And what if I don't want to?" A beat passed.

"I know this might not be fair to bring up right now, but that doesn't make it any less true. I hoped that of all people, you would understand not wanting to open up about a past for fear of being judged," I said, holding her gaze. "Isn't that the reason you still haven't told me about your relationship with Noah?"

"Jin," she warned, her tone exhausted.

"What happened between you and Noah is your truth to tell, and I never wanted to pressure you into speaking on it until you're ready. Yet despite knowing so little of what hell he put you through, I know enough to understand he and I are not the same. I don't hurt people for the sake of being malicious. I only did what I did to protect the people I loved. Keeping the truth from you was wrong, and it was more about my own insecurities than it ever was about trying to break your trust. While I don't expect you to ever forgive me—I sure as hell don't forgive myself —I want you to understand, I am not Noah. I never will be."

Her gaze dropped to the composition book in my hand. She said nothing, only stared at its worn edges.

"While I was in jail," I continued, forcing myself to fill the suffocating silence. "The first panic attack felt like a one-off—something I could ignore and pretend never happened, but after the third one, I was referred to the on-site psychiatrist. Dr. Mendoza taught me the trick about finding a color in the room when I sensed a panic attack coming and encouraged me to journal between sessions. It helped while I was there, but after I was released, I started to write less and less. It became something I only picked up on difficult days, rather than a resource to constantly be utilizing. I didn't start taking it more seriously until I saw how at peace you were every time I caught you scribbling in your notebook. I know part of this is trust, and I want you to have this so we can start the process of rebuilding what we had."

I held out the notebook, but Adeline didn't move a muscle.

I huffed out a breath and thumbed through the pages.

"August 4," I read aloud. "Sabrina was supposed to get the role after her apprenticeship, but I couldn't bring myself to hand it over. How could I after a performance like that? What can I say? Hartwell stole the show."

"Jin—"

"August 12. Every day I get to watch her dance is a little brighter than the last. I can't remember the last time I woke up excited to go to work." I flipped through the notebook until I found the next entry squished between a lopsided checklist and a few budget math problems. "September 9. I can't stop thinking of her. I feel like I'm going crazy."

Between those pages, I lost myself, reliving the version of myself that never thought I would ever be reading this aloud, let alone to Adeline. I was vaguely aware of my name echoing off the high ceilings, but I ignored it and kept reading.

"September 10. HR said it's frowned upon, but there's nothing in the employee handbook that says I can't. I have no idea if asking her will be a mistake, but I would rather live with rejection than regret." Skimming past notes on the beginning stages of planning *Le Cœur Sauvage*, I found the entry I was looking for. "December 22. I would blame Anastasia for getting me drunk at the company holiday party, but I know that would be as much of a lie as saying I wasn't watching Adeline dance all night. It was the first time in a while I saw her smile, and it was borderline addictive. I know it's selfish of me to still want to be with her while she's with someone else, but had Halle not dragged her off the dance floor, I might have spilled my guts to her. I don't know if last night was more of a blessing or a curse—"

The notebook was ripped clean from my hands.

"Jin, please stop. You're overwhelming me. If you want me to read this damn notebook"—she shook it furiously in the air—"then I will do it when I'm ready. If you want me in your life, then you need to accept that I need to do this on my own accord, not because you keep shoving a notebook in my face. You keep claiming not to be him, then please give me this—give me something he never did."

"I—yes, I'm sorry. Take all the time you need, but when you decide to read it, just promise me you'll start with"—I pointed to the notebook—"the beginning of the spring season."

Adeline's focus dropped to the open page. Something must have caught her attention right away, because it wasn't long before her eyes were dancing across the entry. There was nothing I could do other than watch in horror as the composition book clattered against the floor and Adeline stepped away like it was carrying the plague.

Curious what she'd stumbled across, I plucked it off the floor.

. . .

April 2,

The bruises might have faded, but when I close my eyes, I can see his handprint wrapped around the columns of her neck. It makes me sick to my stomach just thinking about the amount of force he had to use for such a deep bruise to blossom across her neck. After everything she's been through, it seems like a blessing she can even find it in herself to smile. Every time I press my lips to the side of her neck, it's my own way of promising I will do everything in my power to keep that beautiful smile on her face forevermore.

I lifted my gaze, but she was already watching me from where she stood in the aisle. Again, her eyes gave away more than she was willing to say aloud—two storms clashing together, and yet despite so much emotion residing there, I could sense her shrinking away from this conversation.

"Talk to me, Adeline. What's going on in that mind of yours?"

Please don't shut me out again.

"Every time?" she rasped, hand brushing over her neck.

I swallowed the lump in my throat, then nodded. "Every time."

Every kiss was a promise, I swore to her. Proof that despite a past riddled with trauma, there has always been a part of her willing to give me her neck and trust I wouldn't hurt her as Noah had. Whether she realized it or not, deep down she knew we were not the same.

"Goddamn it, Jin," she cursed, then began pacing again, hands fisting her inky black hair. "Do you know how exhausting this all is?"

"I want to know," I answered. "Tell me, sweetheart."

"I'm not stupid, Jin." She huffed out a strained laugh. "I didn't run away from our conversation at Charles's apartment for nothing. Logically, I should be able to differentiate what you've done to protect Sophia from what Noah did to me, but my brain was so terrified of putting myself in a position to get hurt again that I ran at the first sign of trouble. It wasn't the mature thing to do, but I couldn't help it; I was terrified. Pushing you away was the safe choice, not the smart one." She stabbed at the air, gesturing to her own journal balancing on the armrest. "I've written about what happened between us no less than a dozen times since, and each and every time I come to the same conclusion: how silly this all is."

Tears blotted out her stormy eyes.

"What Noah put you through was extremely traumatic. It's perfectly normal to feel what you're feeling, and I hope you don't think little of yourself for doing so," I responded, inching my way into the aisle.

"I'm so tired," she heaved, swiping the back of her hand over her cheek. "He's still haunting my every waking moment. Every time someone raises their voice, I flinch, terrified it will be their fist next. I am constantly in pain every day after practice, and I can't even walk into the one place that can help me because I feel like I'm going to faint when I see that blue door. Even when I'm with you, someone I *should* trust, I have to wear my headphones a certain way because I've conditioned myself to constantly be aware of my surroundings in case Noah is lurking somewhere in the shadows. I should be relieved that bastard is dead and I am finally free, but I can't escape him. He's still taking from me when I have nothing left to give."

"Noah doesn't have to win—"

"But he is," she shouted. "He wins every time I struggle to make sense of life without him. He wins every time the memory of him assaults me. He wins every time someone sheds a tear for the life he lived, then condemns me for mine. He wins when I miss out on my chance at happiness when it comes to being with you. God, you have no idea how much he hated you, Jin. He's probably rolling in his grave right now."

I stepped forward. "You haven't lost anything when it comes to us."

"It doesn't feel that way…"

"Do you still want to do this—us?" I asked.

As we held each other's gaze, time seemed to tick by at its own pace. It felt like an eternity before she slowly walked over to me and placed her hand over my heart. I held my breath as Adeline studied her painted nails, tracing over the stitches of my clothes.

"You really hurt me, Jin."

"I know."

"You lied to me."

"I did."

"So much so that I'm scared this might be only the beginning of a heartbreak I won't recover from, but—" She sucked in a sharp breath then lowered her head to my chest, fisting the fabric of my shirt. "You're right, it isn't fair for me to compare what Noah did to me to a mistake you are trying to make up for. I can't bear the thought of losing you," she said softly. "As much as I should step away—at least for some time. I can't do it. I can't *lose* you, Jin."

For longer than I could remember, I have been hopelessly, refutably in love with the woman in my arms. And for much longer than that, I had convinced myself it could never be. I could never love Adeline Elise Hartwell as I should because she would never love me in return. I clung to this sentiment like a life preserver because it was easier to be at home in my heartache than believe I was capable of true happiness.

I wasn't sure if Adeline loved me or ever would, but I would gladly stand by her side through thick and thin, panic attacks, court dates, and all.

"Then let's work through this," I said, voice thick. "Noah doesn't get to win. Okay?"

"I want to work through this together. Just give me time."

Lost in her stormy eyes, I tugged a strand of hair behind her ear.

"All I have is time to give you, wildflower."

A glint of something reflective caught my eye. A diamond-studded band with a crystal teardrop hanging from her earlobe. I knew that earring all too well. The last time I saw it, it was hanging off a corpse.

Chapter Forty

Adeline

Wrapped in a purple bow as bright as a bundle of lavender, the velvet box had been waiting for me atop my duvet cover the second night I stayed at Charles's place. The tiny note attached to the underside of the lid read: *Something to shine as bright as you atop that stage. Good luck, I know you'll be amazing.*

The gift was far too much—I knew that. After some back and forth, I finally accepted the gift and proudly wore it in anticipation of the upcoming show. Delicate in nature, the small curved bands were individually lined with diamonds, all of which led to a crystal teardrop that looked more fitting on the cover of a fashion magazine rather than hanging from my earlobe. The ridges of which I couldn't stop toying with the entire walk from the parking structure to the scarce district streets.

"Do you trust me?" Jin had asked me after discovering the earrings.

That was a loaded question. The concept of trust was much like staring down at the broken shards of a mirror. Under threat of cutting yourself, you can very well mend the pieces back together, but you will always see the cracks in the reflection. It is up to each of us to decide if we are willing to look past them and trust that the shards of glass will never hurt us again.

Jin had lied by omission. More than trust had been broken between us, but weren't relationships by design built on the pillars of imperfection? No relationship was perfect, I knew that. The lack of healthy relationships in my life was abysmal, and it wasn't as if my parents had led by example; however, it wasn't lost on me that couples could easily repair trust with time, patience, and communication. It hadn't occurred to me that someone cared enough to try.

That someone in question had taken a page straight out of my book and written down every drunken confession, painfully blissful memory, and hopeless dream in a composition book nearly as tattered as my heart. I nervously flipped through the pages as Jin sped through the empty district streets for the sole reason of having something to do with my hands.

From November 18, when he questioned if it was acceptable for a grown man to have a crush this bad, to November 23, when he convinced himself it was perfectly fine, to January 14, when he forgot to take his notes for rehearsal because he was so mesmerized by my dancing. It was all there.

The story of Jin without fear that anyone would read his deepest, darkest secrets.

Jin placed his hand on the small of my back as he turned a key I wasn't aware he possessed, and led me into a theater that felt more like a legend than anything else—The Lotte. Having recently moved to the city, there was little I knew about the historic theater other than the fact that it nearly closed its doors forever after a tragic fire. Caleb's construction company was leading the restoration, and by the look of it, it was hard to tell there ever was a fire in the first place.

The Lotte was immaculate. A microcosm of the Entertainment District's rich history that instantly pulled you in and invites you to bask in the gilded ambience. It was like stepping back in time, and there was nothing I wanted more than to get lost between its walls, but Jin's hand was steady on my back, guiding me through several hallways before we were spit out into the main amphitheater. The main seating area had been gutted, creating a leveled surface for the lounge. Tables and chairs had been scarily placed about; the other furniture was boxed up in the darkest corners of the theater.

"Someone will need to be here tomorrow at seven to let the inspector in," a voice said.

Another voice groaned like it was mid-tantrum. "Am I being voluntold or...?"

"If you want to keep your job, then yes."

Two men spoke in hushed conversation near the stage. Bits and pieces of a heated discussion regarding the inspection needed to open the theater doors tapered off into silence as we approached. Completely at odds with one another, the men couldn't have looked more different. Even the way they carried themselves spoke to the lighthearted nature of the one on the left and the rigid, yet commanding posture of the other. They were nothing alike, but I couldn't help feeling that if the man with the scar found it himself to widen his smile, they would be an identical match.

"If this is about the lost footage, then I sure as shit hope you have better news than us. That lead ended up being a dead-end, and we're back at square one," the man with the inky black hair said. "Sanderson isn't returning our calls, and we can't get through to him."

Jin started, "This isn't about the footage—"

"It's about her," the man with the scar interjected, then extended his hand outward. "Adeline Hartwell, the killer balle-rina herself. I've heard so much about you."

"Adeline, this is Antonio and—"

"Erick Destler?" I cut in, staring down at his extended hand. "So have I."

Erick tilted his head, a smirk gracing his features. "It seems like your boss has been whispering in your ear. I'd love to know what that old bastard is saying about me."

I looked at Jin and he gave a small nod.

"Mr. Blanchet—Charles—told me about the conspiracy surrounding his brother-in-law's death and the fire deliberately set to cover it up..." My gaze darted between Destler and Jin, the two men silently communicating something amongst themselves. Trust was not so easily earned for those who had grown accustomed to Judas's deadly kiss. I was in no position to blindly trust anyone, but I had to have faith that Jin hadn't brought me here for nothing. "...is any of that true?"

"Charles gets a sick thrill preying on weakness."

"Destler," Jin snapped.

"I'm not weak," I retorted.

"I never said you were. All I'm saying is Charles likes to use people to his advantage; he did it with Patrick by manipulating his *love* for my fiancée to trap him into a situation that he was never intended to walk away from. If he has something to gain from you, then he would have done everything he could to manipulate you, no matter how strong-willed you are."

"Charles has nothing to gain from me besides my name on his marquee," I explained. "I have no wealth, power, or status."

"Patrick had nothing of value to Charles either, but that didn't stop him from using him to do his bidding," Erick replied. "If Charles found you at your lowest point with promises that seemed too good to be true, then he, without a doubt, has plans for you. He doesn't do anything out of the kindness of his heart."

Jin placed his hand on my back and leaned in to say, "Show him."

"Um, okay. Yeah." Suddenly, all eyes were on me as I tugged a strand of hair behind my ear. Both men subtly leaned in to get a better look, then jerked away when they'd had their fill.

"If you two can make it out of the city within the hour," Erick started, "I can arrange for someone upstate to meet you at a little rest stop on Route 51. They'll give you tickets and passports. It won't be cheap, but it might be your only option right now."

"Are—are you seriously suggesting we skip town?" I asked.

"That"—he pointed to the earrings—"is a problem, and the fact Charles gave them to her means he knows more than he's leading on."

"I still don't understand what the hell is so special about these earrings?"

I was right; when Erick smiled, it did in fact match the man standing at his side. "Well, the last time I saw them, a dead man was wearing them."

The diamond earrings clattered against the nearest table as they slid across the surface. Erick caught them before they could fall off the edge.

"These were originally a gift from Patrick to my fiancée, Krissy," he said, shaking them in his hand. Then, to my surprise, Erick told a story much like Charles had a few nights before. A tale shrouded in misconceptions, forbidden love, and heroic beginnings. It was nearly identical in nature, but the power of perspective shed new light on Patrick's role in all of this. How the beginning stages of an emotionally abusive relationship drove Krissy into Erick's arms with nowhere else to go, and certain measures were taken to ensure she made it out alive. I knew very little of Erick's fiancée, but the more he shared about her journey to happiness, the more my heart ached for the dancer trapped in a relationship she never asked for.

I guessed she and I were similar in that regard.

I had no reason not to trust Charles, for he had given me everything in my darkest hours, but this wasn't the first time someone had spoken out about his character. Once again, I was faced with the difficult choice of whom to trust. Between contradicting narratives and tales of revenge and sacrifice, the only common denominator in all of this was Charles. If the question of faith were pitted between a man who gained more while I danced center stage and the one who wasn't at ease unless there was a smile on my face, then I would always pick the latter in more ways than one.

"Why me?" I asked, and the room fell silent. "Why, of all people, did Charles give me the earrings when I have nothing to do with this stupid rivalry?"

Antonio and Erick both shot a look at Jin.

The smile he flashed me was strained, as if it were more of a nervous reaction rather than something genuine. "Do you remember when I promised to find the piece of shit that had been threatening you, but asked you not to tell Charles what I was doing?" I nodded my head. Erick watched us intently, like he wasn't entirely convinced I was capable of keeping a secret. "You didn't say anything to Charles, right? Not even by accident?"

"No, of course not. I promised I wouldn't."

"Good," he huffed out. "That's good."

"Jin, what's going on?"

"Caleb started meddling in my life, if you can believe that." Jin snorted. "He knew how miserable I was at the theater, so when he heard that Erick was searching for a new executive director, he threw my name in the hat. I had an interview and everything, but Erick was looking for something more than just a director for The Lotte. He wanted information—he wanted to know why his fiancée was receiving targeted threats that were eerily similar to the ones being left behind on your vanity. Erick wanted answers, and so did I."

"You think it was Charles this entire time..."

Jin shook his head. "I can't say for sure, but it certainly feels that way."

The familiar sting of bile burned its way up the lining of my throat as Erick described in exhaustive detail the nature of Krissy's threats and how similar they were to my own. Words alone weren't enough to set me on edge, but it was the photos that accompanied the story that made me sick to my stomach. I slept under the same roof as him, for Christ's sake. What kind of monster toys with people like that?

"Which is why you two should really get the fuck out of town like we already suggested," Antonio cut in from his little corner of the theater, feet propped up on a nearby table, scrolling on his phone like he couldn't be bothered.

Neither of us dignified that with a response.

"He knows, doesn't he?" I said softly. "Charles knows you betrayed him."

"I had a feeling he could sense me slipping away from him, long before I ever started working for Erick. And now...the earrings were all the confirmation I needed."

"What if he's just testing you? What if this is all part of an elaborate plan to test your loyalty, and we're doing exactly what he wants?"

"And what if it isn't?" Erick cut in. "What if he comes for one of us as he did to Caleb? Or worse?"

This was all too much to process in one evening. I was starting to feel myself unravel, and if I was subjected to another truth, I might lose myself completely.

"Jesus," I muttered under my breath, yanking at the roots of my hair. "Jesus Christ. Jin, all my legal shit is tied up with

Charles and Donovan. If he knows the truth and is trying to punish you through me, what am I supposed to do?"

"Leave," Antonio suggested again.

"No," Jin and I shouted in unison.

"How about, I don't know, get a new lawyer?" Antonio shot back.

"*Wow*, that never occurred to me, thank you. I—" I slammed my hand against my chest and froze. "The flash drive. Oh, god."

"What flash drive?"

"Donovan said my only saving grace in this case was the video footage of Noah—of Noah, hurting me. Charles showed it to me one time. It's on a flash drive. Oh, god. He'll never give it up."

"It's red, isn't it?" Jin asked.

That stopped me in my tracks. "Yes." I hesitated. "How do you know that?"

"I think I saw it in his office the other day," he replied, eyebrows knitted together.

"It might be a lost cause. Can we move forward without it?" Erick asked.

"There might be something that can help us, but it involves breaking into my old apartment."

Antonio kicked his feet off the table and rose. "Now, that's something I can help with."

Erick gave him a pointed look. "Don't pretend you're doing this out of the kindness of your heart. You're just trying to get out of the inspection by making yourself busy," he accused.

The man with the crooked nose simply traced a pattern over his heart and said, "Can't both things be true at the same time?"

Feeble is the mind that keeps playing the same game and expecting a different outcome. Having tried my luck once before, I found myself outside of my old apartment, hoping this time might be different. Antonio knelt on the welcome mat, a set of small picks like tools in his hand.

"Hurry up!" I whispered, eyes darting down the empty hallway, expecting Lady Luck to run out any moment.

Antonio shot me a look over his shoulder. "That might be the first time a woman told me to hurry up. Usually it—"

"Keep going, Antonio," Jin added.

He smirked, focusing back on the task at hand. "See, that I am used to hearing."

With a deafening click, the door swung open, revealing a darkened apartment. Andy, being a creature of habit, spent an egregious amount of time with his girlfriend, neither of them willing to sacrifice their rent-controlled apartments in the city. I was betting on the fact that nothing had changed in the time since moving out, and it looked like I was right.

Antonio disappeared into the apartment, hand hovering on his hip. A minute later, there was a low whistle, signaling that the coast was clear.

Much like a novel, life played out in chapters—little snapshots of who we were at any given time. An ever-changing arc of highs and lows. This particular chapter in my life had thankfully closed, but when the familiar scent of essential oils that we used to cover up the neighbor's cigarette smoke hit me, I was suddenly thumbing through the pages until I found myself back in a section of my life I had no desire to reread.

"What's wrong with her?" Antonio asked.

"Give us a second," Jin answered, then threaded his fingers through mine. "Adeline, if you want me to go instead, all you have to do is tell me what I'm looking for."

Tiny little scratch marks cut across the doorjamb where

Andy and Noah had underestimated the dimensions of my desk while moving me in. There were still flakes of the paint that no one bothered to clean up.

"It—" I shook my head, loosening the thoughts. "You won't be able to find it on your own. It's fine. I can do it."

"Are you sure? It's all right to ask for help. I can't even imagine what being back here must feel like."

"Yeah, I'm okay."

Noah had been drunk that evening, claiming he needed to be compensated for his time with beer and pizza if he was being forced to help me move in all day—his words, not mine.

With Jin at my side, I retraced their steps. Over the dent in the wood where he nearly dropped the desk on his toe, past the other scrap in the doorframe where Andy had sworn that if he didn't stop damaging the apartment, he wouldn't get back his safety deposit, and finally to the second bedroom where my desk still stood. A fancy dual monitor gaming system sat atop it that hadn't been there before. It was funny how excited I was to move that thrifted piece of furniture in. It felt like a little piece of me I could have all to my own in space that never felt welcoming from the beginning.

Careful not to agitate my knees, I lowered myself to the rug in the center of the room. Jin followed in suit. Beneath the distressed rug were microscopic initials carved into the corner of the wood panel that, if you weren't looking too carefully, could easily be mistaken for another of the other dozens of scratches Noah left behind. What should have been reported to the landlord months prior had become my dirty little secret.

I pried my fingernail between the panels of wood and lifted.

Jin's breath was hot against my neck as I pulled a crisp white envelope from the gap in the wood boards. Having borne this burden long enough, I found it easier to hand it over to Jin rather than spill its contents. A dozen or so photographs fell into his hand, and all it took was one look at the top of the stack for Jin to turn away and heave a breath.

He had already shared so much with me tonight and been vulnerable in that regard; I guess it was my turn to do the same.

"Noah shattered my phone against the side of the theater the first time he caught me taking photos," I explained, twirling my finger around a strand of the rug. "This was the only way not to leave a digital footprint for him to find but still protected me, if need be."

"The disposable camera?" was all he could muster up.

Until I'd met Jin, I never imagined there would come a time when I would be excited to develop a camera roll. I had twenty-two memories left on my new camera, sitting on my nightstand at home. Funny how things change.

"Noah was easy to love," I offered, hating how true it was. "There was something so addictive about being trapped in his orbit, and after not feeling loved by the people in my life, it was...refreshing. He had a way of making me smile when all I wanted to do was cry after I stumbled into his office on the brink of an all-out breakdown. Or how he made this big, scary city feel smaller when we always had someone to visit or a new place to explore. He felt like a new beginning."

Jin clung to my every word, not daring to flip through the stack of photos.

"It was very early on in our relationship that I became aware of his jealous tendencies—some past relationship heartache he rarely spoke about unless he'd been drinking. I'd recently opened up to him about my own past relationships, so I was trying to be understanding. And, while I was expected to be sympathetic toward his circumstances, there was little reciprocated when it came to my anxiety. There was a clear power imbalance, but I was too close to the relationship to recognize it.

"It wasn't until Halloween weekend that it became so

painfully clear to me. Um..." I tugged at a short strand. "The person I was seeing before Noah happened to be in town for work and decided to stay for the holiday weekend to see some old friends. He didn't know I was seeing someone new and reached out, hoping to grab a drink and catch up. Noah saw the message an hour before we were supposed to meet up with his friends. Part of me wished I'd just stayed home instead of trying to smooth things over and calm him down for the sake of keeping the peace between us. He swore he was okay after we talked, so I slapped on a brave face and tried to salvage what I could of the evening. But my anxiety...I kept drinking, praying it would help. Then Noah kept handing me more drinks—"

The room was going in and out of focus.

"I woke up the next morning with no recollection of what had happened, other than a splitting headache and a deep gash on the side of my knee. He'd been the designated driver for the night, so I turned to Noah to figure out what the hell had happened to me. Apparently, I had been belligerent and completely embarrassed him in front of his college buddies. I broke down and drunkenly confessed all the terrible things I'd been bottling up for weeks about our relationship and my lingering feelings for Marcus, the man I'd been dating prior. Um"—I choked out a strained laugh—"Noah told me the reason I woke up still dressed in the clothes from the night before was that when he tried to get me ready for bed, I screamed at him and told him the only person who could take off my clothes was Marcus."

Jin's eyebrows furrowed. "That doesn't sound like something you would do."

"No, it doesn't." I blew out a breathy laugh. "I— I blacked out, so with no idea of what really happened, I was forced to trust what Noah had told me. I believed every word. He hadn't given me a reason not to trust him yet, but deep down, I had this weird, unsettling feeling every time I saw the cut on my knee in the mirror.

"Anytime I would ask about it, he would flip the conversation back to me and try to guilt me into a confession—screaming at me that drunk words are sober thoughts, over and over again. When I refused to admit I still had feelings for Marcus, Noah eventually broke down and admitted to lying about the entire thing to try to coax the *truth* out of me, somehow painting me as the villain in all of this, like he had no other choice than to manipulate me into doing what he wanted. But Noah wasn't just trying to get a confession out of me; he was also trying to distract me."

Letting the photos speak for themselves, I gently took the stack from Jin's hands and skimmed through them until I found the one from that night. The image was a picture of a picture, originally taken on my cell phone. The divot in the side of my knee was a gooey flesh-like color with a hard black mass in the center. My stomach churned as Jin looked between it and the white scar still painfully visible on my knee.

"It almost looks like the shape of a thumbnail," he pointed out.

"When I woke up, this is how the wound looked. There was no blood on my leg, the sheets, or even the pants I'd been wearing. Nor were there any rips in the jeans...the sober man whom I trusted to take care of me while I was drunk couldn't give me an answer either, and to this day, I still have no idea what happened while I blacked out. Somehow, not knowing was scarier than any of the things he's done to me while I was conscious—it's the not knowing that kills me.

"The first time he hurt me, there wasn't any proof to suggest he'd been the one to do it, but I took a photo of it in case. Little did I know, Noah had been searching through my phone at night and found them within the week. He might have deleted the photo and smashed my phone in a fit of rage, but the photo was somehow still in my drive when I got a new one. After that, I started documenting each time he hurt me with the disposable camera in case I ever found the courage to report it."

Jin sniffled, then wiped the back of his hand over his cheek.

"I wanted so desperately to move past this and pretend the entire thing hadn't happened because, besides the scar on my knee, there was no evidence proving he'd actually hurt me, but the next time he laid a hand on me, I was so painfully sober, I couldn't pretend anymore."

Much like the scratches in the doorjamb and the dents in the wood, these photos told the story of Noah and me—the true story that would never meet the light of day. The small set of bruises lining my forearm from when Noah yanked me into his office a little too roughly after I told him I wanted Daphne, the other physical therapist on site, to work on my knee instead of him. The blistering red scratch marks cutting down my left hip bone were left behind as a warning to stop running my mouth. The bleeding bite mark atop my breast from when I supposedly insulted his masculinity while we were having sex in this very room. The black bruises lining my rib cage like dark storm clouds that took weeks to clear up.

Each photo told a story—a chapter closed.

And despite his every attempt to wear me down, here I was.

Wildflowers are resilient. No matter the location, temperature, or lack of rainfall, they still find a way to bloom. I know you've been through a lot this year, and sometimes it feels like you don't have the right conditions to keep growing, but whether you know it or not, you have always been a wildflower.

Jin caught the tear slipping down my cheek with the back of his knuckle.

"It's okay, sweetheart. You're safe now."

I knew I was, which was why the truth kept spilling from my lips.

"Noah always apologized after hurting me, swore it was an accident, and he would never do it again. The first time was a test. Once he knew he could manipulate me and get away with it, he got bolder, more violent, smarter. He hit me where no one would see, then refused to let Daphne or the other physical therapist work on me so they couldn't report anything.

"I was so scared to leave, Jin. I thought about it nearly every day, but no matter how badly I wanted to, I knew if I did, I would lose *everything* that I have ever worked for." A memory as sharp as the blade I drove into Noah's gut assaulted my mind. The threats spewing from his lips. The way he shoved my knee to the ground and twisted until I went hoarse, screaming at him to stop... "The relationship had been over long before I ever told him I was leaving. I felt like a ghost of who I used to be, drifting through the motions. I poured myself into dance because that was the one place Noah couldn't reach me, but when I pushed myself too hard, I drove myself right back into his arms.

"Sometimes it would help to fantasize about a different life —dissociate during hard times. To think about what it would have been like had I never fallen for his tricks. It was the reason I bought a disposable camera and took photos just in case I had the strength to finally leave one day."

"Adeline"—the photos fanned out between our bent knees as Jin grabbed my face and pressed our foreheads together— "very few people would have had the courage to do what you did. I hope you know that. You are *so* brave, and every day I count my blessings that you broke free."

"It was so scary," I choked out. "God. I didn't think I could do it."

"I know." Jin shushed me with a kiss atop the crown of my

head. "He isn't here to hurt you anymore. You're safe, sweetheart. You're safe."

A bang echoed through the apartment. Startled, I tried to peel myself away from Jin, but he only held me tighter. Antonio sprinted into the room and then skidded to a stop.

"Sorry to break this little heart-to-heart up, but we need to leave. Right now."

Another bang sounded.

"I'd say we have exactly twenty seconds before your old roommate either breaks down the door or calls the cops on us," Antonio said, pointing to the foyer.

"Open the fucking door," he bellowed, punctuating each word with his fist.

I was in enough legal trouble as is; I didn't need to add breaking and entering to the list. Scrambling to collect the photographs, we rushed for the nearest window, heart racing. Antonio had wedged a chair under the doorknob, giving us the head start needed to make it out the fire escape before he could break the door off its hinges.

The entire structure shook as we weaved through the metal labyrinth, Andy hot on our trail. I didn't dare look back, but by vibration alone, I knew he was closing in. Antonio leapt to the ground first, offering to catch me as I free-fell the last three feet. Once Jin appeared at our side, we ran off into the night. The wailing of sirens was distant but closing in every second we wasted out in the open.

Chapter Forty-One

Adeline

Each photo felt like a simulacrum of the truth—a visual representation of my weakness to comply. Another dirty secret to hide away beneath my feet rather than speak of his abuse aloud.

A small voice used to whisper in my ear, pleading with me that if the day ever came, I would have the strength to show someone that envelope. Having listened to the voice in my head for so long, they had conditioned me as thoroughly as Noah had. I never imagined in my wildest dreams that Jin would be the first person I showed them to...

"What do you think?" Jin asked, leaning up against Charlotte's kitchen counter.

She continued flipping through the stack, turning them over in her examination. "I think what you did was incredibly brave, and it was likely a huge risk to get them developed. I've seen countless cases where there's little evidence to support the victim, then it becomes a big who-said-what in the courtroom," she replied, dressed in a pair of satin pajamas.

"So, you think we have a chance?" Jin asked.

Amongst the various secrets he had yet to tell me, apparently, Jin had been hard at work, trying to convince Sophia's firm to take my case pro bono. Something he didn't want me to get my hopes up about in case they decided against it. I wanted to be upset. I really did. But it felt like a waste of my time and energy with so much more to worry about. If tonight had taught me anything, it was that after this mess was over, Jin and I needed to sit down and lay all our cards on the table—no more secrets, half-truths, or sparing each other's feelings. If there was a future for us written in the stars, we couldn't be living in the past any longer.

"No, I didn't say that," she said, handing over the photos with a sigh. "Look. This evidence is good, but it doesn't paint the picture we need. Nothing in these photos even proves that it's Adeline behind the camera."

"Charlotte."

"Jin," she shot back.

"It's obviously her."

"I believe you. I really do. I'm just trying to be realistic about what a courtroom might see. The time stamps show prolonged abuse during the months you lived with Mr. Hernandez, but none of the photos show your face, tattoos, birthmarks, or anything that can link these photos to you personally. These photos would be great with some additional evidence proving the abuse, but it will be hard to stand on its own. Do you have anything else?"

I cleared my throat, but my voice still came out raspy and small. "There's CCTV footage of him throwing me on the ground from the night of his death and photos of my neck taken by RCPD."

"That's great. Paired with the photos, you stand a better chance," she said, offering me a weak smile. "You guys can make yourself comfortable. I'm going to call my boss and see if he's made a decision yet regarding taking your case."

Forty-five minutes later, we left Charlotte's place with more questions than answers. The firm was considering my case, but promises were yet to be made. When we slipped into the car well past ten o'clock, the silence was so loud, it rang in my ears. Jin gripped the steering wheel tight and bowed over, head pressed against it. Each breath came out as a ragged wheeze, and it was several minutes before he could properly regulate his breathing. I simply put my hand on his thigh and reminded him to find something red.

"Thank you," he muttered, hardly a whisper, then shifted the car into drive.

The silence was back. It was several blocks before either of us dared to break it.

"I feel like I've done everything I can and it still isn't enough to protect you," he rasped, eyes transfixed on the red lights ahead. "I don't know what to do. Part of me wishes we could run away from all of this. That I keep driving, and we could leave it all behind. I think we both deserve to have a new beginning where it can be just us two, sharing our lives together."

In a perfect world without consequences, we could drive to the apartment, collect what few belongings we could fit in his car, and never return to the district. We could indulge in Erick's offer and start anew.

I swallowed the lump in my throat.

"As much as I wish that could be true, I think we know that isn't the life we want."

He scoffed. "I would give anything to take you away from all of this."

"Jin," I sighed. "The conditions of my bail don't allow me to leave the city, and if I do, I will spend the rest of my life on the run, and you'd be an accomplice to that. We would never be able to return home. Your baby niece will never meet her uncle, you will never see Caleb and Sophia till the day you die, and I will never step foot on stage again. That isn't the future you deserve after everything you've been through. You deserve more."

"I wish it were that easy."

"Me, too."

A beat passed. "But you could go—"

"Adeline—"

"Please. Just let me speak." I reached for his hand. "You've already sacrificed so much of yourself for your family's well-being. I know what it's felt like to be sitting in a cell, wondering if your dreams will ever come to fruition, and not being sure if you even deserve them because of the consequences of your actions. Whatever we decide"—I sucked in a sharp breath—"we are damned if we do and damned if we don't. What if you went without me? What if you got your second chance to make things right? It would only be temporary, and when the trial is over, we could finally be—"

"No."

"But—"

"Dreams change," he said simply, swiping his thumb over the back of my hand. "I'm not the man I was when I lost that fellowship all those years ago. It felt easier to cling to that hope rather than admit to myself what I really needed. I just—that isn't what I want anymore. I want to be here with you, through thick and thin. No one, including Charles, gets to take that away from me."

Thousands of individual puzzles lay spread before me. Each was a fragment of the truth that I was aware was all interconnected, but I didn't have the means of piecing them together. The trial. The threats. The bail money. The fire. The flash drive. The way Charles attempted to drive a wedge between us. All of it. If I didn't know any better, I would say he was playing chess, and we were playing checkers.

With so little information at my disposal, I knew without a doubt that I didn't want to put the fate of my future in the hands of a man who I wasn't certain had my best interest at heart. A man who took pleasure in using me to play whatever game this was. But if Charles wasn't playing fair, then why did I have to?

"If Charles already suspects you've betrayed him, then neither of us is safe at the theater anymore. You could leave tomorrow, and nothing would change, but Charles needs me. He isn't going to let me leave this company with so much at stake this season, and he might very well hold the flash drive over me to keep me dancing on his stage. I can't win this trial without it..."

"I don't know for certain, but Charles has been wiping surveillance footage from the system since early February. I almost got caught checking them for the March 11 footage...I have a funny feeling that flash drive might be the only copy of that footage existing," Jin admitted.

"Which gives us even more reason to get it back. You said you saw it in his office, right? Well then, if either of us wants the future we rightfully deserve, then we have to steal it from him."

Jin was silent for a moment, pulling off to the side of the empty road to give this conversation the full attention it deserved. He shifted into park and ran a hand over the scruff of his normally clean-shaven jaw—I'd never seen him so disheveled.

"If we take the flash drive, that's it. You can never dance for this company again. I have no idea what Charles is wholly capable of, and I refuse to keep you in a dangerous situation where you could get hurt or worse...are you willing to give up everything you worked for?"

"If I don't get that evidence, then I lose everything regardless."

Chapter Forty-Two

Jin

In the Entertainment District, where the sinners and the dreamers thrived, it was evident which was which. Adeline and I had our heads in the clouds, searching for glimmers of hope while the sinners pulled the strings. If we wanted to clip ourselves free, there was only one alternative: we had to get the flash drive.

Though we couldn't do it on our own.

"Give me one moment," I rasped as we entered the apartment. "I'll come check on you after I finish and let you know what he says."

"Okay," she said, hand slipping from mine.

The door shut behind her, and darkness enveloped me with open arms. I stood frozen in the living room, unable to look away from the tendrils of light spilling out in the hallway from under the door and her shadow dancing back and forth. For the first time in three days, the house felt whole again.

Needing a little space for what I was about to do, I stepped out onto the balcony and braved the elements. A gust of wind cut across my cheek like sandpaper grinding against flesh as I opened the sliding glass door. The cold front sliced through the rising skylines as the lingering winter breeze burned off and spring prepared to take full effect in the city.

"Antonio told me what happened at the apartment," Erick said over the phone. "Did you finally come to your senses and decide to take the offer? The price for two passports will be a lot, but I promise, it will be worth it."

"No," I answered. "Given all Adeline is going through legally, we didn't think it was best to run—that isn't the type of life we want for ourselves."

The line was silent for a beat. "Then why are you calling, Jin?"

Between two rising skyscrapers, the glow of neon lights painted the glass like strokes of a watercolor painting. The mesmerizing colors mingling as one with such grace, it was nearly as enticing as the distant hum of music being carried by the wind. Constructed in ill-fated and harsh times, the Entertainment District loomed a few blocks away, demanding something in return that I wasn't quite sure it was asking for. In a place where the sinners and dreamers were meant to thrive, who was to say I couldn't be both?

"Because I have something you want."

"But?" he offered.

"It comes at a price, and I don't think you're in a position to say no to me right now."

"Okay, Collins. Let's hear it."

"It's clear we aren't safe at the theater anymore, and when we inevitably leave, you'll be no closer to learning the truth than when we started this entire shit show. I'll be gone, and you'll have nothing. There's been enough unnecessary bloodshed already. What if I told you we could finally figure out what Blanchet is up to before he strikes again?

"Charles is harboring evidence Adeline needs to prove her innocence, and if we don't get back, we don't stand a chance in court. I can't get the flash drive from his office without you, and you can't get into the theater without me. Opening night will be the last opportunity for both of us to get answers before we leave."

"If I really wanted to sneak into that theater, I don't need you to do that."

If the price of freedom was unwavering loyalty, then I would gladly carry that burden to ensure her safety. Erick wanted one thing for me, and we both knew it.

"If you do this for me, I will work for you."

"You've already signed the contract—"

"No," I interject. "This isn't about the executive director position."

On the other line, I could hear the muffled sound of footfalls and a door closing. I gripped the ice-cold railing a little harder, waiting for his response.

"Jin, before you agree to this, I need you to know what you are signing up for. You seem like a good guy who had the unfortunate luck of getting wrapped up in this mess, and if you say yes, you'll only be tangling yourself up more."

"I wouldn't have called you if I didn't. I understand what you need from me."

"Do you?" Erick asked. "This might have started as some silly rivalry between family members who are long gone, but now it has *everything* to do with what he's done to hurt the people I love. I should have died the night of the fire; do you realize that? While I bled out, Krissy had to physically drag my lifeless body from the flames before they could consume me, with no way of knowing if I was still breathing or not by the time we were safe. She was willing to sacrifice her life to save what might have very well been my corpse, and every day we have to live with that burden. And while I thank God every day that she saved me, my body will never be the same because of

Charles. I will limp down the aisle when I marry the woman I love. I can't guarantee I will catch her when she falls. I might not be able to run and play with our child if we ever decide to start a family. I am broken, and despite making my peace with that, what I can't ignore is the way Krissy flinches every time she sees a flame spark to life, or when she wakes up drenched in sweat, clenching on to me as if she's scared she might lose me to the flames again, or even the fucking threats on her life left at my doorstep. This is personal for me, Jin. Charles was the first one to draw blood, and the way I see it, he deserves to be repaid for all the pain he's caused, starting with the fire."

"If you're planning to set fire to the theater and hurt innocent people, then—"

"Yes, but not in the way you're assuming," he interrupted. "There's been enough unnecessary bloodshed. I only plan to hit him where it really hurts—his reputation. I have the schematics of the electrical system for the Republic City Opera House and a map of the theater from several years ago that I'm going to send to you. I need you to come down to the Don Juan and confirm they're correct before opening night if this is something you still want to do."

"You were planning something for it all along? Why didn't you tell me?"

"I figured you'd be on a plane by now."

Chapter Forty-Three

Adeline

Having made so many poor decisions in the past, I think I've conditioned my mind to trust myself a little less with each one. Which is why it feels so strange to be so certain of something after learning to fear my judgment rather than respect it. I can't help feeling that Jin, despite his past, had the right intentions, but went about it in the wrong way.

The lies Noah told me are not the same as the truth Jin withheld, but that still doesn't excuse his actions. If there is ever a possibility of a future for us, then we have so much work to do in order to repair what was damaged and move forward. When I told Jin I wanted to try, I truly meant it. If Jin is willing to put so much at risk to fight for me, then shouldn't I be willing to do the same? My hope for—

My pen froze on the ink-stained pages as the back door slid open, and a few heartbeats later, his shadows stretched down the hallway. Jin stepped out of the darkness, the warmth of the desk lamp enveloping him in tendrils of golden light, highlighting the tattered pieces of his soul that had seeped through during his hour-long phone conversation.

"I was just coming to check on you. I'm guessing you

couldn't sleep," he rasped, exhaustion gnawing at the edges of his voice.

Swiveling around in the chair, I tapped the pen against my temple. "Too much going on in here to fall asleep right now. It's been quite the day to process."

"And in about"—he glanced down at his watch—"thirty minutes, you'll have a brand new one to look forward to."

"Oh, lucky me. Only one more day until opening night. Um, did—" My smile fell. "Is everything—"

"Yes," Jin answered, stepping towards the light, "apparently, Erick has been planning to pay Charles back for the threats on opening night all along. The reason the conversation took so long was that we needed to find a way to merge our plans into one. Everything's been worked out."

"Is there anything I can do to help?"

There was beauty in justice—the assurance that for every action, there was an equally deserving consequence. I'd only heard whispers of the fire that ravaged the Entertainment District nearly two years ago, but given all that has come to light in the wake of destruction, an eye for an eye was a deserved fate.

In pursuit of impartiality, I would have as much of a role to play in all of this as Erick and Jin did. Mid-performance, during the climax of the ballroom scene, instead of Carlotta trying her hand at assassinating the king, another type of horror would unfold before the audience on stage. And if all went well, Charles's reputation along with it.

Much like an ember, I could be the spark caught aflame.

Jin explained the plan in great detail, outlining what lengths Jin and Antonio would go through to retrieve the flash drive from the offices, while Erick and Damon locked Charles in his own loge so he would be forced to watch his empire crumble before his very eyes.

"You should really try to get some sleep, sweetheart. It's getting late," Jin finally said.

My hand shot out, fingers wrapping around his wrist.

"Can I ask you something?" I rasped, peering up at him through thick dark lashes. I made no effort to remove my hand, nor did I want to, as his gaze burned into me, pulse hammering against my fingertips.

"Anything, Adeline." My name sounded like honey on his lips.

"I'm still struggling to make sense of everything that happened. No matter how many times I try to rationalize it on a page"—my gaze lowered to the journal where his name was written in rushed cursive, as if I could get my thoughts down on the page fast enough—"I can't wrap my brain around the why. Why risk inserting yourself in the middle of this fight you never asked for? Why do all this to help *me*?"

The sanctity of a promise was all we had after too many truths were shoved away like something to be ashamed of, rather than a means of building trust. We had already shared so much with each other, and if we had any chance of rebuilding what was once lost, it started with this.

"I just want to understand," I repeated, and his pulse quickened beneath my touch.

"I think you already know the answer to that question."

I wasn't sure what was more striking, the lack of hesitation or the words themselves.

"Pretend I don't."

"Adeline."

"Pretend I don't know the answer to that question"—because I wasn't sure I ever would until I heard the words spill from his lips—"and tell me why."

"There are some things better left unspoken. At least for now."

"Jin," I sighed, releasing his wrist. "This entire mess is a shit show, and no matter how we try to plan a million things can go wrong. With so little in my control, I need to focus on what I can so I don't start spiraling. And right now, that's this conversation. You've already done so much to protect me. I don't understand why."

"Because it was the right thing—"

"Don't you dare turn this into some kind of heroic gesture." I stabbed a finger in his chest to shut him up before he could spew out whatever excuse he was about to regurgitate. "Would you have done the same for Anastasia? Or James? Or any of the other dancers in the company, had threats ended up taped to their vanities instead of mine?"

"Do I sound heartless if I say no?"

"A little."

"Then yes, Adeline. I wouldn't have done half of the things I did for you because none of them are *you*. I did all of this for you because it was all I could do."

I threw my hands up and shouted, "Then why can't you tell me? Huh?"

"Because I love you," he blurted out.

The room descended into silence, only the sound of our laboring breaths to answer for. We both froze, neither of us believing the words that had come out of his mouth. There was a war waging behind his burning gaze. Several long seconds passed before he officially declared a winner, swallowed the lump in his throat, and confronted the truth with honor and dignity.

"I am hopelessly in love with you," he said, voice a little shaky, "and rereading those entries only proved that I have been for much longer than I was willing to admit to myself. That's why I did what I did. That's why I am willing to risk everything to ensure your happiness, because without you, I have *nothing*.

"As much as it was slowly killing me little by little, I was well aware that you might never feel that way toward me or ever be in a position to love again when all it had brought in the past was pain. So, I did the only thing I could think of doing. I found my own way to love you."

I opened my mouth, then snapped it shut.

The words presented themselves as a jumbled mess in my head, taking shape and rearranging into nonsense sentences that somehow made more sense than what Jin had uttered aloud. It took far longer than I care to admit for them to finally materialize as the hopeless confession they were.

"Adeline," he heaved. "Say something. Please."

A sob rocked through me that shook me down to my bones.

I slapped my hand over my mouth and gasped, startling both of us.

"Shit." All it took was two long strides, and he was suddenly in front of me, catching tears as they spilled free. "I didn't— Fuck— I'm sorry. I didn't mean you had to say anything. Unless you feel the same way, of course. Not that I expect you to. I mean, please say something so I don't continue rambling on like a lovestruck idiot who can't keep his mouth shut or wait until the right time to—"

Words had failed me too many times before.

Rather than search for the right ones, I crashed my lips against his.

Fate had woven us together—two souls bound by the same invisible string that only began to pull tight the moment our eyes met in that audition room. This kismet blessing had seen us go through hell and back, the string of which had somehow helped us find our way to each other despite so many attempts to sever the connection.

This was the precipice of spring.

Jin was the seasons changing.

Breaking our kiss, I pressed my forehead against his, ready to tell him just that, but when I opened my mouth, nothing came out. I tried again to no avail.

"If this truly is my only life to live," he mumbled against my swollen lips, fingers threading themselves in the hair along the nape of my neck, "then I will spend my every breath loving you. And if I'm blessed with another, I will find you in each and every version of myself and swear the same vow."

The invisible string wound itself within my chest, threading through the various valves of my heart. Each thrashing of the organ wasn't of my own free will; instead, another tug on our connection by Jin's design. I was bound to him and would be forevermore, but as much as I tried, those three little words never left my lips.

Having loved and lost before, it wasn't until now that I realized that it had never been love at all. They had always been beautifully spun words used to distract and manipulate me into staying. Due to the careless actions of another, the power of expression was lost on me. Although I may not be ready to utter those words aloud, it is because of Jin that I know he will be by my side until the day I do.

I cupped his cheek. "In every life, I want it to be you."

The last word came out as a gasp as Jin lurched forward, his lips upon mine. Despite not saying the words aloud, that confession alone was enough to unlock something within us—something carnal. I hooked my arms around him and deepened the kiss, borderline feverish for his touch.

With so much vulnerability laid out before us, it seemed only natural to let our defenses down and act on everything left unspoken. To feel the string shrink in size little by little as our hands explored this naked truth and shed the layers of ourselves that didn't belong in this next chapter of our lives.

It would always be Jin.

In this life. And the next.

I tugged at the hem of his shirt. Jin didn't waste any time yanking it off and tossing it aside, my tank top following soon after. Desperate to feel closer to him, I shoved him backward toward the mattress, falling atop him to straddle his narrow hips.

Leaning in close, I breathed the words, *may I touch you,* along the columns of his neck.

Jin tensed up beneath me, every hard muscle going taut.

"You can do whatever you want with me," he rasped, a little out of breath.

"Can I tell you what to do?" I said, dragging the flat of my tongue along the side of his neck. At first, his only response was a wounded groan, his nails slightly digging into my ass.

"Say the word, sweetheart," he finally said.

"Hold still," I rasped, dragging my lips over his collarbone.

Jin let out a hoarse laugh that quickly dissolved into a series of laboring breaths as I kissed my way down his sternum. The softest parts of my body slithered down him in slow, leisurely motions.

"I know what you're doing," he breathed.

I pressed a kiss to his navel, eyes peering up at him through thick dark lashes.

"I don't know what you're talking about," I drawled.

"This is for what happened in the kitchen—" A sharp hiss filled the space between us as my breast brushed over his erection. I pushed myself up to kneel between his thighs.

"No," I said, staring down at how beautiful he looked sprawled out before me. Hair a little disheveled. Cock straining against the fabric of his jeans. His hands fisted in the sheets like it was the only way to keep his promise to hold still. "This is about showing you how much I care for you."

Two things could be true at the same time, I suppose.

"But you need to hold still while I do this"—I pulled the end of his belt through the first loop, then froze—"can you do that for me, Jin? Can you hold still while I show you how much you truly mean to me?"

His lips parted, lost for words.

Then he finally found it in himself to nod his head.

The long twisting veins lining the back of his hand were raised against his skin as fingers clawed into the sheets. Out of the corner of my eyes, I watched his grip waver and tighten as I purposely drew out every movement. Savored the way his eyes lit up when I fisted the base of his cock as I stroked in a weeping upward motion. Reveled in how the cadence of his laboring breath changed when I closed my swollen lips over his crown. My mouth and hands worked in tandem, pleasuring him inch by inch as he struggled to keep a leash on what little control he possessed.

"Adeline." He groaned my name as if it were the answer to every neglected prayer.

Jin's back arched off the mattress, and he threw his head back as I zeroed my attention on the crown of his cock. My name spilled from his lips again, and instead of stopping as I promised myself I would, I kept working his shaft to see him come undone by my doing.

"Can I tell you a secret?"

"Fuck—" he bit out, chest heaving. "Yes. Please."

There was a sense of wonder in his dark brown eyes that glistened in the tendrils of moonlight. The look of wonder bled into lechery as I tossed my panties aside and Jin rushed to shed his own clothing. I shoved my finger square in his chest, sending him crashing back to the mattress.

I clicked my tongue, pretending to be disappointed.

"I thought you wanted to hear my secret."

"I do," he responded, staring up at me, awestruck.

"Then hold still like a good boy, and I'll tell you," I whispered, hooking my fingers around his waistband and dragging his pants down his toned thighs. Much like the last of my clothing, Jin's boxers met a similar fate, tossed into the darkness surrounding us.

"Actually, I have two secrets," I continued, crawling over him to straddle his lap once more. He swallowed the lump in his throat as I grabbed the base of his cock. "The first one has to do with our first date"—I lined him up between the apex of my thighs—"the night after you took me to the Delten Botanical Gardens, I booked an appointment with my primary care doctor. It's been more than a week since I started taking the pill."

His chest rose and fell in quick succession as the crown ran through my wetness.

"And the other?" he asked, eyes burning into me as I slid down farther.

"The other has to do with you," I rasped, lowering myself down an inch, "I need you to know falling for you has been the biggest blessing in my life."

"I love you," he choked out.

"Then fuck me like you mean it."

My back hit the mattress before I could make sense of what had happened. Pinned beneath the crushing weight of Jin's body, he drove into me with one swift thrust.

The darkness enveloping us seemed to hold its breath as Jin remained unmoving atop me. I reached up and brushed a slick strand of ink-black hair from his eyes to find he was already searching mine.

"I don't know how it's possible to love someone this much and still find myself falling a little more every day," he mumbled, holding my gaze as he slid out to the crown then back into me. "I don't understand how one person can bring me so much happiness without even trying"—another thrust—"and I sure as hell don't understand how it's possible for something to feel so right."

"It's because we were always meant to find one another," I moaned.

"Always," he echoed.

Pleasure was not bound by limitations. It was merely the accelerant to set us ablaze. It burned brighter within me with each punishing thrust. Each filthy confession of lewd dreams and sinful desires whispered into my ear. Each time I clawed my way down his sweat-slick back in an attempt to hold on as he drove me toward perfection.

I was burning alive, but I'd gladly burn with Jin by my side.

Chapter Forty-Four

Adeline

The sanctity of a promise was all we had when nothing about tomorrow was guaranteed. Every whisper in the dark breathed upon my skin. Every vow to put ourselves first in hopes of a new chapter of our lives that wasn't bound by fear or the dictates of others. Every stolen moment we could cling to the following day, where we spent more time curled up in a mess of sheets than worrying about how little time there was—though that wasn't so easily done when there was still so much to prepare for.

Though the sacrosanctity of time ensured the inevitable would transpire, there was only so long we could hide in this room, feasting on the flesh we had starved ourselves for so long before finally facing the cruel world beyond these walls. Reality eventually caught up with us, and before I knew it, I was crossing the threshold of the stage door once more, fingernails biting into the palm of my hand as the inevitable prevailed.

It was okay to be scared, but it was never okay to give up.

That sentiment echoed in my heart with each crunch of rosin beneath my toe, every snap of a pointe shoe hitting a brick wall, and each thrash of my heart in an all-consuming reminder that fear was constantly present.

Yet as constant as fear was, so was Jin.

As they wove purple and white flowers into my braids, Jin sat at my side, determined to banish it away and put a smile on my face. It was astounding how little it took to settle my nerves and keep troubling thoughts from spiraling with a partner who truly made me feel seen. Something about his calming demeanor and easy smile felt like a promise in itself that everything would be okay...but there were signs.

There were little cracks in his mask that manifested themselves in other ways, much like our time in the hospital right after Caleb's accident. The mindless tapping of his legs as he sent messages back and forth to Erick or a glance at the set backstage as if the curtain he replaced for the real one this morning might grow legs and walk away.

As unwavering as Jin's loyalty was to the people he cared for, he was more inclined to share his kindness with others than the burden it weighed on him to put others' needs before his own. I knew all too well the toll that could take on one's soul. So, I took his hand in mine to remind him that I was here for him too, not caring who saw us leaving the studio together.

We turned the corner, and a familiar door came into sight. In the span of two heartbeats, I was certain of three things that made me stop in my tracks.

My heart, as fragile as it may be, didn't quicken in response.

The memories of that night felt somehow out of reach.

And I, without a doubt in my mind, felt safe.

Turning to the man who made part of that possible, I said, "Maybe it would be a good idea to get my knee taped before the show."

"It wouldn't hurt. If you give me a second, I can grab the—"

"No, it's okay," I interrupted. "I think I can get it myself."

His dark brown eyes bounced between me and the door. "Are you sure?"

Painfully aware of what had happened the last time I attempted to step foot in the physical therapy room, I understood where his hesitations lay, but with a squeeze of his hand, a kiss on the cheek, and a promise to be waiting outside for me, he sent me on my way. Step by step, I carved a new path, something I couldn't have even fathomed doing a week prior.

"I'll be right out here if you need me," he reminded me as my hand wrapped around the doorknob.

Nothing had ultimately changed about the room. Skid marks still lined the floor where Noah dragged his desk across the room to place it under the air vent so he wouldn't get hot. A collection of birthday cards and poorly drawn doodles were pinned to the bulletin board in the foyer. The resistance bands were still located on the second shelf because Noah knew I couldn't reach them if he placed them any higher. The physical therapy room felt like a microcosm of the past, as vivid as the memories still threatening to haunt this place.

Part of me knew they always would. The past was still desperately trying to claw its way to the present. The only difference now was that I was determined not to let it win.

Post-traumatic stress disorder would likely be something I would struggle with for the rest of my life. A terminal sentence I never asked for but would ultimately be my burden to bear. With tools at my disposal, people who would drop everything to keep the memory of this place at bay, and a willful spirit, I wouldn't let something as silly as a memory dictate my life.

A memory couldn't hurt. What I did or didn't do with it would.

Daphne, our physical therapist, patched me up with some kinesiology tape and sent me on my way. I emerged with more than a twinge of pride blossoming deep within my chest, knowing this final day at Republic City Opera House had left me a better person than when I entered it all those months ago. I squandered my fear, rather than letting it win. Something I never imagined possible as Jin took his hand in mine and leaned in close.

"Tell it to me one more time," he whispered for my ears only.

"Well, that depends on what time of the night you're referring to. There was the time on the couch or when I was on top—"

"Not that I'm opposed to that," he rasped low against the shell of my ear, "but no."

With a quick glance of our surroundings, I leaned in and said, "Rather than go to James when the theater goes dark, that's my cue to run for the candelabra stage left."

"And if you can't?"

I tapped the single match tucked in the bodice of my costume.

"I'll be waiting for you off stage. Find me the moment the flame catches," he said in a firm tone. Anytime we could bear the thought of tearing ourselves apart from one another, Jin insisted on spending what little time we had left meticulously going over the details. With a mere thirty minutes until showtime, nothing had changed. "Can you do that for me, Adeline?"

With a nod of my head, Jin crashed his lips against mine, consuming me in the process. Kissing him felt like turning a new page—bringing with it an end to this chapter in our lives and vowing the next would be better than the last.

"I don't think I can ever thank you enough for what you've done for me," I whispered against his lips.

"You can start by telling it to me one more time."

"Well, when the theater goes dark—"

"No, the other thing, silly."

"Oh," I said, stretching the word out, "you want me to keep telling you how much you mean to me, and the ways I showed you last night. I'm not sure if I should. It might go right to your head."

He silenced me with a devastating kiss that stole the air from my lungs.

"I love you, wildflower," he rasped, caressing my cheek.

As resilient as the wildflower may be, it took more effort than I was capable of to tear myself from his arms and go our separate ways. Switching out the curtain for the ballroom scene was only the beginning of all Jin would have to risk for my sake, and there was still much to be done. A strange tugging sensation wrapped itself firmly around my heart the more distance he put between us. I stood frozen at the end of the hall, the valves of my heart constricting in response.

"Jin—" I blurted out.

Having endured the worst of the winter, it was a miracle to see the snow start to thaw and life return as the seasons prepared to change. Spring was right around the corner, and all that separated us from seeing our dreams come to fruition was one more harsh winter night. Bound by the same dream and the invisible string that had brought us together, it should have been as easy as breathing to speak the words aloud, but as our eyes met and reality sank in, those three little words stalled in my throat once more.

"Yes."

"I—"

They felt more like a goodbye rather than a promise.

"Just— Please be safe, Jin."

He smiled, and it fractured something within me.

"I promise, sweetheart."

As he disappeared amongst the cast and crew, the words

tumbled from my lips more like a prayer than a promise or a goodbye.

"I love you, too," I mumbled to myself.

But not every prayer was answered.

"Ten minutes till showtime," our stage manager shouted.

Much like a well-oiled machine, dancers, cast, and crew alike sprang into action. Each was making their final preparations before the curtain drew open for a crowd of more than a thousand in attendance. The closer I drew to the thick, red curtains, the more the roar of laughter, conversation, and instruments being tuned merged into one, until it was merely a continuous buzzing that wedged itself so firmly between my brain and skull that I had no other choice than to back away.

"You look as white as a ghost," James said.

"I think it's the makeup," I replied dryly.

"It's okay to be nervous. I threw up on two separate occasions before my first performance as *danseur noble*"—he toyed with the folds of the curtain, mindlessly—"and almost a third time on stage. Anyway, what I'm trying to say is, if you're going to throw up, don't do it on stage."

"I'm not going to throw up."

He leaned in and bumped my shoulder. "Might give them something else to talk about besides the article. I bet half those idiots are here because of what *Republic Press* wrote. Blanchet really knows how to sell a story to drive sales. Anastasia said it's a full house."

According to the whispers circulating backstage, my refusal to be interviewed by Ms. Riviera had only added fuel to the fire, shrouding this case in even more mystery and allure. Everyone wanted to see the "Killer Ballerina" grace the stage. It didn't surprise me the slightest that Charles would capitalize on the opportunity to drive up sales—

"What do you mean, Blanchet knows how to sell a story?"

"I saw him talking to the journalist the night of the showcase," he said plainly as if it were common knowledge. "I guess it makes sense, all publicity is good publicity if you know how to use it to your advantage."

A violin bow snapped on the other side of the curtain. The reverberation slithered its way beneath my skin as more instruments joined in; the sensation brought a painful memory with it.

"Which is exactly why I'm going to do what I can to help you."

"I thought—"

"Shh"—Charles raised his hand—"while I may not be able to make this entire mess disappear, that doesn't mean I can't flip the narrative in our favor—I have people who work for me that can defend you in court. I can make this night a distant memory overshadowed by the future you deserve, but you need to do exactly as I tell you. Can you do that for me, Hartwell? Can you play along until I can make this right?"

The alternative was a wasted life. A future written in Noah's blood that I didn't have the means to wash away. The promise of tomorrow had been ripped away.

"You've suffered enough. Let me take that burden from you," he said softly.

Blanchet extended a hand toward me.

The memory faded, and James took his place.

"—doesn't mean I can't flip the narrative in our favor," I mumbled under my breath.

"What?"

Driven by desperation and the will to survive, I had taken his hand in mine under the impression that this deal was my only hope. I had made my peace with the fact that the price of his services would always be my talent, but if I had always been the investment he intended to keep, why facilitate the threats?

"It still doesn't make sense," I mumbled to myself.

If this was never about my talent, then what would happen if I stepped on that stage and failed to follow through? What would happen if Jin couldn't find the flash drive and his betrayal was discovered? What is the price of failure when we didn't even know what game Charles was playing?

There was another snap of the bow. The reverberation had slithered its way up my arm, threaded itself between my ribs, then struck me right in the heart with such force it faltered for a beat. The shock to the system made my body attempt to right itself, but by overcompensating for my weakened heart, it started palpitating at a rate my body couldn't keep up with.

I sucked in what little air I could.

"I— I need a moment." I stepped back. "Excuse me."

"I was only kidding about throwing up," James called over his shoulder.

Clutching my chest, I bobbed and weaved through the crowd backstage. The familiar sensation of sand being poured into my lungs had returned. The individual grains of sand were rubbing my insides raw. Having been in this exact position countless times before, despite the way my heart knocked against my ribs, there was a strange sense of comfort that washed over me, knowing this would come to pass as all the others had before.

"Five minutes," someone yelled.

Amongst the chaos, it was difficult to make out colors and shapes as the world spun around me in a blur. My heart lurched when I couldn't instantly find something red to cling to, but my mind remained focused, directing me toward the dressing rooms where I knew I would find something red on my vanity—Jin had made sure of it.

The stench of different floral arrangements smacked me in the face upon entering the room. Dozens of brightly colored amber and crystal vases lined the circumference of the small space, masking the subtle notes of sandalwood and spice until it was too late.

The first pop of red I saw was the carnation pinned to Charles's tuxedo.

"What a shame," he drawled from his place on the leather chaise in the corner of the dressing room; a man I vaguely recognized as security staff stood behind him like a shadow stretching outward at high noon, "I thought Jin would have been with you. He hasn't left your side all morning."

The sand churned within my lungs, failing to hide what toll a single breath took in return. Charles's gaze fell to my chest. I remained pinned beneath his stare, praying my body wouldn't betray me further.

"He— He's actually right outside, I don't mind getting him," I said, backing away.

Another shadow slithered from the corners of the room that I hadn't seen before, blocking the only exit with his hulking frame.

"That's okay, Gabriel can find him for us," Charles responded.

The man, whom I could only presume was Gabriel, kicked the door shut on his way out.

"Really, I don't mind, it will be much quicker, and I have to be on stage in a few minutes." I tried the door, but it was locked from the outside.

"No need for that. You won't be performing tonight."

Chapter Forty-Five

Jin

Destler once told me that if time refused to be on our side, then bending it to our will was the only means of taking control of an uncontrollable situation. As uplifting as the proverb may be, that didn't feel entirely possible at the moment.

Sneaking Erick, Antonio, and Damon through the theater's delivery door proved to be a test of my wavering patience when a last-minute delivery delayed our plan by several minutes. Once the catering service was accounted for, I managed to sneak all three men inside undetected using the spare masks and cloaks from act two before parting ways at the entrance to the offices. Erick and Damon seamlessly slipped into the crowd, blending in with the other dancers as they made their way to the loges where they would surprise Charles, while Antonio and I handled the flash drive.

Time seemed to be slipping through my fingers at a rate that defied the laws of physics. Desperation slowly started to nip at our heels as the mantel clock atop Blanchet's bookcase taunted us from afar. Each tick of its hand brought us closer to the end of act one. The office had been completely overturned, with absolutely nothing to show for every wasted minute.

"If you glance at that clock one more time, I can't be held responsible for what happens to it the next time you do," Antonio said as he tore apart a cabinet drawer in search of a false bottom or anything else that could be of any use to us.

Ignoring him, I continued thumbing through a stack of papers.

"You know it isn't going to make time go by any slower," he continued.

"And neither is running your mouth every five seconds," I snapped. Antonio held up his hands in surrender, faking a bruised ego before turning his attention back toward the task at hand. "Just keep working. Please."

The two of us continued working in taut silence, only the sound of ruffled papers and frustrated breaths filling the space between us. Every forgotten document scattered across the hardwood floor and overturned desk drawer clattering at our feet was yet another reminder we were no closer to an answer than when we arrived.

The next tick of the clock rattled around in my skull, making the words scattered across the sales report focus in and out with each lasting reverberation. *Tick.* The files fanned out at my feet as they collided with the floor, and I moved onto the next. *Tick.* Invoices and pay stubs found a similar fate.

Tick.

Then the next.

Tick.

And the next.

Tick.

Tick.

Tick.

The metal filing cabinet drawer slammed shut rougher than

I intended, drowning out the damn ticking for one blissful moment. The drawer didn't latch and rolled open again, giving another opportunity to silence my mind once more. Over and over again.

I could feel Antonio watching me, but I didn't care.

This was it.

There were no second chances—no do-overs.

The familiar searing burn of panic slowly sank its claws into my flesh, making me feel as hopeless as the version of myself I chose to forget. Twenty years old, too naive for my own good, and rotting in a cell while Sophia's safety wasn't guaranteed, and Ethan Bennett roamed free.

I shot to my feet and began pacing, hands interlocked behind my head.

"What the hell are you doing?"

The beast, eager to feast upon my inability to regulate, raked its claws down my spine once more. Instead of breaking new skin, it burrowed its talons deeper into the existing wound, slicing through ligament, muscle, and bone with ease.

"Give me a second," I heaved, lungs contracting. "I'm okay."

"I don't think we have a second."

"I—"

We both froze.

The mechanical clicking of the clock faded away, too distant to ravish my thoughts anymore. The thrashing in my head, a dull imitation of the other, was overpowered by the groaning of wood. The sound slithered its way up my leg and reverberated deep within my bones.

I leaned my weight back and forth, testing the wooden plank beneath my heel.

Antonio shot to his feet and took all but one step before stumbling across another loose floorboard. Taking a page straight out of Adeline's book, we both dropped to our knees and started prying open the old wooden panel separating us with nothing more than stubborn determination and our splintered fingertips. The first few were filled with nothing more than cobwebs and a thick layer of dust, but we kept working our way through the office, one creaky panel at a time. Act two was likely underway, and despite the ticking at my back, I had finally found some truth in proverbs.

"I think I've got something," Antonio shouted over his shoulder as he wedged a letter opener between two panels and attempted to pry it open. "I see something white."

The stubborn bastard took two more heaves and a little assistance from me to finally spring open. In the span of two heartbeats, I experienced a surge of overwhelming joy that could only be achieved from a pure shot of adrenaline to the system, then the immediate crash of realizing what the small rectangular piece of plastic was.

"Holy shit. We found it," he cheered.

"That—that isn't it," I choked out, my arms dropping to my side. "Red. The flash drive Adeline saw Charles using was red. Not orange."

Hidden beneath the plank was a collection of bound, white envelopes and a folded manila folder with torn edges. Tucked neatly between the two was a flash drive.

"Are you sure?" Antonio turned over the bright orange flash drive. "Someone wrote the letter H on the side in permanent marker. Could stand for Hartwell."

Breaking the seal of one of the envelopes labeled Stagecraft Industries, one of the various companies we hired for repairs, I spilled its contents into my awaiting hand. Bound together in a rubber band was a small collection of checks, all adorned with the same red stamp.

Bounced.

I lunged for the next envelope.

"Bounced," I read aloud. "That son of a bitch."

As artistic director, I was privy to some of the theater's finances, but mostly approved budgets for production and investments from donors I'd secured. Charles was adamant about recording and maintaining the financial transactions, and had been long before I was ever hired.

"Jin?"

Over the course of the last decade, I'd borne witness to the steady decline of the Republic City Opera House with a mix of high costs, fierce competition from other district entertainment, and dips in the economy, driving low ticket sales. However, no matter the season, there were always willing investors from the Financial District, ready to throw cash into our endeavors despite it all. I had seen the number myself...

"Jin?" Antonio barked, pulling me from my thoughts. "Care to find out why the hell someone wrote the letter H on this flash drive? Or is it just me?"

"I—yes," I finally said, head reeling.

It felt like a thick layer of fog had descended upon my mind as I attempted to shift focus. I snatched the flash drive from Antonio's hand, crossed the hallway, and cut through the fog blindly for fear of getting lost if I lingered too long. The more distance I put between me and those damned envelopes, the more the fog seemed to lessen with each step, giving me enough clarity to shove the drive into my work laptop and have the file pulled up with a few clicks of the touchpad.

Dozens of small black and white thumbnails stared back at us. I picked one at random, though there was nothing remarkable or even noteworthy, for that matter, of the five-second clip of the backstage hallway. Two figures walked in and out of view, one I recognized, the other I didn't.

Antonio cursed under his breath as he reached around me and clicked on the next video. A ten-second clip of Charles meeting the same man at the stage door entrance, then walking away together.

"Care to explain?" I turned in my seat.

"The H stands for Henri, not Hartwell," he answered, eyes vacantly staring at the screen. "That was Henri Martin with Blanchet, and seeing that they haven't been working together, let alone on speaking terms, since Charles started fucking his daughter, I'm going to go out on a limb and say this isn't a good sign."

"Okay, I understand that, but—" I straightened in my seat. "Did you hear that?"

"No." Antonio was looking at me as if I'd grown a second head.

Straining my ears, I listened for the familiar groan of old wood I knew all too well, but all that answered in return was the distant hum of strings, woodwinds, brass, and percussion marrying into one. Antonio and I switched places so he could continue scouring a fraction of the lost footage as I approached the office door, convinced I wasn't hearing things.

It was distant, but I could hear the familiar glissando effect of a trombone echoing through the old bones of the theater, indicating the betrayals and passion embedded in every note of act two. The king was—

Someone yanked me by the collar of my shirt and sent me careening across the hallway. The lining of my spine hit the back wall with such force that it threatened to dislodge a few vertebrae. I heaved one panicked breath before my attacker's hand closed around the columns of my throat and shoved me down to the ground.

I attempted to shout for Antonio, but all I could manage was a gargled moan.

If I concentrated hard enough around the stars lining my vision, I could just barely make out the sound of my brother's voice, clear as day, mocking my pathetic blow to my attacker's rib and my poor attempt to shove him off of me as I drove my knee into his gut.

I swung again—fuck, I was out of shape.

A gunshot splintered the air, and the hand wrapped around my throat went limp. There was a slight sway of his body, a spray of something wet that painted my lips with the metallic ting of blood, then two hundred or so pounds lifted off my throat.

"What the actual hell is wrong with you?" I seethed, shoving the man's body atop me.

"The next time I save your life, a thank you would be nice," Antonio retorted, tucking the gun behind his back.

"And how do you plan to explain a dead body and a ransacked office when someone comes to investigate the gunshot?" I gestured to the burly man twisted at my feet.

Antonio glanced at his watch. "Doesn't matter. We have to leave anyway."

If the distant sound of soaring notes wasn't telling enough, I peered down at my watch and confirmed my worst fear: our time was up. With no other choice but to abandon our endeavors. Antonio and I collected what remained in the hidey-hole, then rushed to meet Adeline as promised, the wrong flash drive in tow.

Yet another broken promise to atone for.

Chapter Forty-Six

Adeline

The picture of innocence was an illusion, as fragile as the spiderwebs sprawling across a shattered mirror. The mirror was already broken, and I didn't have the means to mend the pieces back together when Charles might very well slice me open with one of them.

"Charles," I rasped, fingernails dragging down the length of the old brass doorknob as I turned in place, "what do you mean I'm not performing tonight?"

"Take a seat, Adeline."

"No." I shook my head, backing up against the door. "I'm fine right here."

"I'm not going to ask you again."

"Jin is looking for me—"

"Sit," Charles shouted, slamming his fist on the armrest. For reasons I didn't quite understand, I took the seat directly across from him. The reverberation of that single syllable rattled around in my head like a relentless migraine pulsating against my skull.

I folded my hands in my lap, then unfolded them.

"What do you want?" My voice was hardly a whisper.

"Glad to see you can still listen," he said, righting himself in his chair as he glanced down at his watch. "We only have a few minutes until the show starts, and I'm not going to waste either of our time. I have something of a proposition for you, *mon étoile*, and I think you and I both know you're far too talented to let all of it go to waste."

"I don't understand—"

The little voice was back and louder than ever.

Much like a battle cry, it repeated the saying over and over again, reminding me that it was okay to be scared, but it was never okay to give up or back down. The only person who benefited when I showed that fear was Charles, which was exactly what he wanted when he raised his voice at me.

If Charles was willing to play games—whatever those games may be—at my expense, then I needed to act as a worthy competitor long enough for Jin, Antonio, Damon, or even Erick, to realize I wasn't on stage. I had to keep him distracted for a little while longer.

Clearing my throat, I straightened my spine and tried again. "And yet I'm not talented enough to perform tonight? I fail to see how this makes any sense when your actions don't speak to your words. What about me being your investment in the future, or was that just another lie?"

"You have always been an investment, perhaps not in the way you thought." On the coffee table separating us was a manila folder. Charles flipped it open and slid it across the glass surface close enough that I could make out the word Starling. "Sebastian has extended the last leg of their show an extra month to accommodate your trial. After the trial's verdict, you will stay with Starling and finish out the remainder of your contract wherever they go."

I snorted. "You're kidding."

"Given everything that has come to light"—he deposited a

ballpoint pen on the contract—"I'm being very generous by allowing you to continue dancing, and I'm not sure if you're in a position to say no right now. The last time I checked, you owe me thousands of dollars in legal fees that Mr. Gonzalez has graciously taken on for your behalf—"

"Fees that you assured me I wouldn't have to worry about."

"I think my exact words were, that's a problem for tomorrow, *mon étoile*," he responded. "If anything, you should be thanking me."

"Thanking you," I scoffed. "For what? Offering me a hand in my darkest hour, only to take it away when it doesn't benefit you anymore. I trusted you, Charles. I gave *everything* to this company, and in return, you put me on your pedestal and promised me the world just to rip it away. You used me and my heartache to spin the narrative of the *killer ballerina* in your favor, only to sell it to the highest bidder when it benefited you. Fuck you and your contract."

"Thanking me," he reiterated slowly, "for giving you a fresh start. An opportunity to leave this all behind and start a new chapter in your life where they don't whisper murderer behind your back or leave threats on your vanity—"

"Threats that you left," I shouted, punctuating each word by stabbing the space between us. All I could do was laugh for fear that the only alternative was crying. "Was it all some sick plan to scare me into signing these papers? So I wouldn't make a fuss and leave because I wouldn't want to stay where I wasn't wanted?"

Charles's smile widened.

"Perhaps you should look more closely before you point blame. I might have known about the threats, but that wasn't me, *mon étoile*. I don't need to resort to threatening to scare you into doing what I want; I have other ways of doing that," he said, pulling out a red flash drive from his pocket. "Sign the contract, and you'll get this back—well, at the very least, Sebastian will hold onto it for safekeeping."

The manipulation of the mind is a dark art only a few can wield skillfully. I'd fallen for Noah's traps far too many times not to see this for what it truly was. While the reason for wielding such a dangerous tool varied from person to person, I was certain Charles wasn't doing this to fulfill some kind of sick narcissistic pleasure, as Noah had. Charles only benefited from this if I signed my name on that dotted line.

I looked him dead in the eyes as I said, "No."

He huffed out a bored breath. "Then you have no one else to blame other than yourself."

There was a knock at the door.

My heart lodged itself in my throat as the shadow of a man slithered to the door.

The rush of excitement was short-lived as a small figure stepped inside. The shadow eclipsed much of their features, but there was no mistaking the golden spun hair.

"Ah, there you are," Charles chirped, rising to his feet.

"You wanted to see me?" Halle rasped, stepping into the room. Refusing to look in my direction, she gave me a chance to study her more closely. While there was variation in her costume design, the matching white spring beauties tucked in braids were identical to mine...

I stood frozen in place, fist clenched at my side.

Betrayal was meant to be the willful slaughter of hope—the breaker of souls and imminent damnation. No matter the degree, it always whispered a lethal promise, swearing to shatter all that had been pieced together. Betrayal came in the form of a friendship long forgotten, and a promise Halle always intended to keep. I couldn't say I was surprised when it hadn't been the first time Halle had broken my heart.

Depicted as the essence of spring itself, there was something so small about the way she lingered in the doorway. Perhaps it was why Charles ignored the question entirely and turned to his partner instead.

"Is there any news from Gabriel about Jin's whereabouts?"

"No," he replied. "Gabriel isn't responding, and the surveillance footage is down."

"Interesting." Charles hummed, finally setting his sights on her. The way her eyes glistened in response made my stomach sick; it was the same look she gave Noah when she thought I wasn't looking. "Halle, *mon chéri*. Hold onto this for me."

She turned the drive over in her hand. "What do you want me to do with this?"

"Did I stutter?"

"But if Jin wants it—"

"If you want to keep your role as Carlotta, then I suggest you shut your mouth and do as you're told." Charles glanced down at his watch. "Now run along, you only have a few minutes until showtime. And for you"—he had me by the wrist, his nails biting the soft flesh as he shoved a pen in my open palm —"by the time I'm back for intermission, I hope for your sake you've made the right choice."

Holding his stare, I spat on his lapel. The saliva soaked through the fabric as it inched its way down his designer tuxedo. Charles released my wrist, grabbed my dance bag off the floor, then made for the only exit. I was roughly shoved aside by his accomplice when I tried to follow after. By the time I found it in myself to rise once more on unsteady feet, the door had shut behind him, locking me inside.

The whine of a violin being strummed echoed through the hall.

I pound my fist repeatedly against the wood, but my shouting was as lost amongst the music as a young Carlotta stepped on stage for the first time in a foreign kingdom. *Le*

Cœur Sauvage was underway, and every wave of the conductor's baton was another heartbeat closer to intermission.

Lining the metal tip with the underside of the door hinge, I swung back, slamming the spine of the book into the base of the screw driver. The old brass pin groaned, rattling around in the bearings, but it didn't move an inch.

The entirety of act one sped by in a blur. As the ensemble took the audience through a perilous journey of heartache, obsession, and triumph, I remained trapped behind closed doors, forced to listen to it all as Halle took my place center stage. The first roar of applause still rattled around in my skull long after the curtains drew back to reveal poor Carlotta wallowing around the slums, unaware how fate would twist its blade, but instead of drowning in the insistent noise, determined to kill my spirits, I proved to be far more determined not to let it win.

Come intermission, I would be long gone.

I would make sure of it.

I kept ramming the spine of the book against the pin with all my might.

By the time the first pin popped free, sweat licked down my spine, and my lungs heaved. I got to work on the second, but it proved far more stubborn. A fiery, persistent aching shot through my muscles as I kept ramming the spine upward. I gritted my teeth and cursed the damned thing over and over again until the back of my eyes stung.

Bang.

"Come—"

Bang.

"—on, you—"

Bang.

"—stupid pin."

The next bang reverberated up my arms. The sensation felt as if someone had taken the screwdriver and used it to split my ulna down the middle. I jerked back, realizing the banging wasn't coming from inside the dressing room.

"Hartwell, are you in there?" a muffled voice called out, jiggling the doorknob.

"Yes." The book clattered to the floor as I shot to my feet. "I'm in here, but I can't get out; it's locked."

"Stand back."

As stubborn as the door was for me, it proved to be quite the challenge for Antonio as he repeatedly rammed his shoulder into the solid wood. With one hinge gone and the other holding on by a thread, it eventually bent under the pressure and splintered open.

Antonio stumbled inside, awkwardly leaping over the door. Notably alone.

"Before you even ask"—he raised a hand as I opened my mouth—"we split up."

"Antonio—" I gasped.

"You weren't on stage, and Jin was already freaking out because we couldn't find the flash drive. Last I saw him, he was heading toward the stage."

Nothing more than a series of neuron pathways and hormones being pumped through the brain, it was strange how the nature of danger took shape in our minds. Such a tiny section of the brain enabled one of four responses: fight, flight, freeze, or fawn. With a tendency to freeze or fawn when faced with fear, I didn't think twice when I grabbed Antonio's arm and ran toward danger, weaving through the chaos backstage as dancers transitioned from scene to scene.

We slipped seamlessly into the crowd, only to be spat out in a secluded corner of the room. I crouched behind a costume rack, pulling him down with me.

"Put this on," I heaved, still a little out of breath.

Antonio leered at the fabric. "I'm not putting on the tights."

"Fine," I said, snatching a nobleman's robe and three masks off the adjoining cart, "wear this instead. I'm trusting you to find Jin and give him one as well. Then bring him to stage left as soon as—"

"Where's the stage left?"

"This is stage left."

"But this is the right side of the stage."

"Antonio," I said slowly. "I don't know you very well, and I'm going to give you the benefit of the doubt, but now is not the time to ask questions. Charles is using the flash drive to lure Jin out of hiding. I will do my part to cause a distraction on stage, but you need to find Jin before that and be ready to grab Halle. She has the flash drive."

Antonio nodded, seeming to turn over the word in his head. "Same plan with a few modifications. Got it."

With the silver and black mask in place, he attempted to rise. I yanked him back down by the hem of his robe. "If anything happens to him—"

"Don't worry"—he batted my hand away, then smoothed out the fabric—"I already saved his ass once today. No, thank you, I mind you."

"Promise me," I demanded, gritting my teeth.

"All right, killer. I promise," was all he said before running off.

Having earned the role of Carlotta so early in my career, believing it was based on merit and talent rather than selfish endeavors, I had trained for the role so thoroughly that I could feel my muscles tense up, anticipating each step as I crept to the outskirts of the stage. The familiar melody beckoned me forward to indulge once more. The notes had etched themselves upon my bones with such painful clarity that it felt like a love letter to what heartache, joy, and benevolence had threatened to consume me these last few weeks.

It was a reminder of how far I'd come and what possibilities awaited me ahead, despite what opportunities had been ripped from right under me.

I clutched the velvet curtain as I leaned forward to get a better look at the stage.

Haloed by a ring of wildflowers as vibrant as the twinkle in her watery eyes, Halle had seamlessly stepped into my pointe shoes and assumed the role of Carlotta. It wasn't until I was seeing it with my very eyes that it finally sank in. The significance of what this role meant to her and the security it promised. I couldn't even begin to imagine what lengths she went to finally get it. There was more to Halle's story, but the question was, was it a story worth retelling?

Betrayal was betrayal. I didn't think I could stomach any more.

Though she seemed to be the exception, not the rule. I trained my eyes toward the heavens, where box five loomed from its dark corner of the amphitheater. The little voice emerged from the recesses of my mind, silent yet curious about what I might do next. I felt a swell of life as a twinge of excitement pumped through my veins at the mere thought of Charles being forced to watch his reign come to an end.

Erick might have a score to settle, but he wasn't the only one.

It was hard to tell from my vantage point, but there was movement in the box.

A heartbeat later, Erick and Damon rushed for the balcony's edge, white-knuckling the railing. It was difficult to make out the fleshy, white scar cutting across his cheek, let alone any facial expressions, but as the two men quickly searched the stage and then rushed out of sight, I didn't need to see a thing to know that if I didn't act now, only more heartache would follow.

If Charles was lurking somewhere in the theater, then this was it.

King Philippe had opened the castle gates, and guests poured into the ballroom with childlike wonder as the corps de ballet took their place. I leaped into action, slipping into a role I never asked for, but felt fitting for someone always destined to play Carlotta, a maiden driven by her own virtuous ambitions and the pursuit of civil justice. Carlotta was destined to sabotage a bloodline and topple a kingdom to fan the flames of revolution—she and I were more alike than I once thought possible.

The music swept me away with its rich melody and willful spirit.

When my gaze clashed with Halle's across the stage, her mask did little to hide the shift in her glistening green eyes. The shades of earthy green dulled within her irises as her pupils expanded to bottomless black pits. Eyes have been known to be a window into one's true self—a reflection of emotions desperately trying to claw their way out, no matter how we suppress them. Halle foolishly gave herself away as we twirled past each other.

As elusive as the ghosts that supposedly haunted this theater, I ducked out of view.

Halle misstepped, whipping her head around as her partner spun her around the ballroom. The masked figures slowly closed in on her to represent Carlotta's inner turmoil regarding whether or not to drive her blade through the king's heart to save another—a life for a life. Those green eyes of hers darted back and forth, searching the crowd as they inched closer with each note.

With the thunderous clap of a cymbal, the crowd started to part.

What was meant to be a final decision in a perilous journey —fate releasing its hold on Carlotta and allowing this choice to be made of her own free will—was now my opportunity to bend fate to my will.

Before the final dancer could step aside, I appeared at her side. I roughly knocked my hip into her, and she went tumbling sideways. The standing candelabras fell like rows of dominoes, one after another, until the last wick caught on the dust curtains.

Shades of forest green erupted into hues of blistering red and oranges as the flames danced in her vision. I loomed over her, reveling in how the world dulled around us.

"It doesn't even hurt, Hal," I said calmly, flames licking at my back. "I'm not surprised anymore, just disappointed in myself for ever trusting you in the first place. Where is it?"

Halle shook her head, crawling backward. "I'm sorry."

I reached out for her. "Where did you put the—"

In a futile attempt to strike my knee, Halle drove her heel into my shin as hard as she could. I stumbled back, narrowly missing her attack. She took the slight moment of hesitation as an opportunity to slip through my fingers, disappearing amongst the chaos unfolding on stage.

Before I could rush after her, an arm wrapped around my torso and yanked me away from the curling flames.

"No, I need—"

I turned in their hold, ready to swing, but my heart stalled instead.

The thick, curling smoke crunched in my lungs, but as I took in Jin looming over me, I could finally breathe properly. While the mask obscured most of his defining features, it was the way his eyes burned into me that was more intense than the flames roaring to life at my back.

"Jin," I heaved, crushing him in my arm, prepared never to let him go. "I—I couldn't get out. I couldn't find you anywhere."

"I'm here now, sweetheart," he said, eyes swimming. "I'm here."

The world around me blurred in and out of focus as I took in more of my surroundings. Those brave enough rushed on stage to extinguish the growing flames, while others cowered in the presence of the ever-shifting beast. The curtains weren't enough to satisfy its endless hunger; the flames jumped about the stage, consuming anything foolish enough to be caught in its path.

"I thought you said the sprinkler system was supposed to go off," Antonio said, rushing to our side.

"It should have," Jin answered, arm tightening around my waist.

The deafening wail of an alarm rang through the speakers. *May I have your attention, please? A fire has been reported in the building. For your safety, please leave the building through the nearest emergency exit.* The announcement was meant to instill order and squander fear, but each time it repeated, those rushing for the glowing green exit signs grew more impatient—more desperate. With so few capable of fitting through the narrow doorways at a time, some guests resorted to jumping the stage and braving the elements for the promise of another emergency exit backstage.

"Jin"—my voice shook with vigor—"the flash drive."

"We need to leave," Antonio shouted over the roaring flames.

"We couldn't—" Jin started, but his voice was swallowed by the clashing of metal and wood. Segments of the backdrop came hurling down toward the stage, shaking the foundation of the building as it collided with the ground. Those trying to extinguish the flame lunged out of the way, narrowly dodging the raining debris. The old stage didn't stand a chance, as it bent and splintered under the crushing weight of the beams that soon followed.

"Adeline. We need to go," Jin said, yanking me off stage. "Now!"

Determined not to face a similar fate, we sprinted off stage, ignoring the harrowing cries for help and hisses of warming metal. Hand in hand, we barreled into the unknown only to be confronted with the mess awaiting us backstage. A sea of bodies crowded around the emergency exit, kicking and clawing their way toward the front as panic pulsated through the masses with each wail of the alarm. With no other choice to escape the flames, we braved the storm, wedging ourselves between sweat-slick bodies that all had one thing on their mind: survive at any cost.

"Jin," I quavered, unsure what I was even asking for by saying his name aloud, only that I needed to know that he was still with me. Jin's fingernails burrowed themselves into my flesh as the crushing weight of the masses pressed us in more firmly.

The sea had a mind of its own, bending and stretching to the whim of the crowd. And much like an actual storm, we were all at its mercy.

Jin's hand left mine, and all hope with it.

Chapter Forty-Seven

Jin

Fresh blood traced down the contours of my fingers, flowing into the love line of my palm. In an anguished attempt to hold on, Adeline's nail had curled into my hand and broken skin as she was torn from my arms.

Each of us was at the mercy of a merciless storm.

A guttural cry clawed its way up my throat as I desperately called her name. The sound of my voice was swallowed up amongst the chaos as easily as her small figure disappeared in the crowd. The familiar burn of panic shot through my veins as I lost sight of her completely.

"Adeline!" I shrieked, attempting to wrestle my way back to her, but much like a rip current, the more I struggled, the further I was swept away. "Adeline! Where are you?"

The nature of panic swore nothing good—it was a plague upon the masses that infected them one by one. Once someone was marked for death, they only regarded themselves in a single-minded resoluteness that only cared for survival, rather than how their actions affected others.

The crowd had bottlenecked toward the mouth of the exit,

spreading this disease upon the mind as they all clawed their way toward the glowing green sign.

Pressure closed in on either side, shifting the organs within me as they hopelessly fought to function properly. An elbow knocked into my gut, rearranging it in the process. Each breath felt thinner than the last as my lungs shrank half in size. My heart pounded against fractured ribs, one inhale away from collapsing entirely.

Inch by inch, the merciless storm swept me away.

The epicenter of the infection was at the mouth of the exit. Those marked fought and shouted to break free, and when the crowd had had enough, they surged forward. Like the cork of a shaken champagne bottle, once the first few individuals sprang free into the alleyway butted up against the theater, the rest came spilling out. Myself included.

My chin collided with the asphalt first; the sudden snap of my jaw made my skull rattle from the tips of my teeth to the top of my aching head. I attempted to pick myself up, and instead was sent crashing back down as the tip of a heel wedged itself between a vertebra. The copper tinge of blood seeped down my throat and soaked the grooves of my swollen tongue.

My fingers curled in the gravel as I attempted to rise once more, but I was sent crashing back to the earth. The next person who trampled over me did so with such force that my teeth sliced through the first few layers of my tongue. It made me wonder if I could still mutter a prayer, or at the very least apologize for leaving Adeline like this so soon. While the prayer never left my lips, someone must have been listening because all the weight atop me lifted.

"Thank you," I mumbled, staring up at Antonio looming over me.

"See, was that so hard?"

"Adeline," I choked out, a spray of blood painting my lips. "I lost her in the crowd."

"I lost Damon and Erick, too. And neither of them is answering their phones."

"I have to find her." I weakly shoved him away, but I only made it two steps before he had me by the arm and yanked me backwards. "She needs me, Antonio."

"She's a smart girl. She knows where to meet us." A protest was on the tip of my tongue, but Antonio beat me to it before I could find the words. "Unless you want to get trampled to death, we need to get the fuck out of the way."

Faith wasn't so easily found in a place like this, but Antonio was right; if I intended on keeping my promise to Adeline, then putting myself in a position to get trampled to death wouldn't let faith prevail.

As I fought a wave of dizziness, Antonio slung my arm over his shoulder and led me from the darkened alleyway. Fully capable of walking on my own, it felt nice to let him bear some of that weight for a moment as we weaved through the chaos spilling out into the street.

"I—I didn't mean to let her go," I said under my breath.

"I know, buddy. I know."

When Erick, Damon, and I went our separate ways, everything had felt so simple. The makings of a plan designed to threaten the very thing Charles cared for the most. I frantically searched every face we passed, praying I might find her in the crowd, but all I saw in return was reminders of how our failure had caused more destruction than Charles ever had.

Yet another broken promise at Adeline's expense.

I'm sorry for hurting you again, wildflower.

On the corner of Fifth and Lextin was a small park that cut through the bustling city—and our designated meeting spot. Putting my faith in Antonio, I allowed him to lead me from the darkness into the soft glow of the street lights looming overhead. From our vantage point down the block, it was difficult to make out the faces, but there was no mistaking the burst of movement disappearing behind one of the many trees that lined the perimeter of the park.

I held my breath until my lungs burned as the figures took shape.

"See, I told you—"

One of the shadowy figures was roughly shoved to the ground.

Antonio dropped me and broke into a full sprint.

"Erick," he shouted into the darkness. "Fuck—Damon."

An officer had his knee pressed between Erick's shoulder blades.

Damon caught sight of Antonio rushing for them, and, unable to sign, he shook his head, and Antonio stopped short. His cousin, on the other hand, couldn't muster up the courage to look him in the eyes as the officer slapped cuffs on his wrists.

"I don't—I don't understand," Antonio heaved, then turned to me as if I might have answers he was searching for. "Jin?"

"We need—"

My phone rang, cutting me short.

The black, reflective screen showed an image of Adeline smiling from ear to ear, holding the dollar bill we hung on the wall of The Tavern. The words *terribly complicated*, barely visible in her elegant handwriting.

My gut twisted into knots as I fumbled to answer it.

"Adeline. Thank God," I sputtered into the receiver, clutching it a little tighter. "Where are you? We're at the park waiting for you."

There was a long, insistent pause that lingered for what felt like a lifetime.

"Jin," Charles finally replied. "Let's see who can find her first."

Then the line went dead.

Chapter Forty-Eight

Adeline

The summer before kindergarten, Melissa had insisted we all load into the car and drive the three hours up the coast to spend her birthday at the beach. Memories of that day were as distant as the fleeting moments we shared as a family that were anything other than miserable, though there were still fragments of that day that will forever be ingrained in my mind. The warm glow of my shoulders burning in the summer sun. The little critters burrowed themselves in wet sand as we frantically attempted to shovel them out. A wave twice my size, swallowing me whole.

As the crowd surged forward, I was suddenly that helpless girl at the mercy of the sea, sucking down one desperate breath after the other with each wave crashing over me. Anytime I thought I had my bearings, another wave would disorient me—pulling further out to sea. And much like that fateful summer day, for reasons I didn't quite understand, the sea decided to spit me out on the coastline after it had its fun.

I toppled over, narrowly catching myself as the ground came rushing for me.

While I was spared by the treacherous sea, others hadn't

been so lucky—Jin had been swept away. I frantically searched for him in the crowd, but even on my tippy-toes, the waves were too large to peer over.

I called his name, but my voice was cast away by the sound of the alarm overhead. The persistent blaring pulsated against my skull, sending any rational thoughts adrift as I tried and failed to make sense of what was happening and what to do next.

I lifted my hands to my ears, needing to silence the world around me and wrangle my thoughts back into place. Something red caught my eye.

Crusted beneath my fingernail was blood—Jin's blood.

Drips had slithered their way between the skin where my cuticle and nail met. My mouth went dry, and a chill ran through me with such force it felt feverish. Having not seen blood coat my hand since that fateful night, my mind and body actively worked against each other. One, considering how strange it was that two men could be so different yet bleed all the same, while the other attempted to pull me back into a distant memory.

I took a shaky breath in, then blew it out.

Memorizing the sight of my trembling hand, I nearly missed it. The flash of a white tutu with gold embellishments sewn into the fabric. Halle stopped short at the sight of all that awaited her near the emergency exit. Whatever decision she made in her head must have been a quick one, because rather than take her chances, she ran off to find another means of escape.

The tip of my index finger ran over my bloodied cuticle.

There had already been so much blood spilled, and I feared that there would only be more if Charles saw things through. If he was determined to use the evidence as a means of bending both Jin and me to his will, then he would likely stop at nothing to see Jin atone for his supposed sins and my inability to comply with everything he gained from me signing my name on that dotted line.

While I might not be capable of throwing myself back in the sea to find him, I could brave a different storm to save him.

I crept out of view, using the various boxes as cover as I trailed after her. With a little quick thinking and dumb luck, I passed a worktable backstage and snagged a pair of fabric shears from the countertop. The familiar weight of them in my hand made weaving through the thick curtain feel like I was being sucked back in time. The irony wasn't lost on me, but I refused to walk this path both alone and unarmed.

Stepping into the theater felt like being transported between the pages of Dante Alighieri's literary work. Blistering flames curled their way up toward the heavens. The farthest corner of the sprawling fresco was met with long, thick scorch marks that tarnished the sky and distorted the melting faces of the cherubs.

Perhaps I hadn't survived the crowd surge after all and was now condemned to the seventh circle of hell. Forced to drown in all the blood I've spilt forevermore. A fitting end for someone who couldn't find it in themselves to mourn the life I took any longer.

It was perhaps why I grieved for this building more than I ever did for him. Republic City Opera House had more of a home than anywhere else, and it fractured what was left of my broken heart to see more than one hundred and forty years of rich, lyrical history threatened to be reduced to ashes. The flames danced in my vision as unshed tears brimmed in my lash line.

This was never our intention. We never meant to hurt anyone or stoop to his level, for that matter—it was always meant to incite fear, not instill it.

"Oh, god," I gasped, hand covering my mouth.

Accepting its fate, the opera house groaned in response as if it were weeping in solace. A final goodbye after gracing the Entertainment District with its presence for so many years. There was another groan, then a sharp, hissing pop.

"I'm sorry."

The tears rolling down my cheeks were suddenly washed away.

I peered up, startled.

An endless spray of water cascaded down from the heavens, making quick work of extinguishing the flames. The two elements fought for dominance, one lashing out at the other. I watched as the flames eventually shrank back in fear, and all I could do was laugh in relief as I was soaked down to the bones.

The theater had been spared by one fate but commended to another.

I had all but a second to savor the overwhelming sense of relief before the sound of footfalls came rushing toward me. I sprinted down the wing steps and narrowly ducked behind a row of seats as someone burst through what remained of the curtains to investigate the faulty sprinkler systems, finally roaring to life.

Halle stood center stage beneath the shower; her costume clung to her frail body.

From my vantage point, I carefully followed her line of sight across the theater. More concerned with the last few guests leaving through the emergency exit than this turn of events, she shot down the steps to make her escape.

Though dreams were short-lived.

The tiny glimmer of hope embedded in her forest-green eyes turned ashen as quickly as the flames that had once threatened to consume the theater as my hand shot out and wrapped around her ankle in passing. By the time her chin connected with the rough, scratchy carpet, I was already on top of her, pinning her down with my weight.

"Where is it?"

"Stop," she wailed, but I didn't listen.

"Give me the damned flash drive," I shouted over the incessant spray of water as I pawed at her costume.

"I don't have it. Charles took it back. Stop."

Our eyes met—

It took a few more beats before I noticed that one of the voices roaring in my ears didn't reside within my head as the others did. This one was coming from behind.

"Noah," a familiar voice called out.

"I don't have it," another voice cried, thrashing beneath me. "I swear."

There was always something about her smile; the mere suggestion of it could warm an entire room and spread with the quickness of wildfire. I often looked toward her on especially hard days, hoping to feel an ounce of her happiness in any capacity. Which is why it broke my heart to see Halle in the doorway, that smile of hers slowly fading as she took in the sight before her—

"No." She shuddered. "No. No. No."

Hope still glimmered in her forest-green eyes, but with each passing heartbeat, I watched it slowly leach away as the initial shock wore off and reality finally set in.

I blinked rapidly, banishing the past away.

Time righted itself once more, and reality no longer held such fluid motions. Memories of the past felt like shards of glass wedged between the grooves of my brain, an unbearable sense of pain that dulled the more I ignored them, but when something or someone plucked the pieces free, I was forced to view them with such clarity that it felt like time had no meaning. This one in particular hadn't been wedged in as deeply as the rest, but as I peered into Halle's fear-stricken eyes, I had the haunting realization I hadn't turned over the piece of glass...

"Halle," I rasped, wearily, all the fight leaving me, "why were you there? The night that Noah died. Why were you still at the theater?"

The woman I had once considered my closest friend aimed for my knee once more, but I had her wrists pinned above her head before she could strike.

"You knew, didn't you? You knew Noah was cheating on me." The contours of her soft features twisted into an ungodly sight as a shriek clawed up her throat. "Is that why you didn't leave when you said you would?"

She shook her head, teardrops rounding her cheeks.

"Answer me!"

"No," she wailed, the single syllable turning into a guttural cry.

"Why were you still protecting him?"

"You didn't deserve his love."

"And you did?"

"Yes."

The thud of heavy footfalls echoed off the high ceiling. I slapped my hand over Halle's mouth as two figures emerged on stage. The man I recognized from the dressing room fought for words as he attempted to justify what he thought he heard, while Charles's sky-blue eyes roamed the theater with predatorial stillness.

From our hiding place, tucked between the rows, Charles couldn't see us. I smothered Halle's relentless screaming with my hand to make sure it stayed that way. Though Halle, to her defense, put up quite the fight, raking her nails down my forearms and hands in an attempt to throw me off.

I shushed her. "Stop doing—"

At first, I thought my eyes were playing tricks on me—that

the flash of red was from my hand, not hers. Though fate had been known to be cruel in the past, why stop now? The entire side of Halle's index finger and knuckles was stained the lightest shade of red—the shade Claret Rouge, to be exact.

"God," I muttered to myself, rearing back.

While fate might get its sick pleasure from watching me suffer, the question was, who was crueler? Halle, or the circumstances that had brought us here?

"She's over here," Halle shrieked, clambering away. "Help!"

Those piercing blue eyes found me from across the theater that instant.

Nothing about the composition of a pointe shoe was designed for running, but that didn't stop me from stumbling to my feet and barreling down the row. The ridged, inflexible nature of the shank contorted my muscles in a dull aching pain as I rounded the last chair and shot up the middle aisle.

Charles and his companion split up, taking either aisle along the outskirts of the theater. Their shadowy figures were visible out of the corner of my eye.

The carpet sloshed beneath my feet as the dull aching expanded upon itself like building blocks being stacked one atop the other. The crushing weight zeroing in on my knee as I attempted to push my body beyond reason and ignored my known limitations. The glowing green exit sign loomed in the distance, a beacon of hope that felt so close yet wildly out of reach as my body actively worked against me.

I darted left, cutting through row sixteen.

The green emergency exit sign appeared to me like a smudge on the horizon—a glowing white beacon that promised if I braved enough of the storm and reached it, I would be safe. The mere suggestion of freedom pushed me a little harder with the promise of all that awaited me on the other side.

If I reached the door, I could wake from this nightmare once and for all.

As my foot hit the threshold, I was violently ripped away from the dream-like state. Fingers curled around the ends of my hair, and with one quick twirl around his fist, he sent me careening back into him. It felt like each individual strand was being plucked from my scalp as he tugged me closer. A guttural cry crawled up my throat as I swung the scissors over my shoulder, aiming blindly. By the third swing, he had two bony arms wrapped around me, one digging into my gut, the other pinning my free arm to the side.

The scissors clattered to my feet, and any glimmer of hope along with it.

Much like a shadow, Halle clung to Charles as they approached.

I used to believe that for someone of his age, there was so much life residing in his crystal-blue eyes. Paired with the theater's grandeur, it always felt magical to be graced by the presence of both. And now...scorched marks haloed him like a crown of fiendish delight. As he collected the scissors off the floor, he looked more like the bringer of death rather than the haven he preached of.

"Some habits die hard, I see," he grumped, running the sharp tip of the scissors along the underside of my jaw in a poor imitation of a loving caress. I jerked away, every hair standing in response to its cool bite. "What? Are we not willing to face the consequences of our actions?"

"Not mine," I said through gritted teeth. "Yours."

"No," he corrected, an unnerving smile curling his lips. "This is about your actions, *mon étoile*—it always has been. For someone who likes to play God, deciding who does and doesn't live, you sure are an ungrateful bitch after everything I've done to clean up your mess."

"It. Was. Self-defense."

"Was it?" The point dug in enough to feel a twinge of pain, but not enough to break skin. "And yet I don't recall you ever reporting Noah's behavior to human resources or filing a police report? Confiding in a friend? Or even trying to leave him?"

He paused, raising an eyebrow.

"No, you waited until it was too late to confront the consequences of your actions, and Noah paid the ultimate price for your mistakes. This is your last chance, Adeline," he continued. "Sign the papers and put all of this behind you once and for all. Don't make another mistake before someone else you care about gets hurt."

The only mistake I ever made was accepting Charles's *help*.

"You," I sneered, then turned my attention to his faithful shadow, "and you can both rot in hell. Then you can finally be with Noah like you've always wanted."

All the color drained from her face. "You fucking bitch—"

Charles cleared his throat, cutting her off.

How ironic for her to call me a bitch when she was the one rolling over for him. It made me wonder if fame was all she was getting in exchange for her obedience. How much of Halle's tattered soul did she have to sell to earn her role? Was the cost merely to do Charles's bidding, or was there more?

He leaned in close and said, "Then you are worthless to me."

"We both know that isn't true," I retorted. "It—"

Charles was shoved aside. I could hardly make sense of what had happened until I peered down and found the shears sticking out of my abdomen, Halle's slender hands still clutching the handle.

"What the *fuck* did you do?" he seethed. Taking her by the laces of her costume, he used them to hurl her against the nearest wall.

Time held no meaning, and my brain and body processed at different rates. I lifted a trembling hand, expecting the cruel bite of pain, but instead, the summer sun gently caressed my skin as I stood on the shoreline once more. I was four years old, watching the water lapping around my feet, then retreating back to sea.

"I—I don't know." Her voice shook. "You said she's worthless—"

"Do you have any idea what you've cost me?"

"No," a small voice choked out, her shadow curling into itself on the floor.

The water drew farther—farther than I could have ever swam on my own. I remembered standing along the shore, so taken aback by how picturesque the entire coastline was. Sun glistening off the water. Islands, a distant smudge on the horizon. Laughter everywhere I turned. Too distracted by the false promise that every weekend might be like this one, I was blindsided by the wave rumbling to life offshore.

The undulating wave crested overhead.

My trembling fingertip brushed the rubber hilt of the shear.

I was crushed beneath the weight of an entire ocean.

The pain had no beginning or end—it was an endless stream of consciousness that took sick pleasure in seeing me feel every agonizing second of drowning on dry land. There was only the blood seeping between my hands and a blistering, fiery pain that made my organs feel like they were being flayed over an open fire as my vision blurred.

God—there was so much blood.

I was aware there was shouting all around me, but I couldn't piece the words together into complete sentences. All I could focus on was collecting the blood slipping through my finger and attempting to put it back in my body.

It kept spilling out of me.

I couldn't stop it.

Death was a cruel bastard, demanding life as retribution for my actions. If he wanted my soul in exchange for Noah's, then so be it, but if I only had a few more breaths left, I wouldn't let them go to waste. The last thing I remember was the blades sliding out of my abdomen with a sickening whish, then commending Charles to the same fate.

Chapter Forty-Nine

Jin

Dark luminous clouds hung low in the night sky. The aroma of fresh rainfall curled the hairs in my nose as I ran blindly into the looming darkness. The rubber soles of my shoes slid against the slick city streets as I chased after the wail of sirens and the roar of the crowd gathering outside the theater. Husbands clung to their disheveled partners, strangers helped strangers during their time of need, and friends called for one another as more people spilled out of the emergency exits. Their faces, a sympathy of horror and confusion, married as one. Some counted their blessings, reconnecting with their loved ones, making it out of the building unscathed. I, on the other hand, wasn't ready to count mine until a certain ballerina was safe in my arms once more.

The crowd split down the middle as two massive fire trucks and an ambulance sped through the streets. I sprinted after them, not thinking of anything but reaching her. Their wheels splashed the blood, dirt, and grime of the district streets as they shrieked to a stop. First responders filed out, some gravitating toward those who needed immediate medical attention while others rushed into the unknown dangers lurking in the theater.

More concerned with the persistent chaos, no one noticed me slip inside.

Nor did they notice the sickening amount of blood flowing down the gradual slope of the aisle, only to be washed away slowly but surely as the sprinklers persisted overhead. Racing against a ticking clock, I followed the trail of blood out of the theater and through the lobby. The sheer amount of which was impossible to comprehend.

And they surely didn't notice as I crumpled to my knees when my legs gave out in the empty alleyway and cried into the darkness closing in on me on all fronts.

The trail of blood had ended.

And all that remained were wilting purple and white wild-flowers.

Acknowledgments

Having spent a lifetime with anxiety's not-so-gentle voice whispering in my ears, writing Our Wasted Vows was incredibly important to me. Adeline, as a character, is someone I connect with on a deeper level, and through her journey, I hoped to show others who suffer from anxiety and PTSD that we are not defined by our pasts, nor the voices that rattle around in our heads. We are far stronger than we think and will never be defined by a voice that doesn't deserve to be listened to. If you take anything away from this story, I hope you remember that it is okay to be scared, but never okay to give up.

With that being said, I still struggle immensely with my own mental health, and that in itself has caused me a great amount of heartache over the years and robbed me of so much joy when it came to publishing my debut novel. Yet despite not always believing in myself, I have been overwhelmed by the people in my life who have believed in me when it felt impossible to do on my own. From my husband, who has always been my number one fan and the person who taught me what being a wildflower meant, to my mother, Danine, sister, Tess, and mother-in-law Karena, who are constantly screaming about my book from the rooftops any chance they get, to my amazing friends who show up to every book event to cheer me on. Thank you, Shelbie, Alyssa, Sydney, Josh, and Sierra, for being my biggest cheerleaders.

A special thank you to my fellow writers. Stumbling across that random thread and deciding to meet a bunch of strangers off the internet on a whim ended up being the best decision I could have made. You all have created such a loving and nurturing community that I can always turn to when I'm confused, stressed, or just need a good laugh.

And lastly, thank you to the readers who have believed in me every step of the way. None of this could be possible with the love you have showered this series with thus far. It had given me so many opportunities I never thought possible, and I am deeply grateful for it all. I promise to continue creating stories that shine a light on mental health representation, empowering women, and are too spicy for their own good. Thank you for putting your faith in me. I am so excited to finish this series and see where this career takes me next with all of you by my side.

About the Author

Riley Andrews was born and raised in California, then moved to Arizona for college and never left, despite the heat. She writes spicy, dark romance inspired by beloved Broadway musicals. If she isn't stressing about her next project, then you can find her daydreaming about her next trip or getting lost in an art museum.

instagram.com/rileyandrews_author

tiktok.com/@Rileyandrews.author